Sage Cane's
HOUSE OF
Grace
AND FAVOR

A Town Will Only Rise to the Standards of Its Women

Books by C.C. Harrison
Running from Strangers
The Charmstone
Picture of Lies
Death by G-String

Writing as Christy Hubbard
Sage Cane's House of Grace and Favor

For more information
visit: www.SpeakingVolumes.us

Sage Cane's
HOUSE OF
Grace
AND FAVOR

A Town Will Only Rise to the Standards of Its Women

Christy Hubbard

SPEAKING VOLUMES, LLC
NAPLES, FLORIDA
2020

Sage Cane's House of Grace and Favor

Cover design by Hannah Linder

ISBN 978-1-64540-331-9

To the stalwart women of the Old West who endured hardship and sacrifice to help open the American Frontier.

The West demanded much from them.

All they expected in return was survival.

What they got was a place in history.

Acknowledgments

To all the people who believed in me, thank you. I couldn't have done it without you. Thanks especially to editor Brittiany Koren for urging me to stretch and reach.

Huge thanks and appreciation to my agent Terrie Wolf of AKA Literary for her kind words always, for cheering me on, and for forgiving my occasional impetuosity. You're the best. Thanks for inviting me into the Wolf Pack.

Thank you to my daughter Barbara who loves this book more than the others, and who encourages me endlessly to write more like it.

Tremendous thanks and gratitude to Kurt Mueller at Speaking Volumes who saw something in my writing that spoke to him.

During the course of writing this book, I referred to many historical resources including: *Pioneer Women, The Lives of Women on the Frontier* by Linda Peavy and Ursula Smith; *Seeking Pleasure in the Old West* by David Dary; *Saloons of the Old West* by Richaerd Erdoes; *Settling the West* by the Editors of Time-Life Books; *The Gunfighters; Showdowns and Shoot-Outs in the Old West* by the Editors of Time-Life Books; *Portraits of the Old West* by Frederick Nolan; *Simple Methods of Mining Gold* by Terry R. Faulk; *Keeping Hearth and Home in Old Colorado* by Carol Padgett, PhD.; *The Gentle Tamers* by Dee Brown; *Soiled Doves* by Anne Seagraves; *The Prairie Traveler* by Randolph B. Marcy, Captain U.S. Army; and many others.

Introduction

Parlor houses in Old West mining towns were a way of life and often a means of keeping the peace. Popular belief in some of these remote towns was that by having someplace for tired, lonely miners to go for conversation and companionship, it reduced the frequency and severity of violence and lawlessness in the streets.

Over time, a contradiction grew between contempt and reverence for parlor house girls. In some growing mountain towns, parlor house girls were often the best dressed, best fed, and among the wealthiest of the citizenry. They were more attractive, more intelligent, and more accomplished in culture and the arts than many society ladies. Some men discovered that parlor house girls even made good wives.

Parlor houses often occupied prime real estate in the best part of town, and offered an atmosphere that was both sophisticated and discreet, as well as a luxury of furnishings and decor surpassing other homes in these growing communities. In most mining districts, they were the cleanest places in town.

This is the story of how the women in one such establishment transformed an entire Colorado town.

Chapter One

1859—The Rocky Mountains

It was a hot and dusty rib-cracking ride getting to the town of Fairplay Creek, and though Sage Cane wasn't a tearful and fearful sort of woman, the trip from Independence had occasioned one episode of the former, and at least a dozen of the latter. She pushed her high-topped lace-up boots against the wagon's footrest, and braced her travel weary body in anticipation of the next bone-jarring bump. Her already bruised elbow banged against the wood-slatted inside of the wagon as the rutted road dropped out from under the iron-rimmed wheels.

"Driver!" she hollered out the window at the man sitting up front. "Please. Can you go slower?"

"Yes, ma'am." Deputy Acer Morrow curbed his youthful exuberance, reining in the horses, but only a little. "Just anxious to get back is all. Sorry, ladies."

Sage glanced at Odelia Maclean sitting on the wooden bench across from her, holding on to the edge of the seat to keep from bouncing out of it. A determined, stiff-upper-lip expression held her features, but her eyes were puffy with fatigue. They'd met in Denver and had quickly become friends during the three days they shared a hotel room—out of necessity to save on expenses—while waiting for the feeder stage from Fairplay Creek. When it had finally arrived, Sage was more than a little dismayed to find it was not a stagecoach at all, but the modified, covered buckboard in which they were now being jounced around.

As the road smoothed out and the wagon slowed, Odelia allowed a weary smile. "I've never been away from home before," she said. "I guess I'm a little nervous."

Sage smiled back, and patted her new friend's hand in reassurance. "Me too, Odie."

"Thank you for hiring me to work at your hotel in Fairplay Creek," she said. "I wasn't sure what kind of job I'd be able to find once I got there. I don't know anything about the area except that it's not part of Kansas Territory. I've heard it's just wilderness."

Sage didn't know much more than that, either, but she was eagerly looking forward to it, and felt fortunate to have made a friend before she arrived. Odie would be a big help since Sage had no experience running a hotel, and Odie said she'd worked at a boarding house before. Sage hired her on the spot.

Bravely, Sage battled the tiny flutter of misgiving that had been companion to her excitement ever since she'd left Independence four weeks ago. A million questions about what her future held swirled in her mind, but she stilled them by reminding herself that she had nothing to lose by going West, and maybe there was something to gain.

The wagon trip from Independence, Missouri to Denver had been so new and strange. She'd ridden through country that seemed to contain nothing except itself, and hadn't noticed enough people living on the land to hold it down.

Hostile Indians were a constant unseen presence and the reason for the two outriders accompanying their transport wagon now. The Winchesters crooked across the outriders' forearms were probably what discouraged the Indians from approaching the wagon as it rolled through the prairies, but she imagined she could feel their dark, disapproving eyes on her back as they passed.

The three days she'd spent in Denver had been a welcome reprieve, though the noise and confusion had made it all but impossible to get any real rest. Within minutes of leaving the booming city yesterday morning, they'd passed a straggle of settlements at the base of the Rockies and been immediately swallowed up by wilderness. Only a few miners' shacks dotted the mountainside.

There were no sounds outside the wagon save the wooden-spoked wheels and horses' hooves on the dirt as they rode first across shallow gullies and through thinning chaparral, then up steep, rocky trails barely wide enough for the wagon.

Last night they'd stopped at a road ranch near the foot of Kenosha Pass, a regular overnight stop for coaches from Denver, but it had offered little comfort. No water for bathing, cold beef and stale bread for dinner, and she'd had to sleep on a dirt floor wrapped in her own blanket. This morning she woke up cold and hungry. For the first time, Sage began to wonder if she'd done the right thing by leaving Independence.

Suddenly the driver cracked his whip and the wagon lurched forward picking up speed again, throwing her against the back of the wood slatted seat. A startled squeal escaped Odie's lips as she flung her arms and flattened her hands against the sides of the wagon to prevent being tossed from her seat to the floor.

"We're almost there, ladies," Acer shouted. "Hang on."

Dust billowed and the wagon bounced over the rutted track as the horses' feet beat the ground. Trunks, hatboxes, and duffels jostled and pulled against the restraining ropes that held them in place. Sage prayed they wouldn't fall off, because she wasn't sure she could get the driver to go back for them if they did.

"Yahoo," hollered Acer, working the horses up to a full gallop. "Hee haw! Giddup!"

Up ahead she thought she saw a collection of buildings but dirt and grit swirled up in her face forcing her to close her eyes and bury her nose against her shoulder. She hung on with both hands as the wagon jolted and swayed over the uneven road, the driver yahooing and whooping all along, his whip snapping the air as the horses thundered ahead. The outriders galloping alongside were equally anxious to reach town, and joined in with Acer's hooting and hollering.

"Haw! Haw! Giddup!"

As they neared the town, Acer put his foot hard on the brake and threw his weight onto it while at the same time pulling back on the reins to slow the team, though he kept up the ungodly shouting. At last the horses came to a stop in front of a building adjacent to a large corral in poor repair, rails scattered everywhere. People in the street and on boardwalks turned to look, and some came running over as the horses snorted and pranced in place.

"Fairplay Creek," yelled Acer, as he jumped nimbly to the ground. "The biggest little boom town in the Rockies!"

Sage had to take a moment to catch her breath before looking around, and when she did, her heart sank as she laid eyes on the falling down rows of buildings that lined the rutted street. It didn't look like a town at all; it was more like a camp. Up ahead, a freight wagon with a team of ten yoked oxen clogged the street in front of an unpainted, hastily put together structure bearing a sign that said GENERAL STORE. Dogs and burros wandered loose in the dung-littered street.

She exchanged an uneasy glance with Odie. "Oh, my heavens," she whispered.

"Christ a'mighty, Acer," a voice boomed from outside the wagon. "How many times have I told you not to do that? It kicks up too much dust and scares the horses in the livery."

"All the Overland stage drivers do it," the deputy defended himself.

Sage saw that the gruff voice and inhospitable greeting came from a tall, well-built man with a craggy face, wearing a black, high-crowned Stetson with a silver Concho hatband. He was also wearing a badge so she assumed he must have some official capacity.

"That may be, but you're not driving a stage," the man roared. "You're driving a converted freight wagon, dammit. Now get your passengers out of there, and take those horses to the barn for a feed." After shouting orders at the young deputy, the man went down on one knee to look at the axle.

Without waiting for assistance, which she wasn't sure was forthcoming anyway, Sage hastily brushed the dust off her gray wool traveling suit, and climbed awkwardly out of the wagon. Odie followed behind.

"How do you do. I'm Sage Cane." She extended her hand to the man, but instead of taking it, he stared at her. In his eyes was a look as though he saw something coming from far away, but it wasn't close enough yet for him to make out what it was.

But then the moment passed, and he stood up, gradually collecting himself. He touched his hat brim. "Howdy, ma'am," he said, nodding first to her and then to Odie. "I'm Bridger Norwood, town marshal."

"I'm the new owner of Wild Mountain Honey." Sage reached behind her and eased Odie forward. "And this is Miss Odelia Maclean, my bookkeeper."

After his initial reaction, the marshal's expression retreated, and Sage found herself a little piqued at his display of indifference. She'd come a long way and a slightly more hospitable welcome would have been appreciated. She certainly didn't expect to be greeted by a big, scowling lout who reeked of whiskey.

Acer untied one of her trunks and tossed it on the ground where it landed with a *thunk*. She winced at his rough handling of her things, then peered up the street.

"Would it be too much to ask for directions to the Wild Mountain Honey Hotel?" she asked. "My friend and I are quite exhausted from traveling, and we'd like to get some supper." She didn't add that she knew she smelled to high heaven and sorely needed a bath.

"Hotel?" Bridger took a stance with his feet set wide and his hands on his hipbones. A Colt .45 was strapped to his leg. "Well, it's not exactly a hotel," he said.

"Oh, it's not? What is it? I understood that my Aunt Honey owned a hotel."

He studied her indulgently as if treating himself to the satisfying sight of a delicious meal he was about to devour. Frankly, she thought it quite insulting, but was too hungry and tired to put the man in his place. All she wanted was a bath and a bed.

"I guess you could call it a . . ." He stopped to consider. "A boarding house." Then, without shifting his bold look, his chin came up along with his voice and he growled at Acer who was unhitching the horses. "Acer, you take care of the team, and I'll bring the buggy round from the wagon barn so I can take these lovely ladies and their bags up to Wild Mountain Honey." He lifted his hand to his hat and dipped his head. "Wait here. I'll be right back."

After he disappeared around the corner of the building, Odie placed a tentative hand on Sage's forearm. "Do you think it's safe to go with him?" she whispered.

"Of course, Odie. He's the marshal."

Odie flared her eyes and compressed her lips in an expression that said being a marshal in a remote mining town didn't necessarily guarantee their safety, and Sage was forced to amend her answer. "At least, I hope it is," she said.

Bridger rolled up with a buggy and a one-horse hitch. He put their trunks and bags in back, then offered his hand, helping Odie in first, then Sage. He picked up the reins and taking a firm grip on the seat rail, pulled himself up beside her. The buggy was small, the seat narrow, a tight fit for three people, and Sage squirmed uncomfortably. Trying to be inconspicuous, she eased as far over toward Odie as she could, but the heat from Bridger's leg where it lay along the length of her thigh seared clear through her skirt and petticoats. She tried to ignore it by giving her full attention to the town.

There was only one word for it. Raw.

It started as a collection of tents and huts high up in the hills and straggled down to a flat of land on which streets had been laid out in a rough grid pattern. Along the main drag through town, sorry-looking wooden buildings had been thrown up by the prospectors and merchants who'd come to cash in on the gold rush that had begun last spring. Between these unpainted structures, canvas tents and lean-to shacks served as temporary shelters for the new arrivals, and apparently for those whose mines had yet to pay off.

As they rode, Bridger nodded to passersby, commenting now and then on the signs of boomtown prosperity that were beginning to transform the town—a newly constructed bank, two new gambling halls, a laundry. Most of the saloons, their doors flung wide open appeared to be thriving. The false-fronts of the newer buildings blocked out most of the view of the snow-capped jagged peaks of a mountain range in the distance.

"Fairplay Creek's a nice peaceful town," Bridger pointed out. "Might not look like much now," he allowed, "but with the number of people pouring into the goldfields, it's bound to grow. Already started."

Sage could see that, and began to feel more optimistic about her future. Along with the growth of Fairplay Creek, the hotel's fortunes were bound to increase and hers along with it.

Bridger traded subdued greetings with a well-dressed man carrying a sheaf of papers coming out of the Land Office. He was one of the few men Sage had seen not dressed like a miner.

"That's Ramsey Thorogood," said Bridger. "He's a pretty important fellow. Currently making himself a fortune selling lots he only paid a few hundred dollars for three months ago." He took a thoughtful moment. "Yep, everyone'll be rich if things keep going along the way they are."

At the edge of town, Bridger slapped the reins and clucked to the horse, turning the buggy left on Seventh Street, a gently rising much used dirt road, its name crudely marked on a boulder at the intersection.

She could see vacant lots staked out in measured parcels along the secondary streets stretching into the distance. They'd only gone a block when Bridger pulled the horse to a stop in front of an imposing, two-story brick building on the corner.

An elaborate painted wooden sign partially covered by overhanging tree branches said WILD MOUNTAIN HONEY, and Sage's heart soared at the grand looking establishment. Filigreed cast iron roof-cresting topped the house like a royal coronet. First and second story windows were tall and stately, and a wide front porch swung around to spacious covered verandas on both sides. Shiny copper roofing sloped gracefully over the front entry, a magnificent carved oaken door with stained-glass sidelights.

Bridger tied the horse to a hitching post, then helped Sage and Odie from the buggy. Sage couldn't take her eyes off her lovely new home as they walked the white stone path and climbed the steps. Without knocking, Bridger opened the door and led them inside.

Sage found herself standing in a cool, marble-floored foyer. A sweeping staircase, its dark wood banister gleaming with polish, curved up to a spacious landing. Around its perimeter were six tall doors, all closed. More closed doors lined either side of a long upper hallway leading away to somewhere at the back of the second floor. Beyond the staircase on the ground floor, the hall extended to accommodate more doors opening to other rooms.

From the ground level entrance hall where she stood with Odie and Bridger, arched entrances to the right and left led into enormous, elaborately decorated parlors. In each, gilt framed mirrors glittered on crimson-papered walls, and the windows were draped with purple velvet that hung to the floor in crushed fabric puddles. The ceilings were high, the details elegant.

Red plush settees and gold brocade sofas provided the seating. Gleaming cherrywood end tables held cut glass lamps with fringed red and pink satin lampshades. Instead of a registration counter where hotel guests signed in, the parlor on Sage's left featured a fully stocked bar complete with brass foot rail in front, and paintings of nude women on the wall behind.

As she took it all in, a horrible gut-wrenching realization struck her and she gathered her skirts and spun to face Bridger.

"This isn't a hotel!" she accused.

The marshal shrugged, palms up. "I told you it wasn't."

"It's not even a boarding house. It's a—" A burst of anger rolled through her jamming the words in her throat. She stared speechless at the rooms and furnishings so far removed from what she imagined Aunt Honey's genteel hotel would look like.

Struggling to regain her voice so she could speak her feelings, she turned to Odie for help in verbalizing what she was seeing.

"Odie, this is a—" she began, but stopped again, surprised to find her friend gazing around the garish rooms with open curiosity and a rapt smile.

"Yes," Odie nodded. "It's a brothel, Sage, and it looks like a mighty fine one, too."

At that, Bridger stepped to the foot of the curved staircase, removed his hat in a grand sweeping flourish, and called up the stairs.

"Hey, girls! Come on down and meet your new landlady!"

Sage lifted her eyes to the second floor landing as one by one, doors opened, and women in various states of undress emerged. Some of them were yawning and rubbing their eyes as if they'd just awakened, some smiled pleasantly, and they all looked at her with curiosity. They came down the staircase chattering like a flock of sparrows and stood together at the bottom. Three or four of them widened their smiles at Bridger and assumed a bold, suggestive pose, which he ignored. A tall, fleshy, red-haired woman in the back was trying ineffectually to cover the tops of her creamy breasts which were bulging out at the neckline of her silky kimono.

With tears blurring her vision, Sage brushed each of the women with a hard, narrow gaze stopping at Bridger.

"I'd like to speak to you privately," she hissed. "Outside."

Gathering her dignity and her skirts, she lifted her chin, and marched out the door to the front porch, a lump filling her throat. Bridger followed.

She swallowed several times before she was able to speak again. "Why didn't you tell me this was a *parlor house*?" Mortified, she felt the blood surge to her face when she said the words.

"You didn't ask," Bridger said simply. He stood self-assuredly in front of her, one long leg cocked, his thumbs hooked loosely in his belt.

Arrogant was what he was, and now with the veil of optimism gone from her consciousness, she took a good look at him. He was older than she'd first thought, probably closer to forty than thirty-five. He'd put his hat back on, and auburn tufts of hair escaped from under it, curling a little over his sunburned neck and ears. He needed a haircut and a shave, and possibly a bath. A glossy, rust-colored sweep of mustache topped a wry smile. He looked at her without speaking, his cool green eyes holding steady on hers.

Reality sank in and it took great effort for her to hold her composure. "Are you telling me my aunt was a madam?"

"I'm not telling you, but the truth is she was."

11

Sage's voice turned shrill. "Well, I'm not. And, I won't be. This is my . . ." She fumbled for some word other than bordello. ". . . place," she finished unable to think of anything else. "And I'm closing it effective immediately."

"Now, Miss Cane, there's no need to be hasty. Look, come on back inside and meet the girls. They're not so bad. I know them all."

"I'm sure you do." She put heavy emphasis on each word.

"Oh, I don't mean like that. Come on in and say hello." He reached for the door and put his other hand on her spine as if to usher her inside.

She batted his hand away and rounded on him. *"Don't. Touch. Me.* Don't you ever put your hand on me again."

His eyes flashed then grew dark. He was clearly taken aback at this. He looked for all the world like a man unjustly accused of a crime he didn't commit, but she didn't give a damn.

She was inexplicably riled at him, blaming him for a turn of events not of his doing, but his touch had burned like an insult, stabbed like an assault on her moral fiber. Overcome by shock and embarrassment, she spun away and stumbled down the steps, her feet grinding on the white stones as she ran down the path.

Chapter Two

Sage wiped at the ridiculous tears beginning to spill over and kept walking, though she had no idea where she was headed. It wasn't like her to cry easily, but the past six weeks had brought her a whole lifetime of reasons to cry. First her dear father's bankruptcy, then the humiliation of Rodney Weatherspoon leaving her at the altar, and a week later the shock of her father's death. Now this. She hadn't even been in Fairplay Creek an hour and already she was welling up.

She took a handkerchief from her handbag and dabbed at her eyes. Had her father's lawyer known Wild Mountain Honey was a parlor house and not a hotel? He'd handled all the family and business affairs before her father's death. Why hadn't he made it clear when he told her about the inheritance from Aunt Honey's estate? Perhaps because it had been, regrettably, her only option as well as her last resort.

Then other questions came to mind. How long had Aunt Honey been a madam? Is that why her name was never mentioned at home? Did that have anything to do with her death? And more immediately, what was Sage going to do now?

She had to figure something out, and quickly. Right now she was too tired and hungry to grasp an idea long enough to consider it even if an idea had come to her. *Oh, my Lord, what have I gotten myself into?* She felt like an intruder in someone else's nightmare.

The sun was low in the sky, its golden orb touching the top of the mountains. At the bottom of the hill, she pointed herself toward the center of town and the noise wafting out the open doors of the saloons. As she got closer, the food smells made her stomach roll. She was light-headed, feeling faint from lack of food. She had to eat, and stopped at the first eatery she came to that looked halfway respectable. It was a small frame structure put together with unpainted timbers. She could see through tall street-side windows that, unlike the saloons, there were plenty of empty tables inside.

When she entered, two men at the back interrupted their conversation to gape at her. An old man sitting alone at a corner table turned dejected eyes in her direction, then quickly slipped back into his misery. Ignoring the male scrutiny, she seated herself at a table next to the window. Something that looked delicious was bubbling on the burner behind the low counter. A young, raw-boned boy about fourteen with a stained towel tucked into his waistband came over.

"What'll you have, ma'am?"

"That smells wonderful," Sage said, indicating the steaming pot on the stove. "What is it?"

"Rattlesnake stew," the boy replied, then grinned impishly at Sage's horrified reaction. "Just jokin' with ya, ma'am." His smile showed a broken front tooth. "It's beef stew, honest."

Dubious, but so hungry she might have eaten it if it were rattlesnake stew, she ordered a large bowl. "Do you have any bread to serve with that?"

The boy nodded. "Yes ma'am, and a crock of butter, too. I'll bring it right over."

True to his word, he was back in a minute with her meal.

She ate hungrily, ignoring the back table where the two men were now openly staring. The first few bites of food stilled the hunger spasms. Her breathing slowed, and she felt her energy returning in waves, strength flowing along her limbs into her brain. Her head stopped spinning, her panic ebbed away, and her mind cleared. Little by little, the true gravity of her situation settled over her shoulders like a shawl.

Hells bells, she was in a pickle.

She looked out the window at the rough men in the street. She didn't even know where she was exactly, except that it was a two-day wagon trip from Denver. But it felt like she was at the ends of the earth. Able to think rationally now, she mentally calculated the contents of the money pouch in her handbag and recognized instantly that she didn't have enough money to go back to Missouri. And even if she made it as far as Denver, where would she live, what would she do there?

Settling her spoon alongside her bowl and chewing thoughtfully, she became aware of the increased activity in the street. In the short time since she'd arrived in town, it had gotten busier. There were more horses, more wagons, and more people—mostly men, she realized—in and out of the makeshift shops.

Across the way was a tin shop she hadn't noticed on her ride through town. Next to it was a barbershop, and on the other side, an assay office where they tested the purity and grade of the ore brought in from the mines. Further down was a gunsmith. Nothing for women, everything for men, and her anger flared again as she thought about what she'd actually inherited—something most definitely for men.

For just a moment, the tenuous grip she held on her emotions slipped, and her future loomed up before her: dark, empty, and forbidding. Here she was, twenty-eight years old, no money, no longer marriageable, jilted, broken-hearted, and stuck in the middle of this raw, wild country with no home and no means of support.

In the street, a buggy clattered by with Bridger at the reins, looking straight ahead, his features still and set as if hewn from one of the freshly felled logs she saw piled around town. He was alone, and the back of the buggy was empty. He must have unloaded her trunks and left them at Wild Mountain Honey.

Then she remembered that Odie was there, too. Poor, dear, innocent Odie in her brown broadcloth skirt and her proper no-nonsense white ruffled blouse. Her thoughts faltered as she was suddenly struck with the notion that Odie might not be so innocent after all. Not only had she not seemed appalled at finding Wild Mountain Honey was a parlor house, she appeared to take some delight in it.

Sage emptied her bowl and pushed it away, but still she sat by the window fingering the napkin in her lap, unsure what to do or where to go.

A small commotion erupted in the corner of the room as a man wearing a grimy apron, big and burly with a frizzy gray beard, hovered over the table where the sad-looking man sat alone. They were arguing, the furious man Sage guessed to be the owner driving his forefinger into the tabletop, angrily making a point.

Ignoring the dust-up, the young boy who had brought her food came back to collect her empty dishes.

"What's going on?" she asked, putting some coins on the table to pay for her meal.

The boy shrugged. "He wants a bowl of stew, but he can't pay. Oscar wants him to leave."

Sage gazed at the man. He was wearing shabby work clothes.

"Is he a miner?" she asked.

"Wants to be." The boy shrugged again. "So far he ain't worked his claim." He reached for the money on the table, but she stopped him. "Here," she said, handing him some bills instead. "Take out enough for him, too."

On his way back to the cashbox, the boy veered off to say something to the owner who stopped yelling and looked over at her. The old miner looked at her, too, the lines around his eyes crinkling in an embarrassed but grateful smile.

She inclined her head in acknowledgement then turned back to the window. How many other people were there in Fairplay Creek without the means to buy even a simple bowl of stew? She remembered reading in an Independence newspaper that most of the miners heading west were men set adrift by the financial panic after the wildcat banks closed.

Across the street, Ramsey Thorogood, dressed in a dove gray suit and new-looking shiny boots, a gold watch chain draped over his vest, stood on the boardwalk talking to three much older men also dressed in business suits. And that's when it struck her.

The disparity in Fairplay Creek—everything for men and nothing for women. Falling down shacks and brand new buildings. People who appeared to have a lot, others with nothing. A burning knot of fear coiled in her chest, and she closed her eyes and stifled a shudder. She didn't want to be one of the ones with nothing.

A floorboard creaked nearby and through downcast eyes, she saw a pair of boots coming toward her, a tan duster flapping around denimed legs. They stopped next to her table.

"Howdy, Miss Cane."

Slowly she raised her head, taking in the hand-tooled leather belt, the silver badge, the broad shoulders, the tawny mustache, and the emerald green eyes staring down at her seeming to take her measure. The faint odor of whiskey drifted to her nostrils, and the muscles in her nose involuntarily clenched.

* * * * *

Bridger thought he knew what he was going to say, had the words fixed in his head, but the sight of her white-blonde hair and blue-green eyes wiped everything from his mind except thoughts of Elizabeth. When Sage had stepped out of the feeder stage in front of his office that afternoon, his heart had crashed against his breastbone, and he'd thought that somehow his prayers had been answered and Elizabeth was miraculously returning from the dead. He'd stared for several moments, unable to speak, and he knew he'd come across as rude and oafish. He made an effort to mind his manners now.

"May I sit down?"

She turned her heart-shaped face up to him, a face that he guessed would light up if she ever smiled, but he hadn't seen a single smile since she'd arrived. Her eyes shimmered with anger. They were red-rimmed, and she looked like she was ready to cry.

"I'd rather you didn't," she replied with a sniff, but he dragged out a chair with his foot and sat down anyway, buckling his long legs under the table.

"You wanna eat, Marshal?" the owner called from behind the counter.

"No, thanks," he replied not taking his eyes off Sage. "I've had my supper."

A silence stretched out as she stared at him, her expression thorny. She was obviously distressed. What he was going to tell her was going to distress her even more, so he decided to work into it slowly.

"What are you going to do?" he asked.

"I told you. I'm closing it. I am not a madam," she said with a disdainful sniff.

"Well, maybe not," he drawled, "but it wouldn't be a good idea to close Wild Mountain Honey."

"And why not?" Another haughty sniff sucked the air between them.

"Damnation, woman. Will you stop doing that?"

"What?"

"That. That sniffing thing. You got a cold?"

She pressed her lips and set her chin in a stubborn line, stiffening even more—if that were possible. The pupils of her eyes pierced him like fine, sharp dagger points.

Damn, this woman was a heap of botheration. That's where the similarity to Elizabeth ended. He let her simmer a moment, then said, "You know, your aunt was very well liked by just about everybody in town. It was a sad day when she died."

"And how *did* my aunt die?" Sage asked, fixing him with a hot accusing stare.

"Some trail trash passing through shot her. After she left the gambling hall."

"My aunt gambled?"

He looked at her a moment without speaking. She truly was uninformed about her own kin. "Let me put it this way. Honey Wild gambled a lot."

Sage's lips parted in surprise. "Oh." It came out on a bubble of air.

Bridger narrowed his eyes and inquired. "Just how close were you and your aunt?"

A wistful sigh escaped her, and her features softened a little. Memory flickered behind her eyes.

"She lived with us when I was a child. After she left, we never heard from her again. At least, I didn't."

Bridger nodded. No wonder she's upset to discover what Honey's been up to all those years. He went on.

"Honey was on her way back to the . . ." He stopped and cleared his throat and started over. "She was on her way home," he emphasized, deliberately not saying parlor house to avoid setting her off again, "when she was attacked and robbed. There'd been a stranger at her faro table, and he'd lost a lot of money and had a big, mean mouth about it. He was still complaining when they threw him out. We figure he waited outside, then followed her, and jumped her before she reached home."

"Did you arrest him?"

Bridger shook his head. "He must a rode out the same night because we never saw him around again. When Honey didn't come home, Miss Priscilla, the cook at Wild Mountain Honey, went out looking and found her in the alley. And of course, her winnings were gone. Miss Priscilla found the lawyer's name and address in Honey's personal papers, and I wrote him to see if there were any heirs."

"I'm her only heir," Sage said quietly, her eyes lowered.

Bridger didn't say anything, letting her have a moment. "She'll be missed. She provided a great service to the town."

Sage raised a delicate eyebrow. "I know what she provided."

"I don't think you do," he replied, his voice taking on a hard tone. He was losing patience with her superiorness. "Some of these miners here are damn fools, but some of them aren't. Some of them, probably a lot of them, are going to be very rich some day soon. But right now, Wild Mountain Honey is the only warm, clean place they have to go for any kind of social life and entertainment. It's a better home than the shacks and dugouts they're used to. Let's say it's a social necessity for the well being of the miners. Hell, if it weren't for the girls at Wild Mountain Honey, most of them wouldn't even bother to wash their face."

Her eyes were on his and she seemed to be listening, but he couldn't tell if she really understood.

"What I'm trying to say is, after your aunt got here and opened her place, Fairplay Creek became a real peaceable town. Didn't used to be so. With some place to go at night and especially on weekends, we don't have bored, angry miners getting drunk enough to shoot up the town. Most of them behave themselves pretty good now. Makes my job easier," he added with a small smile, trying for a bit of levity.

He could see she didn't get the humor. Instead, her eyes took on a hard-edged remoteness.

"Mr. Norwood, I can sympathize with you not wanting to work very hard," she paused, making the point, "but it really has nothing whatsoever to do with me."

"Oh, but it does, Miss Cane," he said, rising to her taunt putting menace in his voice. The way he spoke, growly and mean, usually scared people, and it was his way of avoiding gunfights. He didn't like using that tone on women, but she was getting his hackles up.

He reached in his duster and pulled a folded piece of paper from an inside pocket. He unfolded it and smoothed it out on the table between them, turning the paper so she could read it.

"What's that?" she asked, her lips pursed.

"If you look closely, Miss Cane, you'll see that it's the deed to Wild Mountain Honey."

"But . . . but . . . ."

"And if you look closer still, you'll see that it's my name on it." He tapped his finger on the parchment. "Honey Wild signed over the deed to me a month before she died."

"But that's impossible. I'm her heir," Sage protested.

"Yes ma'am, you are. But you only inherited the furniture, the girls, the business, and the proceeds. Everything inside. But not the building or the land. They're mine." There was an almost imperceptible note of panic in her face, so he pressed his advantage. "You might want to reconsider your decision, ma'am."

He uncoiled his long length from the chair, put two fingers to the brim of his hat, and strode out the door.

* * * * *

Thunderstruck, she watched him go. If he'd left her a choice, she didn't notice it.

His stunning revelation had knocked her breathless, but she understood precisely the implications of what he'd told her. He was her landlord and if she didn't keep a parlor house open in his building, he'd find someone else who would. Or maybe he would himself, but in either case, she'd be left homeless.

She sat back in her chair and heaved a sigh of resignation. Why ever would Aunt Honey sign over the deed to the marshal? She briefly considered that they might have been lovers, but shook off the notion. *Him?*

Through the window she saw Bridger cross the street, pull Ramsey Thorogood aside, and speak privately. Ramsey listened intently, a serious look on his face. She could tell they were talking about her, because Ramsey glanced once toward the window where she sat.

A reasonable woman, she saw the wisdom in being pragmatic, especially now that she had no where else to go. If she stayed, she'd have a roof over her head, at least for the time being. And he'd said the proceeds from the business were hers. What did those proceeds amount to, she wondered. Hopefully they were enough so she and Odie could get by. She couldn't forget Odie. She'd promised her a job. There had to be a way to make this work.

"Excuse me."

She turned to see the miner whose meal she'd paid for standing a few feet away. His face was worry-worn, his demeanor downcast. He showed gray at the temples though he wasn't that old.

"Yes?"

"Mighty grateful for the meal, ma'am. I'll pay you back. Double. Just as soon as I get enough money to buy tools, so I can work my claim. I promise you that. You can count on it."

"You're very welcome, sir," she said.

He dipped his head, and shuffled away closing the door behind him.

The sun had gone down some time ago and darkness was coming in over the mountains. Anxious to be off the street before the hour grew late, she extricated herself from napkin and chair, picked up her handbag, and went outside. Candlelight showed through the windows of the shops as she turned toward what she now had to accept as her home.

The din, piano music and laughter, from the saloons swelled out the doors as she passed. Only some of the storefronts had boardwalks, built or not built according to the inclination of the lot owner, and there were no streetlamps. But Bridger was right about one thing. Gold was bringing a lot of changes to Fairplay Creek. Signs of growth were everywhere. At the rate it appeared to be going, in a month she might not recognize the place.

She stopped in front of a hardware shop set up in a tent. Picks and axes and gold pans hung from a rope out front. Curious, she looked at the prices. The strategies of prospecting were beyond her, but she could see that it took a goodly amount of money to get started.

Night was falling quickly so she hurried on. She noticed a doctor's shingle newly nailed to a post, even a crudely lettered harness maker's sign. Everywhere huts were being replaced by more solid structures, some were being built of stone. But she didn't see any churches, or schools. Surely there were some children in this town. That young boy who served her stew must attend classes somewhere.

On the sides and ledges of the mountain, and out by the river, camp-fires and lanterns burned next to the dusky light of lantern-lit tents. She heard the echo of hammers crushing rock, shovels digging dirt, miners working into the night. Bridger's words came back to her. Some of them were going to be very rich.

She detested having to admit it, but she was being given an opportunity to make a living, a living that could eventually take her out of this godforsaken place and back home to Independence. She didn't have to participate in the activities at Wild Mountain Honey. Much as it went against her grain, all she had to do was think of it as a business, and run it as if it were any other.

23

She was a lady with proper manners and the ability to converse politely. She could read, write, and do her numbers. She appreciated music and poetry, and she was smart. At least as smart as these other people who were making a living in the New West. Smart enough to come up with a plan.

At Seventh Avenue, she turned toward Wild Mountain Honey and made her way along the gently sloping street. Up ahead, the parlor house's leaded windows glowed with light. Candles flickered inside, and sparkling crystal chandeliers spun rays of diamond light in all directions. As she neared, she heard music and people laughing. She stopped at the end of the white-pebbled path and looked at it from a new perspective, through the eyes of a businessperson. There was no denying the architecture was beautiful. She could always redecorate and replace the vulgar furnishings inside.

The sign over the veranda was partially hidden by an enormous evergreen. A wind blew up rattling the branches aside, and for the first time she was able to read the entire sign. WILD MOUNTAIN HONEY PLEASURE PALACE. She hadn't seen the last two words until that moment because of the thick curtain of greenery.

Just as she started up the path, the door flew open. The sounds of music and laughter poured forth as if a levee had burst then were abruptly cut off when the door closed again. Odie rushed out into the moonshadows with outstretched arms.

"Oh, Sage. Are you all right? I was so worried."

"Yes, I'm fine." She returned Odie's warm hug, and started up the front steps.

"No," Odie whispered. "Not that way. Come around back. There's a private entrance."

Odie led her in through a storage room, and past a pantry and a kitchen where a young black woman was working at a huge iron stove. The merrymaking coming from the front parlors could be heard clearly through the walls. The laughter was loud, the conversation spirited, the language colorful. It sounded to Sage like a swearing competition was being held in the other rooms.

"Follow me." Odie, her eyes shining with excitement, took Sage's hand and led her up a stairway to an anteroom at the top. The lighting was low, the furniture looked comfortable. It smelled of lavender. On the right, a long hallway angled off to the front of the house where the second floor landing overlooked the front door.

"The girls' rooms are down there," Odie said. Quickly she shut the door, closing off the passageway. The sounds of revelry from the other part of the house were further diminished to an almost inaudible murmur.

Straight ahead were two sets of glass-fronted double doors trimmed with wide moldings. The doors were thrown wide, and Sage could see they led into private suites that together appeared to take up the entire rear of the second floor. She followed Odie into the larger of the two. A massive stone fireplace covered one entire wall. Arranged in front of the hearth were a round dining table with four chairs, and a patterned divan. Leaded floor-to-ceiling bay windows looked out over hundreds of miners' fires pinpricking the black silhouette of the mountain outlined against the charcoal sky.

Closets and cupboards, more than she'd ever seen in a single room, took up another long wall. Off to the side was a sitting area with a desk, a chair, and another divan. Her trunks, opened but not completely un-packed, were on the floor next to a huge four-poster bed.

"I hope you don't mind," said Odie, "but I've moved into the room next door. It's smaller, but quite suitable enough for me. I thought you'd be more comfortable in here."

"Oh, this is lovely," Sage said begrudgingly, unable to keep herself from admiring the rooms. Furnishings and draperies were tasteful and of good quality, vastly different from downstairs, more along the lines of what she imagined her aunt would choose. She touched the polished mahogany table, ran her fingers over the silk brocade upholstery.

"I started to unpack for you, but . . ." Odie averted her eyes and let the words slide away. Sage looked at her inquisitively, inviting her to go on.

"Well, the, uh, guests began arriving, so I went downstairs."

Sage nodded tiredly and gave a robust sigh, accepting the undeniable truth of her situation. She'd become a madam, albeit a reluctant one, albeit a temporary one, but a madam nonetheless. She caught sight of herself in the full-length mirror across the room. Her light colored hair looked dark and damp, and hung in limp strands down her neck and over her ears. There were grayish smudges under her eyes as if someone had wiped ash-covered fingertips around them. Her skin was pale, her face drawn.

Odie inquired warily. "Are you sure you're all right?"

"Really, I'm fine. I just had to get some air and some food." Then an afterthought. "Did you have supper?"

"Yes," Odie said, her voice animated. "There's a cook here. Miss Priscilla. And I've met the girls, too." She eyed Sage as if gauging her reaction to that.

Sage nodded again and dropped onto the divan in front of the fireplace, unbuttoned her jacket, and slipped it off. Slowly she loosened the buttons of her lace-collared blouse. The sight of the big feather bed with four plump pillows and a puffy quilt sent tremors of exhaustion through her body.

"I need a bath," she said with a shudder.

Odie pointed to a closed door. "There's a bathtub in there. With piped-in water. Miss Priscilla is busy right now, but the girls showed me how to heat it." Odie stood and made a move to go do it, but Sage's staying hand stopped her.

"In a minute. Sit down, please. I want to talk to you."

Suddenly downcast, looking like she expected the worst, Odie took a seat on the brocaded sofa next to Sage. Her features crumpled with worry, and she rushed to speak up before Sage could.

"The marshal told me what you said. About closing it. But I was hoping you'd change your mind. It's quite comfortable here really, and . . ." She spread her hands, palms out in entreaty. "It's a roof and a warm bed," she said plaintively.

"Yes, I know," Sage answered, and Odie hurried on.

"And forgive me if I sound mercenary, but—" Odie lowered her voice and widened her eyes. "You have no idea how much money is coming into this place. We could just, you know, live here, we don't have to . . ." She indicated with a toss of her head the activities that were presumably going on at the other end of the house.

Then her composure cracked. "If you close it, I don't know what I'll do. I can't go back to—" A sob bubbled up breaking off her words. "Can you just think about it?" she implored in a tremulous voice before breaking into huge, breathless sobs.

Sage pulled Odie's hands into her own, and squeezed them reassuringly. She didn't know what it was Odie didn't want to go back to, but it must be something horribly frightful to make her cry that way.

"Please don't cry, Odie." She tightened her grip on Odie's fingers. "I have thought about it, and I've got an idea."

* * * * *

The next morning, Sage opened her eyes to sunshine pouring in through the windows. The house was still. She stretched and yawned. It always amazed her how a full stomach and a good night's sleep could change a person's view of the world.

27

She slipped out of bed and looked outside at the cerulean blue sky, then threw up the sash and breathed in the crisp mountain air. She heard the faint clank and rattle from the mine areas, the miners already at work, or perhaps having worked through the night.

Dressing quickly, she opened her door and stepped into the anteroom. The front part of the house was silent, and she assumed the girls were still asleep. Putting her ear to Odie's door, she heard stirring, and knocked softly.

"Come in." Odie's voice was absolutely lilting.

Sage turned the knob and stepped in to find Odie in front of the mirror putting the final pins in her glossy brown hair. On the dresser was a large black box with brass trim and hinges.

"Good morning." Odie smiled at Sage in the mirror, excitement again dancing in her eyes. She gave her hair a pat, took one last look at herself in the mirror, and turned.

"I have a surprise for you."

"What is it?" Sage wondered with a twinge if she could take any more surprises.

"It's in here," Odie said, putting her hand on the box. "Look." Her fingers fumbled with the latch, and she lifted the lid. The box was filled with money. "This is from last night," she said looking at Sage expectantly.

Sage stared with disbelief, and drew in a breath.

"The girls still have to be paid," Odie went on cheerily, "and there are probably some other bills. I haven't found your aunt's papers and accounting records yet." She paused. "But this should be enough to cover everything, don't you think? To pay my salary? With some left over?"

Sage swallowed and gripped the edge of the dresser to steady herself, her eyes locked on the bills, coins, and gold nuggets in the box.

"Yes," she replied, her voice breathy with relief. "There should be enough left over." Enough to set her plans in motion sooner than she expected.

Chapter Three

Marshal Bridger Norwood sat looking out the window of his office. He rolled a cigarette in his lips liking the taste of the fresh tobacco, squinted his eyes against the sun's glare, and gazed down the dusty street at Sage Cane. She walked with determination, resolutely picking her way up, over, and down the intermittent boardwalks. Her handbag swung from her arm.

He studied her with more than a little interest. In talking with her last night, it had crossed his mind to wonder if she really was Honey Wild's niece, or an imposter of some kind. She didn't seem to know anything about her relative and so far as he could tell, there was no family likeness or similarity.

None whatsoever.

"I think she's gonna close it."

Ramsey Thorogood, sitting with his expensive boots propped on the visitor's side of the marshal's desk, dropped them to the floor with a thud and leaned forward.

"What?"

"You heard me," Bridger replied absently, his attention on the street.

It came as no surprise to him that Sage churned up a lot of attention as she walked along. Men stopped to stare. A few of them tried to engage her in conversation, but after nodding politely, she kept walking. Her pace in her sensible flat-heeled shoes was sure and steady, her determined stride long and sure under her full skirt. She swung her legs from the hip taking good full steps, not mincing and tentative like some women. The motion caused the hem of her skirt to flip up a little over the toe of her shoe each time she stepped forward. Flip, flip, flip. He could almost see her ankles.

"Listen here, Bridger. You told me last night you talked to her and showed her the land title."

"I did."

"You said she looked scared."

"She did."

Sage stopped in front of the hardware. The proprietor poked his head out of the tent flap, and she said something to him. He came out to talk to her, and after chatting a few minutes, she walked on. What the hell was that about, Bridger wondered. Then she turned into Oscar's where she'd had supper the night before. For breakfast, probably. But no, in a short time she came out and continued walking.

"Then why are you telling me now you think she's going to close it?" Ramsey demanded.

Positioning the unlit cigarette in his mouth so he could form words around it, Bridger swung his chair to face the real estate investor. "She doesn't seem to have the same characteristics Honey did."

"She's a woman, isn't she?" Ramsey Thorogood snorted a laugh, his face turning serious when Bridger didn't join him in the gibe.

Bridger was reflecting on Sage Cane. Somehow, he didn't see her running a house of ill repute. She didn't have the sensibilities it required. She was too far removed from the ways of the world, at least the world as it was known in Fairplay Creek. Honey Wild, on the other hand, had a vigorous appreciation for its pleasures.

"You can't let her close the whorehouse, Bridger. Wild Mountain Honey gives the miners someplace to go and something to do. Keeps them out of trouble. No major mining company is going to set up operations in a lawless town."

"You're right about that, I reckon," Bridger drawled.

"And now there's talk of bringing a railroad spur to Fairplay Creek. The track will end adjacent to my land, and I plan to build a hotel across from the station. The railroad won't come to a town where it's not safe to walk the streets."

"I expect you're right." Bridger gazed at the man. He wore a dapper vested suit every day, rain or shine, warm or cold. Bridger supposed it went along with his new image as a powerful man with influential friends. Right now his face was turning red and he was glowering across the desk.

"You know what your job is," Thorogood said, with barely concealed anger. "To keep the peace in this town. I don't care how you do it. But the first time things get out of hand, you're out of a job. Understand?" He stood. "The first sign of trouble, you're off the payroll."

Bridger, knowing Thorogood could make good on that threat, tried to keep his face impassive, but couldn't stop his jaw from clenching. Without another word, not that any more were necessary, Ramsey Thorogood strode out the door.

Damn, I need a drink.

Bridger took the unlit cigarette from his mouth, threw it on the floor, and ran his hand down his face, his cheeks and chin whiskery under his rough hands. He fought down a burning pain that swelled in his chest, but couldn't ward off the memory of that day two years ago in Nebraska Territory. And of Elizabeth with the white-blonde hair.

It was as clear in his mind as if it happened yesterday. She'd come into town that day to shop bringing Jenny with her, the little girl clinging shyly to her mother's skirts. He hadn't wanted her to come, but she said she needed things for their new baby on the way. There'd been some tension because of a gang of outlaws camped over the rise where the street ended on the prairie. They'd caused a ruckus the previous night at a saloon, and as the deputy on duty, Bridger had gone over to quiet them down. It got ugly. Words were exchanged, guns were drawn, but no shots were fired, and in the end, the gang rode out.

But by noon the next day, rumors were flying that they were coming back for a piece of his hide. And they did. Two hours later, with unmistakable menace, they rode into town, stopped in front of the sheriff's office and issued a challenge from across the street. Bridger and the sheriff, and the other deputy, an old-timer, went outside to try and ward off any trouble, but bullets flew almost immediately. People in the street dove for cover. Women and children screamed and ran for safety. The lawmen, dodging bullets, returned fire. When it was over, two of the outlaws were dead in the street, and the other two were making dusty tracks out of town.

But the screaming and wailing didn't stop. Bystanders caught in the crossfire lay in the street covered with blood. Jacob Blakely's boy was sprawled over the supplies he'd just loaded into the family's farm wagon. The preacher, his wife sobbing beside him, was bleeding from a hole in his chest. Two men who'd come out of a saloon were crumpled on the ground, their guns still in their hands.

And then he heard Jenny crying, her little girl voice rising into hysteria. She was on the ground next to Elizabeth, patting her mother's cheeks. "Mommy, wake up. Mommy, please wake up."

But Bridger knew Elizabeth would never wake up again.

After that, there were ugly rumors and lots of questions including plenty that had no answers. It was never exactly clear whose bullets actually killed Elizabeth. Some of the townspeople speculated it was the outlaws'. Others speculated it was Bridger's. Bridger tried not to speculate because doing so ripped his heart open, even now.

He swallowed hard against the leaden knot forming in his throat, snatched his hat from the rack on the wall, and kicked open the front door. It slammed shut behind him as he crossed the narrow strip of ground separating his office from the Diamond Rio Saloon. He motioned to the barkeeper as he entered, holding up a hand with four fingers extended. With his boot propped on the foot rail, he lined up the shots on the bar in front of him knowing that after he downed those, he'd be able to stop speculating. For a while.

* * * * *

By mid-morning everyone in town knew Sage Cane was the new madam of Wild Mountain Honey. With not far to go, word traveled fast. Some of the men on the street broke into smiles at her approach and stared at her as she passed by. Others made lewd comments behind her back loud enough for her, and anyone else nearby to hear. The few women she encountered ignored her neighborly nod, and with tilted noses and pinched mouths, demonstrated their displeasure of her.

She was humiliatingly aware of their scrutiny, and deeply stung by the insults and snubs. Incredibly, she'd gone from being decent to disreputable literally overnight. Her embarrassment turned to anger, but she kept her face impassive, refusing to be distracted from her immediate business at hand. She vowed that one day she'd be seen as respectable again. Until then, she'd build a wall around herself through which no pain could penetrate.

Her next thought came unbidden. Rodney Weatherspoon! The man who promised to love her forever. The man to whom she'd given so much of herself. The man who'd left her at the altar, jilted and alone. Everyone in Independence had whispered about it.

She closed her eyes and suppressed a shudder. Never mind that Rodney was known as the rogue of Independence, a fortune hunter extraordinaire who had already trampled half a dozen hearts, she'd believed him when he said he loved her. A woman in love believed everything. Believed anything.

Her cheeks burned in remembrance as blood rushed to her head in a maelstrom of hurt and embarrassment. The pain of his leaving had settled in her bones and she couldn't shake it.

She was ashamed of herself. For falling in love so badly, and for what she'd done. A pain squeezed her heart at the memory. Thank God she wasn't with child.

Leaving Oscar's, she walked briskly, her destination in sight. Dust blew off the side of the mountain as the wind caught loose dirt being dug up by the miners. The ever-present sounds of hammering and the smack of pickaxes puncturing the mountainside echoed dully down to the street. She heard the shaker boxes, and men calling to each other down by the river as they rocked the sluices back and forth. Sage took some comfort from the clatter.

When she reached the new bank, she pushed open the brass-handled doors and entered. Inside, it smelled of new wood, fresh paint, and varnish. And money. Until this morning, standing beside Odie gaping at the cash box, Sage hadn't realized money had a smell.

She stood a moment, letting her eyes adjust from the brightness of the sun. When they did, she saw a man officiously reviewing some documents at his desk. A nameplate identified him as Martin Gardner, Owner and President. Just the man she wanted to see, but she would have recognized him anyway from the description Odie had given her. Bald head with a few stringy strands combed over, broad paunch, gold nugget ring on his little finger. Mr. Gardner had been a guest at Wild Mountain Honey the previous evening.

Turning up her lips in her most fetching smile, she approached his desk. The bank president didn't look up, but instead lifted his hand and waggled an impatient finger indicating she should wait while he finished what he was doing.

Sage didn't wait. "Good morning, Mr. Gardner," she said interrupting him. "I'm Sage Cane."

He lowered his arm and looked up, a surprised smile spreading across his face. The veins of his cheeks were close to the skin, pale reddish-purple, but clearly visible. The expression in his eyes transformed from annoyance at the interruption to relish at the sight of her. He raked a hungry gaze from her hair to her shoes, and back again. She thought him repulsive, and scrunched her toes and bit the inside of her lip to keep from saying so out loud.

"I'd like to open an account with your bank." She took a seat without being invited, and primly rested her handbag on her knees. "But I need to be accorded your highest level of confidentiality."

"Oh, Miss Cane, you can be assured your secrets are safe with me," he said, at which she smiled demurely.

"And yours with me, Mr. Gardner. Yours with me."

* * * * *

When Sage returned from her errands, she heard voices coming from the kitchen and found Odie sitting at a long wooden table having coffee and talking to the cook whom Sage had not yet met.

She greeted Odie, then smiled at the beautiful black woman stirring pancake batter in a large bowl. Her eyes were lovely, alive and intelligent, seeming to view the world with courage. She had the look of having been born both wise and proud.

"Hello, Priscilla. I'm Sage Cane, Honey Cane's niece."

The cook wiped a hand on her apron and extended it. "I'm a free black," she said without rancor. "It's Miss Priscilla, if you don't mind."

"Pardon me. Of course. Miss Priscilla," Sage replied and took the woman's hand. It was strong and long-fingered, the same color as the coffee in Odie's cup. Their gazes met and Sage knew instantly this was a woman of character.

"Nice to meet you, Miss Sage. Can I pour you some coffee?"

"Yes, thank you," she replied taking a seat next to Odie.

Just then, the sound of footsteps could be heard on the front staircase, the girls coming down for breakfast. Sage found herself apprehensive. She'd never met a soiled dove and didn't know what to expect. And she hadn't forgotten how rudely she'd run off yesterday.

The girls entered the kitchen, some of them laughing, others yawning, and Sage soon discovered she needn't have worried. They were friendly, attractive women with smiles that were disarming and self-assured, and they welcomed her warmly, introducing themselves with confidence. She found them to be as different from what she'd expected as it was possible to be.

Chantal Seabrook had luscious pouty lips that revealed beautiful white teeth when she smiled. A sprinkle of soft freckles danced across Melanie McPhee's nose and cheeks. Natalie Bennett was aging, but becomingly with bone structure that would keep her beautiful as long as she lived. Poppy Merriweather had a slender nose and the lean, fine carriage that signified upper crust breeding. Verbena Jones was small and slender with exquisite porcelain skin, and she wore tiny bells around her ankle. She looked much too young to be what she was.

For the moment, their names swirled in her head as she tried to connect each one to a face. To complicate matters even more, they all had nicknames as well as given names. Chantal was called Fat Mabel, though she wasn't fat; Poppy was called Dirty Alice, though she wasn't dirty; and Natalie was called Tiny, though she wasn't tiny. Verbena's nickname was Frenchy and Sage thought she might have been.

Every one of them, collectively known as the Honeys Odie had told her, were beautiful enough to invite and hold a man's glance, with lively personalities and silky voices guaranteed to keep a man interested and listening. No wonder the miners liked coming here, Sage thought. From what she'd seen so far, the handful of other women in town were hard-bitten and lacking in refinement.

The Honeys bombarded her with questions, curious about her background and where she came from. They admired her hair, inquiring with envy if the striking ivory color was natural or if she'd done something to achieve it artificially. They were disappointed to learn it was natural and therefore not available to them in a bottle.

As they sat down to Miss Priscilla's breakfast of hotcakes, bacon, and biscuits with real butter, the conversation turned to a more serious matter. They were worried about what was going to happen to them now that Sage had arrived.

"Are you going to send us away?" asked Chantal.

"Will we have to move to another town?" Natalie wanted to know.

"We really like it here, Miss Sage. We don't want to leave," implored Poppy.

"Most of us don't have no place else to go." Melanie's eyes held a sheen of unshed tears.

Sage put down her fork. She hadn't thought of that. She'd only thought of herself and Odie. Smiles slowly faded on the faces of the girls and worry shadows stirred behind their eyes as they waited for her reply. Closing the parlor house would put these women out of a home as well as at the mercy of . . . Sage quaked inside. God only knows what they'd be at the mercy of.

She gazed around the table, looking from one face to the other, trying to read their stories in their eyes. Could it be that some of these women were here not by choice, but by circumstances, just as she was?

Sage shook her head. "No," she said emphatically. "No one has to leave unless they want to."

"Good morning," called a cheerful voice. The latecomer, a ravishing red-haired beauty, swept into the kitchen. It was the woman Sage had seen the day before trying to close the edges of her robe over breasts. She stopped abruptly when she saw Sage.

"Good morning," Sage said, and introduced herself. "What is your name?"

Dimples appeared in the other woman's cheeks and her eyes twinkled. "My name is Piroska Gorsky," she replied in a lovely deep-throated Hungarian accent, "but people call me Turtledove." She dipped her head toward her voluptuous chest. "Because my breasts are so big."

Sage fell into laughter and the others joined in. Then, while Miss Priscilla presided over her kitchen and everyone ate heartily, Sage excused herself, and went upstairs to get ready.

* * * * *

The moon had just cleared the rim of the distant mountains making the snow-capped peaks shine like silver against a black velvet sky when a soft knock came on the door of Sage's private suite. Her guest had arrived.

She turned from the window and seated herself at a gleaming cherry-wood kneehole desk, folding her hands on a sheaf of ledger sheets, which held the grim details of her aunt's financial position before she died. Though the nightly revenues at Wild Mountain Honey appeared to be substantial, the cost of maintaining the parlor house was significant. Kitchen expenses were high. They ate well, providing the girls with the best food available. Chickens tended by Miss Priscilla out back provided fresh eggs, but boarding fees for the cow kept at the livery so they could have milk, butter, and cream were considerable. The furniture was expensive and, it turned out, not completely paid for. Medical care for the girls by the local doctor, wages for a combination piano player-bouncer they called The Professor, soaps, creams, any number of things she hadn't counted on, took part of the money. Plus there was Aunt Honey's debt, and her own brought with her from her father's estate. There would not be as much left over as she had first thought. What she was about to do was risky at best.

The knock was repeated. She reached into the desk drawer, and closed her fingers over a small pistol she'd found earlier, apparently put there by her Aunt Honey. She took it out and hid it in the folds of her pale peach-colored skirt. A woman can't be too careful, she reminded herself.

"Come in," she called.

Odie swept open the door, ushered in a man, then retreated, closing the door softly. The man entered the room with halting steps as though taking care not to soil the carpet with his boot soles. He came to a stop a few feet in front of the desk. He held his hat in one hand, and with the other, slicked his hair back off his grizzled but washed face. His pant legs were tucked into well-worn boots she could see he'd attempted to clean. From the quizzical look on his face, it was clear he didn't know why he'd been summoned.

"Got your note," he said. "The boy from Oscar's come up to my dugout and give it to me this afternoon."

"Thank you for coming." She studied his sharp angled face trying to read his character in his features. "I'm Sage Cane."

"I know who you are."

"I'm sorry, but I don't know your name."

"Miller. Josiah Miller. Named after my daddy." He offered a tentative smile and shifted his feet.

"Please sit down, Mr. Miller."

He looked as if he expected her to snatch the invitation away, but after a moment's hesitation, sat on the chair in front of her desk. His fingers fidgeted around the brim of his hat. "Thank you again for the meal at Oscar's."

She inclined her head in a gracious nod, and smiled, an attempt to put him at ease she wasn't sure was working. "You're welcome again. That's why I've asked you here."

His brows dashed into a frown and he hitched forward, his anxiety increased manyfold. "Sorry, miss, I'm still not able to pay—"

"Yes, I know," she stopped him, and smiled again trying not to let her own uncertainty show. She didn't know anything about him, didn't know how he'd respond to what she was about to say. But desperate circumstances required desperate measures, and Lord knew she was desperate. "That's what I wanted to talk to you about."

Some of the tension in his shoulders released, but he remained seated on the edge of the chair. She tried to hold his gaze, but he avoided hers. She guessed he was a man used to paying his debts promptly and was now greatly mortified that he was beholden to her. More so, perhaps, because she was a woman. And a madam.

"How long have you been in Fairplay Creek, Mr. Miller?"

"About three weeks," he answered. He seemed about to say more, but something made him change his mind and he didn't go on.

"You have a mining claim here?"

"Yes, ma'am, I do. Up at Buckskin Ridge, near the lode up there."

Sage was familiar with Buckskin Ridge. The proprietor of the hardware had told her that's where most of the newcomers were heading.

"But you have no tools with which to work it?"

"No." His face crumbled in shame and it was only with great effort he was able to bring it under control. She thought if he were alone, he might have cried.

"And why is that?" she asked gently.

41

He cleared his throat several times before answering. "The crossing from Chicago was hard. Harder'n I thought it would be. My wife took ill on the way and died when we reached Denver. After I paid the doctor and undertaker, there weren't much left. Just enough to get here an' register a claim."

Half of her mind listened with empathy, understanding his grief, while the other half smothered the emotion and focused on survival. Hers and his, for if he were agreeable to what she had to say, their survival would be inextricably tied together.

"Tell me about your claim, Mr. Miller."

He seemed leery about giving away any more information, so she attempted to set his mind at ease. "Forgive me if I sound like I'm prying, but I have a reason for asking. I don't think you'll be sorry for confiding in me."

Somewhat satisfied, he told her. "The claims are laid out in hundred-foot holdings up there. I posted my Notice of Claim my first day here. Went to the Land Office the next day and registered it. It belongs to me fair and square, all legal like."

"How much do you expect it to produce?" she wanted to know.

"Well, it's near a lode. Rumor's got it two veins meet close by. The slope is about right, and the water don't run too fast. Got a better chance'n most of striking it rich, if I can get the gold out."

"What tools do you require to do that?"

"Ma'am?"

"I'm asking what you need, Mr. Miller. Maybe I can help you. What do you need to work your claim? Do you have anything at all?"

The man shook his head from side to side. "I don't even have a shovel. I planned to buy tools here."

"I see." Using the prices the hardware proprietor had given her that day, she did some quick calculations on a piece of paper. After a moment, she looked up.

"I can give you enough money for tools and supplies for six months, enough to buy a burro, a tent, gold pans, shovels and picks." Her gaze swept him. "A change of clothes. Sturdy boots. Food if you fix it yourself in camp instead of eating in a saloon or at Oscar's. In return, I want part ownership of your claim and a percentage of the gold you bring out each week."

He stared at her, hope fighting incredulity for possession of his face, and gave a nervous one-note laugh. "Why would you do that?"

"I have my reasons." She didn't want to be pressed for them. Something told her it was best she kept her motives to herself. If Bridger Norwood got wind of what she had in mind, he might throw her out now.

Josiah was silent so long, she wondered if she'd offended him, and her heart picked up its beat. "Are you interested in making that sort of an arrangement?" she asked.

A coal of hope smoldering in his eyes flamed to life. "Why, yes, ma'am. I expect I am." A grin started.

"There is a condition, though. You must keep this transaction secret."

He nodded eagerly.

"I don't want people knowing our business," she went on. "If one word leaks out about our agreement, I'll see to it that your mining supplies are immediately repossessed." She didn't know if she could actually do that, but wanted him to think she could.

When he nodded again, she opened a drawer, took out the papers she'd spent the afternoon preparing, and handed them to him.

"Can you read?" she asked.

"Yes, ma'am," he replied.

"Then read these carefully before you sign," she told him. "Please take your time."

* * * * *

Bridger yawned and rubbed his eyes, then swung his chair away from his desk so he could stretch. He wasn't used to so much paperwork. It was only since some of the townsfolk, men like Ramsey Thorogood, organized an unofficial legislative body to provide some immediate structure and authority for the fast growing town that collecting taxes and issuing business licenses was taking so much of his time.

Of necessity, Acer Morrow had taken over most of the routine peace keeping duties like settling disputes, calming disturbances, and hauling drunks off the street. When he wasn't mooning over Verbena Jones up at Wild Mountain Honey, that is. The boy was in love, wanted to marry her. Bridger blew a cynical gust of air at the thought. Hell, Acer knew as well as anyone that men didn't marry tarnished goods.

He turned his chair around, signed his name to the bottom of the license for the new all-night laundry run by a Chinaman from San Francisco, blew on the ink, then fanned it with his hand. He halfway suspected the only reason he got the job as marshal was because he could read and write. Didn't matter. It was a job that paid and he was grateful for it.

His head felt hollow and his mouth tasted like cotton. He supposed he should go home. The cabin up on Fourmile Creek was becoming a refuge that every day he was increasingly reluctant to leave. He'd become a solitary man by choice. Liked living in peace and quiet, surrounded by nature, aspens and pine trees, not another soul within a half a mile of his spread.

He looked out the window, then with a long, exhausted sigh, put his pen down, squared the stack of papers on his desk, and stood up. He was done for the day.

He slipped on his trail coat, but before stepping outside, drew his forty-five and checked its loads, as was his habit. Satisfied, he holstered it, leveled his hat, and walked out the door locking it behind him.

His horse, a mahogany bay named Tumbleweed, stood waiting patiently tied to a rail of the corral next door at the livery, one hind leg cocked. Bridger swung into the saddle and settled himself, resting his hands on the saddle horn, thinking about taking one last ride through town. Didn't hurt to stay visible, remind everyone there was law about. He could collect the five-dollar license fee from the new laundry owner. Make sure there was no trouble brewing in the streets. Check out the saloons. Maybe have a drink.

When his boot heel nudged the horse, it made a blowing noise and turned toward the center of town. Toward the sound of piano playing, loud voices from the whiskey mills, shouting from the gambling halls. It all blended into a raucous cacophony that Bridger hardly noticed anymore.

He rode slowly, picking his way through the crowd, his body rolling slightly in the saddle keeping time with the gait of his horse. Up ahead a crowd milled around the Shouting Post. Without a newspaper in town, the only way to spread news of any kind was to shout it in the streets, or post it on what had come to be known as the Shouting Post outside the bank. Posted notices usually announced new businesses, job openings, men seeking work, or goods available to buy, sell, or trade. There was only one reason a crowd as large as this one congregated, and that was to read about the latest gold strike in the camps.

Curious, Bridger angled his mount toward the bank, but before he was close enough to read the hand-lettered sign, some of those gathering turned to him, confusion and anger on their faces.

"Are you gonna let her get away with this, Marshal?" a voice demanded.

"Who does she think she is orderin' something like this in Fairplay Creek?"

Bridger dismounted. "Hold it, boys, let me get a look at it." He shouldered his way through and read the sign on the Shouting Post.

NEW RULES FOR GUESTS OF WILD MOUNTAIN HONEY
Effective immediately
No profanity or vulgar language will be allowed
Smoking will be limited to the east parlor ONLY
Two drink limit per guest per evening
All those who have not taken a bath
will be turned away at the door
NO EXCEPTIONS

It was at that moment Bridger knew Sage Cane was going to be a huge pain in the ass.

"What's pro-fan-ity?" someone asked.

"Cussin', you old goat!"

"How are we supposed to go someplace without cussin'?"

"What're ya gonna do about it, Norwood?"

"Marshal, is that legal?"

Other men had joined the restless crowd and it was beginning to stir. Chests expanded, fingers folded into fists, holsters shifted. Bridger, rankled himself, faced them, holding up both hands as if to fend off their indignation.

"Calm down, boys. It appears Miss Cane isn't used to our ways here. I'll take care of it," he assured them. "I'll go talk to her right now." Angry grumbling transmuted into murmurs of approval as he grabbed hold of his saddle, pulled himself up, and threw his leg over.

Damn, that woman was an aggravation. She had a lot of nerve bringing her prissy ways here, trying to tell others how to live like she was God's own All-High-and-Mighty. He reined his horse into the passing crowd and struck out for Wild Mountain Honey. At Seventh Street, he turned and kicked the bay into a trot. Temperatures during the day were warming, but the night air was still cold and brittle. He could see his breath, and the bay's.

At the top of the rise he dismounted and wound the reins around the hitch rack in front of Wild Mountain Honey. Through the windows he saw people moving about, some of them dancing. Skirting the stone walkway, he proceeded to the back of the house, passing the log pile and Miss Priscilla's fenced off chicken yard. He threw open the back door, and stomped in.

Miss Priscilla was in the kitchen at the chopping block slicing apples, and startled at the sound of his step. "Lordy, Marshal. Don't you know better'n to sneak up on me when I've got a knife in my hand?"

He grumbled an apology as he hurried past, heading for the stairs leading to the second floor.

"Marshal, wait. You can't go up there." Miss Priscilla dropped the knife and followed after him. "That's Miss Sage's private quarters."

"I know what it is," he growled, starting up the steps, then stopping abruptly as astonishment filled the very pit of him. Josiah Miller was clattering down the steps on the balls of his feet, an undeniable sparkle in his eye, and a smile as wide as Kansas Territory pasted on his face.

"Howdy, Marshal," he greeted, putting his hand to the brim of his hat, then "'Scuse me, Marshal," as he turned sideways to squeeze past.

Hovering on the edge of a nonspecific anger, Bridger gaped at Josiah Miller's back, then turned his stare to the top of the stairs. Well, I'll be damned. She's taking customers.

The outright deceitfulness of the woman stunned him, freezing him where he stood, one foot raised on a step above. She'd sat across from him at Oscar's with her uppity sniffs and prudish manners pretending to be so high-minded and honorable. Her words came back to him, pinched and mocking in his memory: *I am not a madam.*

Then shock yielded to humiliation and he felt like a damn fool. He bounded to the top of the stairs and glared at the glass-fronted doors. They were closed, but light filtered through thin, gauzy curtains. He marched across the anteroom and knocked hard, rattling the glass panes.

"Sage Cane, I want to talk to you!"

There was no reply, so he pounded harder. "Do you hear me? Open up," he roared.

When there was still no sound from behind the closed doors, he flung them open and barged in, his trail coat billowing out behind. Sage was sitting at her desk, stark terror in her eyes.

"What kind of a fool do you think I am?" he bellowed, taking long strides and pointing his finger at her nose. But he skidded to a stop when he saw the pistol in her shaking hands, pointed directly at him.

Chapter Four

Bridger, big and imposing, his presence filling the room, gaped at Sage.

"How dare you barge in here this way? These are my private quarters. I demand that you leave at once."

Bridger, his green eyes locked on the weapon Sage was holding, reached out a supplicating hand, and took a tentative step backward.

"Not until we talk," he said. Some of the bark had gone out of his voice, but the look on his face would have soured milk. "Put the gun down," he said, his tone considerably subdued.

Sage forced herself to reorder her thoughts, putting good sense ahead of fear and righteousness. Slowly, she placed the gun, the feel and weight of it unfamiliar in her hands, back in her lap, tucking it into the folds of her skirt. But her anger didn't abate.

"You have no right to come into my room uninvited," she fumed, so incensed she could hardly get the words out. She clenched her fists to stop her hands from shaking.

"What's going on here, dammit?" he spat, apparently emboldened now that the gun was out of sight.

"I'll ask you not to use those words when speaking to me."

"Just which of those words do you object to, Miss Prissy?"

"Profanity is not allowed in this establishment," she said. She tilted her head and looked down her nose at him. Nothing could sway her from her decision.

"Well, that's one of the things I'm here to talk to you about. I saw your sign on the Shouting Post."

"Then you know what the new rules are," she said, her defenses rising.

"You can't impose those kinds of rules."

"And why not, may I ask?" She lifted her chin, boldly meeting his gaze straight on.

"Because that's not the way we do things in this town. The men cuss. They spit, and to some of them baths are not all that important. Even if they had a place to take one, which they don't. And they drink more than two drinks a night. A lot more," he said, lifting his brows to underscore his meaning.

"Well, they won't here," she replied. "You can't tell me how to run my business."

The corner of his mouth quirked up in a one-sided grin, and he took a moment to study her. "So. You're going to keep this place open?"

"It appears to be the prudent thing to do. Do I have a choice?" She let her gaze fall away, afraid he'd see a hint of defeat in it.

"No," he conceded. "You don't."

"Then I intend to run it the way I please."

Bridger stood there, inhaling deeply. His eyes roamed the room as if he were looking for something or someone.

"Is there anything else you wish to discuss, Marshal?" she said, her eyes meeting his.

"Yes," he said. "What was Josiah Miller doing here just now?"

Her breath released in an incredulous rush. "What concern is that of yours?"

"Look, sister, don't answer my question with a question. What was he doing here?"

She quickly compressed her lips before the truth leapt out, her mind frantically searching for a logical lie. "You know what business goes on here," she said, the words slipping out before she could stop them. Instantly mortified at what they implied, she berated herself for letting her wits be dulled by the need to hide the truth of her intentions.

Bridger looked at her a moment, his eyes storming. "Indeed I do, missy." He took a few steps toward her, stopping six feet from the desk. His jaw twitched.

"Tell you what," he said, softening his expression and nodding as if some vague suspicion had just been confirmed. "I'm not a bad fellow. Some of the girls could swear to that, and your aunt too, if she were alive. I don't get rough, I have a soft touch."

There was no mistaking his insinuation, and her cheeks began to burn with shame. She started to retort, but he interrupted her.

"I pay good. I don't have any diseases or lice. And, I already took a bath. How about it?"

"I beg your pardon!" Heat raced down her neck into her chest searing the breath from her lungs. It took superior control to keep from slapping his face.

"Oh, come now, Miss Cane. Everyone knows why you're here."

Boiling with rage, she struggled to get words out, but only managed a series of squeaky unfinished sentences. "How dare you suggest . . . I would never . . . . Why, I should . . ." she sputtered unable to contain her fury any longer.

"All right, all right," he said, backing away, both arms raised in mock surrender. "I'm willing to give you some time to think about it." His face turned irritated. "You women, you're all so touchy."

"I'm not touchy! And I don't need time to think about it! Get out! Leave my house this instant."

His eyes widened and he raised his eyebrows in pseudo astonishment. "Your house?" he said. "Have you forgotten who holds the deed to this place?"

"Get out!"

Overcome with rage, Sage pointed to the door and stood up, too late feeling the gun slide from her lap and crash to the floor, discharging with a deafening roar through the opening under the desk.

Bridger's mouth fell open as he grabbed his upper arm. He fell back against the wall, then slid to the floor crushing his hat.

* * * * *

Bridger sucked breath as Doc Holden poured a stinging liquid directly into the torn flesh just above his elbow where the bullet struck. Fiery pain raced up into his shoulder and spread.

"Passed clean through," the doctor said, peering intently through tiny round spectacles at Bridger's arm. "Missed the bone entirely." He grinned. "You're lucky."

The doctor wrapped the wound, fixed a sling to hold Bridger's arm, then handed him some pills. "Take these."

Bridger swallowed them without waiting for water, then closed his eyes and tilted his head back imploring the pain pills to kick in.

He was also trying to temper his frustration, and keep the lid on his can of cuss words. Since Elizabeth died, he'd taken to using language not learned at his mother's knee. But he had learned how to mind his own business and was sorely angry with himself now for not doing so. What Sage Cane did was no concern of his, but for some reason the sight of Josiah Miller coming down those stairs had set him off.

He winced again, but this time it was at the memory of the hurt he'd put on Sage's face. The blue-green eyes had gone opaque, a mask to cover the pain his words had inflicted. He only hoped he hadn't been jackass enough to send her packing. The notion greatly distressed him, and not just because Wild Mountain Honey would close. He had to find a way to keep her in Fairplay Creek.

Just then hurried footsteps pounded the porch outside, the door flew open, and Acer rushed in, apparently having just heard the news. "You goin' to arrest her, Marshal?" he asked, out of breath.

"No," said Bridger. "It was an accident."

"She's a little hell wind, ain't she?" Doc Holden said, snapping shut his medicine bag.

"No, she's not," Bridger replied. Then, "Never mind you old saw-bones. It's none of your business." He plopped his hat on his head, grimaced at the hole in the sleeve of his duster, put it on anyway one side draped over his shoulder, and stomped toward the door.

"Come along, Acer. There's work to do."

Chapter Five

Afternoon sun pouring in the south window of Miss Priscilla's kitchen flooded the room with warmth and light. In the distance, up on the mountains, the chinking of picks and axes, and the clatter of ore carts provided the ambient background music of life in Fairplay Creek.

Miss Priscilla stood at the stove stirring a pan of venison and rice flavored with cinnamon and allspice. Loaves of bread, a dozen or more of them, still warm from the ovens, were arranged artfully on the sideboard. Marvelous pastry tarts stuffed with cinnamon, sugar, and apples meant for dessert that night were cooling on the window ledge.

The Honeys had retired to their rooms after their mid-day meal to nap or read or prepare themselves for the evening. Poppy and Verbena had gone into town to enjoy a stroll and shop for personal items.

Sage sat at the long oaken table with Odie, lists and ledger sheets spread before them, going over the kitchen accounts. With her plan to become financially independent having been set in motion by virtue of her business arrangement with Josiah Miller, her spirits were elevated this afternoon.

She'd made a similar arrangement with only one other miner. In the interest of discretion, she chose carefully whom she did business with gauging the integrity, work ethic, and moral fiber of each prospect on pure instinct. That, and whatever information she gleaned from casually overheard conversations between the Honeys, who, it seemed, were privy to a great many secrets of their gentleman guests. Choosing the right miners to bankroll would take time. And beyond that, she knew it could take many months before her ventures paid off, if ever.

Meanwhile, her financial circumstances, though not dire, bore watching. She strove to maintain a delicate balance between providing for the needs of the house, which she knew would expand as the town grew, while at the same time having enough cash on hand to negotiate the best deals and give her the strongest bargaining power when opportunities with other miners came along. A great deal of patience would be needed to make it all work.

A week had gone by since Bridger had stormed out of her room, scowling in pain and outrage, his right hand clutching his left arm, blood seeping between his fingers. Much as she thought she wanted to at the time, she thankfully hadn't killed him.

But her encounter with Bridger that night clearly illustrated an important truth. Runaway emotion did not mix with business. Letting her personal feelings compel her to act impulsively would lead to mistakes and could derail her plans. It was important that she maintain a serious minded stance. Fortitude was necessary. And resolve.

She brought her thoughts back to the task at hand, reviewing the list of provisions needed for the coming week.

"I notice we are low on milk," she said to Odie. "Do you think we need another cow?"

Odie replied thoughtfully. "We can afford it as well as the extra livery fees required. What do you think, Miss Priscilla?"

The cook gave a plaintive shrug while she continued preparations for the evening meal. "We can surely use another one. And I'd like to plant a bigger garden, but Lord knows I got enough to do now. Don't know how I'd have time to tend to anything else."

It was true. Miss Priscilla worked long hours, slept only a few, and rarely left the house. Almost all of her waking hours were spent seeing to the needs of Sage, Odie and the Honeys. She didn't seem to have friends in town and Sage hadn't seen anyone call on her, not that they would at Wild Mountain Honey. But Miss Priscilla never complained about it.

Odie finished adding up a column of figures, made an entry in the ledger book, then closed the cover. "Is there anything else?"

"No, we're finished for today," Sage said. "Thank you."

Odie picked up the ledger books, gathered her notes and lists, and went upstairs. Since she kept practically the same hours as the Honeys, she took quiet time in her room each afternoon.

Alone with Miss Priscilla, Sage took a moment to watch her standing at the stove stirring a pot. She moved deliberately with confidence and an efficiency of motion acquired during many hours working in a kitchen. She spoke well and directly, and Sage suspected she had nobility somewhere in her heritage. How had a high-born black woman ended up in a town like this, with a job in a place like this?

An upwelling of gratitude suddenly filled Sage's chest and she spoke her feelings. "Thank you, Miss Priscilla. For all you do, for taking care of all of us."

The spoon the cook was using to stir the pot slowed, then continued as before, and the black woman spoke without turning around, her voice soft. "You're welcome, ma'am. I was thinkin' you'd turn me out when you came."

"Oh, certainly not!" said Sage. "We need you here. Odie and I couldn't manage without you."

Miss Priscilla set aside the stirring spoon, put a lid on the pot, and turned around. Her dark sharp-angled face was damp with perspiration, and she raised her arm to wipe her brow with her sleeve. "I surely appreciate that," she said and smiled, her white teeth a striking contrast to her dark skin.

Sage returned the smile, then stood. "I'll be out for the rest of the afternoon. I have some errands in town." As she turned to leave, she noticed Miss Priscilla studying her, a quizzical expression on her face. Sage paused and turned back. "Yes?" she said, inviting a question.

Priscilla hesitated and seemed to change her mind, but apparently curiosity overcame reluctance, and she spoke. "If you'll forgive me for askin', Miss Sage, I was just wonderin' how long you planned to stay in Fairplay Creek. You don't seem like the type to get much enjoyment from it."

"Did my aunt get enjoyment from it?" Sage asked, eager to know more about the beautiful mysterious woman who'd fascinated her so during those impressionable childhood years.

"Oh, a fair amount," the cook conceded. "Towards the end, though, she spent more time in town than she did here." There was a pause. "She gambled, you know." This last was added in a near whisper as if it were too scandalous to speak of out loud. Which Sage thought was ironic considering their own circumstances.

"So I understand," Sage replied. That's where the money went. After Odie had completed her audit of Aunt Honey's books and unpaid bills, she'd personally visited each debtor and made repayment arrangements. The merchants were only too glad to keep the accounts open and continue doing business with Wild Mountain Honey Pleasure Palace. Sage suspected Odie was allowing at least some of them to take it out in house trade. She closed her eyes and shuddered, then reminded herself of her resolve not to let emotion get in the way of business.

"Do you know anything about the man who killed my aunt?" No one spoke much about it, but Sage was openly curious about the murder. It was her nature to want to bring closure to any unfinished business.

"No, ma'am. Rough towns like this tend to draw the unlawful, especially at first. A red-haired stranger had been around the saloons for some days before. Folks think he did it, but no one's seen him since."

"Had he been a guest at Wild Mountain Honey?"

"No. I'd know if he had been. I hear the girls talkin' every day. About the men from the night before. No one mentioned a man with orange hair and they would of if they'd seen him here."

Sage was certain of that. The girls gossiped about the townsfolk just as the townsfolk gossiped about them. The men of the town shared many secrets while their heads lay upon Wild Mountain Honey pillows, and Sage suddenly wondered if her aunt had been privy to something that led to her death.

"Tell me. Did my aunt ever …" Sage paused, "… entertain gentlemen?"

"Oh yes, now and then," said Priscilla busying herself at the chopping block. "She had her special favorites."

Sage quickly stifled an urge to ask who the special favorites were though she had an idea who at least one of them was. She remembered with some discomfiture what Bridger had said about Aunt Honey vouching for him, and her face grew warm knowing he hadn't been referring to his character but rather his prowess.

She ducked her head, turning away from Miss Priscilla in case her thoughts could be read on her face. "I'll be back by supper time," she mumbled, and promptly left the kitchen.

* * * * *

Sage found the main street of Fairplay Creek crowded and noisier than ever. A newly arrived lick-skillet mix of settlers, miners, and misfits looking tired and travel worn, were scurrying around seeking the quickest way to get situated, get fed, and get rich.

She made her way along the bustling boardwalks thinking that she should get herself a one-horse hitch and buggy for her near daily excursions into the town proper. Priscilla said Aunt Honey had a neat little two-seater, but had to sell both the buggy and the horse to pay a debt. There was a buggy maker across the street, but she did not veer off to visit it and look at his wares. She would do it later, she decided, because right now she was heading straight for Mueller's Shirt and Overall Company.

The front of the store was freshly painted, the brass doorknob newly shined, but all of it layered with dirt and grime and the never ending dust from the street. A sign in the window said Purveyors of Cassamere and Corduroy Pants and Coats, All Men's Clothing. With her head high and her chin tilted maybe a little too much to make up for her nervousness, she strode in causing the bell on the transom to ring and headed directly to the wall where the coats were hanging. The half dozen customers inside, mostly men, abruptly stopped what they were doing and turned to follow her progress through the store.

She paused in front of a rack jammed with new looking outer garments, perusing the selection of coats in various shades of black, gray and brown.

"Good afternoon, Miss Cane." The fawning high-pitched voice came from behind her, and she turned to see a tall, painfully thin man with light colored hair swept back off his forehead, the comb marks clearly showing.

"May I help you? I'm George Mueller, the owner." His smile had an oily quality to it.

"How do you do."

"Welcome to Fairplay Creek."

"Thank you."

"I hope you are enjoying our little town."

"Yes, it's lovely," she said for politeness sake. She'd never say she found the town not to her liking.

"I see you're looking at our new shipment of coats. They just arrived by mule freight yesterday."

Sage nodded and ran her hand along the row of garments on the rack.

"But I'm afraid we don't carry women's clothing," he informed her.

"It's not for me. It's for a man."

At that, the expressions on the eavesdropping customers sharpened, and some of them took a step closer the better to hear the conversation.

"Ohhh . . ." Mueller stretched out the word as if in sudden understanding. Sage could tell by the look on his face he was curious about the identity of the man, and the background listeners were dying to know, too.

"Well," Mueller said, bringing his palms together and turning to the rack of clothes, all business now and eager to make a sale. "Did you have a particular cut in mind?"

"Yes. A duster."

"What color?"

Sage hadn't considered that. She pondered the duster Bridger had been wearing when the bullet tore a hole in the sleeve. "Dark brown," she said.

Mueller took one off the rack and held it by the hanger, turning it front and back for her to see. "Here's the latest duster from Mr. Levi Strauss in Oregon City. Large patch pockets on the front, a storm flap, and inside privacy pockets. The muleskinner told me yesterday that Mr. Strauss is experimenting with a new fabric called denim, but this one is made of serviceable canvas. It's sturdy enough to keep out wind and rain, has a special silk lining for warmth, and an extra long vent in back fits easily over a saddle. Your man will see years of wear from it."

"I'll take it," she interjected, interrupting his discourse, irritated at the words "your man". The other customers were openly gaping.

"What size?"

That stumped her. What size do jackasses wear, she wondered. "It's for Marshal Norwood." She spoke barely above a whisper, covering her mouth with her fingers to keep her words from reaching the ears of the gawkers.

"Oh, the marshal," George Mueller said, surprised, and loud enough for everyone in the store to hear, maybe even those passing by outside.

"I noticed that hole in his sleeve," piped up one of the customers, a man, grinning unabashedly. The woman standing next to him, apparently his wife, blew out a breath of repugnance, lifted her skirts, took the grinner by the arm, and marched them both out the door.

Mueller pulled a well-cut, dark brown duster off the rack, and checked the size. "This ought to fit the marshal."

"I'll take it," Sage repeated.

"Don't you want to know how much?"

"How much?" she asked, wishing he would keep his voice down. The onlookers were enjoying the show.

"Thirty dollars."

Now it was Sage's turn to gape. Thirty dollars! She inhaled deeply, nodded once, and headed for the counter. Mueller followed behind carrying the duster. At the gold scale, she withdrew a money pouch from her reticule, measured out thirty dollars worth of gold. "Can you deliver it today? I'll pay extra."

"Why, yes, I suppose I can." The store owner's eyes gleamed as Sage slid some coins on the counter. "Would you like to enclose a note?" he asked. "Or will Marshal Norwood know who it's from?"

At that, Sage's defenses shot up. She didn't know why she felt combative at the sound of his name. The feeling was instinctive, almost protective, as if the very mention of his name might overwhelm her if she didn't resist.

Calming herself, she replied. "If you would be so kind as to lend me paper and a pen, I'll write a note."

Mueller reached under the counter and produced a sheet of paper, took a pen from his shirt pocket and handed it to her, his expression bland as oatmeal. Sage scribbled a terse one-line message and signed her name.

None of the customers had stopped staring since she entered the store. She knew they'd heard practically every word of her exchange with Mr. Mueller, and the gossip mill would grind for days about it. She was sure everyone in town knew by now she'd shot the marshal, but she wondered how many knew it had been an accident.

Well, fiddlesticks, let them talk! She hadn't meant to shoot him, but he wasn't going to die, and replacing his damaged duster made her square with him now. She would pay her rent in full and on time, but other than that, they had no further business together.

She left the store, cheeks burning, but head still high, then dodging wagons and horses and people, dashed across the dirt street and down a block to the Land Office.

* * * * *

Wooden boards creaked under Bridger's boots as he crossed the landing and opened the door to his office. He was more than a little annoyed. He'd just spent most of the afternoon running errands—delivering delinquent tax bills, collecting taxes or arguing about them, greeting newcomers and explaining the law to them.

New people thought all they had to do when they came into town was pitch a tent, and they were in business. Bridger had to tell them they were required to file the appropriate business license applications, then wait for approval. The system had been set up to keep out the con men and flim flam artists.

And his day wasn't over yet.

He couldn't go home until he finished what he called his "sit down" work. Before the day was over, he had to review a pile of new license requests, reconcile the tax accounts, document recent arrests and fines, do the bookkeeping, and make the bank deposit. Administrative duties were taking so much of his time, soon he'd have to talk to Ramsey Thorogood about bringing in another deputy or two to do the peacekeeping work. No doubt Thorogood would agree. He had what all men needed but many lacked—imagination and vision.

Bridger hung his hat on a hook, and his duster on the coat rack next to the door, then sat down at his desk and sighed, letting his eyes drift to the activity outside the window. From where he sat, he had a view of almost his entire block, both sides of the street. He could see even further if he got up and leaned into the windowpane.

His arm, still in a sling, itched under the bandage. Doc Holden said it was a sign of healing, and the itching would stop when the bandage came off. Bridger hoped that would be soon. It was embarrassing having to go around town with his arm bandaged and in a sling, especially when everyone knew how it got that way. He might as well have been carrying a sign that said Winged by a Woman.

He could still see the look on Sage's face when the gun went off— first disbelief, then panic. After that, he was kind of dazed, but he thought he remembered her coming to him, alarm in her eyes, her soft hands touching him. He'd probably imagined it, though—cold, hard woman like that.

He picked up a pencil, worked it under the bandage, probing for the itch. The hubbub outside had increased, and he turned his attention to the street.

There were many more people about, some of the miners coming in from the camps, and business at the saloons was picking up, not that they lacked willing customers at any time day or night. Along with the influx of new folks come to make an honest living was an assortment of desperate characters lured by the prospect of acquiring gold without digging for it. Yep, they were going to need another deputy real soon.

A dust-covered wagon loaded with household goods and mining supplies clanked by, a young man holding the reins, his discouraged wife next to him, looking angry and tired, with a tiny baby on her lap. Two older children sat on a canvas-wrapped bundle in back, their eyes taking in the spectacle of it all.

As Bridger fixed his gaze on the flurry outside, he caught sight of Sage Cane on the other side of the street coming out of the Land Office, tucking a piece of paper into her bag.

She turned down the boardwalk, her steps crisp and deliberate. Before she'd walked half a block, a high lonesome lurched out the batwing doors of the Salt Creek Saloon and, swaying on his feet, tried to engage her in conversation. When she ignored him and kept walking, he reached for her arm.

Bridger's chair scraped back as he quickly stood, clapped his hand on the pistol holstered to his thigh, and started for the door. But he relaxed when Sage shook off the drunk and continued on her way, back stiff, shoulders straight. Her white-blonde hair was wound into a tight bun at the back of her head. Severe hair for a severe woman. He couldn't see her face, but he'd have bet it held a severe expression.

He was so engrossed in watching Sage Cane advance up the street, he jumped when his door opened and a young boy came in carrying a large package.

"This is for you, Marshal," the boy said, depositing the wrapped bundle on the desk.

"Who's it from?" Bridger asked irritably, disgruntled to have been caught gawking out the window.

"I dunno, but Mr. Mueller said there's a note inside. He give me a nickel to bring it here." The boy grinned, showed the coin, and left.

His curiosity spiked, Bridger made a great effort of opening the package one handed, finally tearing at the paper and string with impatient fingers. Letting the paper drop away, he lifted the duster, and gave a low admiring whistle. It was a duplicate of the one he already owned, except this one was of finer quality, and it, of course, didn't have a bullet hole in the sleeve.

Laying the duster aside, he bent down to pick up the note that had fluttered to the floor, and read the one line message.

He went stone still, and a hard knot of misgiving formed in his chest, the kind that came on those times he knew he'd made a horrible mistake.

"Oh, hell," he said out loud, closing his eyes and shaking his head. He purely wished it was possible to turn back time, at least this afternoon's hours of it. He opened his eyes and read the note again. *I always pay my debts*, it said, which was exactly what he'd counted on. Only now, he had a feeling that he was the one who would end up paying.

Chapter Six

By the time Sage finished her errands and returned to Wild Mountain Honey, the sun was nearing the tops of the western mountains. She'd willed all thoughts of Bridger from her mind, refusing to be distracted from her goal, reflecting instead on her future. It was time to find more miners whose needs were similar to Josiah Miller's so she could make similar business alliances. She wasn't going to depend on just one or two endeavors. That was too risky. She needed to spread her risk—and the opportunities—over a broader plane. Already she'd begun setting money aside for such investments.

Priscilla had just finished mopping the floor, and was wringing out a mop when Sage entered the kitchen.

"Watch your step, Miss Sage. Floor's still wet in places. Supper's all ready. You go get yourself freshened up while I set out a plate."

"Thank you, Miss Priscilla. I'm starving."

Suddenly the cook's attention was pulled to the window, and she propped the mop against the wall, snatched up her apron, and headed out the door, wiping her hands. "Lordy, there's that Indian child again."

Out in the yard, an Indian boy was chasing a chicken inside the fenced-in wire pen. He gave up on the chicken when he saw Priscilla coming, and turned to flee, but she was quicker and grabbed the back of his tattered shirt when he tried to scoot under the chicken coop. He was so thin, his body was little more than a layer of skin over bone. Despite that, his dark eyes danced with spirit as he tugged his arm from Miss Priscilla's grasp.

"I told you before," scolded Miss Priscilla. "Stay away from my chickens, you hear?" She tightened her grip on his arm and was hauling him off the property when Sage called out and stopped her.

"Wait. Bring him here."

"He's been stealin' chickens and rummaging in my garden," the cook complained. "I chased him away three times last week." She thrust the boy in front of her, and marched him to the porch where Sage stood. He'd stopped struggling, but was poised to run if Priscilla let up on his arm.

Sage gazed thoughtfully at the sullen faced boy. He was dirty beyond belief, and his clothes hung from his body mere rags. His feet, which she doubted had ever entertained a pair of shoes, were caked with mud. The calluses on the bottoms were so thick, she could see them.

She had heard there were some Indian encampments over the rise just out of town. He must have wandered off.

"What's your name?" Sage asked gently, but he didn't answer, glaring at her in response.

"Where is your family?" Her voice was soft and reassuring as she tried to draw him out, but he returned only silence. The defiance flashing in his dark eyes was razor sharp behind a shimmer of fear.

"Do your mother and father live nearby?" she tried again, but still the boy did not reply, his chary expression unyielding.

"Miss Priscilla, please take him inside and give him some of that venison on the stove, and one of those cinnamon tarts."

At the mention of food, the boy's face showed a ripple of interest, and he licked his lips, apparently unable to help himself.

"But give him a bath first," said Sage.

"No!" the boy shouted, and tried to yank his arm away again.

"Ah," Sage said, and smiled. "So, you do understand English. Do you speak it, too?"

He set his jaw and lifted his chin. "When I want to," he answered, his voice rebellious.

"Where do you live?" she coaxed. "Tell me."

"There." He pointed with his chin at the woods bordering the yard. "I sleep under the sky."

"Not anymore," she said. "You can stay here until your parents come for you. I'll pay you 20 cents a day to help Miss Priscilla in the kitchen. You can help in the garden, too."

She looked at Priscilla. "Fix him a cot next to the stove. He can sleep there until his family comes for him." Sage turned to the boy. "But first, a bath."

He began struggling in earnest, but Priscilla's strong fingers held him. "You smell," she said, giving his arm a little shake. "You're having a bath. No food until you do."

Reluctantly, he let Priscilla lead him away.

Sage fixed herself a plate, set it on the table, then took a pencil and small notebook from a drawer in the sideboard. While she ate, she jotted some notes, did a few calculations, and made a list of things she needed to do.

Priscilla returned with her freshly bathed charge. His long, raven-black hair was tied back with a string, and she guessed him to be about eleven years old. He was nice looking now that the dirt had been washed away, though his cheeks were sunken, his eyes hollow and ashy. But he was a lot less surly, no doubt anticipating a full stomach.

"I found some men's clothes in the laundry shed that someone left behind," said Priscilla. "They're too big for him, but he can roll up the pants and sleeves. I threw the shirt and britches he was wearing in the burn barrel." She heaped food onto a plate and put it in front of him. He picked up a spoon and began eating hungrily, scooping big mouthfuls.

Sage waited a few moments until the food's calming effect took hold, then tried again. "Won't you tell me your name?"

"Cheveyo," he said around a mouthful of venison. Though the fight had gone out of him, wildness still sparked in his eyes.

"Is that good?" she asked, indicating the food.

He nodded slowly and shoveled another spoonful into his mouth, staring at her the while.

"Well, Cheveyo, if you behave yourself, and do what Miss Priscilla tells you, you can eat like that every day. You won't have to steal from the henhouse. You won't have to sleep in the woods."

His eyes drilled into her, but he kept eating. She doubted she'd get anything more from him tonight.

"Well, then. I'll say goodnight." Sage put her fork on her plate, closed her notebook, and stood. "Now that Cheveyo is here to help, at least for a while, you can plant that other garden you've been wanting," she said to Priscilla.

"Yes, m'am, I surely can," the cook replied and smiled.

"And I'll speak to Odie about buying another cow."

"That would be just fine," the cook replied, obviously pleased. "Oh," she said, remembering. "The marshal was here this afternoon. He brought this. Said to be sure to give it to you." She took an envelope from a shelf above the kitchen sink and handed it to Sage. "Said you need to take care of this right away."

Dubious about what the marshal would bring her, Sage reached for it as if she were afraid it would snap her fingers. Gingerly she opened the flap, took out a piece of paper and unfolded it. It was an overdue notice for a tax bill Aunt Honey had neglected to pay, with an exorbitant late fee added on.

A wave of exasperation rolled over her and she released a pent-up breath.

"He is the most insufferable man I've ever met." Her hands shook as she refolded the tax notice and stuffed it back into the envelope. "He's arrogant, he's rude, he's a . . ." She ran out of the kind of words a decent woman could say, especially in front of a child. Gritting her teeth, she let her breath seep between slightly parted lips. It took all her self-restraint to dampen her frustration, reminding herself once again of her resolve to tend to her finances, her only way out of Fairplay Creek.

Miss Priscilla quirked the corner of her mouth in a quick half smile. "Most people think he's a decent sort," she said. "He's got a hard job keeping peace in a town like this. The girls all like him," she added.

"But that's just it. He's the marshal. He shouldn't be coming here." Involuntarily Sage's mind calculated the actual number of days since he had been there. Six.

"But Marshal Norwood is a single man," Priscilla said as if that explained absolutely everything.

"Well, yes, but still," Sage replied, stubbornly standing her ground.

The cook, her hands in soapy dishwater, stopped what she was doing, her face in a frown, head cocked to one side. She looked at Sage straight on. "Fairplay Creek is a hard two days ride from any civilization. Where else is he to go? I'm sure you've noticed that except for the Honeys, and you and Miss Odie, of course, the rest of the women in this town are no prize."

Sage had noticed. It was rough going for those few women living in this raw town of derisive males with very little privacy anywhere, and it showed on their faces, and in the sag of their shoulders. They lived in tiny, cramped quarters, mere shacks or cabins with dirt floors, sometimes just dugouts carved into the side of a hill. They wore heavy, high-topped shoes, and layers of coarse, threadbare clothing, the back hem of their skirts pulled up between their legs and tucked at their waist in front. Some even wore men's clothes and boots. Style was not much a concern to them by necessity, as the accouterments of fashion were not available even if they could afford them. Gunpowder was far easier to come by than face powder.

Their days were consumed with survival: hauling water, chopping wood, tending gardens, preparing meals, caring for children, or livestock if they had any, or trying to make a little extra by taking in washing or mending while the husbands worked the mines or gambled in the saloons.

Or, she shuddered, spent their time and money at Wild Mountain Honey.

Sage slumped against the sideboard. She looked again at the envelope in her hand. The tax bill. Due in ten days. The total amount would severely deplete her investment savings account, and possibly delay construction of the new facility she planned. Disappointment tried to drain her of energy, but she fought it off. This was a setback, nothing more. Certainly not a defeat. There was a way to resolve this matter, she just hadn't thought of it yet.

"Thank you, Miss Priscilla," she said, straightening. "I'll see that Odie takes care of this right away. Good night."

Chapter Seven

Sage slipped out the front entrance of the bank where she'd gone to make a deposit, and walked briskly down the boardwalk toward the marshal's office. The tax bill was due.

Ten days had gone by quickly, each one filled with almost frenetic activity as she focused on her goal. She'd made business arrangements with two more miners, and was hopeful about the outcomes. None of the mines she'd invested in had paid off yet, but several other mines in the camps had. Reports of new strikes were coming in at the rate of two or three a week, and the lucky miners could be counted on to spread the news of their sudden wealth. Josiah had told her he'd panned a few flakes, but wasn't ready to declare a strike, though he had a happy glint in his eye.

Cheveyo was still sleeping on the cot in Priscilla's kitchen. His parents had not yet come for him despite the sign she'd pinned on the Shouting Post. It occurred to her finally that his parents might not be able to read, and by extension, neither could Cheveyo. A few minutes spent asking him to identify simple words she'd written on a piece of paper proved her suspicions true.

Consequently, she'd scoured her personal library for books suitable for a child, and had begun holding reading classes in her private parlor every morning at nine for Cheveyo, and Oliver Mackey, the boy from Oscar's, who turned out to be Oscar's son. The boys were making great progress. Oliver had asked to take a book home to read.

The business section of the town had spread another whole block into the wilderness. Another billiard parlor had sprung up she noticed, and another smithy. Further down, she saw a new doctor's shingle, two new lawyers, a new clothing store—for men, of course. Next to a new feed store, a fortuneteller had set up for business under a rustic arbor composed of dead boughs and twigs.

Sage hurried along on foot, having postponed the purchase of a horse and buggy. She'd briefly considered renting one, but didn't want to add to her debt. Every dollar coming into Wild Mountain Honey that wasn't required for the maintenance and comfort of the house and the Honeys was going directly into her investment account.

When she reached the block of buildings that included Bridger's office, she stopped and studied the door from across the street, trying to build up the courage to face him. She hadn't seen him since the night he stormed into her rooms, and it distressed her that some part of her brain was marking time and creating an awareness of the exact number of days that had gone by.

She sorely wished she didn't have to go in there, but knowing she couldn't put it off a day longer, straightened her shoulders, and crossed over. After a few calming breaths to stem her nervousness, though her fingers continued to twist in the drawstrings of her reticule, she opened the door.

It was a large room smelling of oiled wood with big windows looking out into the street. A door to a hallway leading to the cells in the back stood open. Wanted posters were stuck up on the wall. A Remington rifle leaned against the wall in the corner.

Bridger was at his desk bent over some paperwork, but he looked up quickly when she came in, his green eyes bright with surprise at the sight of her.

She was determined to remain aloof, was even trying to work up a snit, but the sight of his arm in a sling and the rueful look on his face was so pathetic, her heart swelled in sympathy.

"I'm sorry about that," she said, indicating his arm with a slight dip of her head.

"Did you come here to finish me off?" he asked.

She let the sarcasm go, and instead opened her handbag and got right down to business. "No," she answered, taking out the tax bill. "I came to talk about this."

"What is there to say? Honey didn't pay it. Now you owe it."

Sage stood uncertainly shifting her weight from one foot to the other. She had hoped Odie would handle this, she was so much better at this kind of thing. But Odie had taken to her bed with a headache and sniffles, and Sage had insisted she stay there.

Nervously clearing the emotion from her throat, Sage faced him squarely, and let the words tumble out. "I was wondering, Mr. Norwood, if payment arrangements could be made. This is a rather large amount, and uh, I wondered if I could pay it off a little at a time."

A sly smile played at Bridger's lips as he studied her, and his eyes took on a mischievous twinkle. "Why certainly," he said. "What did you have in mind? Exactly?"

"I can pay you exactly five dollars a week," she answered, ignoring what sounded like but she hoped wasn't an inappropriate insinuation. "That will allow me to dispose of this debt by the end of the year, and still accumulate enough to pay the subsequent taxes in full. Without late fees," she emphasized, trying hard to keep the vinegar out of her voice.

His face was unreadable as he took in her words, studying her with those disconcerting eyes. They were the kind of eyes she'd fallen for once, the kind that had attracted her before, but never would again.

"Yes," he said finally. "That would be acceptable. When did you plan to make the first installment?"

"Today." She reached into her bag, took out the money, and handed it to him. "I'm good for the rest of it. I always pay my bills, you can ask anyone in Independence. I'm paying my father's bills, too."

"Thank you," he said simply, and put the money in his desk drawer. An awkward silence descended, weighty and fecund. He didn't move, nor did she and the air swelled with expectation. She couldn't help noticing there were a few specks of gray in his coppery hair.

"I hope you're on the mend," she said, to break the uncomfortable silence, wondering why she didn't just leave. His eyes held hers until she lowered them, but she didn't like looking at his arm in the sling, either. Instead, she let her gaze drift to the coat rack next to the door.

He noticed, and got to his feet. "Thank you," he said again. "For the trail coat. It's fine. It fits fine."

"Yes. Well. I'll be on my way," she said stiffly. "Thank you for your cooperation."

Without waiting for a response, she scurried out the door, embarrassed. She'd acted like a fool, standing there gawking, unable to think of anything to say, but unaccountably her thoughts had gotten all jumbled up when she'd looked into his eyes, and her feet wouldn't move.

Well, so be it. She had no time to worry about what Bridger Norwood thought of her. She couldn't afford to be distracted in that manner. She had plans. Plans that didn't include him.

* * * * *

Bridger watched as she strode past his window without a backward glance, and disappeared into the crowd gathering around a freight wagon delivering potatoes, butter and coffee to the general store. She'd been a little sharp around the tongue, he thought, but when she'd handed him the money, he'd noticed she had elegant hands with long tapered fingers. They were probably soft, too. Yeah, he thought with some pique, they'd probably never done a lick of decent work.

Working out a payment plan with her was not a problem. He had similar arrangements with others in town. If she didn't come by with the payments, he'd go there and pick them up. It would be an excuse for him to go and see her. Not that he wanted an excuse to do any such thing.

But he did wonder why such an arrangement was necessary. Plenty of money went into Wild Mountain Honey. He didn't know precisely how much, but judging from what Honey had gambled away, there was a sizeable amount. So far as he could tell, Sage didn't gamble, so money should not be a problem. The picture of Josiah Miller clomping down her stairs jarred his memory, but he shook it off. That was her business, not his.

He turned his attention to the stack of trade license applications he'd been reviewing before she came in. He signed his name to several of them, approving a new hardware, a dance hall, and a tentmaker, and set them aside. He planned to deliver them later and collect the fees at the same time.

He was so occupied when Acer came in.

"Mornin', Acer."

"Howdy," replied the deputy, yawning.

Bridger looked up and studied his deputy. He looked drawn and tired, but his eyes still held the eagerness of youth. Long hours spent breaking up fights and rousting rowdies out of saloons plus more hours spent with Verbena didn't leave many hours for sleep.

"You all right, son?" Bridger asked.

"Yeah." Acer sat on a wooden chair at the service counter. After a moment, he said, "I'm thinkin' about askin' Verbena to quit Wild Mountain Honey."

"You're what?" said Bridger, in surprise.

Acer nodded. "I'm thinkin' about askin' her to marry me."

"Marry you?" That was unexpected. He'd heard about men marrying women from those places, though not often, and he'd never heard how it turned out. "Don't go making any hasty decisions," he warned.

"I'm just thinkin' is all." Acer tilted his chair back against the wall, stretched out his legs, and tipped his hat over his eyes.

Bridger returned to the license applications, reading, signing, and setting them aside. "Well, I'll be," he said, after a minute. "Someone's going to build a public bathhouse."

"Yeah," Acer said from under his hat. "The muleskinner brought in a load of washtubs and piping from Denver. I saw some men load it in a wagon, and head west toward Seventh Street. Looks like construction's about to start."

"Well, that will take care of one category of complaint from the miners," said Bridger, thoughtfully. Especially since Sage had imposed the new bathing rule as requisite for admission to Wild Mountain Honey. Most of them had no place to take a bath in the winter months when temperatures made outdoor bathing impossible. He was pleased at the idea of such a facility, the first in town. He took a moment to ponder the application, then picked up his pen to approve it, but stopped when his eyes went to the space where the business owner's name was written in— Sage Cane.

There had to be some mistake. Building a facility of that nature was an expensive proposition. Where would Sage get that kind of money? Wasn't she just in here asking to pay her delinquent taxes in installments?

"Where did you say they were building that bathhouse?"

Acer roused himself, but just barely. "At Wild Mountain Honey," he mumbled. "Verbena told me."

Bridger scraped back his chair, reached for his hat, plopped it on his head, and slipped his trail coat over his shoulders.

"I'll be back later," he said. "I'm going out to deliver these business licenses."

He strode directly across the street into the Land Office where he confirmed via public record the purchase of the vacant lot adjoining Wild Mountain Honey. The owner of the property was none other than Miss Sage Cane. The transaction had been paid for in full. In cash.

What was going on here, he wondered. What was she up to? For someone who didn't want to stay in Fairplay Creek, it sure looked like she was putting down roots.

Chapter Eight

Sage woke to warm sun streaming in her windows, and the sounds of hammering below. She stretched indulgently, extending her arms over her head, lengthening her spine, pointing her toes. Slowly she released the tension in her muscles, then hugged herself under the covers, the thrill of Josiah Miller's happy news still spinning in her head. He'd found a nugget in his pan along with more of the glittering flakes, and expected to hit a vein very soon. Jubilation fairly burst from her, but she dared not tell a soul. She hadn't even told Odie yet.

Throwing back the feather quilt, she slipped on a dressing gown, then went to her bedside window and opened it wide. A gentle breeze blowing off the still snow-covered peaks carried a hint of spring, but the mountainsides were greening up nicely, and the air was ripe with the newness of spring. Soon wildflowers would carpet the slopes with color, sending up more of nature's perfume.

Next door, construction of the public bathhouse had continued apace, the finishing touches now being applied.

Hurriedly she dressed, pinned up her hair, and opened the double doors leading to the anteroom. Delicious smells from the kitchen wafted up the stairs making her mouth water. Odie's doors were also wide open signaling that she was awake, and voices drifting up from the kitchen, along with the aroma of coffee and yeasty biscuits, indicated she was downstairs talking to Miss Priscilla.

"Good morning." Sage entered the kitchen, greeting them with a smile. She accepted a steaming cup of coffee from the cook, and after taking a sip, said, "Mmmm. The best, as always."

Priscilla beamed at the compliment. "Hot cakes today, Miss Sage. With fresh butter and warm syrup."

"Perfect." Sage took her place at the table across from Odie who offered a fragile smile, and Sage wondered not for the first time if she was all right. A faint worry line had taken up residence between Odie's brows, and when she lifted her coffee to her lips, Sage noticed the fingers holding the mug shook a little.

"I hope you slept well. Did the hammering from the construction wake you?"

"No," Odie replied. "I was awake when they started. And you?"

"I was wakened in the night by someone playing the flute. I thought it was a dream at first. It sounded like it was coming from one of the front rooms upstairs."

"Yes," replied Odie. "That was Verbena. She only had one guest last night. Acer Morrow. He asked for only music."

Sage knew that men sometimes requested time with a special Honey for talk or company. Fully clothed, no sex. They liked coming here for the food, the music, the conversation, appreciated a soft shoulder and sympathetic ear. Sage wished Wild Mountain Honey were a place where men and women met and talked and got to know each other properly, a place of grace and refinement instead of what it was.

"I suspect Verbena might be leaving us. And that would not displease me," Sage admitted. A warm wave of pleasure washed over her at the thought of the pretty young girl who wore bells on her ankles becoming a good man's wife.

"The soaps and towels for the bathhouse will be arriving soon," said Odie. "If spring rains didn't wash out the wagon road, the mule freight from Denver should arrive tomorrow. If so, we can open the bathhouse next week."

"Wonderful," said Sage.

"Oh, that reminds me. The girls asked if they'll be assisting in the bathhouse." Odie paused. Sage knew she was trying to skirt an indelicate subject, but, in the end, there was no way.

"You know," Odie went on, "if they'll be paid more for, um, bathing the guests. Or, um, bathing with them."

Heat warmed Sage's cheeks. She didn't like discussing those kinds of details. It was a painful reminder of what she'd become, but as much as she wished it were otherwise, she couldn't remove herself entirely from the activities of the front of the house.

"No, but they can tend the entry if they desire, collect bathing fees, sell soaps, hand out towels. If they are skilled enough, they can tend to the barber and tonsorial needs. Remind the girls it's a public bathhouse, open to everyone in town, not just the men."

"Of course," Odie said, and then fell into silence again, concentrating on her breakfast.

Thoughtfully, Sage studied her friend. Odie wasn't what one would call pretty, but she had an inner beauty that glowed like a beam of loving light. All the Honeys liked her for her kindness and compassion, the merchants in town respected her integrity and prompt payment of their bills. She was an efficient manager, and because of her sharp mind for numbers the ledgers were precisely kept. But to Sage, she was more than an employee. From the day they arrived in Fairplay Creek, they'd formed a bond that went beyond friendship. To Sage, it felt like a sisterhood.

But Sage was worried. Though reserved by nature, Odie lately seemed withdrawn, her thoughts turned inward to some secret place within. Conversation, once so lively and spirited, had become difficult, especially if it wandered away from the present to the past.

Out of respect for her privacy, Sage refrained from asking questions about Odie's life before their meeting in Denver though she wondered about it increasingly. She suspected a fire of passion and strength burned within her friend, kindled by hard times and despair.

All three women, Sage and Odie at the table, Priscilla at the stove, startled at the sound of the front gate crashing open against the side of the house. Shouting from outside and the sound of footsteps pounding the dirt drew their attention to the windows where they saw a woman rounding the corner of the house, running toward the back door, skirts pulled up to her knees so her feet wouldn't tangle in her petticoats. Acer Morrow appeared close behind.

"Stop," he cried. "Stop, thief!"

The woman lumbered up the porch steps and pounded roughly on the back door. "Help me! Please, help me!"

When Priscilla threw open the door, the woman fairly fell into her arms. Acer took a leap onto the porch and made a grab for her, but Priscilla pulled the weeping woman out of his reach, and blocked his way.

The woman was sobbing hard, tears streaking the dirt on her face. "Please don't let him take me," she begged, ducking behind Priscilla. "I didn't mean any harm."

Quickly, Sage stepped forward, hands planted firmly on hips in a stance meant to be reckoned with. "Acer!" she demanded. "What's going on here? Why are you chasing this woman? Can't you see she's with child?"

"Mr. Gallagher caught her stealing food from his general store. She put some apples in her pocket, and she's got jerky up her sleeve. Look there," he said, pointing a finger at her wrist. "You can see it."

Sage could indeed see jerky poking out from the edge of her grimy sleeve, but instead of admonishing the woman, Sage put an arm around her shoulders, and helped her to a chair.

"Come, sit down," she said, then, "Would you like something to drink?"

Priscilla offered a cup of water, which the woman accepted and drank thirstily.

"Now," Sage said in a soothing voice. "What's this all about? Did you steal from Mr. Gallagher's store?"

The question produced a fresh onslaught of tears making it difficult for the woman to answer. "I was going to pay it back, honest." Deep hiccoughs interrupted her words. "It's just that I was so hungry."

"She said she worked here," Acer put in. "But I've never seen her, so I knew that wasn't true. She owes Mr. Gallagher for what she stole."

"Oh, but it is true," said Sage, facing him directly, her hands on her hips again, challenging him. "She does work here, and you can tell Pete Gallagher that he'll be paid whatever he thinks he's owed. Odie will take care of it this afternoon."

"But she—" Acer began stubbornly, extending an accusing finger.

"I'll take care of it," Sage assured him, patting his upper arm, and ushering him gently toward the door. "You won't be bothered by her again."

Acer hesitated, his eyes going uncertainly from Sage to Odie to Priscilla, then back to Sage. Grudgingly, he nodded and touched the brim of his hat in farewell, his expression still stony. "Well, that'll suit me just fine. I got too much other work to do with the marshal being over in Hamilton City and all. Till he gets back, I got my hands full."

"I'm sure you do," said Sage. "Thank you." She continued to nudge him gently, encouraging him to take his leave.

"While he's gone, I'm supposed to uphold the law."

"And you're doing a fine job, too. I'll be sure and mention it to Marshal Norwood. Goodbye, Acer."

Sage firmly closed the door. Odie prepared a basin of warm water, and handed the woman a washcloth and a towel so she could clean her face and hands. Priscilla filled a plate with hotcakes and bacon, and put it in front of the woman who had calmed down enough to tell them her name was Emma Ford.

Emma poured out her story while she ate.

"My husband got tired of working so hard on the mine with nothing to show for it. One day he just up and left leaving me behind in the dugout. I haven't seen him since. I stayed there until the food ran out, hoping he'd come back, but he didn't. I walked into town this morning." She finished chewing, swallowed, and touched a napkin to her lips. "I was on my way here to ask for a job. I want to be a Honey."

The other three women looked at each other then at Emma.

"But . . . you're going to have a baby," Sage replied, stating the obvious.

Emma's face reddened. "I know," she said, lowering her eyes. "I mean after my lying in. I need some way to support myself and take care of it."

Sage looked at her sadly. "Have you done that kind of work before?"

Emma shook her head. "No. I was a school teacher in Texas before my husband brought me here.

At that, an idea bloomed in Sage's mind, one that she'd been nurturing for some time. "Tell me," she said, taking a seat next to Emma. "If you were a teacher, you must be able to read and write."

The woman nodded.

"And do you know history, and your numbers, too?"

Emma nodded again. "And a little music."

"All right. I'll give you a job. But not as a Honey. I teach morning lessons to two young boys, but if you would be willing to take over that task—for wages, of course—I'll fix up a small classroom in the barn.

There's an extra sleeping room in Miss Priscilla's wing. You can stay there until you find more suitable quarters. Would that be agreeable?"

Emma put down her fork and looked at Sage, gratitude filling her eyes and making them gleam. "Yes, it would. Thank you."

"Well, that's settled," Sage said, smiling.

"When you're ready, I'll show you to your room," chimed in Odie. "When is your child due?"

"About two months."

Sage and Odie exchanged a pointed glance. "Don't worry," Sage told Emma. "We'll see to it that you have a proper place in town for your child to come into the world. It won't have to be born here."

Odie stood and smoothed her skirt. "Come along, then. There's fresh linen in the back hall closet. I'll help you make up your bed."

Emma placed her napkin on the table, then put her arms around Sage. "Thank you," she whispered. "Oh, thank you. You're nothing like I thought you'd be."

"You're welcome," Sage said, returning Emma's warm hug. "Go along now with Odie. She'll show you where everything is." Emma and Odie departed, leaving Sage alone with her thoughts.

Emma's parting remark, though meant kindly, pierced a hole in Sage's heart. Because it was true. No one in Fairplay Creek knew what Sage Cane was like, what kind of a woman she really was. To them, she was a madam, someone to be snubbed on the street and whispered about behind her back. Rough men lounging on the benches outside the saloons felt free to leer at her, and make suggestive comments. Sometimes they reached out for her arm when she passed.

For safety's sake, she'd begun carrying a tiny walnut-handled derringer in her reticule ever since a drunk outside the Salt Creek Saloon accosted her on the sidewalk. Her other gun, the one that had belonged to her aunt—the one that had put a bullet through the marshal's trailcoat—

was too heavy to carry on her person, but she kept it handy in her room. She hadn't had time to practice with the derringer yet, but the gunsmith showed her how to pivot the barrel to put the bullets in. Despite its small size, the weight of it in her handbag was comforting. It was probably time she stopped walking everywhere, too.

"Miss Priscilla, where is Cheveyo?"

"At the livery milking the cows."

"Do you think he knows anything about horses?"

"I expect all Indians do," Priscilla answered absently, her hands busy in the sink. "Why do you ask?"

"I'm going to buy a horse," declared Sage. "And a buggy. I think a carryall would be most practical. Cheveyo can take care of it for me, as well as groom and feed the horse. I'll pay him extra. And when the men have finished building the bathhouse, I'll ask them to build a stable for it next to the barn. Then we can keep the cows here, too."

"That would be convenient," said Priscilla.

That decision made, Sage examined a curious bubble of emptiness that had materialized in her chest when Acer said Bridger had gone to Hamilton City. Quickly, she dismissed it. She didn't intend to form any kind of dependency on Bridger Norwood just because he was the marshal. She couldn't let herself need him in any way. Her safety, like her future, was up to her.

Everything was up to her.

* * * * *

After helping Emma Ford settle in, Odie retired to her room, closed the curtains against the brilliant sunshine, and collapsed into her rocking chair. Hours later she was still there, rocking slowly, a tear-stained handkerchief pressed to her face.

The Maclean women were cursed, surely they were. All the women in her family had suffered the same fate, and for a while she thought she'd escaped it. Thought the Maclean curse wouldn't define her life the way it had her mother and grandmother.

When she'd been rescued from that brothel in Cripple Creek, she thought she'd broken the trail of pain and heartbreak that had dogged the women in her family for generations. Until a lack of good alternatives led her to make the same wrongheaded decisions the others had.

It was uncanny how she always knew when her past was catching up to her. She could feel it. A finger of fear would begin poking her belly. Then pain, mild at first, would slither across her forehead and lodge between her eyes.

She was afraid she'd never escape her past, because even in this isolated frontier outpost, that fingertip had begun poking again, so faintly at first that she ignored it. Now a debilitating fog of pain held her head in its grip.

She'd hated having to tell Sage she was too sick to go talk to Bridger about the tax bill. Even as she spoke, she was afraid her shaky voice had betrayed her, betrayed what she was hiding. But, no. Dear Sage had patted her arm in sympathy and told her to stay in bed.

Remembering how uneasily the words had rolled off her tongue, Odie quelled a sob and held a breath. She couldn't let Sage down like that again. Sage depended on her, and Odie's future depended on Sage's success. She *had* to pull herself together if she was ever going to be free.

Grim resolve straightened her shoulders. She got to her feet, wiped her eyes with a fresh handkerchief, draped her shawl over her shoulders, and headed out to settle up with Pete Gallagher for the food Emma Ford took from the store without paying.

Chapter Nine

Hamilton City was twenty miles from Fairplay Creek and linked to it by twisting roads and rough mountain passes Bridger easily navigated now that his shoulder was mended and his arm out of the sling. The townspeople of Hamilton City, and the nearby farmers and ranchers were waiting for the arrival of the railroad, an event delayed by lack of growth. Until now.

When Bridger reached the outskirts of the town, he immediately saw signs of development along the main street—a farm equipment and supply store had opened, the old mercantile had doubled in size, and a newly erected church thrust its steeple into the sky.

There were more people about, too, families, not just single men, and horses and buggies everywhere, though the population hadn't grown as dense as it had in Fairplay Creek. In comparison, Hamilton City was an oasis in the mountains. Quiet, peaceful, inhabited by gentlefolk, due mainly to the fact that there were no saloons, no gambling houses, and no bordellos within the city limits.

Bridger turned his rented two-horse rig down a dusty track and into a wide yard fronting a farmhouse. Smoke came from the chimney, and in the fields behind, stock grazed. Scattered across the valley beyond were other farms.

"Papa! Papa!" A little auburn-haired girl came running out of the house onto the porch, the screen door slamming behind her.

"Whoa," he said to the horses as the child, her skirts and petticoats flying ran across the hard dirt to meet him. He wound the reins around a fence post, and jumped out of the wagon box just in time to scoop her up into a bear hug. Squealing with delight, she wrapped her arms and legs around his bulk.

"Papa!"

"Hey, Princess," he said, while the child planted wet kisses all over his face. "Oh, I've missed you, Jenny."

"Papa," she scolded, cupping his cheeks in her hands and looking directly into his face. "I don't like you being gone so long."

"I don't like it either, honey, but Papa has to work." He gave her another hug. "How are grandma and grandpa?"

"They're fine. Grandma made me this new dress. Do you like it?"

He put her down and held her at arm's length so he could take a good look at the dress. "Grandma Martha made that? It's mighty fine."

"She made it for church, but said I could wear it today 'cause you were comin'."

The screen door squeaked open and a woman came out on the front porch, smiling. Bridger approached, and she tilted her head, presenting her cheek for his kiss.

"Hello, Martha," he said, then hugged her warmly.

"Come on in, son. I've got stew on the stove. It's hot and meaty with lots of potatoes, just the way you like it."

"Mmmm. I can smell it," he said, and his stomach rumbled.

Pop Sven came across the yard from the barn waving and smiling. "Howdy, Bridger," he called.

"Howdy, Sven." Bridger walked out to meet him, and there followed manly hugs with mutual backslapping and vigorous handshakes. Sven's hands were big with a grip to match, and his eyes, Elizabeth's eyes, under a full head of white hair were bright and alert despite his years.

After the rig had been put in the barn, and the horses fed and watered, they sat down to supper. Jenny chattered away, allowed to dominate the supper table dialogue only because her father was there, telling him about school, her new best friend, and the new kittens out in the barn.

"Can I show you later?" she asked.

"Sure," he replied.

Then, after a moment, "When can I come with you, Papa?"

"Soon, baby, soon," he told her. "Don't you like it here?"

"Oh, yes, but I miss you."

She had Elizabeth's heart-shaped face, and Bridger's auburn hair, but the personality was genuinely her own, an intriguing combination of both of her parents' good characteristics with none of the bad. Of course, Elizabeth hadn't had any bad points.

After the kittens were visited, and Jenny went down for the night, story read, prayers said, the grownups settled into the parlor.

"I hear there's lots of changes in Fairplay Creek," Sven observed while Martha poured coffee from a fresh pot. "Railroad ought to be there soon. Word is an advance party of investors is planning a trip to Fairplay Creek end of the year to scout out a logical site for a station."

"How do you hear so much, Sven? Way out here?"

"Muleskinner comes through twice a month," put in Martha before her husband could answer. "When he's here, Sven takes up half his day gossiping about goings on in the other towns along the route."

"And while I'm doing that," Sven said in a mock whisper, "she's in the mercantile getting the same news from Mrs. Murphy though I expect with much more interesting detail."

They laughed, and the room filled with companionable good cheer. Bridger and Sven stretched their boots toward the fireplace letting Martha fuss over them.

"More coffee, Bridger?" she asked.

He held out his cup and nodded his thanks.

Sven slurped noisily from his steaming mug. "Hear tell Honey Wild's niece arrived. Caused quite a stir in town when she made some new rules up at her aunt's place."

Bridger glowered. "That old muleskinner needs to mind his own business and concentrate on getting his freight delivered on time."

"What's she like?" Sven asked, his curiosity about the new madam getting the best of him.

"Sven," Martha warned, with a sidelong glance. "You know, I don't like discussing such people in this house." But after a long silence stretched out in the room, Martha's own inquisitiveness took over in spite of her good intentions. "I hear she's nothing like Honey was."

Bridger rolled his eyes. "Can we talk about something else?"

Two sets of eyes looked at him expectantly.

"All right," he said, edging the irritability out of his voice and giving in. "If you want the truth, she's nothing at all like Honey Wild, so much so that I wonder sometimes if she really is who she says she is."

Sven's eyebrows popped in surprise. "Is that a fact?"

Martha leaned forward, her love of intrigue barely concealed. "Really? Who do you suppose she is?"

"Oh, dang, I don't know. I haven't given it that much thought," he lied.

"Look." Changing the subject, he retrieved an envelope from his pocket and handed to Martha. "I wanted to let you know beginning next month, I'll be able to give you more money. I'll be hiring another deputy to help out. Ramsey Thorogood said he'll be giving me more responsibility and a raise along with it."

"Thank you, son, but we don't need this," Martha said, indicating the envelope. "We can take care of Jenny. After all, she's our only child's only child. It's not necessary."

Bridger insisted. "I know, but I'm her father and I want you to have it."

After a moment, Martha handed the envelope to Sven, their gazes colliding in explicit though silent communication.

Bridger picked up a picture of Elizabeth that was on the table next to him, and gazed at it thoughtfully. "I miss her so much."

"We all do . . ." Martha's voice caught, preventing her from saying more. Sven cleared his throat, hard.

"She wouldn't want me to take Jenny to a place like Fairplay Creek," intoned Bridger. "Not yet. She's safer here in Hamilton City. At least for now."

"Jenny can stay with us as long as you need her to. Why, we'd be downright lonesome without her," said Martha, trying for lightheartedness but wiping away a tear.

"Wouldn't be the same her not bein' around." Sven smiled sadly, clearing his throat again.

The three of them, all that remained of a family, sat before the flickering fire, not speaking, making peace with or struggling with their memories. When the flames turned to embers, they said goodnight. At dawn, Bridger went quietly into Jenny's room for a hug and a good-bye kiss. Then he hitched up the rig and left for Fairplay Creek, tears filling his eyes, spilling down his cheeks. Hastily, he wiped them away, blaming them on the wind.

Chapter Ten

Sage reached for a towel, stepped out of the tin tub, and dried herself quickly. She put on a blue striped cotton skirt and white shirtwaist, pulled on stockings, and slipped her feet into comfortable low-heeled shoes. Today was the day. She was going to unlock Aunt Honey's clothespress, a task she'd been postponing since her arrival in Fairplay Creek.

She had whole mornings to herself now that the responsibility of reading lessons for Cheveyo and Oliver had been put into Emma Ford's capable hands. Over the past month, they had been joined by two other boys at the request of mothers who, to their credit, were willing to overlook the location of the makeshift school—the barn behind Wild Mountain Honey—in exchange for a chance at a future beyond mining for their sons. All four boys had taken well to their lessons and advanced rapidly, so Emma had added mathematics and social studies.

Sage picked up the knife she'd purloined from the kitchen and studied the locked cupboard. After she'd moved into Aunt Honey's rooms, she and Odie had sorted through her Aunt's fine garments of silk, tulle, and cashmere. But a large cherrywood clothespress between the tall windows had remained locked when no one could find a key to open it.

She slid the knife into the crack between the double doors and pried at the lock. Wincing at the sound of splintering wood, she nevertheless increased the pressure on the knife, levering until the lock gave way. When the doors popped open, her eyes widened and she caught her breath sharply.

"Oh, my," she said, taken by surprise at the contents. Despite the heat stealing into her face, she stared, mesmerized.

The clothespress was filled with corsets, but not the heavily boned, plain white and ecru colored coutil corsets she and the ladies of Independence wore. These were the finest French corsets Sage had ever seen, made of moiré silk and satin with gussets and stiffeners of soft cording sewn into the bodices to slenderize the waist and round the hips, to lift and in some cases, accentuate the breasts.

Most were fashioned in delicate pastel colors—pale pink, yellow, light green, but to her amazement and delight, some were made in colors she'd never imagined a corset could be—bright violet, intense magenta, bold blue, and red. And though she'd seen black corsets before, never had she seen them with such lush and extravagant decoration.

Each lovely undergarment was detailed with ribbons, bows, and fancy embroidery, glove-fitted to mold and shape a woman's figure, all artfully designed to enhance a woman's natural beauty. Hardly an edge escaped embellishment by velvet, real lace, ribbon, or miniature ruffles.

A stunning possibility came to her. Maybe Independence ladies did wear corsets like this only she hadn't known it!

It was a thought that brought a wave of wicked pleasure undulating through her middle. Unable to suppress a slightly naughty giggle, she gazed at the elegant undergarments. These corsets were not meant to be covered up or locked in a closet, she realized. Clearly, they were meant to be worn, and seen. She blew a straggling lock of hair out of her eyes.

Odie! Odie would surely want to see them.

Excitedly, she stepped round to Odie's door and knocked, knowing she was disturbing Odie's quiet time. "Odie?" she called softly, and knocked again.

The door opened. "Yes, Sage, what is it?"

Sage wrapped her fingers around her friend's wrist and tugged. "Come. You must see this."

Odie followed, her face a picture of puzzlement. When she peered into the clothespress, she made a sound that started as a gasp, but ended as a merry laugh. "Oh, my," she said, mimicking Sage's words but with far more gaiety in her inflection. Openmouthed, she placed her hands alongside her cheeks and gaped.

"They're beautiful," she exclaimed. "Where did you get them?"

"They were in here. I pried the doors open. They must have belonged to my aunt."

"But where did she get them? There's no corsetiere in Fairplay Creek?"

"She must have ordered them. Or made them. I'll ask Miss Priscilla if she had a sewing machine."

Fascinated, Odie began taking the corsets out of the closet admiring them one at a time. Sage went up on tiptoe and dragged a box off the top shelf. It was filled with elegant hairpieces, enormous masses of curled and puffed hair, coiled chignons, and looped braids. Feathered and jeweled hair ornaments were tucked into a velvet drawstring bag.

Sage reached into another box. "What's this?" she asked, holding up between two fingers a cup-shaped wire contrivance with padding in the rounded protrusions. It was pink and white, embroidered with flowers.

Odie recognized it right away. She took it from Sage and held it up to her chest. "It's a bust enhancer. You wear it like this."

Together they lay what looked to be wearable confections on the bed, stroking the soft fabrics, touching the tiny bows, letting silky fringes slither through their fingertips.

Odie picked up a pale green corselette trimmed in pink rosebuds and held it at arm's length. With a mischievous smile, she pressed it against her body, then crossed the room to look at her reflection in Sage's long mirror. The color brightened her face and brought a sparkle to her eyes.

"I'm going to try it on," she said, excitement making her a little breathless. "May I?" Without waiting for an answer, she added, "You try one on, too."

"Oh, no! I can't," Sage protested.

"Yes, you can. Come on," Odie coaxed. "It'll be fun. No one will see us." Odie selected a corset of burgundy silk trimmed in pink lace and black ribbon, and held it out to Sage.

"Here try this one. It looks like it will fit if you tightlace it. The color suits you."

Sage opened her mouth in further protest, uncomfortable at the audaciousness of Odie's suggestion. Then, surprised at the enjoyable feeling of boldness pumping through her veins, she relented, grinning. "All right." Quickly, she crossed the room to close and lock her doors. "But just one."

Normally lacking in such daring, Sage slipped out of her skirt and shirtwaist, removed her serviceable everyday corset, and put on the corset Odie had chosen. The silky black laces of the front fastening slid easily through ribbon eyelets as she cinched and tightened and cinched some more.

In spite of her misgivings, she was moved to admit it felt incredibly delicious on her body, and when she saw herself in the mirror, was awed at the way she looked in it. Her breasts swelled magnificently above the delicate pink lace bordering the scalloped edge. Her waist, small by nature, looked even more slender above the curvaceous line of her hips.

Odie's fingers flew as she quickly unlaced the pale green corset she'd tried on, and chose another of yellow brocade with a flower design.

Sage approved of Odie's choice. "That color is perfect for you," she said, getting into the spirit of it, and smiling as delight animated her friend's face for the first time in weeks.

The two friends, giggling unabashedly, stood before the looking glass, turning round and round, admiring themselves and each other. The sound of hurried footsteps pounding up the stairs, and Priscilla's voice, shrill with urgency momentarily froze them in place.

"Miss Sage! Miss Sage!"

Sage ran to the doors and opened them a crack to find the frantic cook, hands wringing, face wrought with anguish, as she reached the landing at the top of the staircase. "Come quickly," she cried. "Emma's baby!"

"What?" said Sage and Odie in unison.

"I think it's coming," Priscilla cried, heading back down. "Cheveyo came in to tell me Miss Emma collapsed during lessons. I sent Oliver for Doc Holden!"

"We'll be right there," Sage said. Odie and Sage dressed hurriedly throwing their street clothes on over the fancy corsets, and ran out to the barn.

Emma lay on the floor knees drawn, her face a mask of agony and fear, hands clasped over her taut belly. Cheveyo and his classmates poised anxiously in the doorway, nervous, uncertain, eyes wide with wonder in the age-old posture of males throughout centuries helpless in the face of the horror and miracle of childbirth.

"You boys run along," Sage said, shooing them away, but they didn't move. She knelt next to Emma and looked into her terrified eyes.

"My baby's coming," Emma croaked. "I guess I was wrong about when it was due."

Sage placed her hand on Emma's damp forehead, feeling the heat. She turned to Odie. "Have you ever birthed a baby?"

"No. Never."

"Neither have I," said Sage.

Suddenly, Emma's fingers clamped on Sage's forearm, as a spasm wracked her body. "You've got to get someone here who knows how to catch this baby!" she cried when she could take a breath.

"I'll get Turtledove," said Priscilla. "I think she used to be a mid-wife."

Cheveyo and his friends still lingered at the door leading to the barn. "You boys, scat," Priscilla scolded as she ran past, but they ignored her.

Cheveyo stepped forward. "Miss Sage."

"What is it, Cheveyo?" she replied over her shoulder, not looking at him. Gently she stroked Emma's forehead.

"I know about babies and how they get born. I helped my sister."

"That's very brave of you, Cheveyo, but you'll be more helpful here if you go with Priscilla. All of you boys go," she told them. "Get pillows, clean blankets and quilts, and bring them here. We need to try and make Miss Emma comfortable."

Thankfully, the boys took off without argument across the yard to the back door of the house.

Emma's eyes widened in astonishment when her water broke in a great gush between her legs just as Turtledove came running into the barn.

"Let me see," Turtledove said, kneeling next to Sage and slipping her hand under Emma's skirts. She withdrew it after a minute and nodded, confirming what was quite obvious.

"The baby's coming, but don't worry. I've delivered lots of 'em. Bring hot water and plenty of towels." Turtledove looked around and shook her head distastefully. "What a place to bring a baby into the world."

Oliver returned at a fast clip, sweating, out of breath. "Doc Holden can't come," he announced, his voice climbing an octave. "Someone got hurt up at the mines. Doc went up to the camps."

Turtledove brushed Emma's hair back from her forehead with her hand. "There, there," she cooed. "You just do what I tell you and it'll be fine. I've done this before."

Emma's tortured eyes collided with Turtledove's. "But I haven't," she squealed in fright, then groaned as another contraction gripped her.

Wakened by all the shouting and door banging, some of the Honeys drifted out of the house and across the yard to peer into the barn with offers of help and words of encouragement.

"Not much you can do right now," said Turtledove, her kind eyes on Emma's face. "Emma here's gonna do most of the work. Everyone else best go inside and wait. It's gonna be a long and hard labor."

Emma moaned and screwed up her face signaling the onset of another painful contraction just as the boys returned, their arms laden with pillows and bedding. They dropped them next to Turtledove and retreated to stand in the doorway, their eyes big as saucers.

"Everyone out," Turtledove ordered. "Except you, Tiny, could you stay? And Odie? Help me with the bedding."

Helplessly, Sage turned toward the house followed by the others.

Cheveyo sat down on the back porch steps with Oliver, the other boys having run off.

"We'll wait here," he told Sage, his eyes serious beyond his years, and filled with concern. "In case, you need us."

Sage drifted a hand over the child's head and down his face to cup his cheek. "Thank you, Cheveyo. You're a good, brave boy."

Inside, some of the girls returned to their rooms, but Verbena and Poppy sat in the kitchen with Sage. Priscilla fussed, setting out coffee and cookies and bacon scones. The women sat around the table, not speaking, their glances occasionally connecting in silent commiseration as the minutes ticked slowly by. There was no need for words. Sage knew that each woman in her own way was aware of what needed to be done. Silently they prayed for the safety of Emma and her baby.

Somewhere in the profound stillness, Sage heard a drumbeat, an insignificant sound at the threshold of hearing, and like a door opening in her memory, she thought of the 4th of July parades she'd loved when she was a girl in Independence. Her father always carried her on his shoulders so she could see over the crowd. How she'd loved the music, the prancing horses, the drummers marching in time, stepping as one, the sun glinting off musical instruments and the brass buttons of their uniforms. She wondered at the mind's capacity to store such details.

The sound grew louder, coming into the present, louder and closer. Only it wasn't the spirited, uplifting rhythm of a parade band. It was loud and harsh, and was soon joined by voices, some singing, some shouting, coming from outside near the front of the house.

Alerted, Priscilla set down the coffee pot she'd been cleaning and headed toward the front door, wiping her hands on her apron as she went. Sage, Verbena and Poppy followed as Priscilla threw open the front doors intensifying the din of music and chanting. Cheveyo and Oliver pushed past her and ran out onto the porch, their eyes alight.

"Miss Sage! Miss Sage! There's people out here, yelling and singing."

Sage went to the window. With both hands she parted the brocade drapes and peered outside. Three hitch wagons pulled by thin, rawboned horses had been purposely driven onto the lawn in the front of the house. Hand lettered signs on the sideboards of the wagons crudely painted in gaudy shades of red and yellow declared Preacher Fry's Gospel Society, Come to Save Your Soul.

People, mostly men, but some women, were climbing out, chanting and singing. They wore garments of coarse black fabric, the women clad modestly, fully covered from neck to wrist, skirts hanging to the dirt. Sage couldn't understand what they were saying, but there was no mistaking the admonitions on the signs they were waving at the end of long wooden poles.

"Sinners Repent! Embrace Glory! Abandon the Devil! Repent or Burn In Hell!"

The preacher, dressed in a long black frock coat, white shirt and string tie, jumped from the wagon bench and walked up the white stone path until he was standing near the foot of the front porch steps. He was long-legged and cadaverous, donning a wide brimmed low-crowned black hat. When he raised his arms aloft, the drum pounding stopped, and the discordant singing faded away, but his followers continued to hover in or near the hitch wagons, tense and pugnacious, looking ready to do battle with the devil himself.

Preacher Fry's voice was commanding as he lifted his chin and called out to the house. "You cursed women indulging in wickedness. You harlots. Repent! Repent! Come live a life of purity and spirit." His eyes were ablaze, almost like live coals, and his look was fierce.

The words brought burning disgrace to Sage's face, and she backed away from the window, letting the drapes fall in place. Heart pounding, she strode to the open front entrance where she took a determined stance in the doorway. Verbena and Poppy tiptoed up behind to peer nervously over her shoulders. Melanie came running downstairs and hurried over to see what was happening.

Priscilla took Sage's place at the window, glaring boldly through the glass, gripping a fireplace poker like a cudgel. Oliver and Cheveyo hung over the porch railing gawking at the drama unfolding on the lawn.

Head high, back straight, Sage stood on the threshold and stared at the preacher, refusing to cower under his judgmental stare.

Preacher Fry slowly lowered his arms and laid a big-knuckled hand on his chest over his heart in an affectation of reverence. The little finger of his right hand was missing, the knuckle joint long healed over into a thick opaque stub where it had been roughly severed. He fixed his gaze on her and with a look of benevolent reproach asked, "Sister, shall I pray for you?"

Her answer was quick and defiant. "That won't be necessary." Her voice was strong and steady, but she could feel perspiration soaking her underarms. It ran down her side dampening the burgundy corset she was still wearing.

"But we're here to save you, sister. We've come to blast the devil clean out of your hearts." His manner was of someone who had offered a gift but been rebuffed.

"We don't need you to do that. The devil does not reside in our hearts, but rather in those who judge us," she said, though a part of her didn't completely believe this. Her eyes looked into his, straight and clear, unflinching, hiding, she hoped, the shame and uncertainty tearing her up inside.

Preacher Fry shook his head slowly, his sly grin revealing a row of discolored teeth. The tip of an overly long eyetooth caught on his lip.

"Yes, you do, sister," he said with a sanctimonious sneer. "This town is a sanctuary for the devil."

"You have no right to come here and insult us. This is a fine town with upstanding people."

"But you don't even have a church," the preacher admonished.

"Yes, we do," Sage shot back without thinking.

A murmur rose and fell through the gathering. Someone tittered.

"Well, where is it?" the preacher challenged.

The crowd, their shouts stilled, waited for her to answer.

"It's not built yet," she replied, the words spilling out of her mouth unimpeded by thought. "But it will be. By next spring," she was then compelled to add.

Preacher Fry stared at her a moment, his expression supremely skeptical. There was movement behind his eyes, decisions being rapidly evaluated and discarded. After a moment, he turned his head, and called out to his followers.

"Unload those wagons!"

Behind him, black clad men and women with hostility in their faces lowered the wagon gates and dragged out poles and bundles of canvas. Working together they began pitching tents on the lawn.

"Stop that," Sage shouted, waving her hands in a shooing motion. "You can't do that. You can't stay here!" When they ignored her, she lashed the preacher with a sharp look. "You are trespassing and I demand you leave at once."

At that, Preacher Fry's followers took up shouting again, their faces resolute.

Sage's eyes swept the group. A woman with gray hair and a wizened face stepped away from the crowd and pointed at the porch where Cheveyo and Oliver stood gaping.

"There's children living in that sinful house," the woman croaked in a voice as rough as the serrated edge of a knife. "Repent you sinner women. You vile godless gender, providing sinful services to men and boys." She began banging a tambourine, her face aglow with determined self-righteousness.

Behind Sage, Melanie, who had begun weeping fretfully at the earlier recriminations now backed away with a gasp and burst into sobs, but Poppy, anger visibly rolling through her body, tried to push her way onto the porch with raised fists.

Sage stopped her. "Let me handle this," she whispered. "Please tend to Melanie and Verbena." Reluctantly Poppy did as she was asked. Sage stepped out onto the porch and faced the throng who continued to chant raucously.

"You are doomed, sisters," someone shouted while others defiantly continued setting up camp.

Pointing past the preacher, Sage called to them again. "You there. You must leave at once. You can't stay here. This is private property. Move your wagons. Take down those tents!"

They ignored her and continued their incredible din, singing, shouting, blowing horns, shaking tambourines, fingering makeshift stringed instruments. Someone was pounding the drum again signaling the glory shouting to begin anew.

Sage caught the sudden movement of one of the women in the flock as she picked up a chunk of horse dung from under a wagon and threw it. The clod hit Sage in the chest and splattered in her face, the shock of it knocking her back a step and buckling her knees. Instantly, Cheveyo and Oliver were at her side, clutching her arms to keep her from falling down.

"Cheveyo, go get the marshal," ordered Priscilla.

Quickly, Sage regained her balance and stopped him with her hand on his arm. "No," she declared stubbornly. "I'm all right." Swamped with humiliation and anger, Sage braced her legs and stood firmly, her voice low. "Go to the barn and check on Emma." The boys took off at a run as Priscilla, using her apron, wiped Sage's face and brushed at the mess on the front of her blouse.

The Honeys gathered at the railing overlooking the front foyer entrance, chattering nervously. A few of the bolder ones descended the grand staircase, then clustered together at the bottom, unsure what to do.

By this time, word had raced down to Main Street and along the boarded walks that there was trouble at Wild Mountain Honey. Townspeople had joined the crowd to see what was going on; businessmen, card players, shoppers, newcomers, saloon patrons. Scores of people, walking fast, some running, were drawn by the clamor that was quickly turning into an uproar. Miners leading burros or driving wagons, coming in early from the camps in the mountains behind Wild Mountain Honey stopped to gawk or join the throng.

Preacher Fry, seeing a growing audience, took the advantage. Playing to the crowd, he raised his voice, directing his comments to them.

"My brethren," he intoned. "I would now warn you against these wretched women, these sisters of the devil."

A dust covered miner pushed his way to the front of the crowd. It was Josiah Miller carrying a dirt caked pick and looking bone-tired. With a glance at Sage, he spoke to the preacher in a firm but courteous voice.

"Our object here is to get rich and stay that way. We don't want any trouble. The lady asked you to leave and I suggest you do it. Take your people and move away from here."

"We don't bring trouble, brother. We bring glory and blessing." Preacher Fry was not about to give up.

"We don't want blessings from phony self-appointed preachers like you," Josiah said, and some of the other bystanders concurred in unison.

"Take your people and your wagons and your tents, and get out of town." This from a young miner Sage had seen at the assay office, but never at Wild Mountain Honey. Harry was his name.

The preacher's followers ignored Josiah and Harry, their murmurs rising into shouts. There was pushing and shoving, and the shouts accelerated into anger. Rocks were thrown. Someone fired a gun, someone else screamed, but Sage couldn't tell whether anyone was hit. The crowd worked itself up into a frenzy as the townspeople rushed the trespassers and tried to wrestle them off the property. The miners, their arms and shoulders muscled and rock hard from wielding picks and shovels, grabbed some of the intruders and tried to physically force them back into their wagon. Horses whinnied and shied. One of them reared, almost knocking the wagon carrying the drummer and the horn player on its side.

Lightning exploded behind Sage's brain as a rock struck her on the side of the head thrusting a sharp pain through her skull. Her hands flew to her head and she staggered, but fought to remain standing.

Suddenly a torch was lit, and through a haze of pain she saw someone running toward the house shouting, "Let's burn it down." Others followed, some veering off toward the barn.

"Emma!" Sage screamed. "She's in the barn having a baby. Someone has to get her!"

A flurry of fistfights broke out, and some of the townsmen took off running toward the barn to stop the torch carrying ruffians.

Inside the house, the Honeys clung to each other, some weeping in terror and confusion. Miss Priscilla's voice carried above their cries.

"Stop carryin' on so. Pull yourselves together. Come help me get Emma and the others. Now!" The girls did as she instructed with no one holding back.

"Oliver!" she shrieked out the door. "Run get the horse and buggy out of the barn!"

That was the last thing Sage heard before consciousness slipped away and she crumpled to the porch.

Chapter Eleven

Sage lay on her wooden four-poster, her chest rising and falling with peaceful breathing. Bridger, in a chair pulled up close to the bed, his hat resting on a delicate end table at his elbow, didn't know where to put his eyes.

Everywhere he looked, there were corsets and ladies undergarments strewn about. When he and Doc Holden had carried Sage upstairs, they'd had to remove them from the counterpane before she could be placed on top of it.

It wasn't that Bridger didn't like looking at ladies' fineries and under-things. He rather enjoyed it especially if they were layered over silky skin, but he was afraid Sage would wake up and catch him at it which might embarrass her.

He had to admit that, at first, he'd been taken aback at the sight of them. He had no idea Sage wore such elaborate unmentionables under her mostly prudish outerwear. He would have guessed what she wore under would be just as priggish and dull as what she wore on the outside. That didn't appear to be the case.

The house was quiet, closed to business for the night because of Emma and her new baby girl both of whom were resting in one of the downstairs rooms, tended to by Miss Priscilla and Turtledove. All the other girls were catching up on some much needed sleep, their nerves and sensibilities no doubt shot after the excitement of the day.

The riot had been quelled with the help of some burly miners and saloon patrons who had forcibly escorted the itinerant preacher and his followers well out of town. Miss Priscilla's chicken coop was burned to the ground, but thanks to a quickly formed bucket brigade made up of willing townspeople, only a part of the barn was destroyed. Sage's horse and buggy had been salvaged, and put in an undamaged paddock.

The doctor had examined Sage's head injury, declaring the bump not serious though it bore watching, so had administered painkillers and a sedative to help her sleep. Since she wasn't the only one requiring his ministrations, he'd asked Bridger to sit with her a while applying cold compresses to her forehead. The only other persons he would have trusted to do that were busy with Emma and her baby.

Bridger's gaze fell on Sage's lips. They were slightly parted and though her breathing was even, a vague frown troubled her brow. Her hair was loose, having fallen out of its pins, and he wanted to thread it with his fingers just to feel its softness. Suddenly he gave his head a shake and snuffled out a coarse breath. He was acting like a damn fool over a woman he had no interest in whatsoever.

And why not, some part of him wondered?

Why wasn't he interested? She was beautiful if a bit sharp around the tongue. This was no empty-headed woman, but a strong-willed one, determined. She seemed sensible and somehow respectable, her profession notwithstanding.

Sage stirred restlessly, moaned softly and shifted position, flinging out an arm. The edges of her blouse fell open and Bridger caught a glimpse of the embroidered camisole underneath. Doc Holden, after applying ice to the bump on her head, had diffidently untied her burgundy corset, loosening it so she could breathe more easily. She was still in a faint at the time, otherwise Bridger was sure she'd never have allowed the familiarity.

The lamp was dim, and muted light softened her features. Her fragrance drifted up to his nose, something floral. He tried not to be distracted by it, and by the way her pretty camisole moved in accord with her breathing. An ache of loneliness was building in his chest, and he wondered what it would be like to lie down with her, to smooth away her worried brow. Comfort her.

Or did he want her to comfort him?

Deliberately, he pulled his eyes away, and gazed around. He remembered the night he'd burst into this room after passing Josiah Miller on the stairway only to find himself facing the business end of a gun. He winced thinking about what happened next.

He fixed his eyes on a black lace trimmed corset laid over the arm of the sofa. It had belonged to Honey, he remembered, and he tried to conjure up a picture in his mind of what it would look like on Sage. The vision pleased him and brought a smile to his lips. When his gaze turned back to Sage, her eyes were open, staring at him.

* * * * *

So it wasn't a dream. Bridger had stayed with her, tended to her. Her breeding required that she object to his being there alone with her, but with such a tremendous throbbing in her head she lacked the will to protest.

He was smiling. She couldn't help thinking that he smiled quite wonderfully, if a bit devilishly, but those silly thoughts were banished when the events of the past hours rushed back to her mind.

"Emma," she said and tried to sit up. A dizzying pain knotted itself around her head and she fell back weakly.

"She's fine," Bridger said. "And the baby, too. A little girl. Dawn Allen."

Gently, he lifted the compress from her forehead, re-soaked it in the washbasin on the floor next to the bed, squeezed out the excess water and placed it back on her brow. It felt cool against her skin.

Remnants of smoke lingered in the air, and she remembered men running with flaming torches. "The house is still standing, I see," she said and closed her eyes.

"It is," he confirmed.

Bridger picked up the pain pill Doc Holden had left, put it in her hand, poured water from a pitcher and held a cup for her while she drank. "But I'm afraid Miss Priscilla's chicken coop is a total loss. And the barn needs repair."

Slowly, she lay back and sighed, staring at the ceiling. The chicken coop could be replaced easily enough. But what about the barn? She hoped repairs wouldn't cost too much, though she was grateful it wasn't completely gone.

"What about Preacher Fry's Gospel Society come to save my soul?" she asked dryly. Her mind burned with the memory of the venomous words he spouted, and the vile names he'd called her.

"They're gone. All of them." Bridger filled her in on the details of the preacher's unceremonious departure, and the subsequent fire fighting efforts.

"Where's Odie?"

"Sleeping. She was worn out from helping with the birth. Turtledove and Miss Priscilla have taken over. They're downstairs with Emma and Dawn Allen. Odie closed the house for the night. She didn't think you'd mind."

Sage shook her head setting off a lead ball of pain rolling inside her skull. "I don't mind. What about the girls?"

"All fine. None of them hurt. They're sleeping."

"They probably need it."

"That they do. Doc says you're not to worry about anything. He said you are to stay in bed and posted me here to make sure you did."

She waved away his concern, and started to sit up again, poking at the pins falling from the coil at her neck. "No, I've got things to do," she began, but the hammering in her head increased in intensity and a wave of dizziness brought nausea. With one hand on her head and the other on her stomach, she fell back to the pillows, grimacing.

"It's that medicine from the Doc," said Bridger. "Makes you woozy. You're supposed to sleep."

"Thank you, Marshal, but you don't have to stay with me. Surely you have some peace keeping to do in town. What with Wild Mountain Honey being closed, the men must be tearing the town apart." Despite the pain in her head, she tried for sarcasm, but Bridger didn't rise to it.

"No, it's been quiet. Acer's handling everything, but . . ." He stopped not completing the thought, and scowled.

"But what?" she asked.

"Well, I got word from one of the freight drivers that the federal marshal in Denver is looking for some rough men. One of them is headed this way. Name's Riker. Charles "Shooter" Riker. He's a mean one. Shot a man in a saloon in Denver. The driver brought some wanted posters with his picture. Asked if I'd hang them around town. Told him I would."

"You'd best do that, then," she said, her voice barely above a whisper, the words slurred from the effects of the medicine.

"You'll be all right?"

Feebly, she waved a hand through the air, dismissing him, then let it drop on the counterpane. "I'll be fine," she answered, feeling herself begin a slide into a sort of twilight slumber. His farewell came to her as though from a distance, and she didn't hear the door close when he left.

Her thoughts went to the barn and she wondered exactly how much of it was damaged, and whether she could continue classes for the boys. Emma would be lying in for several weeks. They'd need to find her a place to live. She couldn't stay here with a baby. Would she still teach classes?

Sage floated in a half sleep, half awake stage that made her feel as if she were rising up off the bed toward the ceiling. Bridger's smile lingered in her mind. She wouldn't admit an attraction to him, but she couldn't help being aware of his maleness when he was around even though he had the wandering eyes of a man who couldn't be counted on.

She pushed away thoughts of Bridger Norwood and turned her mind to the empty miles between her and Independence. How soon before she could go back? How much of her savings would she have to spend to repair the barn? Perhaps she'd been too hasty in purchasing the land next door and contracting to build the bathhouse, but it had seemed a decent thing to do not just for the girls, but for everyone given the paucity of bathing facilities in town.

She sighed, too tired to think about it now. She'd figure something out tomorrow. She was on her own. It was up to her. Everything was up to her. Somehow she'd find a way.

Chapter Twelve

The floorboard creaked behind her, and Odie instantly came awake. Someone was in her room.

The room was hot, almost to suffocation, but she sensed a presence behind her, felt the air displace when it moved. Holding her breath, she inched her hand under her pillow until the tips of her fingers touched the derringer, a twin to the one Sage carried in her reticule.

Suddenly, he was on her back, crushing her chest against the mattress, pinning her arms beneath her. One of his calloused hands pressed the side of her face into the pillow while the other grappled between her legs.

"Shooter!"

"That's my name," he growled, then squeezed his meaty fist on the tender flesh of the inside of her thigh. She gasped and drew a ragged breath through her teeth.

"Please," she begged. "Leave me alone."

"Leave you alone? That was the mistake I made in Dodge City, wasn't it?" His drunken tone was bantering but no less threatening. "Leaving you alone so you could run off and make me a laughing stock. A man who couldn't hold on to his own wife." He squeezed her thigh again, painfully digging his fingers in, shoving her face into the pillow, cutting off her cry of pain.

The odor of stale sweat and many days on the trail drifted in sickening waves from his body. His breath was foul from drink and anger, the whiskey stoking the fire that burned in his belly, releasing the rage she knew resided in his soul even when he was sober. He was capable of great cruelty. He'd hurt her many times, and she was terrified of him. Frantically, she tried to get out from under the crush of his body, but his weight imprisoned her allowing little more than ineffectual thrashing of her legs on the mattress.

"Don't fight me, Odie. You know what happens when you fight me. What I have to do then. What you make me do."

She did know. With sinking heart, she remembered clearly the slaps and punches, the crushed nose, the broken cheekbones and swollen eye sockets. She stopped struggling, but couldn't keep her body from shaking.

"How did you find me?" she rasped.

His laugh was low and menacing. She could feel his breath on the back of her neck. His voice grated in her ear.

"Weren't hard," he hissed. "The ticket agent at the stage station remembered you buying passage to Denver. The desk clerk at the hotel in Denver saw you get on the feeder stage with that other one. That snooty one with the yellow hair." He wrapped Odie's long braid around his hand and yanked on it, pulling her face close to his.

"She's next when I'm through with you. Now, be a good girl and spread those legs."

"Shooter, no. Please." She struggled again, but he easily subdued her.

"I was hoping I'd find you with another man so I'd have a reason to kill you both. Too bad."

He was incredibly strong, his arms like steel. He hauled her up and flipped her over onto her back, then fell on top of her, crushing her breasts with his barrel-like chest, shoving his knee hard up between her legs.

"Stop! You're hurting me! I can't breathe!"

She grappled against his grip, straining to shove him off, but it was an uneven contest, defeat was inevitable. Life with Charles Riker had taught her that it was best to deny him the gratification of seeing her in pain, of hearing her beg for mercy. But her body fought of its own accord, trying to buck him off, desperate to break contact with a madman.

Her strength quickly subsided. She stopped flailing and lay helpless beneath him, her breath ragged and shallow.

"Now, how's it going to be?" he snarled. Their lips were almost touching and spittle sprayed on her face. "Hard? Or easy? Before I kill you anyway."

The knife point against her throat caused her heart to pound against her chest, and that's when she knew. He wasn't going to let her live. He didn't need the knife, his grip could crack her bones, snap her neck. She was too terrified to cry out. The gun under her pillow might as well have been out in the yard.

Steeling herself, she tried not to cringe, not to shrink away from him as he lifted his hips, pulled open his pants, and pushed himself roughly into her. The tip of the knife pricked her skin, and she held her breath, expecting it to plunge deep into her neck at any moment. She heard a whimpering sound and realized it was coming from her.

He finished with a grunt and she braced for the blows she knew would come next. They began almost immediately. He pinned her arms with his knees and pounded her face, her head, her mouth with his massive fists. She heard a tooth crack, then tasted blood where the sharp edge cut into the inside of her mouth. Hard blows pummeled the bone over her right eye and lights exploded inside her head. His fist plowed into her ribs. There was another crack followed by hot burning pain.

Delirious with pain, unable to speak or move, she felt him straddle her again, his knees on either side of her hips. The knife was back at her throat. His drunken fingers fumbled as he tried to force himself into her again.

Ears ringing, her head swimming with pain, she was close to losing consciousness, but inside her fevered brain something base and primitive commanded her to live. An overpowering will to survive flickered, then flamed to life. In delirium, she prayed Shooter was too distracted with what he was doing for his booze befuddled mind to notice her hand sliding under the pillow, reaching for the derringer. Her fingers touched it, then it was in her hand. Nausea turned her stomach over.

Suddenly Shooter jerked as a bullet exploded from behind, drawing blood as it grazed his neck before embedding itself in the bedboard above her head. Odie forced her swollen eyelids open to slits and over Shooter's shoulder saw Miss Priscilla standing at the foot of the bed holding a smoking revolver in steady hands.

"Get off her, mister," she hissed. "Get your fat ass off her. Right now."

With a roar, Shooter rolled off Odie and hurled himself at Priscilla. "You goddamn bitch!"

Another shot rang out, and his hands flew to his crotch, his eyes wide with pain and surprise. Blood spurted from between his legs and trickled through his fingers, and he barely had time to open his mouth before a third bullet tore a hole through his heart stopping his scream.

* * * * *

Sage woke with a grunt. A harridan with straggly ropes of hair like snakes sticking out from her head, stood over her holding a candle.

"Sage! Wake up," Odie rasped. "I need you."

The sleep-inducing effects of the pain pills reluctantly ebbed away as Sage leaned up on her elbow. "What? Odie? What is it?"

"My husband," Odie whispered, her voice breaking on a sob.

Sage blinked twice. "You have a husband?" she asked, trying to shake off the numbing sedative and come fully awake. "Where is he?"

"You have to come with me. Please." Odie folded her fingers around Sage's arm and pulled. When she moved, the candle flame flickered and glowed, reflecting on her battered face and swollen eyes. Her nightgown hung in tatters and was stained with blood.

Sage gasped and slowly pushed herself up, dropping her feet to the floor. "Dear Lord! What happened to you?"

"Hurry," Odie said, grinding out the word, pulling Sage toward the door. "Hurry."

Odie roughly dragged Sage into her room and closed and locked the door, silencing the click of the latch. Priscilla was sitting in a chair, rocking back and forth, her arms wrapped tightly around her middle. The posture seemed essential to holding herself together.

A man lay on the floor. His britches were open, his front covered with blood.

Three pairs of eyes stared in horror. No one spoke until Sage managed to whisper, "That's your husband?"

Odie nodded.

Sage's eyes traveled over Odie's battered face. "He did this to you?"

Odie nodded again and began weeping. "His name's Charles Riker. They call him Shooter."

Sage passed a hand over her eyes, pressed the eyelids with her fingertips, then pinched the bridge of her nose. "Oh, dear God," she said on a rush of breath.

Miss Priscilla stopped rocking and began a whispered narrative. Fear and desperation pitched her voice into an unnatural range as she began to explain.

"I got up with Emma and the baby. I was in the kitchen rinsing a washcloth in the sink, and thought I heard noises coming from Miss Odie's room. Then I heard her cry out. I didn't like the sound of it, so I grabbed the gun and came up." She gestured to the body on the floor. "He was beating on her somethin' awful."

Miss Priscilla's eyes moved to the knife that had fallen from Shooter's hand, then to the gun at her feet where she'd dropped it.

"I had to help Miss Odie. I couldn't let him do that to her." She began to sob, shoulders shaking. "He would have killed her."

Sage sank into the cushions of the upholstered settee, sighing deeply. She cocked her elbow on the arm of the sofa, spread her fingers over her face, and buttressed her head in her hands, trying to take it all in.

Odie, no longer able to hold herself upright, had gone down on her knees in the middle of the floor and stayed that way weeping, her face awash in tears and blood. Slowly, Miss Priscilla got out of the chair, wet a cloth from the pitcher, knelt beside her and pressed it to Odie's face. Her movements were as gentle as a mother's soothing a child who'd taken a fall.

Over Priscilla's shoulder, Odie's swollen eyes bored into Sage.

"I'm sorry I didn't tell you." She wept noisily, then gulped. "That he was after me, I mean." She sniffed wetly. "When I met you in Denver, I'd spent all my money getting that far. And then we shared a room at the hotel, and you offered me a job . . . I had to say yes, it was my only way out. I had no more money and no place to go. I thought if I could only get far enough away, to a wilderness town like Fairplay Creek he wouldn't find me, and I'd never see the worthless bastard again. Never have to say anything to anyone." Tears flowed, drenching her cheeks.

Sage recalled their first night in Wild Mountain Honey, how Odie had pleaded with her not to close it down and put her out of a job. She realized now that this is what she had feared, this is what she'd left behind and dreaded having to go back to.

Sage returned Odie's gaze and was swept up by a wave of sympathy.

"Several weeks ago, I'd heard some gossip at Gallagher's General Store," Odie continued. "I overheard the bullwhackers talking, telling tales and exchanging news from the other towns along their routes. I heard one of them mention Shooter's name. Someone had seen him in Denver." She was overcome by a deep sob that convulsed her body. "I prayed he wouldn't come here."

Miss Priscilla was gently wiping Odie's face, cooing comforting words.

"What are we going to do, Sage?" Odie wailed.

"I don't know. Let me think."

"They'll hang me," Miss Priscilla said matter-of-factly. "Folks won't put up with a black killing a white man. Don't matter none that he was beating Miss Odie to death. When they find out, they'll hang me."

"No, they won't," said Sage. "I won't let them."

"They'll hang me for sure," Miss Priscilla said again, her voice breaking. She dropped the cloth and covered her face with her hands. Her sobs collapsed into whimpers and somehow that was more pitiful than screams.

"Stop it," said Sage. It came out harsher than intended, but she knew with thudding certainty that what Miss Priscilla said was true. They'd hang her, and Bridger Norwood would be helpless to stop them. "Stop it. Both of you."

Sage stood uncertainly, swaying a little. "We have to get him out of here right away. The authorities are after him. Marshal Norwood is hanging wanted posters sent up from Denver. There's a reward, so everyone will be looking for him. They know he was headed this way."

She stared at the window. The night sky was dark as pitch, but in a couple of hours the sun would peek over the rim of the mountains. Sage knew they didn't have much time.

"Miss Priscilla, will you please bring the horse and buggy to the back door?"

Priscilla's eyes, glittering with tears, widened. Odie stared and her mouth dropped open. Sage didn't have to explain. All three knew what they had to do. No one had to speak their intentions out loud.

"Take the shovels from the barn and put them in the back," Sage instructed.

Without a word, Priscilla left the room.

Sage gathered Odie where she was slumped on the floor, helped her to a chair and stripped off her torn nightgown. Taking camisole, petticoats and a dress from the clothespress, Sage began helping Odie into clean clothes.

Odie gasped, her breath shuddering when she lifted her arms into the sleeves. "My rib," she breathed. "I think it's broken."

Hurriedly, Sage ripped a bedsheet into strips and wrapped them around Odie's middle, pulling them snug for support.

"That should help a little. I'm sorry I can't do any more."

Odie nodded and Sage helped her finish dressing.

By the time Priscilla returned, Shooter's body was wrapped in blankets from the bed. Wordlessly, with Odie grimacing from the effort, the three women carried the body down the back stairs. They stopped at the bottom outside the kitchen where Cheveyo was stretched out on his cot next to the stove. Worriedly, Sage glanced at him.

Miss Priscilla shook her head and mouthed, "He's sleeping."

Sage nodded and they continued through the storage room and out the back door.

Shooter was heavy and it wasn't easy lifting him into the back of the buggy. Irritated at being disturbed before morning, the horse snorted and danced, jostling the buggy making it difficult, and they almost dropped him. Finally with a great heave, they managed to hoist the body over the side and it landed with a thud. The horse whinnied, snorted and stamped his feet again, making a racket. The women froze.

"Whoa," whispered Sage, grabbing the bridle, settling him down.

"Odie and I will take care of this," Sage said to Priscilla. "You can," she tilted her head toward Odie's upstairs room and the bloody mess remaining, "take care of the rest."

Miss Priscilla nodded. "Yes."

From inside the house came a baby's cry, the insistent mewling sound of a newborn. Priscilla frowned, exchanged quick worried glances with Sage and Odie, then hurried inside to help Emma with the baby.

Sage lifted the reins, clucked to the horse, and they began to move. Odie sat stiffly, one hand in her lap, the other pressed to her ribs. Behind them in the wagon bed, the shovels clanked together sending a piercing ring into the night air. Odie, averting her eyes from the bundled blankets, reached back and moved the shovels apart.

Sage directed the horse away from the main street, guiding him along the freshly graded side streets, past FOR SALE signs and stacks of fresh cut lumber. On the outskirts of town, away from the noise and the lights, a new residential section was beginning to spread. The buggy bumped along a rutted lane, past dugouts and tents and shanties.

Cloaked in the black of night, neither woman spoke. Sage kept her mind blank, unwilling to examine the meaning or repercussions of what she was doing. Maybe what Miss Priscilla did was wrong, but what Shooter did was wrong, too. Who was more wrong? Was anybody right? She didn't know, but she wasn't going to let Miss Priscilla hang for saving Odie's life. And for—*God help me for thinking this*—for killing someone who deserved to die.

* * * * *

The sky was grey but the tops of the mountains were pale pink when, hours later, Bridger came to check on the house. He rode around to the back forming a wide berth around Wild Mountain Honey, his bay's hoofs making a dull clopping sound in the hard packed dirt. He reined the horse to a stop in the trees and looked at the house. It was quiet. Nothing moved.

The back door creaked open and Cheveyo stepped out onto the porch. The boy was rubbing his eyes, his mouth open in a wide yawn. He trotted down the steps and through the dirt to the barn where he unhitched Sage's horse from the buggy, brushed it down, put it in the paddock, and tossed some feed into the trough. Then, using buckets of water and a rag, he returned to the buggy and washed away layers of reddish-brown dirt.

Curious, but with something telling him not to let his presence be known, Bridger waited on horseback in the shadows. When Cheveyo finished his chores and returned to the house, Bridger nudged the bay closer to the barn, staying hidden in the trees.

Up against the wall just inside the barn door were two shovels layered with the same dirt Cheveyo had washed from the buggy.

Bridger rested his hands on the saddle horn, narrowed his eyes in thought, and wondered if this was something he needed to remember. Or if, as was often the case in a rough and tumble mining town, it was something he best forget.

Chapter Thirteen

On the first Wednesday of the month, Cheveyo hitched the sorrel to the buggy and walked it to the back porch of Wild Mountain Honey where Sage waited on the steps.

"I go with you?" He held the reins as she stepped into the buggy, sat down, and arranged her skirts. "It's late. Maybe full dark when the meeting's over."

"No, thank you, Cheveyo," Sage replied, pulling on her gloves. "I'll be fine. I don't expect the meeting will last till then. You stay here and read that book you borrowed."

"Yes, Miss Sage."

He handed her the reins then stood barefoot on the bottom step. Though Miss Priscilla had an easier time getting him to take baths and wear the freshly laundered clothes she laid out for him, Cheveyo had drawn the line at wearing shoes on a regular basis.

She clucked to the horse and flicked the reins. "Mind you help Miss Priscilla in the kitchen if she needs you," she reminded as the buggy moved away.

"Yes, Miss Sage."

The business section of town had further spread its boundaries with buildings and hastily erected shanties taking up both sides of the street. On one of the new corners, she noticed a large parcel of land had been graded. A sign said it was the site of a hotel, the first in Fairplay Creek. From the looks of the foundation, it was going to be huge, taking up the entire corner stretching almost a full block on either side.

There was still no newspaper in town, so the Shouting Post in front of the bank remained a popular source of information. As she rode past, her heart gave a dull thud against her chest bone when she saw Shooter

Riker's face gazing meanly from a tattered wanted poster, its picture and the words faded and bleached by the sun. The posters were all over town. Bridger had even insisted on putting some up in Wild Mountain Honey figuring that would be the first place Riker would go.

It was, she thought.

At least she hoped it was. She hoped no one had seen him in town who might later wonder where he was now.

She'd left the posters up in the parlors and public rooms, afraid it would draw attention if she insisted they be removed, but her heart turned over every time her eyes fell upon it. She was sure Odie's did, too, judging by the way she lowered her gaze whenever she encountered one. Miss Priscilla tore down the poster in the kitchen and burned it in the stove.

After Sage and Odie had buried Shooter in Hatchett's Draw, and later set his horse loose with a smack on the rump near the Indian camp, Odie stayed in her rooms for several days because of the injuries to her face. When the ugly dark blue bruises began to fade, she covered them with powder before she would venture out. No one spoke of that night again.

Sage worked her way down the street that was as wide as a pasture avoiding the clusters of gawking tenderfoots and greenies. Every one of them had the lean and hungry look of the newly arrived. Some had eyes that glistened with excitement and adventure, others already looked dejected and disappointed.

She slowed as she approached a crowd that had circled around a teamster who was putting on a show, cracking his bullwhip through the air with great flourishes to the delight of the onlookers.

The bullwhacker, a sight a buzzard would have gazed upon with delight, interrupted his exhibition to brag loudly about his prowess with the long whip he used to control the oxen that pulled his freight wagons.

"Why, I've sliced the britches off a man wearing them without touching the man's skin," he boasted. "I'll bet anybody a pint of whiskey I kin do it again."

A tenderfoot obviously having spent too much time in a saloon stepped away from the crowd. "I'll take that bet," he said, swaying drunkenly.

With great drama and to resounding encouragement, the grinning young newcomer staggered to the middle of the gathering and bent over with his rear end toward the bullwhacker. A hush fell, the bullwhacker stepped back, the whip cracked, and the tenderfoot yelped and executed what Sage thought was the highest jump she had ever seen.

"Owww!" he yelled, his hands to his seat. "That hurt!"

"Well, tarnation," observed the bullwhacker with exaggerated astonishment. "Looks like I owe you a pint of whiskey."

The crowd roared.

Sage shook her head. She could ignore the rascality of some of the sharpies and harpies who came to town, but not when it came to cruelty. Some of them carried their practical jokes too far. She longed to see a measure of civility in town, but guessed she'd be back in Independence before it arrived in Fairplay Creek, if ever.

Suddenly she heard shots and reined up her horse. A young man and a girl came barreling up the street, their horses at a gallop, yelling at the tops of their voices, the boy firing his revolver. He appeared to be well lit from whiskey, laughing and shooting into the air. The girl, who couldn't have been more than fourteen or fifteen years old, was equally noisy as she rode by, long hair streaming behind, wearing nothing but drawers and a chemise.

Sage turned to watch as people in the street, hooting and hollering and cheering them on, dove out of the way to avoid being trampled. Sage was shocked at the young girl's bold display, then realized she'd never seen that young man at Wild Mountain Honey. And it further occurred to her that he might very well be getting for free what visitors to Wild Mountain Honey were paying for.

She watched a moment as the couple disappeared into the crowd at the end of the block, and lamented the lack of a decent place in town for young people to meet in a socially acceptable manner.

Still shaking her head, she continued on to the general store where a meeting was being held to discuss some of the needs of the town—fire protection, for one—and whether or not it was time to form an official town council.

She wrapped the reins around the hitch rack in front of Gallagher's General Store next to a saddled horse. It stood patiently, head down, occasionally stamping its feet to rid its legs of flies. She recognized it as belonging to Bridger.

Lifting her skirts, Sage went up the steps and stood in the doorway looking over the gathering. Meager, she thought, given the number of people in town now, but at least some of them, the ones who were there for the long haul, wanted input into the future of the town.

Pete Gallagher had pushed the clothes racks and merchandise tables up against the walls to make room for chairs and benches. Men dressed in buckskin, slouch hats, boots, moccasins, armed with knives and revolvers suspended from their belts, and miners aplenty made up the crowd. Some of them were accompanied by their wives. That is, the wives who weren't too exhausted from the grueling attempts at keeping a decent home in the hovels some of them lived in. For a woman who cherished cleanliness and fine things, this town must prove to be a huge disappointment.

Head high, shoulders back, Sage strode into the room and took a seat in one of the back rows. Whispers of her arrival flowed through the crowd like wind over a wheat field, and conversation dwindled as heads turned in her direction. She could see the resentment in the women's eyes when the men pressed forward introducing themselves to her. She knew what the women thought of her. A young woman alone, a madam no less, a lure for their husbands.

Well, if they knew how to keep their men home at night, places like Wild Mountain Honey wouldn't thrive in towns like this, she couldn't help thinking.

Her eyes swept the group and she saw Bridger standing at the front of the room off to the side. He was clean and groomed, his hair tied back and mustache trimmed, wearing his new duster. He was talking to Ramsey Thorogood, but turned to look at her.

Their gazes connected, hers faltered, and for a moment the conversation and crowd noises faded into the background as she nodded in his direction.

Hello.

Smiling, he returned her nod.

Hello back.

A beanpole in miner's clothes took a seat next to her, and she scooted aside to make room for him on the bench. He dipped his head and touched his hat in greeting, then crossed his arms and turned his attention to where Ramsey Thorogood and his associates were taking seats at a long table facing the crowd. She noticed they'd begun wearing gold nuggets on neck chains, and so had some of the miners as they'd prospered.

She caught Josiah Miller looking her way. He winked and grinned. She lifted up her lips in a tiny smile, acknowledging the wink. She knew what that wink signified. He'd made a strike. A big one. He hadn't yet announced it. The assayers were still determining exactly how rich the ore was, but Josiah had assured Sage her portion would be sizeable.

She looked for the other miners she'd staked and partnered with, five of them by now, but they weren't in attendance. As her eyes swung over the group, she caught sight of one of the women talking to Bridger. She was standing in a provocative posture, hips slightly forward, head tilted back flirtatiously, beaming up at him.

Involuntarily, Sage's eyes narrowed. Who's that? she wondered, feeling a strange twitch in her heart.

Ramsey Thorogood snapped the lid of his watch closed, slipped it back into his vest pocket, and started the meeting.

"Welcome, and thank you for coming," he began, then got right down to business.

Real estate prices had increased, and this news was cheered as he went into great detail. His announcement that several mines had come in sent the crowd into an uproar. When it settled down, he introduced some of the new business owners. All men, Sage noticed, opening businesses that served men—saddlemaker, hat maker, tonsorial parlor.

Bridger stepped forward to give a report on the number of new business licenses issued, the amount of back taxes collected, and here he flicked a glance at Sage who narrowed her eyes at him. Then he introduced his newest deputy, a husky, broad-faced man who was either half Indian or all Mexican, but his name was Honcho McGillicudy.

"I'd planned to enumerate the number of arrests and detail the various violations," Bridger went on, "but time won't allow for that. There're too many. But the fines collected have increased the town's coffers considerably. Again, the amount is so great, I'm still calculating."

"Thank you, Marshal," Thorogood said. Bridger reclaimed his place against the wall.

Then the discussion turned to the necessity of electing a mayor and town council as the means to ensuring a well run town.

"If we want the stage line to come here, and eventually the railroad, we need to show some organization and leadership," implored Thorogood.

But the townspeople had already begun to get restless, some of them scraping back their chairs and slinking out the door which had been flung wide to admit fresh air. This was all new, and people weren't used to sitting down and confabulating about serious matters especially when the sound of laughter and piano music from the saloons and dance halls drifted up and down the street. Good times called to them.

But many of them stayed, and the proceedings continued, winding down without a decision being made about elections.

"We'll table that until next time then," Thorogood said, as he and the other well dressed men at the table began shuffling papers and gathering themselves to adjourn the meeting. "Now if there's no further business . . ."

"Excuse me."

One of the miner's wives whose husband had already left stood up. Her face was plain with a nose that was humped and slightly off. The hem of her skirt and the edges of her shawl were frayed. Neither garment looked especially clean.

"Yes?" Ramsey Thorogood said. He and the other men up front stared at her. One of them rolled a fat cigar into the corner of his mouth and chomped on it.

"Excuse me," she repeated, "but what about a school?"

The men up front continued to stare with blank expressions. There were shuffling and murmurs from the gathering.

"Schools is for sissies," one of the grizzled old timers in the back said, and stomped drunkenly out the door.

"School?" Ramsey said, as if it were a notion he hadn't heard of. "Well, there is no need for a school. There aren't enough children in town. And besides, we have no teacher."

"She does," the woman said, waving a finger in Sage's direction.

Sage felt warmth creep into her face as everyone turned to look her way.

"At her place," the woman went on. "She's been teaching Oscar's boy to read, and that Indian, too. And some others, I hear. She's got a teacher there. Why can't my children learn to read, too? I got a boy and a girl old enough now to take lessons."

Thorogood's gaze swung to Sage and stopped. "Is that true, Miss Cane?"

"Yes," she answered. "It's true. Emma Ford has been giving lessons." After the barn was repaired classes resumed, attendance having increased by one for a total of five students.

"Why can't my boy and girl have lessons, too?" the woman asked indignantly, looking from Sage to Thorogood and back again.

"Well, they can," said Sage, but before she could go on, a buxom, thick-waisted woman piped in. It was Estella Gardner, the banker's wife.

"You don't want your children going to a place like . . . that," she admonished, tilting her nose as if she smelled something bad. "It's a . . ." She huffed. "Well, you know what it is."

"I know Emma Ford," said the first woman, "and she's a fine woman with a baby of her own. What does it matter to me where classes are held as long as there's learnin'."

"What about a church?" a third woman called from behind Sage.

"Yeah," chimed in a miner showing two gold teeth. "A church is as important as a school."

There were shouts of "Yeah," and "That's right," and a heated discussion ensued about the possible merits and disadvantages of building a school first or a church first.

After a noisy debate, Ramsey Thorogood held up his hands calling for quiet. "All right, all right. Quiet down please." He waited for the hubbub to subside before going on.

"There might be a way to include other children in Emma Ford's classes . . . ." He stopped and nodded at Sage. "That is, if Miss Cane agrees. I'd be willing to work out the appropriate details with her until a proper school building can be constructed." But then he shook his head. "However, a church is out of the question. There's no money for a church. And we don't have a minister, anyway."

The beanpole miner next to Sage stood up, both hands holding his hat against his chest.

"I'm a minister," he said. "Had to close my church in Mineral Springs when the mine there folded and everyone moved away. Came here to try my luck with a pick and shovel. But I'd rather preach the word of God."

Again heated debate coursed through the remaining crowd, some for, some against, but mostly for.

Sage felt Bridger's eyes on her and caught his gaze. He hadn't said anything, but his face was serious and he was listening closely.

"But we don't have a place to put a church," Thorogood insisted, shouting into the crowd.

"Well, she said she was building one," someone else shouted back, pointing at Sage.

Silence fell and Sage looked around to see who had spoken. A husky woman with frizzy hair was glaring at her.

"When that gospel wagon was here, Sage Cane told the preacher she was building a church," the woman said.

"That's right. We heard her," said someone else. "Didn't we?"

There were shouts of concurrence.

"Yeah."

"I heard her say it."

"She promised, indeed she did."

As the shouts grew louder, Sage stood and looked around at the weathered faces with work-hardened features. What they were saying was true. She had made a promise of sorts to these people, many of whom had come to her rescue that day, running off Preacher Fry and his gang, preventing them from burning her house down, putting out a barn fire that could have spread to neighboring structures. Possibly even taken lives.

"Why can't we have the church and school in the same building?" a woman in back of the room suggested, speaking loudly and deliberate over the commotion.

Instantly, quiet fell and all eyes turned to Sage.

"I think it's an excellent idea to have the church and school in the same building," Sage began, "and I intend to keep my promise. I'll finance the construction and meet with Mr. Thorogood next week to select a location and sort out the details. Would anyone object if we added some rooms at the back for Emma and her baby?" Then she nodded toward the miner seated next to her. "And one for the preacher, too?"

Applause and affirmative cheers broke out.

"Let's do it."

"That's an excellent idea."

"Meanwhile, until construction is complete, you're welcome to bring your children to Miss Emma's classes. Just let her know in advance so she can put lesson plans together."

This was greeted with scattered applause and thank yous, and the meeting broke up. Townspeople began making their way out the door, some to go home, some to partake of the entertainment offerings along the street. The bone thin miner next to her held out his hand and introduced himself.

"Preacher Jared Picket," he said. "I'm mighty appreciative. You won't be sorry. God's name needs to be more prominent in this town. What's your name? I'm new to Fairplay Creek, so I don't know you."

"Sage Cane," she said, shaking his hand. "I'm rather new here, too. It was nice meeting you. Good night."

She turned to leave and the woman who had brought up the subject of a school was standing so close behind, Sage almost bumped into her.

"I'm Hattie Murphy," the woman said. "I want to thank you."

"You're welcome, Mrs. Murphy. But are you aware . . ."

"I'm aware who you are," Hattie Murphy said matter-of-factly. Her face was drawn, her eyes tired and framed with wrinkles, the skin gray with the beginnings of a sag. "My husband spends most nights at your place."

Hattie Murphy's words made Sage uncomfortable. She felt like she should say something to that, but didn't know what.

Thankfully Hattie went on. "But I got children. I want to help them find a way out of this place. That'll only happen if they're educated. If you can help me do that, I'd be grateful for it." With that she turned and walked slowly away, shoulders slumped.

As Sage watched Hattie take her leave, an idea took shape, popping fully formed into her head. She considered it briefly, decided it was an absolutely ridiculous notion, and released it.

Chapter Fourteen

After Hattie Murphy left the meeting, Bridger watched Sage hold her position looking like she was mulling something over in her mind. Probably wondering how she was going to pay for a church and a school. Maybe she'd opened her mouth before thinking. Raising a school and a church even if they were combined into one building would be costly.

But one thing was certain, and he took some sneaky pleasure in it. If she kept her promise, and it appeared that she meant to, she'd be in Fairplay Creek for at least another year. Hell, it might take her that long to come up with the funds.

Unaware of Bridger's scrutiny, Sage continued to stand for several seconds, then opened her bag, took out her gloves and slowly fitted them onto her hands, her expression distracted. Bridger was fascinated by the graceful way her hand arched as she smoothed the leather over her long, delicate fingers, and fitted it over her palms. She repeated the motion with the other glove, tugging lightly, then stroking it in place with movements that were like a caress.

He found it quite sensuous and led him to wonder if she was wearing that embroidered chemise and burgundy corset. Or the black one trimmed in lace that had belonged to Honey. Or maybe one of the others he'd seen that night in her room. His mind began forming pictures of how she'd look wearing them. Slender hips, a waist so tiny he could almost encircle it with his hands. Small, firm breasts rising elegantly above the lace, smooth mounds of silky flesh that nestled nicely into his palms.

Now why in hell was he thinking about Sage Cane that way?

Stirrings low down in his belly prompted him to discontinue such musings for surely no good could come of it. Without doubt, he was smart enough to know that.

He made his way down the crowded aisle to intercept her at the door.

"I could use a new jail and a new marshal's office."

She turned, surprised, her startled eyes wide and full of question, examining his face, querying him with a raised eyebrow.

He took a step back, held up his hands, palms out, fingers spread. "Sorry," he said. "That was a joke. A bad one."

She stared at him a moment longer and he felt those blue-green eyes down to his toes.

"Oh," she said, and continued out the door. "Good evening, Marshal."

He caught up to her at the hitch post. Well past dark now, the street was swarming with people, horses, mules, and wagons. Crowds loitered on the boardwalks, their laughter and shouting filling the air.

"Maybe I'd better see you home," he said.

"No, thank you," she replied in a high-pitched, falsely playful voice, not looking at him.

Just then shouts arose. A shoving match had broken out in front of the saloon across the street, and a boisterous crowd quickly gathered, urging on the combatants. Bridger caught sight of Honcho McGillicudy mounting his horse. They exchanged an unspoken message with a nod, after which the new deputy rode over to cool things down before they got out of hand.

Bridger unwound the bay's reins from the hitch post, and tied them to the back of Sage's buggy. A layer of dust had settled on the pebbled black leather, dulling the gleam of the brass fittings.

"What are you doing?" she asked, her fists pressed into her hips, her reticule hanging from her wrist.

"I'm driving you home."

"No, you're not," she replied stubbornly.

"Yes, I am."

Bridger held out his hand, offering to help her into the buggy. "As an officer of the law, I'm duly sworn to see to the safety of the people of this town." He gave her a smile.

When she refused his hand, he climbed into the driver's seat and picked up the reins. A burst of drunken laughter broke out in the street, some young bucks whooping it up and carrying on.

Sage looked in their direction, then sighed loudly. Bridger smiled and held out his hand again. She reached for it, clasping it with more strength than he imagined she could. He closed his hand over hers, aware of how small her fingers felt in his clumsy paw. She lifted her skirts, climbed in and sat down next to him.

"Thank you, Mr. Norwood," she said, fussily arranging herself. She settled in place, straightened her back, and folded her gloved hands in her lap over her bag. "It seems you're determined to come to my rescue whether I need it or not," she said, finally meeting his gaze.

"You're welcome," he said, "and it's my pleasure." He let his smile linger, hoping she might do the same, but she didn't. She turned away and stared straight ahead, her nose in that ever present sniff position. He didn't think he'd ever met a woman who could sit so straight without falling over.

He snuffled a short laugh, flicked the reins and made a sound to the horse which, being well trained, instantly began walking in the direction of Wild Mountain Honey. Bridger's bay tethered behind kept an easy pace.

Bridger had helped her select her horse. The day she'd gone to the livery, he happened to be there and had given her advice though she hadn't asked for it.

"Choosing a horse is like choosing a mate," he'd told her. "If you choose the wrong one, you won't be happy."

She'd glared at him, obviously not appreciating his humor, then left without buying it. But a few days later he saw that she'd purchased the horse he'd pointed out had the best characteristics.

They rode a few moments in silence. He was extraordinarily aware of her nearness. His heart began to thump and it was all he could do not to touch her. He couldn't help glancing over at her, but every time he did, he pictured her the way she was the night of the fire, the night they'd run Preacher Fry off. Lying in bed, she looked so vulnerable, helpless even, the effects of Doc's pain pills softening her rough edges.

But he forced himself to stop thinking along those lines. Helpless was not a word that described Sage Cane under normal circumstances.

"How's Emma?" he asked, to make conversation.

"Fine," Sage replied.

"And the baby?"

"Fine, too."

Their eyes met briefly, the corners of her mouth tilted up a fraction of an inch, and then she looked away.

"Interesting meeting," he said to keep the conversation going. "If the town continues its present rate of growth, I expect they'll have to elect a mayor and town council within the year."

"Yes," Sage agreed. "Last Friday there were so many new arrivals, they were lined up on horseback and in wagons for a mile out of town waiting for the freight haulers to move off and clear the street so they could come in."

"I expect not all of them will stay," reflected Bridger. "Some folks come here thinking there's gold lying on the ground just waiting to be picked up. When they see different, they scratch around a little, then give up and leave. If they have enough money to get a ride out with a teamster, that is. But they're the ones averse to hard work, and they wouldn't survive in this town anyway."

A small group of men standing in the middle of the street deep in conversation moved to the side to let the buggy through, greeting Bridger and tipping their hats to Sage.

"Those who are clever enough to find a way to stay and make a living, well, that's who will help build a firm foundation for this great country and make history here."

"Benjamin Disraeli says increased means and increased leisure are the two civilizers of men," responded Sage. "It will be a fine day in Fairplay Creek when that happens."

Bridger had only a vague idea who Benjamin Disraeli was, so didn't comment.

They chatted some more about the meeting and all the ways the town was changing. Bridger mentioned the number of rooms in the hotel under construction—twenty. Sage commented on the lack of provisions for women in town.

"It'll be good to have a school here, though," Bridger said. "We need some educated boys to help run the town."

"And girls," Sage added with purpose.

"Oh, yes, and girls, too," Bridger conceded. "Maybe when the school's built, I can start thinking about bringing my little girl here to live."

"You're married?" Genuine surprise lit her eyes.

"Was. My wife was killed back in Nebraska Territory."

"I'm sorry," Sage said.

"Got caught in a crossfire. Some very bad men came into town on a Saturday." Bridger told her what happened leaving out details, leaving out the part about not knowing whose bullet actually killed Elizabeth. He didn't want to think about that, let alone talk about it. He especially didn't want to talk about it with her.

Sage listened sympathetically, her eyes warm, her expression compassionate.

"What is your daughter's name?"

"Jenny. Cute as a button. Looks like her Ma. Her hair's like mine, but her smile is all her Ma's." His heart pinched, thinking about her.

"Where is she?"

"She lives with Elizabeth's parents in Hamilton City. They've got a nice big spread there. She's happy with her grandparents."

"But you miss her."

He nodded, but felt tears burning behind his eyes, so cleared his throat and changed the subject before he embarrassed himself.

"So," he began. "Where are you figuring to build that school?"

Sage shook her head and sighed. "I don't know. I saw a sign on a piece of land behind the bathhouse site. Now that the public baths are almost finished, they've cut the street through and platted out some more lots. Maybe there. I'll discuss it with Mr. Thorogood next week."

Bridger let a moment go by. "Excuse me for asking," Bridger said then, "but where are you going to get the money to build that school?" The rude words tumbled out before he could stop them.

Sage bristled, then sighed in high drama, huffing out a breath. "Mr. Norwood."

"Yes?"

"Are my taxes paid up?"

"Yes, I believe they are."

"Has my business license been activated and paid up to date?"

"Yes," he answered, wondering what she was getting at.

"Is my rent paid in full and on time?"

"Yes, it is."

She turned with slow deliberation and laid a look of utter distain upon him. "Then where I get my money and what I do with it is none of your concern."

Bridger's patience fell away, and irritation flared.

"Oh, don't get your petticoats in a twist," he said, annoyed. "I was only making conversation. I know perfectly well where you get your money."

Her mouth fell open, and a flush bloomed on her cheeks. "And just what are you implying? I am running a business, as you well know, since you're the one who forced me into it."

"*I* forced you into it?"

"Yes. *You.* I told you at the beginning I was not a madam—"

"Like I said before," he interrupted, unable to keep the steel out of his voice. "I know what you are. I saw Josiah Miller coming out of your room."

Sage gasped. "How dare you bring that up again?"

"You're right," he said. "I should have checked first to see if you were carrying a gun."

"Why, you are a boorish, insufferable man. And for your information, I am carrying a gun. I always carry a gun—"

"You probably need it to fight off all the men."

Her eyes opened wide, like she'd just been slapped. "Men! What men?"

"All those men you spend time with. Those miners."

He knew what he was saying wasn't true, but it was true about Josiah Miller, and Bridger couldn't stop himself from poking a stick into that particular beehive because . . . .

Oh, hell.

Because he wished she had invited him into her rooms instead of those miners.

By this time, they were in the alley that led to the barn behind Wild Mountain Honey. Sage was livid, calling him names he didn't think she knew, but she stopped yelling at the exact instant he pulled up on the reins.

"Whoa!" he said. The sorrel came to a stiff-legged stop and backed up a few steps.

"Good heavens, what's that?" Sage asked peering at a form huddled on the ground in the moonlight.

Bridger's boots were on the dirt in a heartbeat. Sage clutched the chair rail and scrambled out on her own, catching the heel of her boot in the tangle of her petticoats and almost falling to her knees. She found her footing beneath the tangle of skirts, and followed Bridger.

A woman was curled up in the dust, weeping, and Bridger went down on one knee beside her. Sage crouched on the other side and helped him lift the woman to a sitting position.

"Ma'am? Are you hurt?" Bridger peered at her.

The woman kept her head down and didn't answer, just continued to weep miserably.

"Please let us help you," said Sage. She tried to brush the woman's hair off her tear-swollen face, but when the woman saw who it was, she jerked away from the touch.

Then her face collapsed, and her sobbing rose up with new energy. "It's your fault," she cried, her shadowed expression laden with reproach. "It's your fault he's in there."

"Who?" said Sage. "In where?"

The woman raised her arm and pointed with a shaking hand at Wild Mountain Honey. "In there. My husband. I want him home with me. He brought me to this horrible godforsaken town where I have no family, no friends. I don't know anyone. I'm living in a tent, for God's sake! And I'm going to have a baby!" she wailed, choking on a sob.

141

Sage's heart moved for the troubled woman. "Let's take her inside," she said to Bridger. "I'll have Cheveyo come out and see to the horses."

They put their arms around the forlorn woman and together helped her into the house where she collapsed onto a kitchen chair. Sage brushed a veil of straggling hair from the woman's face, and that's when she saw her eye. It was puffed up and tinged with purple.

Sage caught a breath. "Oh, my."

"Lordy," Miss Priscilla said when she saw it, and immediately busied herself in the pantry looking for something with which to soothe it.

"What happened?" Sage urged.

Haltingly and through tears, the woman related that her husband had moved her to Fairplay Creek three months ago. The plan was to set down roots while he staked a claim and mined it. But after all this time, he hadn't yet broken ground on his claim. Instead, he'd spent all his time in the saloons or at Wild Mountain Honey, and they were almost out of money. She'd begged him not to come here again tonight. They argued, he hit her, and then he left.

Anger quickened Sage's heart.

"What's your name?" Bridger asked.

"Ellen Berger," she answered, and sniffled.

"What is your husband's name?" Sage asked, prompting a curious look from Bridger.

Ellen eyed Sage and hesitated before answering. "Halstead," she said. "Halstead Berger."

"Is he here now?"

Ellen squeezed back a tear and nodded.

Sage promptly spun on her heel, and pushed her way through the heavy oak door and down the hall, sweeping into the smoky east parlor like a turbulent weather front.

The merrymaking in the front rooms continued unabated, but a dozen surprised faces turned to stare, unused to seeing Sage in the parlor during business hours. The piano player, concentrating on his music and unaware of her presence continued banging on the keyboard.

"Halstead Berger?" Sage shouted into the noisy crowd. "Is Mr. Halstead Berger here?"

Raucous laughter gradually subsided and conversations faltered as everyone turned their attention to Sage. Some of the revelers in the west parlor crossed the foyer and gathered at the doorway looking in to see what was going on.

Odie tucked the cash box on a shelf under the bar and stepped out from behind. "Is there a problem, Sage?"

"Halstead Berger?" Sage called again, ignoring Odie and spinning slowly in the center of the room. "Mr. Berger?"

A big, rawboned man sitting on the divan giggling with Poppy Merriwether looked up with an engaging smile. He was young and handsome with blond, curly hair and a likable face.

"That's me," he said, grinning.

"Will you come with me, please Mr. Berger?" Sage asked.

Murmurs and snickers rippled through the room at her softly spoken request. A man guffawed loudly. A couple of others whooped.

"Why, shore," answered Halstead, eagerly jumping to his feet. "Anything for you, Miss Sage."

Without another word, Sage, walking briskly, led the young man out of the parlor, down the hallway, and into the kitchen. He stopped as if his boots had been suddenly nailed to the floor when he saw his wife sitting at the kitchen table.

"Wha . . . ?" He looked at Ellen, then at Sage, and finally at Bridger who glowered at him.

"What is this?" Halstead asked, his breath giving off an aroma of spirits from the bottle.

"You tell me," said Sage, angrily.

"What are you doing here?" he said to his wife, his voice gruff at first. Then he lowered it. "You don't belong here."

"No, Mr. Berger," hissed Sage, straining the words through her teeth. "You are the one who doesn't belong here. You are a married man with a baby on the way. Why aren't you at home with your wife?"

Halstead had the good sense to look at least a little contrite in the face of Sage's admonishment.

"Well, I was just . . . I mean, I . . ."

"You are no longer welcome at Wild Mountain Honey," said Sage with finality.

Halstead's mouth dropped open, but Sage cut him off with a hard look, stemming the argument she saw was forthcoming.

"You are going to be a father. As such, you should be spending your time finding a way to make a living in Fairplay Creek so you can support your family. I don't want to see you here again."

Bridger shifted his weight and cleared his throat. "Well, now, Miss Cane, isn't that a little . . . ?"

Sage ignored him, fixing her eyes on Halstead.

"I mean *ever*," she emphasized. "Do you understand?"

Halstead slid his gaze over to Bridger. From his expression he appeared to be expecting a show of fellowship followed by a reprieve.

But Bridger's voice was tight and commanding. "You heard the lady. Collect your wife and take her home."

Halstead looked a little scared now, but he managed a nod. His face slowly softened, and he turned to Ellen who sat in silence dabbing her cheeks. Her eyes were locked on his and it was clear to everyone in the room she adored her husband.

Gently, Halstead took her arm.

"I'm sorry, Ellie," he said. "Come on. I'll take you home."

Throat tight, Sage warned, "And don't you dare lay a mean hand on her again."

She put her hands on Ellen's shoulders and kissed her lightly on the cheek. "See me if you need anything," she whispered, drawing Ellen into a hug. "Anything at all."

Leveling a fierce look at Halstead Berger, Sage left the kitchen and went upstairs.

Chapter Fifteen

Sage's door was slightly ajar. Bridger could see her standing in front of the fireplace, back straight, shoulders stiff in a posture of anger. Her arms were crossed, hands wrapped tightly around her upper arms, fingertips digging into the soft flesh.

He knocked lightly, his hand on the doorknob. "Miss Cane?"

"Come in, Marshal," she said quietly, not turning around.

Bridger entered, hat in hand, his fingers fidgeting around the edge of the brim.

He cleared his throat to fill the silence. "Good thing we came along when we did."

"Yes," Sage replied, staring at the flames.

A moment went by. "You did the right thing. Sending him home with her."

Her shoulders rose and fell in a sigh of defeat or pique, he couldn't tell which, but when she replied, her tone was wry. "I'm glad you think so," she said, without turning around.

"I, uh, I'm sorry about before," he said.

She didn't respond, not that he expected her to. He pressed on.

"About the rude way I spoke to you on the way here. I know what I said isn't true. About the other miners." It was true about Josiah Miller, he reminded himself, but best not mention it again.

"Anyway, I hope you'll accept my apology. I had no call to say those things to you."

She daggered him a look over her shoulder, then turned back to the fireplace.

Not knowing what else to do, he sat on the divan behind her painfully aware of her repressed fury. Silent moments ticked by.

Finally, she let out a breath and turned to face him.

"It's not fair to the wives," she said. "This . . ." she tossed her head and lifted her eyes to the ceiling, then looked him straight in the eye.

Bridger was at a loss how to respond, and uncomfortable under her acute gaze. Her sea-green crystal eyes didn't waver from his face. She looked at him as if she was waiting for him to say something. He knew what she was thinking, knew what she wanted him to say. But his lips were clamped shut, so she said it for him.

"Married men should not be coming here." She spoke barely above a whisper.

He held up a hand as if to ward off her words even though he saw the good judgment in them. "Now just a minute. You can't bar married men."

"Didn't you just see what I saw?" she demanded, flinging out a hand.

Angrily she threw herself into a high backed chair and pressed the heels of her hands into her eye sockets. "He put a baby in her belly then left her alone in a tent while he spends his time . . ." She lifted her hands and raised her eyes again for emphasis. "Here!" She shook her head, frustrated.

"I don't understand it," she said, an unmistakable look of irritation on her face. "The men in this town have divided up the women into reputable and disreputable. Good and bad with no in between. But the so-called good women have sex, too. Judging by the increased number of children around." She lowered her head again, then quickly raised it. "He gave her a baby. How does he think that happened?"

Bridger shook his head. "You can't do it," he insisted.

"Why not?"

"If you've ever seen the inside of a mine, you'd know why."

She stared at him, clearly expecting more of an answer than that. He tried to give it to her.

"These miners tunnel all day in the dark with nothing but a candle in their hats and one on the wall and dank air in their lungs, their hands worked to the bone. They'd be willing to pay everything in their pockets for an approving smile from a beautiful woman."

"Then they should go home at the end of their work day," she insisted.

"Home to what?" Bridger shot back. "Have you seen the women in town? Some of them eat like slopped hogs."

"That's because the men do!" Angrily she blew out a breath and shook her head. "You missed the point, Marshal. Our young Mr. Berger hasn't done any of that. According to his wife, he hasn't dirtied his pick and shovel since they arrived in Fairplay Creek."

She had him there. He tried to come up with further argument, but she kept talking.

"He has a woman at home who I'm sure would be happy to smile at him day and night. If he was ever there," she pointed out, jabbing her forefinger toward him.

"Well, I agree that's the case with the Bergers," Bridger conceded. "But not the others. Without this place to go to, the slightest provocation sets them off. You think it's wild here now, you should have seen it before Honey opened up."

"Look," Sage said, reasonably. "You may have peace in the town, but the families are being torn apart. I feel responsible for that."

There was pain in her eyes, and accusation too that said he shared the responsibility. He moved his gaze to the hollow of her throat where a little pulse beat. A tight band of guilt squeezed his chest. Part of him knew she was right. This was no place for married men. But the sharp prick of conscience didn't stop the burst of anger that rolled through him.

"You can't bar married men!" he insisted, cutting the air with his hand.

"Well, I'm going to do something!" she declared, standing statue still, refusing to back down.

They glared at each other, sparks practically arcing through the charged air.

Anger flashed in her eyes. She crossed her arms, raised her eyebrows and gave him a look that said, "And what are you going to do about it?"

His lips twisted while he chewed the inside of his cheek, trying to tamp down the frustration that was boiling up in him. When faced with a moral dilemma, he always chose on the side of right. He was angry now because he knew she was right, but he couldn't make himself say so. He stood there juggling principle with common sense and harsh reality.

With effort, he slowed his breath, put his hat on his head, and gave her a curt nod.

Furious, she spun around to face the fireplace, showing him her back.

"Good night," he said with finality.

But he didn't move. Like an idiot, he stood rooted to the spot. His heart was knocking hard against his ribs.

He stared at her back, determination written in the set of her shoulders, her spine stiff with resolve. What did she mean she was going to do something? Exactly what did she intend to do? He didn't know the meaning of her threat. Was it a threat? It sounded like a threat. He took it that way.

His own resolve melted away and he felt himself drawn to her. He put his hand on her arm and gently brought her around to face him. When their eyes connected, he felt a tug.

"Don't go," he said. "Please. Don't leave."

She gave him a look of surprise, eyes round, her lips parted the tiniest bit.

He put his hands on her shoulders to keep her from backing up, then wrapped his arm around her waist and hauled her up against him. His mouth came down on hers, hard and deliberate.

Her arms were still crossed in front of her, pinned now between them. He expected her to resist, but she didn't, and he didn't stop to wonder why. He just kept kissing her.

Was it his imagination or did her lips respond to his? No, of course they didn't, because he was doing something he should not be doing. But oh, how he wanted to do it, had wanted to do it ever since he'd laid eyes on her.

And he hadn't been wrong. It was exactly as he'd imagined it would be, her lips soft and warm, making his pulse thunder in his ears, setting off a pleasurable squeeze in his heart.

The touch of her body seared his nerve endings, sending heat to a place deep inside him, kindling a blaze in the pit of his stomach that threatened to flare up out of control. Before the full power of his arousal became apparent to her, he pulled away. They looked at each other for one stunned second.

"Good night," he said again, and took a step back.

Crazy with wanting, he strode across the planked floor and out the door, closing it harder than he'd meant to, but not going back to apologize. Not for the door slam, and not for the kiss.

* * * * *

If Bridger had stuck her with a hot poker, Sage couldn't have been more surprised. His touch had exploded through her body. The strength shot out of her limbs, and it was a good thing he'd been holding her, because she would have fallen to her knees. Simply remembering the thrill of pressing against him threatened to send her to her knees. Quickly she sat down.

The male scent of him lingered in the room, and she licked her lips, tasting him there. She never imagined a kiss could make her feel that way, giddy and overwhelmed with sensations.

She'd been kissed and more than kissed by Rodney Weatherspoon, but there had never been the sweet torment that sent sweat trickling between her breasts. Based on her limited experience and what she'd heard from other women, most men were more practiced at mauling, squeezing, and rubbing than they were at kissing and caressing. Bridger's lips pressing hers and his arm around her waist had made her heart skip beats.

She touched her fingers to her lips.

They felt hot.

They felt kissed.

She closed her eyes, gradually calming herself. There was no point indulging these feverish musings. She had no intention of falling under his spell, or any man's. Circumstances demanded that she focus entirely on matters of more importance. Including her survival.

Chapter Sixteen

Every so often, Sage found herself having to get reacquainted with the town, it was growing that fast. The business section had expanded its girth from Main Street to include two parallel streets, one to the north called Front, and one to the south called Mineral. As streets, they were hardly more than rutted byways lined with tents and crude wooden frames draped with canvas to keep the weather out. Most of the town's activity and business still took place on Main Street.

But assays were coming in every day with high content gold, and as a result, Front and Mineral would no doubt be developed apace with more saloons and additional businesses in short order. It appeared to have already begun. A dentist had arrived in town, and she'd heard someone was trying to start up a newspaper, but so far had seen no sign of it.

"*Look here*," a sign stuck to a tent proclaimed. "*For fifty cents you can get a good square meal*." Another restaurant.

She lightly smacked the reins and spoke softly to her horse, whom she'd given the name Mandy. As the carriage rolled into town, Sage deliberately focused on the jingle of the harness, the gentle bobbing motion of Mandy's head and the way the horse swiveled her ears taking in the many sounds. But inevitably, Sage's mind returned to what had been uppermost in her thoughts for weeks. The kiss.

It had been a silky, sexy kiss, and she hadn't been able to chase away the memory of it, nor did she want to. Even now, a tingle fingered its way up her spine. And she couldn't stop thinking about what Bridger had said.

Don't go. Please don't leave.

His words had caught her by surprise, and she was inexplicably disturbed by the undercurrent of anxiety they'd produced in her then, and now. Of course she was going to leave. She had to leave!

Stunned, she realized that her plan to return to Independence seemed to bear less urgency than it once did.

Resolute, she shook that wayward notion away with a toss of her head. No. She was leaving.

She forced her mind to what she was about for the morning. She would have to hurry if she was going to finish her errands and pick up the package that was arriving on the freight wagon from Denver before meeting with Ramsey Thorogood in his office.

Without her knowledge or accord, Thorogood had gone ahead with the final construction drawings for the school and church building. He'd also selected a site of his own choosing, a site Sage felt unsuitable, and it appeared he was taking charge of the venture without consulting her on anything even though she was paying for it. At her insistence he'd agreed, though reluctantly, to meet with her today to discuss details of the project. Construction was scheduled to begin soon. The sooner the better as far as she was concerned.

Meanwhile, Emma was conducting reading and math classes in a back room of the recently completed bathhouse next to Wild Mountain Honey. Construction had taken longer than expected due, in part, to a shortage of copper tubs from Denver, but had finally opened for business last week. Emma now had ten students, thanks to Hattie Murphy, who encouraged other mothers to overlook the proximity of the classroom to the parlor house and let their sons and daughters attend. Grudgingly, they did.

Sage pulled Mandy up in front of the bank, wound the reins around the hitch post, and went inside. Her entrance commanded attention as it always did. The tellers, all men, looked up from their work to acknowledge her with lusty smiles. Martin Gardner immediately rose from his chair and escorted her into a small enclosed room where she could make her deposit in private away from prying eyes.

As always, a look of mild astonishment washed over his face when she pulled her deposit from her satchel and laid it out on the table. Bags of coins, stacks of paper money, pouches of gold dust, and handfuls of nuggets all brought a mixture of pleasure and curiosity to his face. Her deposits had grown increasingly substantial and included not only income from Wild Mountain Honey, but from her share of mine proceeds as well. If Martin Gardner wondered about it, he never mentioned it directly, referring to it obliquely instead.

"It's been a good week at Wild Mountain Honey," he remarked coyly, eyeing the riches laid out before him.

"Yes," Sage answered, then lowered her voice conspiratorially. "And I trust you've had a good week there, as well?"

"Certainly. Oh, most certainly," he sputtered. He wrote out a receipt, and handed it to her. "I appreciate your business."

She nodded. "And I, yours," she said with a lilt before taking her leave.

A crowd was gathering in front of Gallagher's General Store and the tonsorial parlor next to it. It was Friday, and the Creekers, as the townspeople called themselves, were waiting for the freight wagons to bring the items they had ordered the last time the drivers had been through. The ox trains could be seen a mile away, a cloud of dust on the mountain marking their advance. The bullwhackers' swear words carried on the air and bounced down the rocky slopes, the crack of their heavy whips echoing against the walls of granite. *Whap, crack. Whap, crack. Whap, crack.*

Leaving Mandy and the carriage in front of the bank, Sage made her way along the boardwalk and positioned herself at the edge of the waiting crowd in front of the new barber shop.

She dipped her head and half hiding her face under the brim of her bonnet, surreptitiously scanned the crowd looking for Bridger. When she didn't see him, she shifted her gaze across the street and down the block toward the marshal's office. No one was on the porch and she was too far away to see in through the windows. His horse wasn't tied up out front and she didn't see it in the livery corral next door. Disappointed, she nudged away a twinge of regret.

Hattie Murphy caught her eye and waved, calling her name. Hattie was one of the handful of women who had begun openly acknowledging Sage on the street after she'd spoken up at the town meeting. With the exception of Hattie and one or two others, the looks thrown her way didn't approach respect, but at least they were a shade less reproachful than when she'd first arrived in town.

Her mind drifted back and she marveled at how much had happened since then. She'd been busier than she'd ever imagined, and though almost constantly surrounded by people with hardly ever a moment to herself, an edge of loneliness had still managed to creep in.

"Good morning."

The voice came from behind, breaking into her thoughts, and she turned, mildly startled.

Honcho McGillicudy, having stopped to greet her, was standing with one foot on the boardwalk and the other in the doorway of the barber shop.

"Well, good morning, Mr. McGillicudy. Nice to see you again."

He took off his hat as he approached her. "Lovely day, Miss Cane," he said.

"Very lovely," she replied pleasantly.

"Waiting for the wagon from Denver?"

"Yes," she said. "I'm expecting a package."

His hair was black and longish, curling gently on his shoulders. He was big with broad shoulders, but he spoke so softly most people would have a hard time taking him for a lawman. He rubbed his chin self-consciously.

"I was just on my way for a shave and a haircut," he said, indicating the barbershop where the tall distinguished looking owner was peering out the window.

"I see," she replied politely.

Honcho stood nervously shuffling his feet in obvious discomfort. After a moment of uneasy silence, he cleared his throat.

"I've been thinking"

She smiled up at him. "Yes?"

"You don't know me," he said. "I mean, we've just met briefly, but I've been wondering if you'd consider having a meal with me some time. Just a lunch over at Oscar's. Or something."

After the words rushed out, his eyes bounced from his boots to her face, his expression shy but hopeful, as he waited for her answer.

Sage was touched, but taken aback at the same time. Such a gentle soul, she thought. Quite polite with manners that came so naturally she imagined they must have been learned in childhood, indicating he certainly hadn't been raised in this benighted town.

"Why, yes," she found herself replying. "Yes, I would. I'd love to have lunch with you."

His face lit up. "That would be fine," he said, grinning with relief. "Just fine." He plopped his hat back on his head and took a step to leave, then remembering, turned back.

"May I pick you up next Tuesday at noon?"

When she nodded her assent, he touched his fingers to his brim and disappeared into the barber shop.

She stood a moment thinking about the invitation, the first since she'd been in Fairplay Creek. Why not have a friendly lunch with Honcho McGillicudy? He appeared nice enough. He'd come over from Leadville, a place she'd never been, and it would be interesting to know about another town in Colorado. She had no designs on him, but it seemed he would be pleasant company. It had been a long time since she'd shared a companionable meal with a gentleman.

And just like that, her mind detoured to thoughts of . . . the kiss.

As much as she hated to admit it, Bridger's kiss had left her feeling as vulnerable as a twig. Memories of his touch—his arm curving around her waist, his lips pressing on hers—made her feel dizzy and pleasantly light headed every time she thought about it. She reached into her bag for a handkerchief, and dabbed at a film of perspiration on her brow just as the first of the freight wagons entered the town throwing up a blanket of dust.

The wagons were heaped with goods and supplies covered with canvas lashed down with ropes and chains. Deliveries of necessities were less erratic than in the past, the freight haulers could be counted on to arrive according to a fairly regular schedule. Come winter, though, they would become slow and undependable again. Winters were hard in the mountains, the high passes became treacherous or impassable, clogged with several feet of snow. Miss Priscilla had told her that last winter a wagon arrived with the mules covered with ice and the driver sitting on the box frozen to death.

Sage watched as the first wagon approached pulled by multiple pairs of oxen plodding through the dirt, throwing up dust. The sound of cracking whips and the teamster's inspired profanity urged the animals forward. Two more ox wagons followed, driven by rough looking men as muscled and foulmouthed as the first. Bringing up the rear was a smaller wagon pulled by a pair of mules. Together, the freighters took up almost the whole street.

"Hell's fire! Stand back, people, I gots to have room for the damn animals and to move about," Shorty Lee Russell shouted to those waiting on the boardwalk. "Devil's balls, I'm doin' the best I can, so don't be pushin' and shovin'," he complained even though no one was. He tended to speak to people in the same loutish manner he spoke to his oxen, though with a smidgen less vulgarity.

Excited conversation rose as townspeople milled about waiting for the freighters to untie the ropes and pull the canvas from the wagons. There were sacks of flour and sugar and beans, boxes and crates of tools, mining supplies, household items and other supplies, and the much anticipated mail.

The ox drivers distributed the mail first, and Sage stood back anxiously waiting for her name to be called. When the letter bags were nearly empty, and the crowd beginning to disperse, Shorty Lee motioned her over.

"Howdy, Miss Sage," he said, his smile showing a row of brown teeth with two missing on the bottom. His red shirt was stained with dirt, sweat, and tobacco juice spatters, his brown canvas pants muddied to the knees. A Bowie knife and pistol were buckled around his waist.

"I got your package for ya." He reached into the mail sack and pulled out a large, thick envelope, and handed it to her.

"Thank you, Shorty Lee," she said, her nose twitching at the smell rolling off him.

"Could only get one, though," the bullwhacker informed her. "The others were sold out. City ladies buy those soon's they get printed. I'll bring 'nother one next time I come through. You kin count on it."

"Thank you. I appreciate you bringing this one," she said.

He smiled again. "I'll be seein' ya up at Wild Mountain Honey in a couple hours, then I got to get on to the next town."

"Well, you'll be happy to know the bathhouse is open now," she made a point of saying. "You will visit it before you come over?"

He looked at her as though he didn't understand what she meant, then comprehension lit his face. "Oh yes, ma'am. You bet. Much obliged. "

She stepped away and too impatient to wait, ripped open the envelope and peeked at the copy of Godey's Lady's Book inside. The issue was a few months old, but she pulled it out of its wrapper and eagerly flipped through the pages of dressmaking patterns.

She'd been a regular reader of the publication back in Missouri and had sorely missed it. On a whim, she'd given Shorty Lee some money in advance and asked him to bring her as many issues as he could get his hands on the next time he came through. She had depended on the journal for fashion and lifestyle news. Of equal interest, were the articles championing women's rights and the editorials espousing other forward thinking concepts of its editor, Sara Josepha Hale.

Mindful of the time and her meeting with Ramsey Thorogood, she slipped the magazine back into the envelope and turned, nearly bumping into a man coming out of the barber shop.

"Oh, I'm sorry, I . . ." she began, but the words dried up when she found herself looking into blue eyes more rakish than ever, the memory of which caused her to shiver imperceptibly. She gathered her wits and greeted the devil himself.

"Hello, Rodney."

His mouth spread in a broad grin and he started to tip his hat, then recognition flooded his face. She could tell by his expression the exact moment in which recollection stirred and he realized who had spoken to him.

"Oh," he said, the corners of his mouth slipping a notch. His eyes darted nervously, and he was momentarily disconcerted.

"Why, Sage. Hello." He swept his hat off his head and held it against his chest.

Sage took a step back and looked him over, taking him in from head to heels. He was wearing a single-breasted frock coat with a velvet collar.

A snowy, frilled shirt showed under his brocade vest. The hat in his hand was a grey felt bowler.

Her gaze fixed on his face, but his eyes darted uneasily, unable to meet hers directly.

"I didn't expect to see you in Fairplay Creek," she said. "In fact, I didn't expect to see you ever again."

Instantly, his brows came together and his expression seemed to liquefy into a mask of contrition. He looked like a boy about to be taken to the woodshed.

"Look, Sage," he began. "I'm real sorry about what happened back home. It was just that I ..." He paused. He had a gentleman's demeanor, his manner almost courtly, but he was bumbling like an idiot now.

"Yes?" she coaxed, arching a brow. She was much more self-possessed than she thought she'd be if she ever saw him again. Being on her own had given her confidence. Having her own money certainly helped.

He puffed out his cheeks and blew out a gust of air. "Well, I guess I wasn't ready to, you know. Get married," he finished.

Her smile was forced but she kept it going. "So I gathered," she said, and waited for him to say something more.

When it was clear he could do nothing beyond clear his throat and drum his fingers on the brim of the bowler, she asked, "What brings you to Fairplay Creek?"

He recovered a little of his composure. "Oh, I've heard about the gaming tables here," he replied. "I've had a bit of luck since I saw you last. Thought I'd see if my streak would hold in the mining camps."

Recently, professional gamblers had begun making their way up the mountain to Fairplay Creek, slick dressed, well turned out men who stood apart from the crowd of grimy dust covered snuff chewers expectorating in the streets. Rodney looked as dapper as they, and she wondered where he got the money to enter that risky profession.

"I see," she said. An awkward silence fell and she tightened her arms around her package. "Well, I wish you luck."

When she started to leave, he put his hand on her shoulder and stopped her.

"I'm really glad to see you again, Sage." His hand stroked up and down her arm in a too familiar way, then it stopped and he left it there. He sidled up closer, and spoke close to her ear.

"I want you to know that I never meant to hurt you. It was just that things happened so fast."

She hardly thought a twelve month betrothal was hasty, but nevertheless held her tongue and waited. While she was no longer angry, a scintilla of hurt and disappointment lingered. She wondered what he'd say in his defense.

"Would you be so kind as to give me a chance to explain? Please. Have dinner with me. Tonight." The pressure of his fingers increased on her arm.

He was looking at her fervently, his blue eyes clear as a lake. How many girls had gazed into them and found them as heart stopping as she once had? How many had been swayed by their influence to do something against their better judgment?

Ironically, it was that very capacity to persuade that prompted her to accept his invitation.

"Why, yes, that would be lovely," she replied, stepping away from him. His hand fell to his side. "We can have a nice talk over a quiet dinner," she went on. "There's a new place that just opened up last week called the Gold Dust Saloon. It has a quieter reputation than the other establishments in town, and private alcoves we can close off with a drape."

A smile started up one corner of his mouth, and he began to look quite pleased with himself.

"For privacy while we talk, I mean," she added slyly. "It's right down the street." She nodded in its direction. "You can't miss it. Shall I meet you there at four?"

He grinned broadly. "I will count the minutes," he said, lifting her hand and touching his lips to her gloved palm.

She sent a smile over her shoulder as she walked away, but let it collapse when she turned around. She hated resorting to deceptive tactics.

In the past, she'd always done what was right and proper, exactly what had been expected of her. She wasn't sure if that had been a function of virtue or cowardice, but nonetheless she'd grown in experience since then. Now she acted out of necessity and an instinct for survival.

Mandy nickered softly and twitched her ears in greeting when Sage returned and untied the reins.

A spiral of anticipation began to form in Sage's chest as she settled herself in the seat bench and adjusted the embroidered pillow behind her back. If her meeting with Ramsey Thorogood went as she feared it would, Rodney might prove to be very useful.

Yes, Rodney, she thought, I'll give you a chance. A chance to do me a huge favor.

She clucked to the horse setting her in motion, and headed for the meeting with Ramsey Thorogood.

* * * * *

"You asked her to eat with you?" Bridger asked, dumfounded.

Honcho was a bull of a man, but conveying to Bridger his morning exchange with Sage, he looked as bashful as a school boy.

"Yeah," he nodded, his smile shy.

Bridger stopped in the process of loading his Winchester, and stared at his new deputy. "What did she say?"

"She said she would. Next Tuesday. Lunch." Honcho's Adam's apple bobbed. "At Oscar's."

Bridger gazed coolly at Honcho who stood there grinning like a damn fool. He pictured the two of them sitting across the table from each other. Honcho big and hulking, dwarfing the chair, and Sage, prim and proper, wearing a crisply pressed shirtwaist with an amber brooch at her throat, her hair tucked into its usual tidy bun. Maybe she'd be wearing one of those fancy corsets underneath. Mulling that over gave him an urgent clench in the pit of his stomach. His face must have conveyed what he was feeling because Honcho's smile faltered.

"Oh," Honcho said suddenly. "She's not taken, is she?"

"No," Bridger replied vaguely, his mind locked on the implications of Honcho and Sage eating lunch together. "No, she's not."

Honcho gave a relieved chuckle, and his smile appeared again. "That's good. For a minute there, from the look on your face, I thought you had designs on her."

"Who?" Bridger returned. "Me? No." He put in a fresh cartridge, slammed home the action, and took aim at the coat rack in the corner to check the sight. "Get ready to ride out with me," he said stiffly. "We've got work to do."

"What happened?" Honcho asked, one hand automatically going to his revolver, the other to his gun belt to confirm its quantity of ammunition.

"I've rounded up a couple of men and we're riding out to Hatchett's Draw a few miles out of town," Bridger answered, peering down the barrel. "Someone said they saw an outlaw we've been watching for in the vicinity. I think it's the drifter that killed Honey Wild." He looked up to explain. "That's Sage's aunt. She used to run the parlor house." Then in case Honcho didn't catch his meaning, he added, "Sage is now . . ."

Honcho spun the cylinder on his Colt .45 and met Bridger's gaze with a long look of his own. "I know," he replied evenly, and holstered his revolver.

Bridger lowered the rifle to his side, then grabbed his hat and slapped it on his head. "Let's go have a look see at Hatchett's Draw," he said, then stormed out the door, coattails flying.

Chapter Seventeen

Rodney was waiting when Sage arrived at the Gold Dust Saloon. If she hadn't needed him, she might have gotten some small satisfaction from not showing up, leaving him waiting and wondering just as he'd left her waiting at the church. However, her need for his help was greater than her need for revenge. He helped her from her carriage, and with his hand on her elbow, guided her through the batwing saloon doors.

The place smelled of new wood, cigarette smoke, roasted beef and beer. The owner had divided up the space with a low wall between the dining area and the bar to separate the diners from the drinkers in an attempt to raise the cachet of his establishment.

There was still plenty of light at the mountain camps at that hour of the day, so the place wasn't crowded like it would be later on, but all the stools at the bar were occupied by miners, their muddy boots propped on a shiny brass rail. Their faces, reflected in the wide mirror on the wall behind the bar, showed a mixture of expressions: sour, serious or gleeful depending on how the day's diggings had gone.

It was the kind of saloon where the glasses were all polished and twinkling, and the man behind the bar was crisp with starch, and meant it when he smiled. Tables and chairs were arranged with seating for four in the space allotted for dining, the room lit by hurricane lamps hanging from the ceiling. A faro table was set up in a separate room at the back, but no one was playing.

When Sage entered with Rodney, several of the miners greeted her courteously, their faces showing surprise not only at seeing her in a saloon, but at seeing she was accompanied by a stranger. She nodded politely in return and headed for one of the private alcoves, Rodney following. Solicitously he helped her off with her jacket, then sat down across from her.

The saloonkeeper came over from behind the bar to take their order, introducing himself as Blake Connor. Rodney ordered whiskey for himself, and without asking, sarsaparilla for Sage, and roasted beef with gravy and biscuits for both of them.

"I'll have a glass of wine, please," Sage interjected, bouncing a meaningful look between Rodney and the owner. "I prefer red, if you have it."

"Yes, ma'am," he replied. "I'll see you're not disturbed," he whispered conspiratorially to Rodney. As he left, he pulled a fringed shawl along a wooden rod, closing off the alcove opening.

When they were alone, Rodney looked at her and smiled easily, his prior discomfort seemingly put to rest. His blue eyes sparkled with color. They'd always been his most arresting feature, and her heart pinched remembering how much trust she'd once put in them. She wasn't sure she could trust them now, but since what she was about to ask of him didn't involve matters of the heart, she was going to take the risk.

She folded her hands on the table and listened politely as he shared news of friends and acquaintances in Independence, talking companionably as if they were old friends. She found herself looking at him with curiosity, and studied him while he talked.

He'd always been a finicky dresser, but now she could see his collar and cuffs were slightly frayed. A button was missing from his vest, and the buttons weren't silver like she first thought; she could see the brass showing through on the worn edges. Loose threads poked from the shoulder seam of his coat. The shine had forsaken the lucky horseshoe stickpin adorning his tie. He apparently hadn't had as much luck at the tables as he'd claimed.

He continued talking, his conversation light, his manner confident and sophisticated. She found herself staring at his lips, fascinated as they

formed words that were smooth and glib, and suddenly they were someone else's lips.

Bridger's lips.

She lowered her eyes and shifted in her seat feeling heat creep into
her cheeks. When she looked up again, Rodney was peering at her
expectantly. He'd asked her a question and she'd missed it.

"Forgive me. What did you say?" she asked.

"I said do you remember that night we went to the Fourth of July
dance at the grange hall? And while everyone else was watching the
fireworks we sneaked out to the picnic grove by the river?"

The heat in her cheeks flamed to fire. She remembered it very well,
and with a heap of misgivings.

"I'm afraid, Rodney, I'd rather not discuss that. Under the circumstances, it is not a night I recall fondly. Considering," she added, with
emphasis.

His face fell, and it was his turn to lower his eyes. He peeked at her
from under his lashes in a manner that in the past she had found quite
charming. But then all scoundrels are charming, she reminded herself.

"I have a confession to make," he said.

"Oh?"

"Yes. I didn't just happen to land in Fairplay Creek on a whim."

"You didn't?"

He looked at her, his eyes serious and intent. "No. I came here because I knew you were here."

"But you seemed surprised to see me," she said.

"I was," he admitted. "I didn't expect to run into you that way. I just
arrived last night and planned to look you up this afternoon. I was caught
by surprise running into you in front of the barbershop first thing this
morning."

"Why did you plan to look me up?" she asked.

"Because I've been thinking about you a great deal. I missed you and realized how much I care for you."

She resisted raising a skeptical eyebrow.

"I didn't want you to think badly of me," he went on. "I wanted to tell you I'm sincerely sorry I ran off without telling you."

Remembering that sorry day, she felt the stirrings of anger all over again. "You left me in a difficult position, Rodney," she couldn't help scolding. "Everyone was at the church and . . ."

He held up his hand, and looked remorseful. "I know. And I'm sorry. It was wrong of me."

She skewered him with narrowed eyes, then leaned back, crossed her arms in front of her, and waited. "You said you wanted to explain."

A vertical crease appeared between his brows, and he shrugged. "The truth is," he implored, "I have no explanation. I simply made a mistake."

To her annoyance, he reached across the table, laid his hand on hers and closed it over her fingers.

"An emotionally costly mistake," he went on. "A painful one. I was hoping you could forgive me," he finished.

The desperation in his eyes told her the truth of it. He was broke, down and out despite the gentlemanly façade he showed the world. Her father's lawyer must have told him about her inheritance, and he'd come to Fairplay Creek hoping to share in what he saw as her good fortune.

"I have forgiven you, Rodney," she said matter-of-factly, gently removing his hand.

"I thought that . . . hoped that, you might . . . we might try again." His voice was beseeching, but she caught the bogus intention behind it. He was the same falsifier he'd always been only now she was going to use that distinguishing characteristic to her benefit.

"I'm sorry, but that's not possible."

Disappointment leaped to his face. "Why not?"

Just then Blake Connor came back with their meals and drinks. He set them on the table, then left, closing the drape once again behind him. Gales of laughter came from the other side.

Ignoring his plate of food, Rodney leaned forward and asked again. "Why not? Is there someone else?"

"No, there's no one else. But I've moved on with my life, Rodney. I'm in charge of an enterprise that takes up all of my time, and I have no intention of getting married now. More to the point, I don't want to get married. No," she corrected herself, shaking her head and waving her forefinger. "I don't need to."

Rodney leaned back in his chair and picked up the tumbler the bartender had put in front of him. "You do seem to have some standing in town," he acknowledged, gazing at her with a look that fell just short of reverence.

Her mouth prepared to smile, but she held it in and picked up her fork.

"Yes, I do," she conceded. "I'm doing quite well. More than well," she pointed out.

"So I've heard." He lifted his whiskey in a silent toast, then dejected, tossed it back when she didn't reciprocate. He pursed his lips and studied her. "I never pictured you as a . . ." He paused. "A madam."

She smiled primly. "There are many things you don't know about me," she replied, then placed a tiny bite of food into her mouth. "Oh, this is good," she said, chewing and motioning with her fork toward his plate. "Try it."

He sliced a chunk off his beef, stabbed it with his fork, dragged it through the gravy, and popped it into his mouth. They ate in silence for a while.

Just as she was wondering if he had enough money to pay for the meal, he placed his knife on the edge of his plate along with his fork, and looked at her directly. "I'll be honest with you, Sage."

"That would be nice," she said, swallowing. "For a change."

He disregarded her remark and went on. "Things haven't been going well for me," he admitted. "I was wondering if, I mean, I was hoping you could help me out with a loan. I promise I'll pay you back."

She set her utensils down and looked at him directly, her head tilted. Still a swindler, she thought, looking for easy money. She didn't think the grime of real work had ever lined his fingernails. At least not since she'd known him. When they met, he'd told her he owned a lumber mill in Canada. Turned out he was a sawyer all right, but not the owner, rather an employee who had been run out of town after being caught in bed with his boss's wife.

"Well, as long as we're being honest," Sage replied, "I must tell you I had an ulterior motive in accepting your dinner invitation."

He narrowed his eyes suspiciously. "You did?"

"But I can help you out."

His face brightened.

"But not with a loan."

His face fell.

"I can give you a job."

He stared, his expression blank. "A job?" he croaked.

She touched her napkin to her mouth and took a sip of wine. "Don't worry," she said, setting her glass on the table. "I don't mean a long term job, and not a hard one. I mean a task. I have something that needs doing, but it requires secrecy."

His features softened, his eyes expressing a hint of interest.

"I will pay you."

At that, he looked at his empty glass, tweaked the drape aside and called for another, then gave her his earnest attention.

"What do you want me to do?" he asked.

"I want you to act as my intermediary in a very important matter, vital to the well being of the children in Fairplay Creek. You will be dealing with some of the most prominent men in town, men who are in a position to directly influence its future."

Rodney puffed up with self-importance.

"I'm confident you can handle it," she flattered, then proceeded to tell him about her ill-fated meeting with Ramsey Thorogood that afternoon.

As she'd expected, Ramsey had only agreed to meet with her as a courtesy. He had no intention of letting her play any significant role in the planning or building of the school, other than taking her money, of course. Clearly he was of the same opinion all menfolk were when it came to women. He thought they were flighty and addled, whose only proper place was at home, in the kitchen, or in the bedroom.

"Important decisions will need to be made," he'd declared, studying her with amused tolerance. Then he'd dismissed her. "These affairs are better left to men."

Holding back her anger, she could have withheld her offer of money, but that would have accomplished nothing. Instead, it would have harmed the children and the town, and not coincidentally, further diminished her honor by tainting her with a broken promise. Rather than waste precious time arguing with him, an argument she knew she couldn't win, and delaying the project, she'd reacted on impulse.

"Well, then we are in agreement, Mr. Thorogood," she replied sweetly. "I'll have my financial consultant contact you tomorrow. He's an investor and will certainly want to be in on the important decision making you speak of."

Thorogood seemed surprised at this, but Sage was sure he wouldn't back down from building the school and church. After all, he had his own reputation to consider, and breaking a promise he made in front of so many townspeople would certainly be detrimental to his desire to be elected mayor.

Rodney listened intently, his meal untouched in front of him.

Speaking quietly so she wouldn't be heard outside their draped nook, Sage leaned across the table, their faces inches apart. If he interpreted her manner as flirtatious it was fine with her. Flattery had always worked best with Rodney.

"I'd like you to meet with Ramsey Thorogood, one of the town's leaders," she said.

Rodney nodded, looking interested and impressed.

"I will introduce you as my advisor and consultant. Your job will be to carry out my wishes and decisions, but present them as your own. That's the only way I'll have an equal say with the other men on the building project."

Sage hated having to use Rodney or any man in this manipulative manner, but she didn't see it as dishonest. She saw it as practical and the most expeditious way to accomplish a very important task that would have great benefit for the town. It seemed to be in the nature of men, especially important men like Ramsey Thorogood, that everything needed to be their idea first, and she'd found it was the clever woman who used that particular male proclivity to her benefit.

Rodney's smile flashed again, and it didn't take more than a moment for him to jump at her offer even before knowing the specifics.

"I'll do it," he said, and again raised his glass in a toast. This time Sage lifted hers to meet it.

Before the town meeting, she wouldn't have needed Rodney's help or anyone's. She had accumulated nearly enough money to take her away from Fairplay Creek back to her comfortable existence in Missouri. But she had promised the townspeople a church and school.

And beyond that, she couldn't just close the parlor house and leave the Honeys stranded. Some of them had saved the money they earned, but many of them hadn't. Some of them had children living with grandparents or other relatives, and were dutifully sending every penny back for their care. She couldn't turn those women out on the street. She felt obligated to help them relocate and get started someplace else in whatever endeavor they chose. That would take money, too.

And she hadn't forgotten Bridger's concern about keeping lawlessness at bay if Wild Mountain Honey wasn't there to attenuate a tendency toward stability. Admittedly, Fairplay Creek wasn't exactly a model of civility now, but by closing Wild Mountain Honey, would she be putting a greater number of people at risk as Bridger feared?

It was a dilemma that weighed on her mind with each passing day. There had to be a way she could keep her promise to the townspeople and still achieve her own goals without anyone being harmed in the process. With Rodney supervising the building project, she'd be free to concentrate on her own plans.

After she filled Rodney in on the details, she took a small pouch of gold dust and some paper money from her bag, and handed it to him.

"Here's an advance on your salary. Use some of this to buy a new outfit. Gallagher's has good quality menswear," she suggested, "but a new clothier has opened up down the block. Patronize whichever you wish, but remember, you will be dealing with the most important men in Fairplay Creek. You'll want to meet them on equal footing."

When they finished eating, Rodney assisted her to her feet, placed some of the money she'd given him on the table to pay for their meal and steered her out of the dining room toward the batwing doors. The evening air had chilled with the lowering of the sun, and she pulled her grey wool jacket tighter.

Miners and other rough looking men filled the street in front of the Gold Dust, their raucous voices rising above the pounding of hammers and the scrape of saws. She and Rodney forced their way through a rowdy bunch milling on the boardwalk blocking the exit.

Across the street, some men were erecting a structure, hastily throwing it together with warped and knotty lumber, the kind tossed aside as unsuitable for building. Six by six corner posts held a platform reached by a staircase of eight steps. It was a gallows. Bridger was standing off to the side with his hands riding his gun belt, studying the scene and looking supremely perturbed.

"What's going on?" Sage asked a bystander crowding at her elbow.

"They caught the son a bitch that killed your aunt," the miner replied, excitedly. "Found him camped out near Hatchett's Draw."

At the mention of Shooter Riker's final resting place, Sage's stomach dropped and her head went into a tailspin. Perspiration quickly moistened her chemise, and she clasped a hand on Rodney's arm to steady herself.

"That redheaded varmint is gonna hang tonight," the miner went on gleefully showing a gap-toothed grin.

"Doesn't he have to go before the judge?" Rodney inquired.

"Already did," returned the miner, swaying on his feet from the effects of the invigorating beverage in his flask. "Had a trial at the Diamond Rio. He's guilty, shore enough."

Over the heads of the swarming miners, Sage saw Bridger's gaze fall on her. When they made eye contact, there was almost an audible click and Sage's heart took a thump, then speeded up.

Leveling his hat, Bridger shouldered through the crowd and hurried over, giving Rodney a spiteful look before addressing Sage.

"What in blazes are you doing here?" He was gritty with trail dust and damp with sweat.

"Having dinner," she replied, flustered at his brusqueness.

Scowling, Bridger dashed a glance through the batwing doors. "In there?" he asked. Then his eyes, registering distaste, darted to Rodney. "With him? I was just in there and didn't see you."

"We ate in one of the private rooms." Hurriedly, she made introductions. "This is my business associate," she said, indicating Rodney. "Rodney Weatherspoon, I'd like you to meet the marshal, Bridger Norwood."

Rodney held out his hand, but Bridger didn't take it. Instead he tipped his hat back with his knuckle, turned down the corners of his mouth and gave Rodney a disapproving glare. For a tense moment, they sized each other up, each one seeming to find the other unsuitable.

"What kind of business associate?" Bridger demanded.

Sage stiffened. "You do have a knack for asking questions whose answers are none of your business, Mr. Norwood," she huffed, irritated at his tone as well as his prying.

Bridger went on as if she hadn't spoken. "This is no place for you. There might be trouble. We got a street full of angry men who are getting ready for a hanging. You best be going."

To his credit, Rodney, exhibiting magnificent gallantry, stepped in manfully. "Excuse me, Marshal, but you've no call to speak to Miss Cane that way."

Bridger jammed his fists on his hips, spreading the edges of his duster to show a holstered gun lashed to each thigh and faced Rodney, squinting. "Who the hell are you to tell me how to speak?"

Bridger looked at Rodney like he was a rattler sunning on a rock, and then the two men faced off like mongrel dogs. Sage put herself between them, while the crowd jostled and swarmed around them. Thankfully,

Rodney was the first to collect himself. He took a step back, smoothed his hair and shot his cuffs.

"Rodney was just seeing me to my carriage," she said in a mollifying tone, hoping to ease the friction.

"Oh, yeah? Well, I'll take care of that," Bridger said. He put his hand on her shoulder to escort her and she felt a thrill of warmth at his touch.

"Bridger, please don't be rude," she hissed, and stood her ground.

"I'm not being rude," he shot back in a loud voice. "I'm talking about your well being. There's gonna be a hanging, and there might be trouble," he repeated. "Now, come on. I'll see you home." He took her arm brusquely and began moving her through the mob, leaving Rodney standing open-mouthed.

Embarrassed and a little annoyed at Bridger's boorish behavior, Sage shook him off.

"I'll see myself home, thank you." She pivoted and called to Rodney. "Thank you for dinner. We'll talk again in a few days."

With that, she showed them both her back, and pushed her way through the throng. At the hitching post, Mandy was prancing nervously. Her ears twitched at the noise and commotion, but she snuffled softly and calmed at Sage's touch.

Without a backward glance, Sage climbed into the buggy, picked up the reins and set the horse off at a trot toward Wild Mountain Honey. Besides wanting to distance herself from what could very well turn into a riot, she wanted to see how Odie was taking the news about the capture at Hatchett's Draw.

Chapter Eighteen

Bridger finished his bath, stood up in the copper tub, took a thick towel from a peg on the wall, and hurriedly dried himself off. The rugged fragrance of the woodland scented soap he'd used infused the air in his small bathing cubicle.

He wrapped the towel around his waist and stepped out of the tub. Using an extra towel, he wiped steam from the mirror over the basin, then shaved his three day growth of beard. After examining his image in the mirror, he picked up a small scissors and carefully trimmed his mustache. Satisfied with the result, he then went to work on the straggles of hair curling on his shoulders, clipping off the ends to even them out.

He was thinking about Sage.

And Honcho McGullicudy.

And Rodney Weatherspoon.

Bridger had disliked that man from the moment he laid eyes on him standing with Sage in front of the Gold Dust Saloon. Who the hell did he think he was acting so possessive, like he had some kind of claim on her? She'd introduced him as a business associate, but he came across as something else. Something more personal, like a suitor.

Bridger's scissors stopped in mid-clip.

Or had Rodney merely been exhibiting well-bred manners? Something Bridger most definitely had not done.

"Huh," Bridger grunted, then went back to trimming his hair, feeling his ire rise again. He couldn't remember a time he wanted to hit someone more. He'd wanted to grind his fist into Weatherspoon's face until his lips were bruised and bleeding. Maybe it would have been better if he'd done that right off instead of letting his anger make a fool of him. He'd acted like an ill-mannered lout in front of her, and not for the first time, either. He knew better, he scolded himself. It's just that Elizabeth had been gone so long, he was out of practice when it came to women and courting.

He lowered the scissors and his eyes went distant in the mirror.

Courting? Is that what he was about to do?

He wasn't sure he would call it courting exactly, but if, as it seemed, Sage enjoyed sitting down to a meal with a man, maybe she'd agree to sit down to a meal with him, too.

Oh, hell, yes.

Of course, he was going to court her. At least he was going to try to.

He took his new shirt and pants from the hook behind the door, and pulled them on. The stiff fabric made his skin itch, but the proprietor at Messrs. J. & R. LeBlanc Clothiers had said he looked dashing and quite the gentleman. Bridger wasn't sure if dashing was the appropriate look for a marshal, but having spurned the embroidered braces and doeskin vest proffered by the haberdasher, he at least didn't look dandified like that over-groomed, weasily tenderfoot Weatherspoon.

He shrugged into a new jacket, adjusted the fit over his shoulders, and smoothed his hands down the worsted. Satisfied with the fit, he took one last look in the mirror, swelled his chest, squared his shoulders, and stepped out of the bathing cubicle where one of the Honeys was waiting.

"Want me to take those to the laundry?" she asked, indicating the bundle of rolled up dirty clothes under his arm.

"Yes, thank you, Maude," he said, handing it over.

She stroked a clothes brush lightly over his shoulders and down his back with brisk little sweeping motions, then turned him around and touched up the lapels.

"There you go, handsome," she said, after a few more whisks with the brush. "You look good enough to eat."

He paid her for the bath with a little extra for the service and the compliment.

A twilight sky glowed above the ridgeline, and campfires flickered up and down the mountainside as Bridger exited the bathhouse. He took a moment to gaze into the distance, going over in his mind his plan for the evening, pumping up the courage to see it through. Rejection was always a possibility and he steeled himself for it.

Leaving his horse at the hitch rack in front of the bath house, he walked the short stone path leading next door to Wild Mountain Honey. Still angry at himself for acting like an idiot the last time he'd seen Sage, he hoped to make amends now.

He entered through the rear storage room and stood uncertainly in the back hall at the foot of the stairs. Since it was still early in the evening, the sounds coming from the front parlors were subdued, conversation was muted, the music low.

He took off his hat and watched Miss Priscilla through the open kitchen door. She was at the sideboard frosting a sweet lemon cake and talking to Odie. He cleared his throat to get their attention, and they turned.

"Excuse me, ladies. Could I talk to you a minute?"

* * * * *

Sitting at her kneehole desk, Sage slowly turned the pages of her Godey's Lady's Book, admiring the newest fashions and sewing patterns. It seemed something new in the way of undergarments was being worn by the most fashionable ladies in the bigger cities like New York and Boston. Called crinolines, they were sort of an underskirt made of whalebone or wire designed to hold skirts out in a graceful bell-like shape.

Fascinated, she pondered the impracticality of wearing such a garment here in Fairplay Creek where spiky nails and sharp edges protruded everywhere, and nearly every doorway was rough-framed in splintery wood and barely wide enough to walk through. Far more practical would be the ruffled women's trousers first worn by Amelia Jenks Bloomer under her skirt. But Sage couldn't deny the crinolines were beautiful, and she sighed with longing, admiring them.

A soft knock came on her door which stood slightly ajar and she looked up to see Odie standing there.

"Hello, Odie. Come in."

Odie looked lovely in a high-necked jewel-blue silk dress snugly buttoned up from waist to chin. The worried frown she'd been wearing for weeks had disappeared. Instead, she was grinning with simmering excitement.

"Bridger is downstairs," she whispered. "He wants to see you."

"He does?" Sage replied, surprised. "Why?"

"Well, he's calling on you, silly," Odie answered.

"Calling on me for what?" she asked, turning out her hands and lifting her shoulders in a shrug. Odie's meaning escaped her. It took a moment to dawn.

"Oh!" She suddenly got the strangest feeling of butterflies in her stomach. "You mean *calling* on me."

Odie smiled. "Yes, and if you want time to freshen, I'll send him up in five minutes."

"Oh, please Odie, I'll need ten," Sage replied, rising quickly, and heading for her closets.

Odie, who hadn't stopped smiling since she opened the door, carried the smile with her when she retreated.

Sage flew to the full length mirror and hastily removed and replaced the pins in her hair to neatly catch up any straggling locks. She pinched her cheeks, though there was no necessity as high color was already forming two rosy circles on her cheekbones.

Standing before the closet that held her best outfits, she stripped off her muslin day dress and took out the peach colored silk, but hurriedly put it back when she remembered what had happened the last time she'd worn it in Bridger's presence. It seemed like forever ago, but even if he didn't remember what she'd been wearing when she accidentally shot him, the memory of that night was still fresh in her mind.

Instead she put on a low cut dress made of shimmering aqua-colored taffeta trimmed with lace along the neckline and at the hem. In her nervousness, her fingers felt useless as thick sausages as she clumsily worked the front buttons. She toed off her house slippers, and was just slipping her feet into pale green silk low-heeled shoes when a knock sounded. Hurriedly, she poked a jeweled hair ornament into her chignon, checked her reflection in the mirror, took a deep breath, and went to open the door.

Bridger stood there, a crooked half-smile showing under his auburn mustache. He was freshly bathed and shaved, smelling of soap and talc, and she took an inordinate amount of improper pleasure in the sight of him.

"Hello, Bridger," she said.

"Good evening," he replied. His gaze moved over her admiringly. "You look nice."

"So do you," she answered. He'd cut his hair, she noticed, and his jacket and shirt looked new. She took a step back widening the door so he could enter. "Come in."

He snatched off his hat and stepped in, hooking a finger under his collar in an attempt to loosen it.

It was disconcerting that the sight of a man could excite her so much. She was afraid he'd see the emotion in her eyes if she looked at him directly, so shifted her gaze away from his face and gestured to the divan in front of the fireplace.

"Won't you have a seat?" she asked, leading the way.

"Yes, thank you," he replied and sat stiffly, carefully setting his hat on an end table.

Sage lowered herself next to him, fussed with her skirts, then folded her hands in her lap, her mind spinning as she frantically tried to think of something to say to ease the uncomfortable silence.

"This is a surprise," she said honestly. It was all she could come up with.

"I came to apologize," he said. "For the other night, the last time I saw you. For the way I acted."

She met his eyes then, stopping a small smile from tilting her lips.

"There was no call for it," he rushed on. "He . . . your friend . . . was escorting you. I had no call to step in and interfere. As you correctly pointed out at the time, I was rude."

"Apology accepted," she said, setting her smile free and hoping he didn't notice her breath had quickened. "You were only doing your job."

"Yeah, well . . ." Bridger cleared his throat, and pulled at his collar again. "And there's something else . . ." His words drifted off.

"Yes?"

"I wondered if you might do me the honor of having dinner with me," he said.

She stared at him, lips slightly parted in surprise as he rushed on.

"Since you had lunch with Honcho and dinner with Weatherspoon, I assumed you enjoyed dining with company. So, I wondered if you might dine with me, too."

He swallowed.

She blinked. "Why, yes. I'd like that very much." She paused. "When did you have in mind?" she asked, hoping she didn't sound too eager.

"How about right now?" he said, surprising her further.

"Now? You mean here?"

He nodded, his eyes shining, his expression hopeful.

"Well, I . . ." she began to object, but was interrupted by someone softly tapping at her door. Bridger jumped up and strode quickly over to open it, admitting first Miss Priscilla, then Odie.

The women entered carrying trays laden with steaming crocks of roast beef stew, plates of Denver biscuits, a bottle of blackberry cordial, one of brandy, and thick slices of sweet lemon cake. Barely able to suppress their grins, they placed the food on Sage's square dining table. As Miss Priscilla, with great ceremony, arranged place settings for two, Odie set shallow bowls of potpourri around the room.

"Enjoy your meal," she said, when she'd finished arranging fragrant candles on the mantle and lighting them.

Miss Priscilla stoked the fire, added a log, and winked at Sage over Bridger's shoulder on her way out with Odie. "Let me know if you'll be needing anything else," she said, and closed the door softly.

Sage sat nonplused, but no less enchanted at the scene that had just unfolded before her. When she was again alone with Bridger, she spoke in a voice airy with delight. "You arranged this with them?"

He sent her a grin that was warm as the noonday sun and a little bashful. "I reckon I did."

She laughed lightly. "Why, I don't know what to say." She studied his face, her heart racing.

He approached, offering his arm. "May I have the pleasure of your company?" he asked, gesturing toward the table where dinner waited.

Before she could answer, he took her hand and placed it in the crook of his elbow. She rose and let him escort her to a chair which he gallantly held for her. After she lowered herself into it, he stepped around to the other side of the table and sat opposite.

Captivated beyond words, she watched him serve her plate first, then his, then pour brandy into his glass and cordial into hers. They began to eat, wordlessly at first, but before long the delectable food had a calming effect that served to break the tension. They exchanged pleasantries, heaping praise on Miss Priscilla's culinary expertise, then naturally lapsed into polite dinner conversation.

"I hear one of the Honeys left," Bridger commented. "Beatrice, was it?"

"Yes," Sage replied. "Her husband came up from New Mexico and begged her to go back with him and she agreed. I sent her off with my blessing."

Bridger spooned a bite of stew into his mouth, chewed and swallowed. "Well, you're about to lose another. Acer told me today he and Verbena have set a date for a wedding. Acer bought a little homestead a few miles out of town."

"Oh, I'm so pleased," she said, leaning back a little. "Verbena has often talked about settling down and having a family. She very much wants children. I'm not sure Fairplay Creek is where she wants to raise them, though," she added.

"Oh, I don't know," Bridger commented. "The town has come a long way from a ragtag settlement of tents and cabins. It's a real community now. Lacking some amenities, but those will come in time."

Sage agreed, and he went on.

"Ramsey Thorogood has invited a consortium of railroad and land investors to come and take a look at how far the town has progressed," Bridger went on. "They'll be here in a few weeks. They should be suitably impressed to see plans for a school and church underway. Do you know when construction will begin?"

Sage nodded. "Next week," she said. " I'm quite excited."

Rodney had been instrumental in moving the project along according to her wishes. He'd proved his mettle and shown a surprising strength of character in his dealings with Ramsey, persuading Thorogood to agree to architectural plans and a location of Sage's choosing. Rodney's charm and affable personality had meshed nicely with Ramsey's despite the latter's overbearing nature. Rodney told her that Ramsey had hinted there was a possibility they might be partners in future endeavors.

Bridger refilled his glass with brandy, then extended the bottle of cordial, offering her some. "You?"

She nodded and held up her glass. He poured and she stopped him with a thank you.

"I heard the stage line engineers have already surveyed a location for a ticket office and boarding station," she said.

Bridger nodded. "Just past the livery, where the new blacksmith shop is opening."

"We'll surely see more people coming in then," she said, sipping from her glass. "And going," she added.

Bridger was silent for a moment. He met her gaze, but shifted it away and changed the subject. "I didn't see any of the Honeys at the hanging."

That was a topic she'd hoped to avoid talking about, but of course there was no way around it. She'd already been derelict in not thanking him for catching her aunt's killer. She did so now.

"Thank you for bringing my aunt's killer to justice," she said, then added, somewhat dismayed. "Even though it was frontier justice."

Bridger shrugged. "Well, that's the way things are done here. He did have a trial," he reminded her.

Though she wondered at the mechanics of the trial and its impartiality, she chose not to comment. There was no point. What's done was done.

"How did you get a judge here so fast?" she asked instead.

"Judge Monroe just happened to be riding through on his circuit. It was either conduct a trial right away or lock the killer up in the jail for a month until the judge came back. I didn't really want him here that long. The cost of his food and keep would come out of the town coffers.

"And besides. Emotions were still running high over your aunt's death. Some of the miners were so incensed they wanted revenge instead of punishment, and weren't willing to wait for a trial. I couldn't guarantee the man's safety. I thought it best to give him a speedy trial, and get it over with."

"What was his name?" she asked. "And how did you find him?"

"His name's Ham Tucker. One of the miners spotted him near Hatchett's Draw. Recognized him right off. It's hard to hide that bright orange hair of his. And Tucker didn't try to. He was proud of it and just arrogant enough to think he could come back here and nothing would happen to him."

She'd slid an anxious glance toward Bridger at the mention of Hatchett's Draw, but his face registered nothing of concern. Quickly, she lowered her eyes and turned her attention back to her meal.

"Why did he come back, I wonder?" she said, idly.

"He said he was supposed to meet his friend. Shooter Riker."

Sage's stomach dropped and she set down her spoon, quickly putting her napkin to her lips. Her eyes touched Bridger's fearing a hint of indictment in them, but his expression held no accusation. Instead, he seemed to misinterpret her look as uncertainty.

"He's the one pictured on the wanted posters," he said to remind her.

She coughed lightly into her napkin. "Yes, I remember," she said, managing to keep her voice from shaking and betraying her. She began eating again.

"So that leads me to believe," Bridger went on speaking around a bite of biscuit, oblivious to the turmoil rising inside her, "Riker is definitely headed this way. I'll keep the wanted posters up until he shows his face."

Sage refrained from commenting, concentrating fiercely on her food, her throat so constricted she could barely swallow let alone talk.

"I expected to see some of the Honeys at the hanging," Bridger said again into the silence. "I thought some of them might want to be there. You know, in honor of your aunt's memory."

"No," she answered, softly. "I asked them not to go."

"Why?"

"It's uncivilized," she said, without looking at him.

Bridger stopped eating, and still holding his knife and fork, rested the heels of his hands on the edge of the table. He looked at Sage, his expression perplexed. "But that's the way things get done in towns like this."

"But that doesn't mean it's civilized," she pointed out.

"Maybe not," he conceded. "But it's practical. And necessary. We can't always wait for civilized ways to catch up to us. Not if we want to keep order here and be relatively safe. Towns like Fairplay Creek can easily be taken over by lawlessness if it's not caught in time and quelled right away."

"You mean like the near riot in front of the Gold Dust the day of the hanging?"

"Well, yeah," he said.

"How did you quell that?" she asked.

Bridger smiled and started on dessert. "Oh, that was easy. Free drinks." He forked off a morsel of sweet lemon cake and popped it into his mouth.

"Free drinks?" Her eyebrows rose.

"Yep. Blake Conner offered free drinks at the Gold Dust so that pretty much ended it."

She rolled her eyes and sighed.

He caught her disapproval and stopped eating. "Look," he said. "Ramsey wants . . ."

"A peaceful town," she finished for him. "Yes, I know. But what you just said contradicts what you told me when I first came here. You said the existence of a parlor house kept Fairplay Creek peaceful. Now it seems Wild Mountain Honey being open or closed has nothing to do with lawlessness or its potential."

He responded with an air of wounded dignity. "Well now, Sage, don't go off on a tangent."

"I'm not going off on a tangent. You said . . ."

"And don't go repeating what I said, either."

Exasperated, he sat back, put his fork down and touched his mouth with his napkin. "Compared to some of the other unruly gold towns popping up in the Rockies, Fairplay Creek is doing all right."

"But—"

He reached across the table and took her hand in his, the surge of its heat up her arm stopping her words from leaving her mouth. Her eyes alighted on his and she experienced a rush of desire that made her breath quicken. She was doing nothing to stop herself from being charmed by this man.

"It appears that is something on which we'll always disagree," he said quietly. "Now, can we talk about something else?"

The cordial was making Sage feel too mellow to argue, so she agreed. Or was it that disarming smile of his that was filling her with warmth inside? They moved back to the divan in front of the fire, Bridger carrying the bottles and setting them on the low table. He held up the cordial, offering to top off her glass.

"More?"

"Just a little, thank you," she replied, and situated herself comfortably against the cushions. She looked at his handsome face, his nose so nicely shaped, his piercing green eyes flickering in the firelight. His lips were so damn appealing. In the past, it had irritated her that she had responded to him in such a heated way. Now, she rather enjoyed the feeling.

"Tell me," she said, gazing at him as she sipped from her glass. "How did you end up in a town like this?"

She watched as Bridger lapsed into thought. "Oh," he said, a faint frown line appearing between his eyebrows, "I guess it was as much by accident as by design. After my wife died, I was pretty lost. I quit my job as deputy right away and let myself be carried away by grief. I mourned hard and for a long time. Drinking became an all day event, and that helped some. Staying liquored up meant I didn't have to think. Or feel."

Fleetingly, she thought of the times she'd run into him in town, a sour look on his face, smelling faintly of alcohol.

"One day Elizabeth's parents came to our cabin and found me passed out drunk, Jenny in dirty clothes, hungry and crying. They took her home with them, then Elizabeth's father came back with Elizabeth's brother Jacob, who beat the shit out of me . . ." He caught himself and sent her an apologetic look. "Uh, knocked some sense into me, I mean.

"I had no memory of the previous three days and when they told me how they found Jenny, I was mortified. Disgusted with myself. They helped me see the wisdom of leaving Nebraska Territory and all the painful memories, getting a new start someplace else. They sold their place and we all came to the gold fields. They bought a small ranch in Hamilton City, and kept Jenny there while I looked for work.

"At the time, Fairplay Creek was barely more than a block long canvas city, but it was growing fast. I knew these mining towns all had a group of influential men looking to get in early and make a profit, or gain influence through politics or some other way. So I asked around for the name of the most important man in Fairplay Creek. Ramsey Thorogood hired me on the spot as town marshal."

Sage wasn't prepared for the gush of emotion that swept her when she heard his story There was so much sorrow in his voice. His eyes were moist and red-rimmed, his features pulled down with sadness.

He pressed his lips together and offered an apologetic shrug. "I don't have the drinking to forget completely under control yet, but I'm working on it."

She could hear the pain in his voice, sense the scars on his emotions. "I'm so sorry about your wife, Bridger. Really I am. Sometimes it seems that the pain of losing someone you love is more than a body is meant to bear."

He swallowed, nodding, and an easy silence passed between them.

Dark night reposed beneath a silvered moon. Through the window hundreds of campfires glowed up and down the mountainside, many times more than when she'd first arrived at Wild Mountain Honey.

"You lost someone you loved, too," Bridger said, after a considered minute. "Your father. That's why you're here, too. But not only that. You had a life back in Independence, a life you loved, I'll wager. You're probably mourning that."

A sudden tumble of memories overwhelmed her. Her life in Independence was nothing like her life here. Days back home had been filled with shopping and theater and friends. With church, and books and dances, and the ladies in her reading group. And, after her mother died, with keeping house for her father, something she never thought of as a chore, but rather something that brought her closer to her remaining parent.

"Yes, I am," she admitted. "And my father, too. He was a wonderful man. I miss him."

"This probably isn't the life you pictured for yourself, is it?"

She lowered her eyes. "No," she admitted. "It isn't."

"What kind of life did you envision?" he prompted.

She lifted her shoulder in a small shrug. "Oh, after my father died, I thought I'd marry Rodney and—"

Bridger bolted upright, slopping brandy out of his snifter onto his hand. "Marry Rodney! You were going to marry him? That greenhorn?" Bridger roared with laughter. "That fancypants?" he choked out. "That blowhard wears a bowler, for chrissake."

Bridger's merriment was so genuine, Sage found herself not only laughing, but agreeing with him about Rodney. She supposed her former fiancé did come across as sort of a con man, a deadbeat with no fear of drowning in honest sweat. Compared to Bridger and the other men she'd come to know in Fairplay Creek, men who nearly worked themselves to exhaustion just to survive, Rodney didn't look like he would last a week in the harsh environment of a Rocky Mountain mining town. And indeed, he might not have if she hadn't employed him.

Still, Rodney held some qualities that were appealing, otherwise she wouldn't have fallen for him in the first place. Only now, thinking back on it, she realized she'd been swept away by his unrestrained charm, and by skills that were mostly unutterable in polite company. She blushed fiercely and her gaze drifted back to Bridger.

She let it linger on him longer than was decent, but she couldn't restrain herself. She loved the rugged look of him, the way his dark auburn hair curled around his ears, the freshly barbered ends of it brushing his collar. Her eyes traveled the length of his legs stretched out toward the fire, boots crossed at the ankles. She was imagining how one of those legs would feel casually flung over hers while she slept, so wasn't prepared for what he said next.

"How many men are you seeing?"

Instantly, the shameless fantasies in her mind shattered like broken crockery, and fell away. Embarrassed, as if he'd read her mind and caught her having impure thoughts, she stared at him, speechless.

"I'm not prying," he hurried on. "I'm only asking because I want to know if I have a chance."

"A chance? A chance for wha—?"

"What I mean is . . ." He faltered and shoved a hand through his hair before going on. "If there's a ring, you know, I'm throwing my hat in it," said Bridger.

"Oh," she said. Then, "Oh!"

He moved toward her and took her hand. "I know we got off to a bad start and we don't see eye to eye on some things, but I'm not a bad fellow." He'd said that to her when they first met on the day she arrived in town, and she had taken it to mean something else.

"I had a wife I was faithful to and a steady job. I've got a good job now, too, maybe even a future in this town if I set my mind to it and have a reason to settle down."

She felt a sharp tug somewhere in her middle.

"I find myself thinking about you at odd moments throughout the day," he went on. "Some days all the time. So what I want to know is, are you still planning to leave Fairplay Creek?"

It was a question she'd begun asking herself on a daily basis. Unfortunately, she was no longer sure of her answer, and took a moment to find words. After some reflection, she replied as honestly as she could.

"Bridger, I'm a respectable woman, or at least I was seen that way back home. Now I'm a madam, an unintentional one, but still not respectable, and as long as I stay in this town, I never will be. Back home I was careful about my reputation. Anyone who knew me back there would never believe where I live now, what I've become." She set her glass on the table and sighed. "I'm not a madam."

Those were words she'd spoken the day they met, only tonight he looked like he believed her.

"I've come to see that," he replied. "And I understand how difficult it must be for you in your present circumstances." His eyes were soft, sincere in their depths. "But as long as you're here, is there a possibility that we might spend time together? Have dinner together? And talk? Like tonight?"

She stared into his steady gaze as a thrill started spinning behind her breastbone. "I think there's a very good possibility of that."

He looked at her with such longing, she felt as if he could see through her clothes. The air in the room was charged.

He pulled himself to the edge of his seat, set his glass on the table next to hers, and reached for her. They moved as one into an embrace that was chaste by any standards with his hands on her upper arms, hers draped over his shoulders, but where he touched her it was as if a lightning bolt shot through her.

The kiss was long and deep, and when it ended, she opened her eyes seeing his at close range, and they exchanged a look full of promise. As if compelled to make good on it immediately, Bridger wrapped his arm around her and pulled her against him. He kissed her more deeply still and she knew she should have been shocked, even shamed by his insistent tongue moving against hers, by the way his hand slid down to her hip and stayed there. Instead she was swept by a longing so huge, she put her arms around his neck and pressed her body into his.

Her heart became a wild thing within her chest, and she experienced a most delicious heat seeping into her body from his. An ache of arousal within her that hadn't made itself known in a long time now clamored for satisfaction.

"Oh, Bridger," she whispered, her eyes closed, her head tipped back while he kissed her throat. His lips moved down to the tops of her breasts and her heart stopped. The sound of a gunshot muffled by closed doors and smothered by the heat of passion didn't register in her mind until a terrifying scream sliced into her awareness.

Chapter Nineteen

The ensuing silence was so sudden and intense that the next gunshot sounded like a cannon burst followed by the sound of breaking glass. Shouts erupted, and screams intensified as they boiled up from the downstairs parlors.

Bridger bolted to the door and raced down the hall to the front of the house where the sounds were coming from. Sage, skirts gathered, hurried close behind. When she reached the balustrade overlooking the entrance foyer, she was stunned to see the magnificent crystal chandelier that had hung from the second story ceiling shattered into a million pieces on the floor below. The bullet that took it down was lodged in the pilaster framing the archway through which she and Bridger had just emerged.

Below, backed up against the inside of the front doors was a man, big as a bull, with massive shoulders. He stood in a posture of defiance, his muddy boots widespread, his arm clasped around Melanie's neck, forcefully holding her in front of him, the barrel of his gun pushed into her waist.

His clothes had seen rough wear. His coarse hair hung in disarray, and most of his face was covered with grey whiskers. Fury etched deep lines around his eyes, and they darted from side to side making him look like a cornered animal searching for an escape. He was a stranger, but despite the rage distorting his features, Sage thought she'd seen him somewhere before.

"Drop the gun," Bridger called down. His voice was strained, but calm. "No need for anyone to get hurt."

"Please don't shoot me," Melanie begged, her voice raspy, fear showing in her wide eyes.

"He already shot Odie," a man in the parlor yelled. The man had his arm around Odie's waist, supporting her. Odie was clasping her elbow to her side, biting back a wail of agony. Blood saturated her sleeve and she was grimacing in pain. She swooned and he caught her, lowered her to a settee. Sage caught a breath and made a move to go down to her, but Bridger's outflung arm stopped her.

Shock had frozen the others in place. The terrified Honeys, their eyes big and round, held their hands over their mouths, stifling screams in their throats. The men, all of whom were required to leave their guns in a locked box behind the bar, stood in helpless silence, weaponless, eager for an opportunity to leap forward and subdue the intruder, shock momentarily rooting their feet to the floor.

The man with the gun raised it to Melanie's head, and lifted his eyes to glare at Bridger. "Who are you?"

"I'm the marshal here, and I suggest you let her go, and then back right out that door and leave."

"I don't have business with you, Marshal. Stay out of it." The air around him crackled with his outrage.

"He's one of Preacher Fry's followers," someone said, and that's when Sage realized why he looked familiar. The last time she'd seen him, he was running toward her barn carrying a flaming torch.

"You best leave, mister." One of the men stepped boldly out of the parlor into the foyer, but halted when the gun veered in his direction.

"Hold it right there," the gunman snarled, "or I'll blow a hole right through ya." To show he meant business, he sent a bullet into one of the pink and burgundy fringed lamps on a sofa table, blowing it to pieces. Three men standing next to the sofa dove to the floor.

Melanie's eyes were squeezed tight shut, tears leaking out.

Bridger's hand slowly slid his coat aside and hovered over his holster, but the gunman caught the movement and swung his aim around to Bridger. "I said stay out of it. This is not your business."

Reluctantly, Bridger backed off. "All right," he said, holding his hands palms out, attempting to appease. His voice was placating. "Just calm down. Let loose of that girl, state your business and be gone. Leave these good people alone. What do you want?"

The wild-eyed man dragged his gaze over the terrified assemblage. "I want what's mine," he said in a reasonable tone of voice before bellowing, "Verbena!"

For an electric moment surprised gasps filled the air. Then came the hiss of shocked whispers.

"Verbena?"

"He wants Verbena."

"What does he want with her?"

"Verbena's not here," Sage called down to him, hoping the falter in her voice wouldn't reveal the lie. Her body quaked as sick fear washed through her.

"Get out of here old man," someone shouted. "We already ran you out of town once, we can do it again."

For a moment, the gunman looked uncertain. Beneath the whiskers, his face was square as a box with no chin to speak of, but the ferocity in his eyes was appalling. Then his mouth twisted.

"Somebody better bring me Verbena or somebody's gonna get hurt," he spat. His eyeballs jerked with frenetic energy as he looked around. His grip on Melanie tightened.

Sage felt Bridger's energy gather, trembling and waiting for the moment of release. Everyone seemed to be holding their breath, afraid the slightest movement or sound would send the man further over the edge and provoke him to start shooting.

"Verbena!" he roared again. "Where are you? Come down this instant, you harlot." His tone of voice and the look on his face indicated he wasn't going to leave until he got what he'd come for.

"What do you want with Verbena?" Bridger challenged mildly, trying to stall.

Sage could feel the nervous tension in his body vibrating on her skin. She could see the strain in his face. His brow was furrowed, his eyes narrowed. Was it her imagination, or was he moving with tectonic slowness toward the top of the stairs?

Before the man could answer, a door opened behind Sage. A hush fell. She turned to see Verbena walking slowly down the corridor carrying a book, her finger stuck between the pages as if holding the place where she'd stopped reading. Only the tinkle of the tiny bells around her ankle could be heard as she came to stand at the balustrade beside Sage. She stared down at the man holding the gun, looking at him with a face like an angry little fist.

"What are you doing here?"

The man's features seemed to melt, and in a voice fractured with emotion he replied, "I've come to take you home, honey."

Sage caught back a breath. Bridger tensed. The others stared, open-mouthed. Melanie wept silently.

Verbena's lips formed a bitter smile and she slowly shook her head back and forth as if he'd made a bad, sad joke. When she replied, her beautiful voice rattled like stones.

"How did you find me?"

A slow grin spread showing yellowed teeth, and his eyes lit. "I saw you. When I was here before. With Preacher Fry. I saw you standing in the doorway, behind that . . ." Suddenly, his mouth curved into a sneer and he motioned with his gun.

"That whore," he spat, meaning Sage.

Sage bit the inside of her mouth to keep from crying out and forced herself not to flinch. Instead she steeled her shoulders and moved her hand, closing it over Verbena's where it clung to the railing in a death grip.

"Do you know this man?" she asked her.

Verbena nodded and drew in a deep struggling breath. "His name's Thaddeus Werner," she said in a voice just above a whisper. "He's my father."

She stumbled on the word *father*, seeming to say it reluctantly, then closed her eyes as a single tear escaped from under her lashes. "I'm so ashamed," she whispered to Sage, throwing her hands over her face, letting the book fall to the floor.

But Thaddeus Werner heard her and choked out a nasty laugh.

"You're ashamed? Ha! I'm the one who's shamed. Too ashamed to step forward and claim you as my daughter in front of Preacher Fry. I didn't want those saintly people knowing my daughter had let herself be dragged into this kind of hell."

Verbena wiped her cheek with the back of her hand and glowered at him. Her eyes were wet with tears, sparking with pain and anger.

"This isn't hell," she said, stepping quickly to the top of the staircase where she pointed a shaking finger. "Living with you, that was hell," she said, impaling him with a venomous stare, moving slowly down the steps.

Sage drew in a breath and exchanged an anxious glance with Bridger. Verbena was inadvertently placing herself in Bridger's line of fire, ruining his chance at a clear shot if the opportunity arose.

"Your cruelty and vindictiveness filled our home. Your unforgiving, judgmental badgering. Your relentless punishments. That's what I remember from my childhood."

Werner looked at her in disbelief, the gun wobbling in his hand, momentarily forgotten. His stranglehold on Melanie loosened. She dropped to the floor and crawled frantically on her hands and knees to the safe embrace of those watching from the parlor. Werner didn't seem to notice as he stared open-mouthed at Verbena.

Verbena's voice grew louder as she spoke. "Here, no one beats me like you beat me and my brothers nearly every day. You beat poor mama half to death, then let her die having a baby."

Werner made a strangled sound deep in his throat and shook his head. Then, oddly, he ignored her accusation and spoke to her as if she were a small child and he a loving father.

"Come along, Verbena. We have to go now. I'm taking you home."

She shook her head, hard. "Get out, Pa. I'm not going anywhere with you."

Werner's face collapsed into sorrow, his whiskery cheeks flooding with tears. "Dear God, the devil has taken over your soul," he lamented. The hand holding the gun began to shake.

Deftly, while Werner's eyes were focused on Verbena, Bridger had edged himself along the railing to stand at the top of the stairs, his hand poised at his side. "Hold it right there, mister," Bridger called down, ready to draw.

Instantly, Werner collected himself, and with a violent motion swung the barrel of his gun until it was pointing directly at Bridger's chest. His finger tightened on the trigger.

"Don't touch your weapon, Marshal," he warned. "I got no qualms shootin' a lawman in this house of the devil."

Bridger froze, but didn't back away, and the two of them locked eyes over Verbena's head.

After several long moments that seemed like years, Werner broke eye contact, turning a beseeching gaze to his daughter.

"Verbena, come on down here. I'll take you home to your mama."

"You crazy old man!" she exclaimed scornfully. "My mama's dead. You killed her."

"NO!" Werner cried. "No, I didn't."

A fog of confusion swept his face, veiling his eyes, blanching the color from his cheeks. Then it ebbed away. "She got sick, is all. And then died. You know that," he insisted.

"No, Pa." Verbena's words came out thick with sorrow. "She wasn't sick. She was havin' a baby and you wouldn't go for the doctor."

"She didn't need no doctor," Werner scoffed, quarrelsome again. A muscle beside his eye began to twitch. He put a finger to it trying to get it to stop. "She had you and the others without a doctor," he pointed out, frustrated at her disregard of his logic.

"But she was having trouble." Verbena was weeping openly now, tears falling and staining the front of her dress. She continued to move down the stairway one slow step at a time. "You could see she was. We all saw she was." Unafraid, she stopped halfway and pointed to the door. "Leave, Pa, and don't come back anymore."

But Werner made no move to leave. Instead, he planted his feet and steadied the barrel of his gun at her. "You're comin' with me," he said, his voice low, filled with menace. "I didn't raise you to be no whore!"

"No? Well, you're the one who taught me everything I know," she shouted.

There was a massive intake of breath. Some of the women began to sob.

Werner's body stiffened and his face flamed red. Spittle sprayed when he spoke. "Why, you whore. You ungrateful trollop . . ." His finger curved on the trigger.

Verbena halted abruptly and for the first time showed fear.

Bridger snatched his gun from his holster and clutched it in his hand as he descended the stairs behind her. "I'm telling you for the last time, mister. Put the gun down." His voice was loud and commanding.

Verbena held up her hand and backed up a step. "Don't, Pa. Please don't shoot. I'm getting married and . . ."

Werner interrupted with savage contempt. "Married! What kind of a man would marry a tramp like you? You're nothin' but a whore and never was anything else."

His hand was shaking so hard he used his other one to hold the gun still, but there wasn't a glimmer of weakness showing in his eyes.

Staring at the gun pointed in her direction, Verbena pleaded with her father. "No, Daddy. Please don't. I'm going to have a baby . . ."

Suddenly, there was instant chaos as the front door flew open and Acer burst in followed by Cheveyo, Josiah Miller, Halstead Berger, and two other armed men. Werner, thrown off balance when the door slammed into him, stumbled forward trying to regain his footing.

Gun quickly holstered, Bridger bounded down the steps two at a time, his boots barely touching them. He landed on Werner, clamped his arm around the big man's neck and squeezed, but the huge body refused to go down. Josiah Miller and Halstead Berger piled on, and it took the three of them to force Werner to his knees. In the scuffle, the mahogany foyer table was knocked over sending a jade vase crashing through the stained glass sidelight next to the door.

Fighting wildly, Werner refused to give up, flailing his arms, the gun still in his hand. Some of the other men attempted to move in to help, but were forced to dodge around in a desperate attempt to avoid the line of fire. At last, Werner's big body was thrown to the floor where he landed with a thud. Someone booted him in the head knocking him unconscious. Someone else booted the pistol from his hand at the same time a bullet exploded from its barrel.

With a squeal of surprise and pain, Verbena pressed her hands to her stomach and dropped where she stood, crimson seeping between her fingers. She slid to the bottom of the staircase, her tiny ankle bells making a pitiful tinkling sound.

The rooms erupted into pandemonium, an explosion of panicked activity. Everyone seemed to move at once with no clearly defined purpose. Talking, screaming, sobbing, swearing. Sage scrambled to where Verbena lay crumbled into a heap, blood pooling around her, but Acer got there first, scooping the young girl into his arms.

"No!" he shouted. "No!" He lowered his head, kissing her forehead over and over. "Verbena!" "Verbena! Please honey, don't leave me! Don't! Please don't die!"

Verbena's eyelashes fluttered closed and her head slumped against his chest. Her arms hung limp as Acer clutched her to him unmindful of the blood pouring from her stomach. Holding her tight, rocking back and forth, his cries were tormented.

Tears poured from his eyes, dripped from his nose and chin, but he ignored them and held on, pulling her closer. He tucked her onto his lap, wrapping himself around her petite frame as if trying to take her up into his own body. His sobs were the mournful sounds of a wild animal howling in agony.

Someone had gone for Doc Holden who now hurried in with the undertaker. They tried to ease Verbena away from Acer so they could look at her, but Acer shoved them roughly away and swore at them, screaming, making a fist, striking out.

Sage put a hand to her mouth, a sob escaped her burning throat. Tears blurred her vision, and she swayed, putting her hand against the wall to steady herself. Bridger saw and rushed to put his arm around her shoulders.

The men dragged Werner out the door and the panic in the room began to subside. Everyone turned to look at Acer, momentarily sharing his grief as he cradled Verbena's lifeless body. A few quickly lowered their eyes or turned away, embarrassed at the rawness of his emotion as he made no attempt to hide his pain.

Doc Holden stood there, head bowed, big hands hanging helplessly at his side, not knowing what to do. Everyone was staring in shocked disbelief.

Sage moved away from Bridger to kneel beside the sobbing deputy. Gently she enfolded his head in her arms and tucked it into her shoulder, crooning softly into his ear.

"Let them take her," she whispered. "Please, Acer. Let them prepare her for God's hands."

A long moment later, Acer sniffed, then got to his knees, tenderly holding Verbena in his arms. He stood, slowly carrying Verbena like a child, her body limp as a rag doll, and walked out the front door without a word. Doc Holden and the solemn-faced undertaker followed assisting Odie, one man on each side. She was white-faced with pain and loss of blood.

When they were gone, Sage's teary gaze tracked slowly around the room going from face to face. Shoulders heaving in an attempt to control her sobs, she swept the room with her arm.

"Get out!" she said, her voice hoarse and agonizingly strained. "Anyone who doesn't live here, get out! Wild Mountain Honey is closed for business. So get out! Now!"

* * * * *

The darkness of night pressed down on the windows of Sage's living quarters, and the chill that always comes just before dawn crept into her bones despite the roaring fire in the hearth. She was on the divan wrapped in a blanket staring at the flames. She was thinking about Verbena and how full of joy she'd been. Her impish face. The clear sweet sound of her voice when she sang. How she played the flute, and sometimes danced and twirled with bone castanets, delighting everyone who watched her.

A single convulsive sob wracked up from her chest, but she forced it back down. This was not a time for weakness. This was a time for strength.

The remains of her dinner with Bridger had been cleared away by Miss Priscilla, and the candles still burned low. It seemed a lifetime had passed since they'd been lovingly lit by Odie.

Footsteps sounded on the stairs. It was Bridger. She'd asked him to come back later, and had left the kitchen door open for him. He came in quietly and she made room for him beside her. He sat, moving slowly as if every bone and muscle in his body ached with fatigue. Shadows suffused his troubled face.

"How's Odie?" he asked.

"Sleeping. Miss Priscilla is sitting with her."

He nodded, then gazed solemnly at the flames flickering on the hearth.

"Where's Werner?" Sage asked after a moment.

"At the jail."

"Is he all right?"

There was a long pause. "He died on the way," Bridger answered finally, without explanation.

Sage took this to mean he might have been helped along. She closed her eyes and a shudder passed through her.

"What about Acer?"

"He's pretty tore up. Doc gave him something to settle him, but I doubt it'll do any good. It'll take some time, but he'll make it. He's young and strong."

She swallowed painfully, her throat tight with sorrow. She had to let some time go by before she could speak again.

"I can't do this, Bridger."

He didn't reply, just sat there with his elbows on his knees, looking at the fire, the reflection of the flames dancing in his eyes. He dragged in a long breath, then let it seep out slowly through his nose. His lips were tight, his face grim.

The fire crackled and a log fell, throwing up a small shower of sparks.

"If the men in this town won't set the standards," she declared softly, "I will." The words came out confident and assured, but inside she felt defeated.

Bridger leaned back and turned to her, opening his mouth to say something. She put her fingers to his lips stopping his words. "I don't want your opinion, Bridger. And I don't want to argue. There's only one thing I want now."

He looked at her, questioning.

"Hold me," she said. "Just hold me, nothing else."

He softened his features and moved closer as she opened the blanket and folded him in it beside her. He wrapped both arms around her and held tight. Her head was on his chest. She could feel him breathe, hear his heartbeat.

"I'm so cold," she whispered, shivering, and he tightened his arms.

They sat in silence until she said, "This is all my fault."

Bridger took a breath to say something, but she went on before he could. "I should have closed this place long ago. Wild Mountain Honey has done nothing but cause trouble and pain for everyone."

Bridger gently put his lips to her hair, but otherwise didn't move or speak. The fire crackled and sparked on the hearth. Coyotes took up a song somewhere far off in the mountains.

She put a hand to his chest, letting her fingers linger as if to draw warmth from his strength. A shiver fluttered through her again and she sighed. "I don't think spring will ever come," she said, sadly.

Chapter Twenty

Sage held the door open at the rear of the bathhouse. "Hurry," she whispered as the wind whipped ice particles inside. A swirling grey mist had hovered over the town for days culminating in this early spring snowstorm.

Hattie Murphy, Violet Gallagher, and Ellen Berger, having finished their baths, hurried out holding on to their bonnets as wind billowed their cloaks around their bodies. Faces lowered against biting gusts and snow that stung their cheeks, they followed Sage through the darkness to the back door of Wild Mountain Honey where Miss Priscilla welcomed them into her warm kitchen.

Nervous conversation ensued as the ladies stomped their boots and shook wet snow from their woolen wraps before hanging them on hooks in the storage room. A fire burned on the kitchen hearth sending a warm glow through the room. The ladies moved near it, holding their hands toward the flame to ease the cold from their fingers.

"Natalie is waiting upstairs," Sage told them. "Tonight she'll be teaching make up, grooming and comportment."

Hattie and Ellen gathered their skirts and headed up the stairs.

Violet Gallagher screwed her face into a grimace. "This corset doesn't fit right. It's killing me," she complained. "I can't breathe."

"Chantal can take measurements and re-fit you a new one," Sage told her. "She's copied a new pattern out of Godey's, and can make it for you in aubergine with an ivory lace trim. I think you'd like it."

"Thank the Lord." Tugging at her corset, Violet fell in behind Harriet and Ellen and followed them up to the comfortably furnished anteroom.

"Don't forget," Miss Priscilla called after them. "Table manners and dinner conversation when everyone is finished with their corset fittings."

"We won't forget," they replied, after which their voices were lost in a chorus of greetings as they were welcomed by the early arrivals.

"Why don't you go on up?" Miss Priscilla said to Sage. "I'll wait in the bathhouse in case anyone else arrives."

"Thank you. And will you send Sarabeth over? She wanted to participate." Sarabeth was the lady barber Sage had hired to perform tonsorial services in the bathhouse.

"I will," Miss Priscilla said, wrapping herself in her cloak.

Sage went up to join the others.

In the anteroom, chairs had been arranged in rows class room style facing a table where Natalie stood smiling and greeting each arrival by name. As one of the more mature Honeys, her calm demeanor served to ease much of their apprehension. For most of the women, it was their first time within the walls of Wild Mountain Honey. Sage knew it was only natural they were bringing whole buckets of misgivings along with them.

She smoothed the back of her skirt and took a seat along the wall next to Odie. Petticoats rustled and chairs scraped as the ladies settled in. A hum of quiet conversation filled the room as everyone waited for Natalie to begin her class.

Before Sage came to Fairplay Creek, she'd heard it said that women and horses had a hard time of it in these far-flung mining towns. Now that she was living here, she'd have to say that horses had it far easier. They were fed, sheltered and cared for with great regard and rarely left to fend for themselves, unlike most of the women. The West was full of women whose youth had been burned away by the struggle to survive both the climate and the harsh living conditions, not to mention the force of their men's characters.

But cowards didn't come to the New West, Sage reminded herself. It took courage and passion and determination.

As a result, the women were forced to become resourceful in order to make it through. They had to develop a certain toughness, become self-reliant and inventive if they were to survive. Unfortunately, those were the very characteristics that disturbed the menfolk who were used to being in charge and running everything, including the lives of those same women.

For that reason, Sage had implemented her plan in secrecy to avoid the inevitable conflict that would assure her failure. Discretion was vital. The men wouldn't have understood and would certainly have felt threatened by any show of feminine assembly, seeing it as a sort of rebellion. But Sage was determined that something needed to be done to bring enlightenment to this community. Money didn't seem to be enough. There was plenty of money around, but obviously money alone didn't bring civility. It was apparent something else needed to be done to cultivate refinement and provide a moral compass to the residents of Fairplay Creek.

When the parlor house was shuttered after Verbena's death, Sage had offered a salary to any of the Honeys who would stay on and help implement her plan. Her bank accounts were flush, thanks to Odie's efficient running of the house. Her mining investments with Josiah Miller and the others were paying off, significantly enhancing her personal assets. She was in a position to give back to the community that had helped her to prosper by raising the status of the women who lived and suffered there. That, in turn, would benefit the entire town in the long run.

She had gathered the Honeys and presented an idea how that could be done.

"You are all accomplished in the art of love and seduction," she'd told them. "I'd like you to teach those very skills to the women in this town. If you will share your proficiencies with them, you'll all be handsomely rewarded later."

Most of the Honeys agreed to stay on, but a few of them left, choosing instead to return to their families, or move to some other house in some other mining town. To help them get started, Sage gave them money for transportation out on the stage that had begun a twice weekly run to Denver. She was eternally grateful to the others who stayed, knowing she would not be able to carry out her plan without them. They worked together for weeks laying out a strategy.

Sage hadn't seen Bridger but briefly, and only in passing since winter had unpacked its wildest punch. Caught up in the fist of a Rocky Mountain winter, most of the miners had temporarily quit working their claims. With the parlor house closed, they spent all of their time in the saloons and gambling houses, or passed out drunk at home.

And just as Bridger had warned, lawlessness escalated. He and his deputies were beleaguered trying to keep it under control. Thievery and hold ups took place in broad daylight. Playful gunfire was not so playful anymore. Public drunkenness, always a problem, had intensified, and was now supplemented by fights and random shootings. The men were edgy, quick to draw down on a fellow miner in a saloon, or on a gambler across the card table over some real or imagined affront.

Acer, grieving the death of Verbena, was no exception. He walked around like someone had hollowed out his insides making him meaner than a wild dog, and more than eager to take his pain out on the lawbreakers. Everyone pretty much understood that was something that could happen to anyone whose beloved had died in his arms. They mostly stayed out of his way.

Sage held on to her grief, too, would not let go of it, because to do so was to accept what happened to Verbena. She had no intentions of accepting it, and she wasn't going to forget it, either. She found strength in her grief and anger, the strength to go on. To make change.

Hattie Murphy was instrumental in helping Sage spread the word, secretly of course, about the charm school classes at Wild Mountain Honey. Hattie convinced the five women who regularly attended town board meetings to sit in on a class or two, and decide for themselves how beneficial they were. Finding them favorable, those women whispered into the ears of other women, and soon not only were town wives attending, but their older daughters, too. Eventually, the few unmarried women in Fairplay Creek asked to be included.

Surprisingly, the logistics of keeping it clandestine weren't difficult to work out. Sage simply designated certain nights as ladies only at the bathhouse. That way if anyone asked or got suspicious, an explanation was ready. The women were simply going to bathe, which they did, but afterwards gathered at Wild Mountain Honey for lessons on grace and manners and seduction. That the women arrived home later than usual was neither noticed nor remarked on by absent or inebriated husbands rendered unconscious by strong drink.

Those attending for the first time usually arrived alone, nervous and unsure if they should be there, anxious about where it would lead. Those who returned brought a friend or neighbor. Now, after only a few weeks, the room was filled and Sage felt gratified as she watched the ladies quietly chatting and welcoming newcomers with feminine affection. She spied Estella Gardner, the banker's wife, present for the first time, sitting alone off to the side. Deep lines of disapproval showed on her face.

But at least she came, thought Sage, remembering how she'd endured Estella's harsh glares of condemnation whenever they had passed in the street. Estella may have come across as cranky and cantankerous but like all the other women there, she loved her husband, wanted to keep him, and was willing to learn something new to accomplish that.

Natalie, self-assured and graceful, stood at the front of the room and lightly clapped her hands. The chatter died away and all eyes turned to her.

"Welcome, ladies." Her smile was wide and genuine. "If it's your first time here, thank you for coming. If you've already attended one of our classes, thank you for coming back." She scanned the faces. "And I see we do have some newcomers tonight. I've posted the class schedule in the kitchen, so please take note of it before you leave. Our class tonight is on clothing and personal grooming. And please remember. All our classes are free. Shall we get started?"

Heads bobbed eagerly.

"All right," she began. "The number one rule that should govern your appearance whether at home or on the street is tidiness. Ladies, please keep in mind that untidy habits and an untidy appearance are most displeasing to the eye."

Some of the ladies shifted uncomfortably in their chairs. A low buzz swept the room as a flurry of hands surreptitiously straightened collars and cuffs, and fingers quickly swept stray locks in place.

"Make an effort to see that your clothes are well-fitting and in good repair. Shabby, basted, and pinned together seams and closures are decidedly in bad taste."

Natalie's kind eyes scanned the gathering. "We must be tidy, tidy, tidy. Your self-respect," and here she paused, holding up a finger for emphasis, "and, ladies, your self respect is important!—demands the decent appareling of your body. You should make a point to look as well as you can, even when you are alone. There is no better enhancer of self-respect than to be properly adorned, and by that I mean clean and neat, wearing fabrics of beautiful color."

"Well, I don't have a closet full of finery," said Penelope Parker, one of three female miners who had trudged up to Fairplay Creek to stake out and work claims last summer. Her voice was as gravelly as the dirt she dug.

"Me, neither," put in Jonelle Brownlee, another woman miner who kept a shack in town.

A chorus of voices joined in. "I sure don't . . ." "Not me." "I only have three dresses to my name."

"Even if you only have one frock, it's imperative that it be as neat and appealing as if it were made of silk and satin. And don't forget to keep your linens and hosiery clean and mended," Natalie added.

There was a disconcerted mumble.

"I know it takes time, ladies. Yes, indeed it does, but the results will make it all worth while. You'll see."

"My husband doesn't give me any extra money for fine fabrics of beautiful colors you speak of," complained one of the wives. She was wearing a frumpy brown dress pinned together at the bodice, its hem hanging in tatters.

Sage knew this woman's husband. She'd invested in his mine and was aware of exactly how much it was producing. He had plenty of money. He just had to be convinced to part with it.

Sage encouraged the frustrated woman. "If you practice the skills you learn here," she said, "your husband will be more than happy to provide you with whatever you need to keep yourself attractive." I'll see to that, Sage declared silently.

The woman, only half convinced, gave a skeptical nod and turned back to Natalie as she went on.

"Make it a point to examine every garment when it comes out of the wash and if needed, mend it then and there. Never use pins to replace missing buttons. And, ladies, pay attention to your bonnets. Make sure they suit your face."

"What do you mean?" asked Gardenia Fortney, the fortune teller who had set up a shop next to the Land Office. "What kind of bonnet would suit my face?"

Natalie studied the woman through narrowed eyes. "Well, you have a long slender face, so be sure to select a bonnet with a soft brim that is wider at the sides than at the top."

Gardenia nodded her thanks.

"For you ladies with a broad or round shape to your face, you'll want a wider brim with trimmings arranged high rather than over the ears. And ladies," Natalie reminded, "plump throats require narrow ties under the chin. Wide ties will crinkle and fold unattractively into excess skin on the neck."

At this, the stouter ladies squirmed and lowered their eyes, uncomfortable at the mention of an overabundance of flesh.

Natalie noticed and added quickly. "Plumpness in and of itself is not a deterrent to grace and charm if the beauty regimes we're talking about are used. The main thing is not to emphasize plump figures by wearing unbecoming bodices and skirts that are too tight. Ruffles and gentle folds of fabric disguise fullness around the middle. And high sleeves and trimmings carried up to the shoulder tend to draw a man's eye up, thereby increasing your height and diminishing fullness of body."

There were nods of satisfaction and relief. Some of the ladies took a few notes, others were writing furiously.

"I think we all have made bathing a habit by now, at least most of us have and if not, it is an absolute must for good grooming. But between visits to the bathhouse, vigorous attention should be made to make sure nails are not rimmed with black, and hair isn't full of dust."

"How are we supposed to keep dust out of our hair?" croaked Margery Moffett, the third female miner. "Except for wintertime, the air is filled with it."

"Brushing," explained Natalie. "Brushing is the safest and most economical method of removing dust from your hair between your weekly washings. If you can't afford to buy hair brushes from the general store, Sage has kindly offered to provide one for each of you."

Thankful smiles were directed at Sage along with a smattering of appreciative handclaps. Sage nodded politely, acknowledging their gratitude.

"And to add some extra shine to your hair, rinse with rain water or vinegar, both of which are readily available for free or at very little cost. Home made apple cider as a rinse works fine."

Heads bent, the note takers scribbled feverishly.

"Clean your teeth daily and keep your breath sweet. Pete Gallagher carries tooth cleaning powder and toothbrushes at his General Store, so there is no excuse for not doing it. No man wants to kiss a mouth that smells, or is foul from disease. If you can't afford to buy tooth cleaning products, use common table salt or crumbs from burnt bread. A little vinegar does a fine job of removing stains."

Ellen Berger raised her hand and spoke up.

"During our trip here from Ohio, we used ashes from the fire on twigs of sage to clean our teeth. Not as pleasant, but it was all we had and it did the job."

A rumble of dissent began. Sage spoke.

"That won't be necessary, ladies. I'll provide toothbrushes and tooth cleaning products for everyone."

A chorus of thank-yous rose, and more hand clapping louder this time.

"Now for makeup." Natalie picked up a tin of powder. "Easy with the powder puff, ladies. Use it lightly and with a gentle hand. Like this." She demonstrated, gently tapping powder onto her beautiful face. "A hairpin steeped in lampblack can be used to darken and outline the eyes. I'll show you." Looking into a mirror propped up on the table, she began making up her eyes.

"But I don't want to look like a Jezebel." Estella Gardner's snooty voice resounded through the room. "Or a . . ."

Abruptly she cut off her comments and stared at Natalie, then at Sage and the other Honeys in the room. "Or a lady of the night," she finished, lowering her eyes, her face flaming.

Not in the least offended, Natalie smiled reassuringly at the banker's wife. "Looking attractive doesn't mean looking like a Jezebel. We can show you how to use cosmetics to get your man's attention and keep it. That's the main thing we want, isn't it?"

Estella gave a little nod, looking like she was embarrassed to even entertain such a thought as that, as if there was something shameful about wanting to keep her man to herself.

"We all know what Natalie says is true," said Hattie Murphy, standing up to face the others, but making her point to Estella. "Our men have been paying a lot more attention to the ladies of Wild Mountain Honey than they ever have to us. Let's learn from Natalie and the others. Now that I've come to know them, they're not much different from us. They're women trying to make it in a man's world, and a harsh environment to boot. I, for one, intend to listen to what they have to say if for no other reason than to make my life easier. I want to keep my husband's eyes on me. These ladies are willing to tell me how to do that, and I'm grateful for it."

Applause and murmurs of agreement followed. "Me, too." "I, as well."

The woman sitting next to Estella took her hand and patted it gently, one woman to another in understanding.

Natalie continued. "The hands of time leave marks on all our faces, no one is exempt. But there is no need to have them placed there prematurely. To fortify against wrinkles, always wash your face in cold water. Add a little bran to the water and rub with a towel for extra glow. That's what I do and I am often complimented on my smooth skin."

"Is there any way to get rid of freckles?" someone wanted to know. It was Clara, the fortune teller's fourteen-year-old daughter.

Natalie's eyes softened as she smiled at the young girl. "Why would you want to? Freckles can be very attractive. Take a look at Melanie." Everyone did, agreeing she looked beautiful and fresh.

"And they're lovely on you, too," Natalie pointed out to Clara. "But if you really want to get rid of them, mix a little lemon juice with milk and apply to your skin at night."

Clara nodded shyly, slouching down in her chair.

"But never, never, never," Natalie admonished the wives, "let your husbands see you do these things. Oh, he may get pleasure from it once or twice, but before long he will find no arousal from seeing you soap your ears, rub bran and milk on your face, twist your hair into curls with rags, or other unlovely essentials to your grooming. His attention should be bestowed on you as the result of these ministrations, not while you perform them."

Everyone nodded, seeming to see the good sense in that.

"Now," Natalie went on, "Odie is going to talk about exercise."

"We get plenty of that," said Nelwyn Foster. She was married to Malachi, the blacksmith. Sage had seen Nelwyn helping her husband in his smithy shop. The woman did strenuous work every single day.

"Well, I'm going to talk about fun exercise, not drudgery," Odie explained, stepping to the front of the room while Natalie took a seat.

Odie faced the women, her hands folded primly at her waist. "The best way to put a fine glow on your face is by exercise," she began. "Take a vigorous walk or run each day to energize and tone your body.

Running strengthens abdominal muscles, so lift your feet high like a spirited horse.

"As you fine tune your body, you can add skipping to your daily exercise. Just don't jump too high or overdo it and be afflicted by perspiration. Otherwise you'll have to take an extra bath or at the very least, wash your face and neck and underarms, and your, um, private parts."

Odie was interrupted by a titter of embarrassment that swept the room.

"Now, now, ladies," Odie chided. "If you can't bring yourselves to think about your private parts, or talk about them without awkwardness at the appropriate time, of course, you won't be able to put into practice the skills Turtledove is going to teach you. She's going to be very specific in her lessons on seduction."

The titters morphed into giggles and hands flew, nervously covering lips or eyes.

Turtledove spoke up from the corner of the room. "How many of you ladies think of sex as vulgar?" she asked.

Slowly, hands inched up until nearly every arm was raised.

"There's too much hullabaloo made about it anyway," piped up Estella.

"Well, let's face it ladies, sex is important to men. That's why places like this thrive." Turtledove gestured to where they were gathered. "Men want and need a woman who knows how to pleasure them. That's why they came here. And that's what we're going to teach you so you can keep them in your bed."

"Some scientists are even saying that sex is essential for good health," Emma Ford offered timorously.

"Oh, pshaw! Who's saying that?" grumbled Estella.

"Well, I don't remember his name, but he wrote a report about it."

"I read it in Godey's," Hattie said. "The editor, Mrs. Hale wrote an editorial suggesting the same thing."

"Really?" someone asked. The others looked around with raised eyebrows as if seeking confirmation from an expert.

"We must let go of our finger-wagging prissiness when it comes to having sex with our husbands," admonished Turtledove. "You must encourage him to say anything to you, and you must not react with outrage when he does. What happens in the privacy of your bedroom, as long as it is not hurtful to either one, should not be gilded with the stain of wrongdoing.

"In my class, you're going to learn about men's bodies, and about your own. The Honeys are going to tell you where and how to touch a man that will give him such pleasure, he won't ever think about going to a parlor house again.

"And, the pleasure is not all his, ladies. There are ways he can give you pleasure, too. It's up to you to tell him what they are."

After a few startled gasps of disbelief, a hush fell in the room until Violet Gallagher spoke up.

"Pete rolls on me like a log," she complained.

"Be patient," Turtledove said. "Under the Honeys' tutoring, sex may eventually satisfy your soul as well as your body. Sex is a sacred expression of devotion and elevated love distinct from the lust they exhibited with the Honeys. It's a natural desire given by God, and the body is the intended means by which to express it. It can and should be a joyous experience using the right love techniques."

"There are techniques?" Penelope asked, her voice pitched up to a squeak of surprise.

"Yes. You'll learn how to touch a man in a way that will give him pleasure and enhance his desire for you."

The reaction from the ladies to this pronouncement was decidedly dubious.

"Haven't any of you ever touched your man for his pleasure?"

Eyes quickly lowered and there was a general clearing of throats and shuffling of feet until someone finally spoke up.

"I did once," said Penelope. All eyes flew in her direction.

"It felt like a turkey wattle," she said.

The room erupted in a thunderclap of laughter that went on and on until the ladies were wiping tears from their cheeks. Young Clara's cheeks flamed and she looked like she wished the floor would open up and swallow her whole. "It looks like a turkey wattle, too," put in Sarabeth, trying to catch her breath, her words impeded by an uncontrollable giggle.

"Well, then you aren't doing it right," said Turtledove. "We'll talk about that next time." She waited for the hilarity to die down before continuing.

"All right. If there are no questions, we'll go on to talk about carriage and grace. Quite a few of the town ladies have already taken this class and you may have noticed them on the street."

"Yes, I saw Bonnie Lee Addelson the other day," declared Pitty Redmond. "She walked down the street as if she owned the world. She looked like she was floating on air, like her feet weren't even touching the ground. And the men stopped to stare as she went by."

"So it seems our teachings are working," said Odie.

"How can we learn to walk that way?" asked Jonelle.

"Posture, ladies. Exquisite posture that is achieved by standing and walking mindfully. Hold yourself erect with your chin well away from your chest and look straight ahead," Odie replied. "Don't plod. Don't mince. Swing your legs smoothly from the hip. Carry yourself with pride and confidence. Every woman is enhanced by graceful movement. Keep your arms pressed lightly against your sides when walking or sitting. This might feel a little stiff at first, but with practice will become easy and natural.

"Also, cultivate your manners and avoid slang. Men look with reverence upon a woman who has a discreet, well-modulated voice. Never speak loudly in his presence unless your house is on fire. Practice a low, clear tone of voice with an easy conversational manner.

"And, ladies, this is of utmost importance. Never find fault with your man, or what he does, unless you do it lovingly and preclude it with a kiss. Refrain from continually reminding him of his mistakes. And never part from him without saying loving words even if you have to say them through clenched teeth."

This brought nods and grins of mutual understanding from everyone.

"Always ensure that when he comes upon you, there is delight in the meeting. Greet him with a loving smile. Men like to be petted and soothed. Remember. What men want most—"

"Besides sex, you mean?" interrupted Hattie Murphy.

Quiet laughter started up again, and there were knowing grins.

"Yes," put in Melanie from the back of the room. "Besides sex, what men want most is to be listened to. Believe it or not, ladies, that's another reason they liked coming to Wild Mountain Honey. When they had a tale of woe or a boast whether real or imagined, they poured it into our ears because we listened patiently and responded kindly."

"Always laugh at his jokes," added Chantal. "Even if you've heard the story a dozen times before."

"And, remember this above all else. You'll never gain a man's affection with complaints, reproaches, or sullen behavior," Odie concluded.

"Here, here," hailed Violet, as the women began gathering their things to leave.

"Please try to come back tomorrow night. Poppy Merriweather will demonstrate how to dress for adornment instead of concealment using intimate apparel. Chantal and Colorado Kate have been busy on the sewing machines creating lovely new designs. Those who haven't already taken that class, come prepared to be measured and fitted for lingerie and nightgowns."

"Now it's time to take what you've learned and put it into practice out there. Smile, everyone," Sage reminded, "and stand up straight!"

Chapter Twenty-One

The bitter spring storm that had unexpectedly frosted noses and numbed toes was gone by Sunday. In its place was sunshine so bright, the green sheen of new growth on the lower elevations was incandescent. Tree branches previously bare and encased in thick coats of ice now sprouted tiny new leaves on their tips. The scent of pine, heady and pungent, perfumed the air. And as if directed by a Divine hand, this glorious transformation took place just in time for the first Sunday service of the Fairplay Creek Community Church, held in the recently completed schoolhouse.

The brass bell that summoned students to classes on weekdays now beckoned folks seeking fellowship and spiritual unity. Townspeople and miners, individually or in small groups, made their way up a gentle grassy rise on foot or by horseback, in wagons or on mules. Some came willingly, some reluctantly, others were dragged—Miss Priscilla's firm grip on Cheveyo's shoulder made him wince as she marched him up the path—but they all arrived with some measure of anticipation and curiosity to hear the first sermon ever to be said in Fairplay Creek.

Inside, the schoolhouse smelled of new wood, the walls, beams and rafters still unfinished. Dark oak benches gleamed with several coats of fresh varnish, brand new Bibles and hymnals tucked onto slatted shelves beneath the seats. Pastor Jared Pickett, looking properly pious in a handsome new suit, white pleated-front shirt, and black string tie stood on a raised platform at the front of the chapel, his expression pleased and a little surprised at the turnout.

Butterflies in Sage's stomach felt like a herd of stampeding buffalo as she entered with the modestly, though tastefully dressed Honeys. Their entrance into the house of worship stirred up plenty of attention. A low murmur started and the congregation openly stared as the Honeys glided primly up the aisle to take seats on the benches Sage had permanently reserved in the name of Wild Mountain Honey. She glanced around before settling into her seat, and noticed with pleasure that the ladies who'd been secretly attending her charm school had learned their lessons well.

Estella Gardner, wearing a new tie-down bonnet with a narrow ribbon forming a bow under her chin, strode in with husband Martin, her hand resting lightly in the bend of his arm. The familiar scowl was gone from her face, and in its place was an expression of supreme self-satisfaction, her lightly blushed lips quirked in a smug smile.

Following in their wake, Waylon Clarke walked proudly if a little bewildered beside his wife Laura, her head tilted at an angle that best showed off her long graceful neck. Beautifully draped in a fringed paisley shawl, her impeccable posture turned admiring heads as she passed.

Violet Gallagher smiled a greeting at Sage and gracefully took a seat across the aisle. When she slid down the bench and pulled her skirts aside to make room for Pete, Sage caught a glimpse of pale purple petticoat ruffle peeking out from under the hem.

A smile played around Sage's mouth. The ladies looked utterly charming and just as she'd hoped, notice was being taken. But it was only the beginning. The next step of her plan would surely turn the town upside down.

A tap on her shoulder interrupted her thoughts and she turned to see Penelope, Margery and Jonelle, the three women miners, sitting behind her. All three flashed smiles and fluttered their fingers in hello. Penelope still had her hair pulled back in a bun, but looser and piled on top of her head. Margery's face was lightly dusted with powder making her skin look youthful and translucent. Jonelle, brushing delicately at her skirt, was sneaking demure peeks from under lowered lashes at Rodney

Weatherspoon seated two rows away. Her freshly shampooed hair hung in soft golden curls down her back. Rodney couldn't take his eyes off her.

Sage felt compelled to let her gaze drift around the room, scanning the faces, looking for Bridger, but he wasn't there and she turned away disappointed. It had been weeks since she'd last seen him, coming out of his office, their eyes meeting across the crowded street. He looked exhausted and in a hurry, but crossed the street and made his way toward her.

"I've been meaning to come up to see you," he'd begun, "but . . ."

"I know," she'd interrupted. "You're busy."

He'd nodded, weariness churning behind his eyes. "I'd like us to have dinner together again some time."

For a split second, she'd had the urge to grip the front of his coat, pull him toward her and plant a kiss on his mouth. But she'd let the moment pass hoping it wouldn't be a moment she'd forever look back on with regret.

"Yes," she'd said. "I'd like that, too."

But it hadn't happened, and a hole had opened up in her heart.

Pastor Pickett snapped the lid of his watch closed and slipped it back into his coat pocket. The room quieted as he stepped to the pulpit, his face beaming. He began by thanking everyone for coming, then offered blessings, and led prayers for peace, prosperity and healing. The sermon that followed was filled with inspiring Bible passages of love and hope for the future of the church, the town and the townspeople. When he was finished, members of the congregation were so moved by his stirring words, they openly applauded him. The collection plate after making its rounds brimmed with coins, bills and nuggets, proof, Sage realized, of just how deeply folks were yearning for spiritual fulfillment.

As parishioners filed out, congratulating and shaking hands with Pastor Pickett at the door, Sage felt a wash of relief when she spotted Bridger standing with Ramsey Thorogood on the front lawn. They looked like they were having a disagreement, their gestures abrupt, their words chopped off as they interrupted each other. Both men turned to look at her, then hurriedly ended their conversation. Bridger gazed at her for several seconds, shoulders slumped. He didn't look well. Was he drinking again?

She started in his direction, but Ramsey hurried forward, cutting her off.

"Good morning, Sage," he said, tipping his hat. He too looked weary, his voice strained.

"Good morning, Mr. Thorogood. Did you enjoy the service?" she asked politely. She felt a twinge of disappointment when over his shoulder, she saw Bridger mount up and rein his horse in the opposite direction. He glanced back once, then nudged the bay into trot and away.

"Indeed. Pastor Pickett and the church are welcome additions to our community. Everyone is sincerely grateful for your generosity."

"Completely my pleasure," said Sage.

"Yes," Ramsey replied, distracted. A lull followed. His fingers tapped a rhythm around the brim of his hat and his eyes wandered, refusing to meet hers. Finally, he took a quick peek over his shoulder as if making sure no one was listening, and stepped closer.

"I was wondering if I could speak to you a moment about a matter of great importance."

"Why certainly," she said, "Is there a problem?"

"Well, yes, there is," he replied. "You're aware that the railway company has been looking at Fairplay Creek for some time now, considering it as a location for a major railway stop."

"Yes. I'm aware of that."

"And the stage line is talking about expanding the route beyond Fairplay Creek and building a transfer station here or somewhere nearby."

"Yes, I'm aware of that, too."

He hesitated and cleared his throat.

"Is there a problem?" she asked again.

"Yes, there is a significant problem. It seems both the stage line and the railroad executives considering those projects are on the verge of withdrawing their offers on the land they were going to purchase."

"Oh, dear," Sage replied, arranging her features in a great show of compassion. He didn't have to explain to her what it meant if that were to happen. His comfortably feathered nest would rapidly fray. She let the silence lengthen, waiting for him to go on.

"The reason they're reconsidering is they feel that Fairplay Creek has become too lawless, rowdy, unstable."

"That's certainly true," she agreed.

"They're afraid folks might not be safe in Fairplay Creek. You know, company management wouldn't want to move their families here to live. And there are passenger liability concerns, as well."

"I see." She paused. "Perhaps you should hire more law enforcement."

"That's one solution," he conceded, his fingers jiggling on his hat again, "but I'm afraid that's not going to solve the problem on a long term basis."

She raised her eyebrows and waited for him to get to the point.

"I have considerable investments connected to the railroad coming here. I, and others," he added quickly, "will be hurt financially, quite severely, if the railroad pulls out of the deal."

"Oh," she said, on a long breath. Her tone was sympathetic and concerned. "Can I help in some way?"

His face lit with hope. "Yes," he said. "As a matter of fact, you could help greatly by re-opening Wild Mountain Honey."

Surprised, Sage's mouth fell open, but before she could reply, Ramsey hurried on.

"I'm prepared to offer you something in return."

"I don't need money, Mr. Thorogood. Though the construction costs of the school were great, I'm far from bankrupt."

"I'm aware of that," he assured her. "It's not money I'm offering you."

"Oh?"

"I'm offering you a position on the town council."

She was totally unprepared for that, but compressed her lips and recovered her composure. "Do you mean to say that if I reopen my place, you're willing to allow me to have some say in how this town is run?"

"Y-yes," he replied, but she could tell it wouldn't be easy for him.

Sage arranged her face into a thoughtful expression. "Well, I don't know," she replied doubtfully, and watched his new found hope abandon him. "I have been thinking about remodeling and redecorating the house. If I decide to accept your offer, would you have a problem if I changed the decor?"

"No, no. Not at all," he said, brightening again. "I understand it's been some time since the furnishings have been replaced."

"Yes, that's so," she agreed. "And I'm wondering if a name change might be in order, too," she added. "Would you object to that?" she asked coyly.

"No, not at all," he said, fairly dancing in place with excitement. "Does that mean you'll consider it?"

"No, Mr. Thorogood. I'll do more than consider it. I'll do it. That is, if I can have the time required to refurbish the establishment."

Thorogood grabbed her hand in both of his and shook it up and down. "Certainly, Miss Cane," he said. "Take all the time you need. Just so I can assure the investors that the lawlessness in Fairplay Creek will end soon." Thorogood swept his hat onto his head, preparing to take his leave.

"When do you plan to announce my appointment to the town council?" she asked.

Thorogood hesitated. His eyes darted and his mouth dropped open.

"How about at the town meeting next Wednesday?" she suggested.

"Well, uh, so soon?"

She nodded. "Yes," she said. "Why not? That would be quite appropriate, don't you think?"

"Yes, I suppose so."

"Fine," she replied. "I'll see you then."

Odie approached, her gaze following Ramsey's departure. "He looks pleased with himself," she remarked.

"Doesn't he, though?" Sage stared after him, satisfaction swelling in her chest.

"And you look like the cat who swallowed the canary," Odie said, turning a curious expression. "What did he say?"

Sage slanted her eyes and flicked a conspiratorial glance at her friend. "He just offered me a position on the town council in exchange for doing something I was going to do anyway."

After the briefest of moments, Odie caught the implication, and her eyes flew open in surprise. "He wants you to re-open Wild Mountain Honey!" she gasped in a loud whisper, eyes twinkling.

Sage nodded, tamping down her own excitement, lips pressed tight to keep from laughing out loud and drawing unwanted attention.

"Well, I guess that makes it official," said Odie, conspiratorially. "When's the big day?"

Before Sage could answer, someone called her name.

"Sage!"

Startled in the manner of children caught sneaking forbidden treats from the pantry, Sage and Odie spun around to see Hattie Murphy approaching at a fast clip.

"Have you heard the news?" Hattie said, catching her breath.

"No. What is it?" replied Sage.

"Someone just found a freight wagon turned over at Hatchett's Draw. The driver's dead, and a passenger was injured. Thirty-thousand-dollars in gold and silver is missing."

At the mention of Hatchett's Draw, Sage's heart slammed against her breastbone as if trying to break free. Odie blanched.

"Oh, no," Sage said, stopping herself from meeting Odie's tortured eyes. "How awful. Have they caught the robbers?"

"No. Honcho just took off to find Acer. Bridger and the deputies are rounding up a search party. They think the robbers are hiding out in the rocks."

Odie's hand flew to her mouth and she swayed slightly. Hattie noticed and laid her hand on Odie's forearm. "Are you all right, dear? Are you ill?"

"No, just . . . just hungry, I guess. I missed breakfast."

Hattie patted Odie's hand. "Oh, you poor dear."

"Let's hurry on home, then," Sage suggested quickly, taking Odie's other arm and giving it a gentle tug. "You'll feel better with one of Miss Priscilla's bacon scones in your belly." They waved Hattie a quick goodbye, Sage drawing Odie toward the surrey at the hitch post.

"What will happen if they find him?" Odie asked in a husky whisper, sounding truly sick. She didn't need to say who she was talking about.

Sage didn't answer, just flicked the reins and set off at a trot. She'd moved through her years decisively, rarely failing to find a resolution to a problem or negotiate any number of bumps and detours along the way. But this was a question to which she had no answer.

"I hope they don't," was all she could reply.

Chapter Twenty-Two

Bridger tilted his head and tossed back a slug of whiskey, then sighed, and enjoyed the burn of it all the way down to his stomach. He signaled the Diamond Rio barkeep for another, pulled his hand down his face and gave his head a shake in an attempt to throw off the weight of his fatigue. Weariness pressed down, drooping his shoulders and curving his spine. His reflection in the backbar mirror showed deep lines etched into the skin around his eyes. He looked forward to going home and getting some sleep, but right now wanted to savor this rare moment to himself.

He nodded his thanks for the refill and Jake moved off to wait on a couple of ragtag cowboys who had just come in slapping their hats against their thighs shaking off the dust. They had shaggy mustaches and masses of hair combed straight back with their fingers. Bridger gave them the peace officer once over. Deciding the strangers weren't looking to cause trouble, he put the glass to his lips, took another soothing swallow, then turned around on his stool and leaned his back against the bar. He swept the room with his eyes.

The sun, just about to drop behind the rim of the mountain, slanted its rays in through the slats in the batwing door making an elongated laddered pattern on the worn wooden floor. Bridger stared at it, realizing he'd never noticed it before. Usually the crowd in the Diamond Rio was so thick all anyone could see was a swarm of bodies through a thick haze of smoke.

Frowning, he turned back around to face the bar. "Hey, Jake."

The bartender ambled over, gave the surface of the bar a swipe with a towel, then rested his forearms along the edge of it. "What can I do for you, Marshal?"

"How's business been lately?" Bridger inquired, curious.

Jake's eyebrows popped. "Kinda slow," he said after a thoughtful moment. Practiced eyes gauged the room, seeming to calculate the day's take. "At least slower than it's been for some time. Used to be customers were spilling out the door into the street."

Bridger nodded, but didn't reply.

Jake shrugged. "Don't get me wrong. I'm still doin' all right. Business bein' slow's not hurting me money-wise, so I don't mind. After Miss Cane closed her place, this place was packed so tight I could hardly pour fast enough, so I don't mind catching a breath now." He paused. "Why you askin'?"

Bridger took another sip, rolled it around, appreciating it before swallowing. "Just wondering," he said. "Something seems . . ." He paused, the corners of his mouth turned down. "I don't know . . . different."

Jake studied the room. Half a dozen men sat at the long bar, leaving another half dozen stools unoccupied. Three tables were filled with card players engrossed in their games. A couple of loners sat at the back. "You mean in here?" Jake asked.

"No," Bridger answered. He tossed his head toward the street. "I mean out there. Anything seem odd to you? Unusual?"

Jake pushed out his lips and dipped his head from side to side as if deciding how to answer. "Well, maybe. I'm in here most of the time, don't get out there much, but well, yeah. I did notice something when I went to the bank yesterday."

Bridger narrowed his eyes at the bartender, inviting explanation. "What?"

"Well, you know how cranky Cash Redmond's wife Pitty is all the time? Always scowlin' at everyone and complainin'? Givin' Cash hell's devil when they're together?"

Bridger could see the woman's sour, disapproving expression in his mind's eye. He flinched inwardly. "Yeah."

"Yesterday morning," Jake went on, "she was in line at the bank in front of me. I overheard her talkin' to the teller, and she was being ..." He paused, the features of his face pulled together in thought. Then he shrugged. "Well, she was being pleasant. Then when she turned around to leave, she looked at me and smiled and said 'Good morning, Jake,' like we were old friends or somethin'. Surprised the dickens out of me, especially when I noticed ..." He stopped again.

"Noticed what?" said Bridger, leaning forward.

"She, um, smelled nice. Like she was wearin' some kind of perfume or somethin'. It was real nice."

"Huh," Bridger grunted, and frowned.

"And her dress. It was ..." Jake cupped his hands and moved them around inches from his ribs and chest letting gestures take the place of words he couldn't seem to summon. Finally he gave up. "Let's just say no one would have any trouble knowing she was a woman, if you get my meaning."

Bridger nodded. He got Jake's meaning, all right. He'd noticed similar things on his rounds through town, in Gallagher's General Store, in the lobby of the new hotel, at the bank, the bakery, even at church. The women seemed to be different, more . . . He searched for a word to describe it, but womanly was the only one that came to mind. And the way the men reacted to them was different, too. They were more . . . Well, manly.

Bridger twitched his mustache.

No.

Gentlemanly was a more accurate word.

At first, Bridger hadn't been able to put his finger on just what it was, not being skilled in the intricacies and subtleties of social interaction, but he took note of a certain delicacy of manners.

Oh, the streets were still crowded as all get out, and there were still plenty of fights and shootings. Just not as many. The jail was empty some nights.

And though some of the men standing outside the saloons still whistled and catcalled to the women passing by, they seemed to be doing it less aggressively.

Along with that, he couldn't help noticing there was a considerable amount of flashes of lace and flutters of ribbon on bonnets and bodices. Soft lilting voices and flirty eyes replaced the usual coarse vocalizations and downcast gazes so prevalent in this harsh environment. The women were speaking softly, walking gracefully, moving sensuously. Their voices were now silken and lilting and pleasant to the ear, and their gazes lingering a moment too long weren't just directed at him anymore, but at other men, too.

And just as Jake had pointed out about Pitty Redmond, they all smelled nice. It wasn't just from the sweet smelling soaps Sage used in her bathhouse. These fragrances were heavier, heady. They reminded him of how the Honeys smelled.

But that wasn't all.

Some of the women were acting kind of strange. He'd seen them walking up and down the side streets and along the river at a brisk clip. Some of them were lifting their knees high, taking big steps, almost lunging.

They were exercising!

While Bridger pondered this, more customers came in and Jake went back to his bartending duties, leaving Bridger to look for answers in his glass. Not finding any, he wiped his mouth with the back of his hand, laid some money on the bar, gave Jake a two-fingered farewell, and stepped outside just as the sun dipped behind a high peak. A sudden gust of wind blew up, and he hunched into the collar of his sheepskin jacket.

The bay nodded and snorted when Bridger untied the reins and hauled himself into the saddle. He stood in the stirrups a minute, stretching his back and his long legs. Automatically, his gaze drifted to the far end of town, in the direction of Sage's house. He wondered what she was doing.

He hadn't seen her except in passing since the night Verbena was murdered. The night she'd closed Wild Mountain Honey. The night they'd almost . . . .

Shit.

He dropped back down in the saddle remembering how badly he'd wanted to unfasten the buttons all the way down the front of her dress and remove the pins from her hair to feel it fall into his hands. He experienced the same quivery jolt he always felt when he thought about it. He wondered if he'd ever be alone with her like that again.

Last month, Ramsey Thorogood had told him he'd asked Sage to reopen the parlor house. Bridger hadn't expressed an opinion, but he secretly hoped she wouldn't do it.

A freight wagon rumbled by, thumping and banging over the holes washed out by spring rains, and he turned to watch it go by.

That's when he noticed the Appaloosa.

It was tied in front of a saloon half way down the block, head down, rear leg cocked, tail flicking flies. Dark, with black spots over a white rump. It was big for an Appaloosa, over sixteen hands, Bridger guessed.

He pulled on the reins, turned his bay and ambled over to take a closer look. As Bridger approached, the Appaloosa snorted and tossed his head flicking his ears in greeting to the bay.

Bridger's eyes fell on the tell-tale jagged lightening bolt of a scar on its hindquarters. It was a horse he remembered from Nebraska Territory. A horse belonging to a friend of Shooter Riker. The last time Bridger had seen this horse was through a cloud of dust as it raced out of town, beating a hasty retreat into the prairie, its rider slumped forward holding his gunshot arm. He'd been expecting this horse to show up ever since he got the wanted posters with Shooter Riker's picture.

Bridger scanned the boardwalk wondering where the Appy's owner was. Probably inside somewhere playing cards or drinking. Quickly, he dismounted and tied up next to the spotted horse.

He approached a knot of men talking and drinking on the boardwalk. "Any of you men see who rode in on that horse?"

His question was met with wary eyes and evasive denials until one of the men spoke up.

"Yeah," he said, swaying on his feet, not yet drunk enough to fall down. "Big guy, broad shoulders, with a gimp arm."

"Did you see where he went?" Bridger asked. The men shook their heads.

"I'm sure he's around here somewhere," one of them offered half-heartedly and turned away.

Bridger eyed an old codger slumped against a wooden post. "How about you? You see where the rider went?"

"I'm shore he's around here somewhere," the old man shrugged drunkenly.

Bridger walked the length of the block scrutinizing faces, stepping in doors to drag a slow gaze through the crowd inside.

When he returned to retrieve his horse, the Appaloosa was gone.

He mounted up again, and headed for home. He made his way through town, then nudged the bay up into a cantor when he reached open country. If he was guessing correctly, the Appaloosa belonged to Trip Mondragon, and Trip had come to Fairplay Creek looking for his saddle tramp partners Ham Tucker and Shooter Riker.

Well, Ham Tucker had been tried, convicted and hung for killing Honey Wild. But where was Shooter Riker? Funny, he hadn't shown up. Most of the freight haulers had seen him at one place or another along the trail from Denver. News from the bullwhackers could usually be depended on, but nobody had yet seen Riker in Fairplay Creek.

Shreds of clouds passed over the moon throwing ragged shadows across the trail, and Bridger slowed his horse to a walk. The air was sharp and cool, the smell of evergreens pungent in his nostrils. For no good reason, it reminded him of the morning he stood in the shadow of the trees alongside Wild Mountain Honey and watched Cheveyo clean fresh mud from Sage's new buggy.

He pondered on that until he reached the packed trail that led to the cabin on his spread. His tired mind was taking his thoughts in directions he didn't mean it to, making connections that didn't make sense. He yawned, his bleary eyes struggling to stay open long enough to put his horse in the barn, and get himself undressed. He needed sleep, and he meant to get it without delay.

Inside his cabin, he hung his coat on the peg next to the door, toed off his boots, unfastened his gun belt and laid it next to the bed within easy reach. He fell onto his mattress and was instantly asleep.

Chapter Twenty-Three

The sound of hammers and saws had stilled, the carpenters gone home for the day, but the smell of paint and sawdust lingered in the air at Wild Mountain Honey.

Remodeling of the house was nearing completion, but there was still plenty for Sage and the Honeys to do. Activities were restricted to the east parlor, it being the only usable and reasonably private room available during construction.

The first round of charm school classes had concluded, but some of the ladies had gathered for final lingerie fittings. Canvas and duckcloth were nailed over the doorways, but failed to keep out the dust and odors from the other rooms. The windows were covered against prying eyes from outside.

Sage sat by the light of a lantern embroidering an elaborate blue flowered trim on a camisole. Odie, whose handwriting was by far the most accomplished, was at the table composing the wording for the invitations to the grand opening celebration.

Chantal and Colorado Kate, damp tendrils of hair falling out of their pins, worked busily at two sewing machines set up in the center of the room. Half a dozen full length mirrors were propped against the walls. Hanging from a rack in the corner, covered with a sheet to keep them clean, was a collection of ball gowns, a luscious assortment of silks and satins, adorned with frilly ruffles and lace, trimmed with sparkling jewels and gleaming pearls.

Sheets had also been spread over the upholstered chairs and settees, new furniture recently delivered with surprisingly little damage via ox team from a cabinet maker in Denver. Sage had paid the freight haulers extra money to keep quiet about the shipments. The carpenters had been paid off, too, though she was sure they'd at least hinted some details of the structural changes they were making to the floor plan.

On top of the sheeting, the seamstresses had laid out newly stitched lingerie; petticoats trimmed with scalloped edges of lace, whisper fine stockings in a variety of colors, delicate chemises made of Jaconet designed to cover the bosom leaving it veiled but exposed. All the undergarments were incredibly beautiful and seductive.

Pitty Redmond stood on a low stool prattling away while Melanie wrapped a measuring tape around Pitty's slender waist. Pitty, who always seemed to know what was going on all over town, was reporting the latest happenings.

Sage's thoughts fell away and she picked up the gist of it in the middle.

"And then, Pete Gallagher says, 'why Pitty, you look nice today.' And I said, 'why thank you Mr. Gallagher. I'll take a small sack of sugar and a pound of flour.' Then Pete said to me, quiet like, 'Why don't I just put an extra half pound of flour in your bag?'" Her eyes sparkled and her smile beamed as she told the story.

"Don't let Violet know he flirted with you that way," piped in Chantal above the whir of the sewing machine. Her feet furiously pumped the treadle.

"Oh, he wasn't flirting," said Pitty. "He was just being friendly."

"Here, try this on," said Melanie holding out a petticoat to Pitty. It was soft with a Broderie anglaise border, and accordion pleating guaranteed to produce an intriguing rustle when she moved. "I took it in a little, it should fit better now."

Laura Clarke turned this way and that in front of the mirror, peering over her shoulder at her reflection with a worried expression. She was holding her skirt and flouncy petticoats bundled up in her arms, examining her bottom which was covered in black silk surah drawers edged with a froth of dainty lace.

"I can't get over how the men in town have changed," she said absently, studying her behind in the mirror. "Yesterday I stumbled on a loose step on the boardwalk and dropped a package. Three men ran over to pick it up. They practically had a fist fight over it." She paused. "Do these make me look fat?" she asked the room.

Colorado Kate looked up from her stitching, straight pins pressed between pinched lips. "Uh, uh," she grunted. The other ladies concurred, assuring her with absolute sincerity that she did not look fat in those beautiful new drawers.

"No, you look fine," said Nellwyn Foster. "I wish I had your tiny bottom." She was holding a bust enhancer to her chest, looking down at herself, her face serious. "The men have changed because we've changed," she said. She turned sideways to take a long final look in the mirror. "I think this fits fine, Chantal. Can I take it home tonight?"

Chantal nodded, and Nellwyn went on. "Malachi commented just the other day the whole town seems to have changed."

Sage smiled to herself, tied a tiny knot in her embroidery thread, then clipped it with her teeth. Yes, signs of domestication were everywhere, and if it continued the way she hoped, women would no longer be accosted in the streets. Gunfights would be few and far between; indeed, they had already diminished. Mothers wouldn't fear for the lives and souls of their children. Families would be able to make Fairplay Creek a destination, a place to settle and live out their lives with children, and eventually grandchildren.

There was still a long way to go for that, but Sage had a plan she hoped would be embraced by the townspeople. If it was, Fairplay Creek would be one of the most desirable communities in the Rockies.

She knew it was risky. Ramsey Thorogood and the others expected to see Wild Mountain Honey reopen like it was before with the exception perhaps of some new paint and wallpaper. They didn't know she had far grander changes in mind.

She held up and admired the camisole she'd been stitching. This one belonged to her, and her heart tripped a little when she thought about how it would look on her, and who she hoped would see her in it.

Dare she harbor such hope?

She'd spent more time with Bridger in the last several weeks than she had all winter long. He was still quite busy, but mostly office work now rather than peace keeping. He'd been able to set a schedule with fairly regular working hours, and he had a day off now and then. He kept to a consistent quitting time so they could dine together several evenings a week.

But not at Wild Mountain Honey.

She'd deliberately avoided being alone with him in her rooms since their passion almost overcame their good sense the night Verbena was killed. Something caught in her chest and she closed her eyes recalling the sweetness of his touch, how the warmth of his hands on her burned through her clothes. Her lips twitched in a faint smile remembering the taste of him, how he smelled, his strong arms pulling her close against his body. Her longing for that again, and more, was overwhelming.

But she wasn't going to make the same mistake she'd made with Rodney by allowing improper intimacies with Bridger when their relationship probably was not going to lead anywhere. How could it? He was a decent man. She was the madam of a parlor house.

Also, she didn't want anyone, including Bridger, to know about the changes she was making to the place. Not until the grand opening. The charm school ladies knew what she had planned, but they'd been sworn to secrecy.

Instead, she and Bridger shared meals and conversation elsewhere, usually in the dining room of the hotel or in a private alcove at the Gold Dust. After the weather turned mild, she often packed a picnic basket and they rode out to Red Hill or the top of Hoosier Pass for the afternoon. Bridger would spread a blanket on the grass, and they'd sit together enjoying the view along with Miss Priscilla's cold white meat chicken sandwiches, potato salad, biscuits, iced tea and sugar cookies.

Later, with the sun high in the sky, they'd sit closer, shoulders touching, holding hands. One time they stretched out on the blanket alongside each other and took a nap in the shade of an aspen. Nothing had happened between them, but it was supremely thrilling for her anyway. She'd never actually fallen asleep next to man.

Now, she wondered what Bridger would say when she made her announcement at the gala, how he'd react. He still held the deed to the place. He had let her and the girls stay on when she closed the parlor house after Verbena's death, but his patience and generosity surely had a limit. He hadn't pressed her on it, and she'd insisted on continuing to pay rent, but still she was sure he had an expectation of what would happen within the walls of Wild Mountain Honey.

Ramsey Thorogood certainly did. He'd asked her to re-open Wild Mountain Honey and she'd promised she would. She just hadn't clarified the nature of its new existence, and he'd assumed business would carry on as before.

A tiny quiver of dread stirred to life. She wasn't worried what Ramsey would think about it, but what if Bridger became angry? She snipped a length of three-ply thread, moistened the end of it on the tip of her tongue, and slipped it through the eye of an embroidery needle. She took a few stitches, placing them just so, touching up the decoration on the camisole.

What if Bridger argued with her about it?

Well, she was used to that. There were quite a few things they'd agreed to disagree on. But would he make demands she'd refuse to meet?

She released a small sigh. He might.

But she wasn't changing her mind and that alone could very well cause an irreparable rift between them. Another reason to maintain decorum.

She looked up at the sound of hurried high heels click-clacking in the hallway outside the east parlor, and saw the edge of the canvas covering the doorway thrown hastily aside. Estella Gardner rushed in, her face flushed, pulling a corset from her bag.

"Chantal," she implored. "Can you fix this? Can you make it fit better? It's not quite right."

Chantal creased her brow and shook her head indulgently. "Estella, I've already adjusted it three times. I can't make it any tighter or you won't be able to breathe."

"Oh, I don't want it tighter," the banker's wife said with a coy smile. "It's plenty tight enough. I want it lower."

The lilt of companionable laughter drifted through the room, and heads bobbed in agreement that lower was probably better. Sage watched them silently, admiring them. It was the unmistakable strength and courage of these women that were going to make a difference in this town and help it survive by making a difference in the men.

"Let me look," said Chantal, rising from the sewing machine and reaching for the corset Estella held in her hand. With furrowed brow she studied it, then shrugged. "There's not enough time to take it apart and do it over. I could take an inch of lace off the top," she offered.

"Yes. That's fine," said Estella, relieved. "And can you put in some of those padded cups, too? Please?"

Chantal smiled, and said she could. Estella leaned forward and squeezed Chantal's shoulders in a quick hug. "Thank you."

Just then a flurry arose as Margery, Penelope and Jonelle, the lady miners, arrived for final fittings of their ball gowns and to select lingerie. They went immediately to the assortment of undergarments laid out on the sheets.

"What color stockings should I wear?" Jonelle asked, picking up a pair made of sheer pink silk.

"Day stockings should be of the same color as your dress," said Chantal, "but for evening, wear black stockings with fancy garters. Especially if someone is going to see them later."

The lady miners giggled, and bubbles of delighted laughter punctuated the excited conversations in the room. Fabrics rustled and skirts and petticoats flew as the ladies removed their clothes to try on their beautiful new garments. Then there were the sounds of gentle ohs and ahs, the ladies admiring themselves and each other.

At the table where paper and pens were scattered, Odie's voice broke into Sage's thoughts of Bridger. "How does this sound for the invitations?"

"Read it to me please," Sage replied.

Odie cleared her throat and read the flourishing script.

YOU ARE CORDIALLY INVITED TO ATTEND
A GRAND OPENING BALL
AT
SAGE CANE'S HOUSE OF GRACE AND FAVOR
(formerly Wild Mountain Honey Pleasure Palace)
TWO WEEKS FRIDAY NEXT.
AN INVITATION-ONLY PRIVATE RECEPTION WILL BE HELD
FROM
7 TO 9 pm - PLEASE BE PROMPT!
Following the reception, the doors will be open to the public

to view the newly refurbished facility.
Music. Entertainment. A buffet.
Two drink limit strictly enforced.
Baths, clean clothes, and good manners are required.
This is a formal affair, so please wear your best and dress
appropriately.

"Oh, that sounds fine, Odie. How soon will the invitations be ready to go out?"

"I can have Cheveyo and Oliver deliver them to the men on the invitation list tomorrow. I'll hang a public announcement about the nine o'clock open house on the Shouting Post the day after that."

Odie continued to peer at the handwriting on the page, thinking. "Do you want to add, you know, the other changes? Tell them about . . . ?"

"No."

"What about . . . ?"

"No," answered Sage. "I think not. I'll announce my plans to the guests the night of the gala. I want them to be surprised."

Odie's eyebrows arched. "Oh, they'll be surprised, Sage. You can be sure of that."

Chapter Twenty-Four

It was seven minutes to four when Martin Gardner closed the ledger book and straightened the accounting records he'd been working on in preparation to ending his day and going home. He was anxious to get there. It had lately become a sanctuary of sorts, and he looked forward to his evenings at home, especially since Wild Mountain Honey had closed.

Estella had done some things to spruce up the small log and stone house; fresh paint in the front foyer, new wallpaper in the sitting room, fragrant candles in the bedroom. It was really quite pleasant. Every evening, there was a warmed crystal snifter and a bottle of brandy waiting for him on the table next to his favorite chair. The chair was also new.

A low rumble in his stomach reminded him that Estella said they were having roast beef and dumplings for dinner tonight, his favorite. She made a ritual of dining these days, the table precisely set with cloth napkins and flowers, the silver gleaming, the food steaming hot.

He glanced up, and his brows bunched in a frown. That Indian boy who worked over at Wild Mountain Honey was standing outside the bank, hands cupped around his face, peering in at him through the window.

Martin quickly stood up, but before he could take a step away from his desk, the Indian opened the door and entered the bank bold as you please. Martin caught the eye of the teller nearest the entrance who pushed through the waist high swinging door, and grabbed Cheveyo by the shoulder.

"You can't come in here," the teller said roughly, spinning the boy around in an attempt to usher him back out to the boardwalk. "You don't have any shoes on."

Cheveyo deftly shrugged away from the teller's grasp, and advanced on Martin Gardner, his hand outstretched. He was carrying something, an envelope of creamy vellum, and offering it up to Martin.

"What have you got there, boy?" Martin asked warily.

"It's from Miss Sage," Cheveyo said, pulling away from the teller who had grabbed him again. "She said to hand it to you directly, and not give it to anyone else." He glared up at the teller who scowled back at him.

Martin took the envelope between his thumb and forefinger so as to avoid touching the boy's hand, and looked at it. His name was on the front, so clearly it was for him. He turned it over and saw that it was sealed. Interesting. Why would Sage Cane be sending him a sealed letter, he wondered with a vague sense of hope and anticipation.

"All right, you can leave now," he said to Cheveyo, dismissing him. The teller smirked, but Cheveyo ducked away and scooted out the front door ahead of the teller's push.

Martin tucked the envelope in his pocket and finished clearing his desk. He took his time locking the drawers, and closing and locking the big vault in back. He bid good bye to the tellers who hurried out with a wave. Martin pulled the shade and locked the door behind them. Only then did he sit back down, take the envelope from his pocket, pick up a letter opener from the cup on his desk, and slide it under the flap.

The paper was of good quality, the envelope lined with a tissue thin covering of gold. Curious, he slid out the heavy vellum, unfolded it, and read the finely inscribed invitation.

A smile started, and he felt a little twinge of pleasure. At last she was re-opening the parlor house, though he wasn't sure he liked the new name. He said it out loud to himself. "Sage Cane's House of Grace and Favor."

After thinking about it, he shrugged, deciding the name was appropriate after all.

He unlocked his desk, carefully placed the invitation at the very back of the bottom drawer, extracted his calendar from the top drawer, marked the date on the appropriate page, and locked up again.

He put his hat on his head, hung his cane from his arm, and went out the back door thinking about the crystal snifter and bottle of brandy Estella would have waiting for him at home in the sitting room. As he climbed into his carriage, he wondered what new surprise his wife would have for him later that night, after dark.

* * * * *

Pete Gallagher opened the envelope Cheveyo had given him, stared at the invitation a long time, brow creased, lips twisting, then tossed it in the trash, envelope and all. He turned back to the job of organizing the sacks of beans, flour, corn, and sugar that had been delivered earlier. He hefted a sack of oats onto his shoulder with hard muscled arms and carried it to the storage room at the rear of the store.

There was a time, last year, in fact, he would have jumped at the chance to attend a private party at the parlor house. Now it didn't appeal to him anymore. Why should he go to Sage Cane's place when Violet was waiting for him at home every evening eager to do things to please him he didn't think she knew about?

It had occurred to him to wonder a time or two where she'd learned those things, but then figured it was probably from those Godey's magazines she read all the time. And that was fine with him.

A sweat broke out just thinking about the way she kissed him now, and how her fingers stroked and danced on his body before he fell asleep. He wiped his sleeve across his forehead, turned out the lights, locked the front door, and pocketed the key. He was closing up early and going home.

* * * * *

Deputy Acer Morrow tore open the invitation Oliver had brought out to him at his ranch, read it quickly, ripped it into tiny pieces and threw it in the fire. He was never going back there. He put his head in his arms and bawled. Oliver simply turned and walked away.

* * * * *

Malachi Foster saw Cheveyo heading for the blacksmith shop, and smiled a welcome.

"Howdy, Cheveyo. What brings you here?"

"Miss Sage sent me with this." He took an ivory colored envelope from a pouch around his waist and held it toward the blacksmith. Eyeing the envelope, Malachi pulled a rag from a pocket of his leather apron and wiped his hands. "What's this?"

"It's an invitation, sir. Miss Sage is having a party. You're invited."

Surprised, Malachi took the envelope, and thanked the boy who immediately spun on his heel and dashed off. The blacksmith watched him go, then turned curious eyes to the envelope, but he didn't open it right away. Thoughts of his wife flooded into his consciousness. Nellwyn had been quite relieved when Sage closed the place last year though saddened by the shooting that killed Verbena.

Nellwyn had always hated it when Malachi went there.

He pushed his thoughts back to the last time he'd visited Wild Mountain Honey, counted the time, and was surprised how many months had gone by. But the funny thing was, he hadn't missed it. He hadn't even thought about it much. He'd been perfectly content to spend his time with Nellwyn. In fact, he looked forward to his time alone with her.

He glanced around to see if anyone was watching, stuffed the invitation into his pocket, and went back to work. He supposed one more visit to Sage's place for a party couldn't hurt.

* * * * *

Ramsey Thorogood snatched the ivory colored envelope out of Oliver's hand, took a bill from his wallet, and handed it over along with thanks to Oliver who whooped with glee when he saw the denomination of the bill.

Ramsey wanted to whoop with glee, too, but kept his calm for the sake of good manners; the dining room was crowded, every table filled. He touched his napkin to his lips, and opened the envelope. When he finished reading the invitation, he let loose a smile after which he apologized to the board members with whom he was having dinner, excused himself, and laid some money on the table.

"Please," he said smiling to his dinner companions. "Allow me to pay for the meal." Then he left.

Back in his office, he lit the lamp, and quickly wrote letters to the railroad investors and land speculators with whom he'd been negotiating. You can be assured, he told them, there isn't a finer place in all the Rockies for a railroad stop, a stagecoach transfer station, and a mining conglomerate. Guaranteed.

* * * * *

Bridger lifted his boots to his desk, crossed his ankles, tipped his chair, and peered glumly at his invitation. Huh, he thought, dejectedly.

She was going to do it just like Ramsey said she would. She'd been vague in her answers when he'd asked her about it, so he should have expected it. Still, he was surprised, and a little disappointed.

He squinted out the window and thought about it.

Reopening the parlor house meant Sage was staying in Fairplay Creek, or at least he assumed she would, so that was the good part about it. But he wasn't happy about the rest. For the thousandth time he heard in his mind the sound of Josiah Miller's boots pounding on Sage's back stairs. He gripped the arms of his chair until his knuckles were white to keep from smashing his fist into the wall. He wished he could forget it.

"Damn," he said irritably. He dropped his feet and let the chair hit the floor with a crash. He crushed out a cigarette on the floorboards and glowered across the room at Honcho who had just opened his own invitation. Bridger watched Honcho's face go from curiosity to pure perplexity. The deputy looked up and saw Bridger staring at him.

"There's rumors she's going to make a surprise announcement," said the deputy. "What do you suppose it is?"

Bridger shook his head and turned away holding on to his scowl. He never knew what the hell Sage was up to.

* * * * *

When Rodney read his invitation, he thought he'd died and gone to heaven. Sage was opening her place again! That was just what the town needed. Just what he needed. All those women and good times available to him any time he wished to drop in. He had plenty of money now, thanks to her, so he could . . . His heart dropped down to his stomach and his smile dissolved as Jonelle's face popped up in his mind.

If he went to Sage's grand opening, would Jonelle think less of him? In the past, he'd spent nights with plenty of loose women. Most of them, he'd never seen a second time, so didn't care what they thought of him. But Jonelle's opinion mattered a great deal. Not that he ever spent a night with her, though he'd like to.

She was the most beautiful woman he'd ever known. He pictured those golden curls and ached to run his fingers through them. She put color on her lips to make them glossy, and they looked so plump and soft.

He'd seen her across the room last evening having dinner at the hotel with her friends, Margery and Penelope. She smiled beautifully when he came in, and peeked at him all evening from behind her pearl-studded fan, fluttering it, hiding her captivating eyes behind it, sliding it down over her breasts. It was very arousing.

He read the invitation again, and began to feel a little sick.

* * * * *

As soon as Odie put hammer to nail at the Shouting Post, a crowd gathered to read the announcement. The menfolk broke into cheers, but the merriment subsided somewhat when they got to the part about the dress requirements. The jovial expressions fell into petulance, hands went to hips in consternation, heads were scratched and shook. They looked around at each other seeking some sort of explanation.

"Does she mean we have to dress up?" one of the men asked Odie.

"Yes," she replied. "That's exactly what she means. That's one of the new rules."

"Sage is makin' more rules?" another man grumbled.

"Sage has made some changes, yes," Odie admitted. "She'll tell everyone about them the night of the gala. See you there," she said airily to the curious eyes and doubtful faces. "And don't forget to bring your very best manners."

But behind her cheerful demeanor, she was beginning to worry. What Sage had planned was going to turn this town upside down. These men were coming to the grand opening expecting one thing, but they were going to get something quite different. She hoped Sage hadn't misjudged their reaction.

Chapter Twenty-Five

"Gentlemen, may I have your attention, please?"

It was the evening of the gala and the invited guests were assembled in the marble foyer of Sage Cane's House of Grace and Favor, waiting impatiently for the parlor doors to open.

An elegant new chandelier, more grand than the one before, was suspended from the ceiling. The garish purple brocade drapes that previously covered the front windows had been replaced with silky panels in a tasteful fawn color. Woodwork, moldings, and the banisters on the grand staircase glowed with the sheen of hand rubbed oil.

Sage stood on the second to the bottom step so she could be seen and heard. It was just after seven and nearly everyone who had been invited had arrived. Except Bridger. Conversation was spirited and it took a while before she had everyone's eye.

"Thank you, gentlemen, for coming to help celebrate our grand re-opening. I'm sincerely happy to see you all here tonight. You are in for an evening filled with food, fun, music and surprises that I'm sure will delight you."

Her words were met with smiles and curious expressions. A sense of expectancy filled the air.

"To begin, Odie will give each of you a number."

Some of the smiles wavered uncertainly, and questions flew.

"What's the number for?"

"Is this a joke?"

"Are you playin' a trick on us, Sage?"

She held up her hands in a plea for silence.

"Please," she said loud enough to be heard over their raised voices, "bear with me. It's a little game we're playing to begin the evening. Sort of a masquerade. It's all part of the surprise. Please, play along. I don't think you'll be disappointed."

Questions abated, but the doubtful expressions remained.

With a nod from Sage, Odie began handing out four inch by four inch white cards, each inscribed with a number. A few of the men looked mildly annoyed, some narrowed their eyes suspiciously. There was a considerable amount of nervous shuffling of feet.

"The east parlor has been enlarged and remodeled into a ballroom. Your surprise is waiting for you in there. When I open the door, you will enter the ballroom and look for a dance partner holding a number that matches yours."

There was a moment of stunned silence until someone asked, "There's women in there?"

Sage smiled. "Yes," she assured them. "They, too, are holding numbers, and the woman holding your matching number is your companion for the evening."

Uneasy murmurs began as the men looked at each other, clearly dubious, not sure what to expect.

Odie swept open the door and stood aside, a musical trio struck up a lively melody, and the men slowly entered the parlor, some holding back.

Mirrored balls spun slowly overhead sending tiny reflections skittering around the room. Pinpoints of light bounced off the ceiling, and skipped along the freshly painted walls and newly varnished floorboards. The framed engravings of nymphs and satyrs going about their business in pastoral settings were gone, as were the pictures of nudes that had formerly graced the room. Gone too, were all the red velvet, gilt, and tassels replaced by the tasteful, subdued colors of a formal drawing room.

The gaudy ruffled and glass bead lampshades had been replaced by new ones, properly pleated in neutral hues of beige and ivory, though the embroidered throw pillows remained. Lavishly draped pale rose-colored curtains swooped back from either side of the windows revealing creamy sheers falling to the floor. Bronze sculptures were displayed on marble stands. Lace covered dining tables arranged around the perimeter of the room each set with gleaming table service for four.

At the far end of the ballroom, the charm school ladies waited, each one dressed in a magnificent flowing ball gown, holding a card with a number. Their faces were hidden behind exquisitely decorated masks, bedazzling arrangements of feathers, beads, and sequins. Jade feathers and turquoise beads replicated seductive feline features. Yellow ostrich feathers and amber trimmed the gold papier-mâché face of a sensuous lioness. Ice blue satin brocade glittered with silver sequins and iridescent peacock feathers swept up into butterfly wings. Each mask could have stood alone as a work of art.

The men, stunned, took a few steps into the room, then hovered uncertainly near the door. Their faces displayed a variety of emotions and Sage wasn't sure if they were awed or intimidated by the sight.

For a long moment, no one moved. Then Pete Gallagher, holding the number three, broke away from the group and strode across the room. Grinning, he walked directly to a woman wearing a black and silver feathered mask holding a card with a number matching his.

"Hello, Violet," he said, removing her mask and kissing her.

The others stared, too surprised to speak or move.

Pete then bowed from the waist, gave his arm a grandiose swing and said, "May I have this dance, my dear?"

As the band, a trio from the Hamilton City First Methodist Church hired for the evening, began a slow waltz, Violet caught Sage's eye.

"I had to tell him," Violet said, apology in her voice. "He was refusing to come to the party. I hope I didn't ruin everyone's surprise."

Pete gently took his wife into his arms and twirled her around the room, a look of pure pleasure on his face.

With the surprise revealed, the married men, beaming with pride, quickly crossed the room to claim their wives.

Martin Gardner, looking relieved, found Estelle wearing a purple, green and gold Venetian half mask sparkling with crystal beads. He put both arms around her, closed his eyes, and they stood in place, swaying together in a long hug, his expression pure contentment.

Malachi Foster made his way over to Nelwyn, walking slowly, his expression shame-faced. He removed her multi-colored Gypsy Queen Feather mask, clasped both her hands in his, and gazed into her eyes.

"Nell, I'm sorry—" he began, but she stopped his words with her fingertips. He turned his face aside, insisting on speaking, compelled to explain. "I know you don't like me coming here . . ." and this time she stopped his words with her lips.

"Don't talk, Malachi. Just dance."

Cash Redmond approached Pitty, lifted her hand and tenderly kissed her palm. Taking great care, he slipped her mask over her head, careful not to muss her hair, and unabashedly kissed her long and hard on her lips, oblivious to the others watching.

"Do we have to stay?" he asked in a loud whisper.

"Yes," she replied, laughing, then lowered her voice. "At least until after dinner."

Watching from the sidelines, the bachelors, uncharacteristically bashful, held back.

"Go ahead," Sage prodded, her touch gentle. "Find out which of those stunning creatures is your companion for the evening." She didn't tell them she'd let the women make that choice for themselves.

Jonelle, impatient, wasted no time and walked directly over to Rodney who was shyly shuffling his feet, looking ready to bolt out the door. For a fancy talking man, he sure was at a loss for words now, thought Sage.

Oscar, who gave the impression he'd gotten most of his talking and all of his laughing done at an early age, broke into a sloppy sideways grin when he found his number matched up with the one Emma Ford held.

Honcho entered shyly, looking for number eight. Poppy Merriweather smiled engagingly at him, holding up her card to show it matched. Honcho smiled in return and didn't appear to be disappointed.

After that, the other ladies were quickly unmasked amidst exclamations of surprise and delight, and the energy in the room became exhilarating. Happy couples glided around the room in time to the music, skirts swaying in graceful motion. Most of the men had two left feet, but did their best to please the women. Ballroom dancing lessons were certainly in order, Sage noted.

Above the music, Sage heard someone call her name and she turned to see Ramsey Thorogood waving to her. He was standing with Gardenia who had asked to be matched up with him. Sage acknowledged his wave with a smile and turned away, hoping to put off the inevitable confrontation she knew she'd have with him. He'd expected her to re-open as a parlor house, and probably felt she'd betrayed his trust. She wondered if Bridger felt that way, too, and so decided not to come.

Cheveyo walked by carrying a tray of canapés. She'd coerced him into putting on a shirt and tie, and along with Oliver, help serve finger food during the party. She put her hand on his arm and stopped him.

"Cheveyo," she said, looking at his feet. "What happened to the shoes I bought you to wear tonight?"

"They hurt my feet, ma'am."

She pressed her lips, and shook her head, then gave the boy a smile. "Oh, Cheveyo," she said, straightening his collar and pretending exasperation. "Whatever am I going to do with you?"

He shrugged, and gave her an impish grin. She smiled after him with affection as he walked away, then with a stiff little bow, offer canapés to Hattie Murphy and her husband Ben.

Bridger still had not arrived. Anxiety tightened its grip on her heart. Maybe she'd made a mistake not telling him what her plans were. Even though his name was on the deed and he owned the place, she'd had no intention of asking his approval of her plans, but perhaps out of respect she should have let him know what she was going to do.

"Sage."

Lost in thoughts of Bridger, she jumped and turned around.

Ramsey Thorogood was standing there, his features set, his eyes determined. "I'd like a word with you."

"What's wrong?" Sage asked. "Surely you're not disappointed to be sharing the evening with Gardenia."

He took a deep breath, turned and motioned to Gardenia that he'd be right back, then faced Sage head on.

"No, Gardenia is lovely. But, Sage, have you forgotten our agreement?" His face was grim and he was all but tapping his foot like an obdurate schoolmaster speaking to an impudent child.

"No, I haven't." She inflated her smile. "Why?"

"You promised to open the parlor house."

"I'm afraid that's not what I promised, Mr. Thorogood," she replied sweetly. "You asked me to reopen the house, and I said I would. But I didn't promise I'd reopen as a parlor house."

"That wasn't my understanding," he pointed out.

"I know," she said, patting his arm in sympathy. Then, "I'm sorry, will you excuse me? The entertainment is about to begin. Melanie's going to sing. She has a splendid voice."

The final notes of a Viennese waltz floated away, and the musicians changed the sheet music on their stands in preparation for Melanie's solo.

Melanie stood to the side facing the guests. Sage introduced Melanie, whose lilting voice captivated the guests.

When Melanie finished her solo, Ellen Berger joined her in a duet of, "Speak To Me Only With Thine Eyes." Halstead Berger, fairly bursting with pride, looked on lovingly. Sarabeth read a poem, then another one, then another, and still Bridger had not arrived.

When the entertainment portion of the evening ended, Josiah Miller sauntered up next to Sage.

"Hello, Josiah," Sage greeted her friend, lightly touching her cheek to his. "Where's Penelope?"

"She's in the ladies room with the others," he said, then smiled. "Congratulations." He glanced around the room. "You've done well."

"We've both done well," she replied.

"Yes, thanks to you. I don't know where I'd be without your help."

"It was, and is, a mutually successful business arrangement."

He nodded, looking pleased.

"What are you going to do when the mining conglomerates come in and want to buy us all out?" she asked him.

"Sell, of course," he replied, as if the answer were abundantly obvious. "How about you?"

"Sell," she said, without hesitation.

They shared a laugh, and a friendly hug. Penelope returned from freshening up, and Josiah went off to join her.

"I can't find anyone with my number."

Relieved to hear Bridger's voice, her heart did a little skip beat, and she turned to find him standing there in the doorway, one shoulder braced against the frame. He was dressed in a new dove grey suit and matching vest. His smile was one of pure pleasure, and he ran a caressing glance down her body, admiring her. His gaze, fixed on the sight of her breasts framed in frothy lace lit a fire under her sapphire blue gown.

262

"Oh, dear," she replied, pretending to be concerned. "Would you like me to help you look for it? Maybe it's upstairs."

He laughed and took both her hands in his, pulled her close and kissed her cheek.

"It's good to see you," she said softly. "I'm glad you came."

"You look more beautiful than ever," he said, his eyes blazing with green fire.

"Thank you."

"So this is the big surprise," he said with a toss of his head indicating the room and all the happy people in it.

She nodded. "There's more."

He rolled his eyes. "Oh, please, no more surprises."

"I'm going to make the announcement as soon as Acer gets here." She paused. "He's coming, isn't he?"

Bridger shrugged. "I don't know."

Doc Holden waved his arm, motioning her and Bridger to his table. Bridger tucked her hand in the crook of his arm and together they walked to where Doc Holden sat with Odie.

"Can you join us?" Doc Holden asked pulling out the two extra chairs.

"Yes, thank you, we'd be delighted," said Sage. "Bridger, why don't you sit down while I check in the kitchen to see how dinner preparations are coming along? It's almost time to serve. And will you keep an eye out for Acer, please?"

As Sage headed for the kitchen, she sent up a little prayer the deputy would decide to come. After Oliver told her how Acer had reacted to the invitation, she'd personally driven out to talk to him. She had no intention of matching him up with anyone, and didn't expect him to spend the entire evening if he chose not to. So he wouldn't think she was being disrespectful, she shared with him how she planned to honor Verbena's memory.

In the kitchen, Miss Priscilla with the help of two young Indian girls, Kayenta and Mischa, were filling platters with thick slices of steaming roast beef, yams glazed with ginger and blackberry wine, chunky white potatoes in cream sauce, and plump ears of sweet corn.

Miss Priscilla had borrowed Sage's carriage and driven out to the Indian camp to hire the girls to help in the kitchen for the occasion. A promise of wages was inducement enough for their Apache warrior father to allow them to leave the camp three days prior. As an added bonus, Sage told the girls they could each select a fancy petticoat to take home. Kayenta and Mischa were wearing the petticoats they'd chosen over their regular clothes.

Sage exchanged a glance with Priscilla who shrugged and said, "They insisted."

Sage suppressed a smile. "Well, you look lovely, girls," she assured them. Kayenta and Mischa giggled and shyly ducked their heads, but didn't stop working.

Turning to Priscilla, Sage asked, "Shall I tell everyone dinner will be served soon?"

"I'm guessing we'll bring the first plates out in about ten minutes."

Sage returned to the ballroom, asked the band to end the dancing in favor of mellower music more suitable for dining. The leader nodded, tapped his baton, and the trio struck the opening chords of Suite in E by Johann Sebastian Bach.

Just then she saw Acer standing uncertainly in the doorway to the parlor, face taut, smile damaged. Sage wondered if he'd ever have a happy moment without Verbena.

"Thank you for coming, Acer. I was hoping you'd be here when I made the announcement. You're just in time for dinner." He let her take his hand and lead him to the table with Odie, Doc Holden and Bridger who all welcomed him warmly. Bridger dragged an empty chair over for him.

Sage picked up a fork, tapped lightly on a glass, and delicately cleared her throat. Conversations fell off as one by one the guests looked her way.

"Dinner will be served in just a few minutes, so would you all be seated?"

Chairs scraped as the guests took seats and settled themselves, napkins unfurled and landed on laps. All eyes were on her.

"I'd like to thank you all for coming tonight," she began. "It's been an evening of surprises . . ."

There were chuckles and titters and sounds of agreement, everyone smiling up at her.

"Now, before we enjoy the delicious meal Miss Priscilla has prepared for us, I have an announcement to make."

A low buzz of curious murmurs rose and fell.

"As some of you may have already guessed, Wild Mountain Honey will no longer be a parlor house." She paused, anticipating angry protests, but none came, so she went on. "Instead, it will be a place for the entire community to come and enjoy the fine things in life of which there are many.

"Fairplay Creek is growing at a rapid rate. You've all worked very hard to bring this growth about. The gold mines have brought prosperity to many, not only to the miners, but to the business owners who support the miners, and those who provide the necessary goods that allow us all to live here in relative comfort. More businesses are opening up every week, and I don't think we can anticipate an end to this expansion."

She was pleased to hear a smattering of applause.

"We have all the essentials of any booming community in the New West. Now it's time for refinement, and for some new ways to enjoy the abundance the gold has brought to us."

The guests, their expressions open and expectant, listened attentively.

"This establishment is now called Sage Cane's House of Grace and Favor, and the new name signifies more precisely the activities that will hereafter take place within these walls. My dream from the beginning has been to make my Aunt Honey's house a lyceum, a place where everyone may gather for lectures, concerts and entertainment. A place of grace and education and intellectual pursuits. A place where decent women can meet decent men."

At this, polite but decisive applause broke out, mostly from the women, but from some of the men, too. Others were blank-faced and looked like they were trying to decipher what she meant.

"It is both wise as well as romantic to make love the sanction of marriage, and the supreme object to search for in one's life. Sage Cane's House of Grace and Favor will assist in that pursuit by offering men and women of all ages a clean, safe place to participate in respectable social interaction and enjoy the highest quality entertainments.

"Here you'll find music and dancing and reading clubs. We'll teach reading and writing to those who've never had the opportunity to learn. We'll gather as a community to discuss current affairs and philosophy and religion. We'll have dancing lessons and art lessons and poetry readings."

She sneaked a sideways peek at Bridger and was relieved to see he was beaming.

"Upstairs is a room filled with books. It's Verbena's old room. Contrary to what many of you may have thought, our dear Verbena spent a lot of time there alone, reading. Books were her passion. She'd often expressed a desire to write one. For that reason, her room will be devoted to the love of books and reading, and open to anyone who enjoys literary pursuits. In her honor, I've named it the Verbena Jones Lending Library and Reading Room."

Acer hadn't said a word and his head was bowed. He swallowed hard as if his throat were constricted, and a tear slid down his cheek. Both Bridger and Doc Holden gave Acer's back a comradely thump.

"Beginning Sunday, two days from now, and every Sunday afternoon following, musical entertainment and poetry readings will be held in the west parlor after church. For those who wish to attend, Pastor Pickett will hold Bible study on Sunday evenings. During the week, concerts and dramas and various other entertainments will take place here in the ballroom.

"Please feel free to form a friendly discussion group on any topic. We'll provide a room and seating. Just let us know when you wish to meet and how many will be attending.

"This program is still in the early stages of planning, so your suggestions are welcome. Just let Odie know what you have in mind and we'll do what we can to help you implement it."

Priscilla, Kayenta and Mischa entered the ballroom pushing serving carts on which dinner platters steamed. Delicious aromas filled the room.

"It looks like dinner is ready to be served, so I'll stop talking now and let you enjoy the feast Miss Priscilla and the girls have prepared."

After a prolonged enthusiastic round of applause, she sat down and took a deep breath, relieved. Bridger was staring at her, his grin crooked, eyes sparkling. Under the table, he reached for her hand and she threaded her fingers through his.

Animated conversations and the sound of corks popping on celebratory bottles of champagne immediately filled the room. She looked around and read a range of emotions on the faces of everyone there. Delight, excitement, anticipation, curiosity, even a little uncertainty, but no one had objected. No one had expressed anger or even displeasure. She smiled at her dinner companions with elation and relief.

"Well, if someone will open that champagne," she said brightly, indicating the bottles in the cooling bucket, "I'm ready to celebrate." Bridger and Doc Holden did the honors, expertly extracting the corks.

"You're quite a woman," Doc Holden said, lifting his glass in a toast. "I truly do admire you. I knew you had character the day I met you."

"As I recall, that was the day she shot you, Bridger," Acer said, managing a small smile.

"Here, here," Doc Holden hailed in jest, raising his glass in a renewed toast while Sage blushed in embarrassment.

"Well, if you don't mind, I'd prefer to forget that," Sage said to Doc Holden. "But thank you for the compliment. I sincerely appreciate your words."

Bridger's arm was resting on the back of her chair. His thumb stroked up and down her bare shoulder, the movement searing her skin and sending a warm thrill of promise into her breast.

Acer spoke up. "Thank you, Sage," he said, "for honoring Verbena that way. She would have loved that. A lending library and reading room named after her. She would have been so proud."

"I wish there was more I could do," she said, laying a gentle hand on his.

Their dinners were served and everyone ate heartily. Dessert was flame-browned peaches in warmed sweet ginger wine sauce, topped with whipped cream followed by coffee and brandy.

At nine o'clock, the open house began and a crowd dressed in finery was admitted. Tables had been cleared of dinner plates, and a fruit and sandwich buffet set up at the back of the room. The band started up a vigorous Two-Step, and the dance floor was soon crowded with revelers.

Word of the changes to Wild Mountain Honey had spread through the crowd while they waited outside, and now Sage was peppered with questions and comments, most of them positive and encouraging. A few of the old timers complained grumpily, but that didn't stop them from enjoying the buffet table and high octane punch bowl.

Bridger had gone outside for a smoke with some of the other men. The ladies freshened up, or sat in clusters primping or gossiping, waiting for their men to return. Some of them kicked off their high heels to relieve their aching feet, some covered yawns with their hands.

Sage spied Cheveyo, an empty tray hanging forgotten by his side, talking to Clara, the fortune teller's daughter. The boy stood a head taller, and Clara, looking demure, gazed up at him adoringly. Both of them blushed furiously when Sage approached.

"Cheveyo, why don't you let me take Priscilla's tray into the kitchen?" she said, reaching for it. "Then you can take the rest of the evening off to spend some time with Clara."

"Thank you, Miss Sage," he said, flashing a grin.

"Thank you," said Clara. They hurried off to sit on a bench near the front door to continue their conversation.

Sage felt a hand on her back and knew by the touch it was Bridger. She turned to face him. The grin on his face was absolutely devilish. "I thought you were going to help me find my number," he said, his lips close to her ear.

"Come upstairs with me," she said. "I have something to talk to you about."

He gave an uncertain little wince and narrowed his eyes. "Uh oh," he said. "Sounds serious."

She dipped her head in concession. "Well, yes," she replied. "It is important."

He took a step back. "Did I do something to make you mad?"

She smiled. "Of course not." His hand was on her bare arm. She liked the way it felt there, warm and casually intimate.

"I'll go up now. You come up in ten minutes. And use the back stairs."

Chapter Twenty-Six

Bridger tossed his hat on a chair and joined Sage on the settee. She'd set out a bottle of champagne and two glasses on a silver tray. He poured for them both, then looked at her with eyes soft and warm.

"Congratulations," he said. "You accomplished what you set out to do." His voice was deep, his words heartfelt. "You managed to bring respectability to this town."

"I hope so," she said.

He was silent a moment. "Of course, there's no guarantee the saloons won't hire upstairs girls."

"All I can do is hope not," she said. She told him about the charm school classes she'd held in secret. "The intent was to instill a healthy sense of marriage and family by educating the women. Now, it's up to them to carry on, and impart to their children what they've learned about the importance of creating a strong family structure, and making their home environment so appealing sons and husbands won't be lured by outside influences. I'll continue holding classes as long as they're wanted. There are newcomers every day and lots of young girls who will be coming into womanhood."

Together they sipped champagne and fell into a comfortable silence.

"I have something for you," Sage said. She reached into her bodice, took out a folded piece of paper, and handed it to him.

He unfolded it. "What's this?"

"It's a check," she replied. "I'm offering to buy this house from you."

When he didn't reply, she added quickly, "If that's not enough, or if you prefer cash, I can make arrangements."

Bridger's eyes went from her face to the check and back again. He pulled in a long slow breath, then let it out as he reached into an inside pocket. He took out his wallet, and removed a piece of paper.

"Here," he said, handing it to her. "Here's the deed Honey gave me."

She took it, but before she could say thank you, he spoke again.

"It's no good."

Her eyebrows jumped in surprise. "What's no good?"

"That deed," he said. He tore her check in half and handed it back. "Honey gave it to me when she couldn't pay off her gambling debts. I gave her the money and she signed over the deed. It was supposed to be temporary, so I never recorded it. I planned to give it back to her."

She gaped at him in blank disbelief. "What?"

"If you check the public records at the Land Office, you'll see the deed to this place is still in her name. Except now that she's gone, it's passed on to you, of course."

"Do you mean to tell me I've been the full owner all along?"

"Yep."

"Why didn't you tell me?"

His eyes alighted on hers. "Because I was stupid, I guess. I thought Fairplay Creek needed the parlor house to thrive. You've proven me wrong. I didn't tell you later, because by then I had ulterior motives. I was afraid you'd sell out and use the money to leave town. I didn't want you to go."

Sage stared, speechless, trying to decide if she should be angry at the deception, or laugh out loud. While she was trying to make up her mind, he put his arms around her and kissed her, softly at first, then more urgently. The joy of letting herself feel desire built within her until she thought she couldn't contain it. He pulled away and gazed at her. She felt his yearning in the tension in his body and in the intensity of his eyes.

"Sage, I love you. Surely by now you know how strong my feelings are." His eyes were shining, his breath warm against her lips. "Do you care for me at all?"

"Bridger, I do, I care for you in the same way, it's just that . . ."

But he didn't let her finish what she was going to say. "Will you marry me?" he asked, his voice husky with yearning.

His eyes were locked on hers, and she wondered if he saw the shock in them. She had despaired that no one, at least no one decent, would ever ask her. Who would want a madam for a wife? Gently, she pulled away.

"I'm going to give you the opportunity to take back your offer of marriage, Bridger."

His hands on her upper arms increased their pressure. "I don't want to take it back. Why would I take it back?"

"You're a fine man, Bridger, solid as bedrock. But I won't have people denigrating you because you married me."

"But you're not . . . you don't . . . you said you didn't . . ."

"No, but I might as well have. Folks take the same view of me as if I did. That's why it was so important that I invest in the mines. I needed to become financially independent in order to survive. In order to have a home, in order to—"

Bridger held up both his hands and waggled them, signaling her to stop talking. "Wait, wait a second," he said, shaking his head, a stunned, dubious expression on his face. "You invested in gold mines? What mines?"

She nodded. "Yes, several. Starting with Josiah Miller's. I met him the day I arrived in Fairplay Creek. He didn't have a penny to get started, so I made a business arrangement with him. I staked him in return for half interest in his mine and a percentage of what he dug out. At the time, I was desperate to acquire enough money to go back home." She shrugged. "And later, there were other miners who needed help, so I set them up, too." She paused, staring at his stricken face. "Then one thing led to another and . . ."

"And you stayed on and became a very rich woman," he finished for her, flabbergasted.

"Yes." She looked into the deep green mystery of his eyes, trying to read his reaction to her mendacity.

Suddenly he threw back his head and let out a rich burst of laughter. "Oh, I've been such a fool. I thought . . ." He captured her eyes with his.

"What?"

"Never mind."

He cupped her chin in his palm and positioned his mouth over hers. She felt the flow of his warm breath. When she moved, her lips grazed his and her breast brushed against his upper arm. The unexpected touch exploded through her body warming her to her deepest part.

Her eyes looked into his, straight and clean, unflinching. Something about him stirred a boldness within her. She'd never had a man take hold of her life like he did. There was something so compelling about him.

His hand moved up between them and he cupped one breast. The feeling of his hand rocked her like a small earthquake, and her breathing grew faster. He bent his head until his lips touched the tender skin between her breasts. His tongue traced fiery lines over that part of her. The room swayed beneath her.

His hand moved from her breast to her waist and he stood up, carrying her along with him. She was helpless to resist when his hands began to slowly unfasten the buttons at the back of her dress. It fell to the floor in a rich rustle of taffeta.

He led her to the bed, and she stood there in total surrender as his hands gently pulled at the laces of her corset, then loosened the hooks one by one. He removed the pins from her hair and let her white blonde tresses tumble free in a cascade around her shoulders. After he removed her camisole and petticoats, she let him lift her onto the soft mattress, marveling that his touch could bring such desire burning inside her.

He undressed quickly, never taking his eyes off her. When he lay down beside her, the sensuous feelings that surged through her body were too much, too overwhelming. She stretched her body against the length of his.

His hands caressed her, slowly, in long gentle strokes, following the curves of her shoulder and her waist, then along her thighs. His touch was light and gentle, and she strained to feel it, moving her body to the movements of his hands. Her breathing grew faster. She brought his face to her and kissed him. Waves of pleasure washed over her. She felt like she was drowning in heat.

"I love you," he said against her lips. He bent lower until his mouth touched her breast. It rested briefly there before he ran his tongue slowly across it.

He moved on top of her and lay that way, holding her, not moving. The feel of him covering her, the weight of him on her was so nice, a small moan escaped her. She raised her hips and parted her legs, embracing him there. He barely moved, but he was inside her, and she was swept up by a rush of exhilaration. Suddenly sensation flooded in, overwhelming her. A lovely explosion inside her washed her in oceans of ecstasy. She clung to him, tight and hot, merging them into one. She raised her hips to pull him in more deeply and they moved together. She wanted to melt into him, and pressed her hands along his back and down his thighs, pulling him more tightly to her even though they could not have been any closer than they were.

She curved one leg over his hips, clasping him, and moved against him. The desire that surged through her body was almost too much. She was lifted up by exquisite sensations, by the heat pouring through her and the joy of taking him in. His movements became urgent and she rose to meet him in time for his shuddering release.

Their rapid breathing slowed in the quiet room. She looked at her fingers deep in Bridger's hair, and waves of pleasure washed over her. She'd never reached such height of ecstasy in her entire life. She wanted to do this with him again and again and again.

He lay beside her and cradled her. She let out a long sigh of contentment, too spent to move. She never imagined it could be this way, had never experienced such height of rapture. A tear escaped from the corner of her eye.

He noticed. "I hope you're crying because you enjoyed that," he said, gently wiping the corner of her eye with his fingertip.

She looked at him through tears. "More than I can tell you," she replied.

He took her hand and kissed her palm, and then her fingers one by one. She felt the shock of desire burst within her once again. He brushed her hair back from her face and looked at her through eyes that seemed to smolder in their depths. "Everything I ever hoped for, everything I ever dreamed of is right here, now, with you. I don't know how I can go on if you're not with me. My life would be meaningless without you."

She laid a hand on his chest, and he gazed deep into her eyes.

"I'm going to ask you again, and I'm going to keep asking you until you say yes. Or until I die. Which will it be, Sage? Will you marry me? Or will I still be asking with my last breath?"

She ran her finger along the fine line of dark hair running under his belly button, concentrating on the heat emanating from his body. How could she say no? How could she not pledge herself to this man who was so good, and honest and decent? He was strong and courageous. He was tender, and God in heaven, he was handsome. The mere touch of his fingertips on her skin sent her into such a state of high elation it made her mind spin out of control.

And he loved her.

But most of all, he was a man she could depend on.

She put her arms around his neck and kissed him long and hard. "Yes, Bridger, I'll marry you. I love you, and I'd be proud to be your wife."

Chapter Twenty-Seven

Overindulgence in liquid spirits had its price. Suffering was to be expected. But Bridger felt it was extreme to be sent to hell because of one last night of celebration as a single man.

His head was cracked in two. Surely it was.

Acer and Doc Holden and Honcho and the others at the Diamond Rio had insisted on celebrating the demise of his bachelorhood uproariously. Toasting and congratulations had begun yesterday afternoon and by the time he reached his cabin, the moon was full up. He didn't remember how he got home. Thankfully Tumbleweed remembered the way.

He dragged his eyelids open and was assaulted by a blast of sunshine pouring in through the window. He slapped his hand over his eyes and winced, then felt for the jagged crack that had undoubtedly split his skull. He couldn't feel it so surmised it was on the inside.

Today was his wedding day. At noon, he would marry Sage.

If he didn't die first.

The taste in his mouth was putrid and even he couldn't stand the stench that emanated from him. The smell of whiskey and something unidentifiable seemed to be seeping from his pores. He couldn't show up at the church smelling worse than the barn barrel after the stalls had been cleaned. A dunk in the icy river would do him a world of good, not just physically, but mentally as well. He just had to make his way down there.

Moving like an arthritic old man, he dropped his feet to the floor with a thump. Jesus, he still had his boots on. It took superhuman effort to pull himself erect into a sitting position on the bed. Something crashed inside his skull and he groaned with pain. He waited for the pounding to subside, then slowly opened his eyes and looked around.

His guns, still holstered, were on the floor next to the bed. His coat was tossed half on, half off the back of a chair. On a hook by the door, hung his black wedding suit, clean and pressed, the crease in the pants sharp as the blade of a knife.

He grinned. Damn, he was going to look handsome in it.

He stood, using the wall for balance. His stomach clutched and swirled, and he swallowed fighting off the wooziness.

He snagged a towel from beside the wash basin and started for the door, but turned back remembering his gun belt. Moving slowly, he bent over to pick it up, but a wave of dizziness sent him reeling. Pain like hot needles pierced his head pitching him off balance. He grabbed for the bedpost to right himself, but his feet slipped out from under him. Down he went hard on his hip, the sole of his boot smacking the gun belt, sending it skidding under the bed where it slammed into the back wall.

Oh, shit.

There was no way in hell he could reach it without dragging the heavy bed into the middle of the room, and he was in no condition to expend anywhere near that kind of effort. Not until he'd had a dunk in the river to clear his head and hopefully, diminish the incapacitating pain in his head and joints.

He struggled to his feet, and rubbing his hip, made it to the door. When he opened it, he saw Tumbleweed standing at the bottom of the porch steps with woebegone eyes, still saddled, reins hanging loose.

"Oh, shit," Bridger said again, and reached for the reins.

"Hey, boy," he said, "I'm sorry." The horse snorted a response, and tossed his head irritably.

"Why'd you let me drink so much, huh?" He spoke softly to the horse, soothing it. "Don't you know I'm getting married today?" He patted the horse's neck. In return, Tumbleweed snuffled and bobbed his head, and backed up, tense and jittery.

"Whoa, there. Whoa. What are you so nervous about this morning? Huh? Bears been out in the night? Or is it coyotes? Did you scare 'em off?"

Tumbleweed's ears pricked forward as if listening for something beyond Bridger's voice. He stroked the animal's velvety nose and patted its shoulder which settled it some.

"Come on, boy. Let's go down to the river and cool off before breakfast."

Bridger knew he invited a fresh onslaught of pain not to mention the dislocation of his head should he try to climb into the saddle. Instead, he put one foot deliberately in front of the other and headed painfully for the river, moving as if he had lead in his boots. Tumbleweed followed on the lead.

The water's edge, just short of a quarter mile from the cabin through an evergreen forest, was a welcome sight to Bridger's beleaguered spirit. Morning sun dappled the surface of the river as the rush of water slowed at a boulder strewn bend, then rippled over a rapids before hitting the shallows further downstream.

The horse lowered his head to drink and Bridger dropped the reins. He sat on a boulder to take off his boots. The metal on Tumbleweed's halter clanked when the horse suddenly raised his head. Overhead, branches fluttered as a flock of birds took flight. A rustling in the trees behind yanked Bridger's attention. He looked over his shoulder to see the Appaloosa emerge from the pine grove, Trip Mondragon in the saddle aiming a Winchester, a look of contemptuous triumph on his face.

Bridger's hand flew to his side, reaching for a weapon that wasn't there as the crack of a rifle and the whine of a bullet sounded almost simultaneously, and sent him tumbling into the river.

* * * * *

Across the afternoon sky, grey clouds were gathering for a serious downpour, and Bridger hadn't yet arrived for the wedding. It was one-thirty, and Sage had been aware of every tick of the clock and every beat of her heart since noon. The parlor was decorated with huge white satin bows and vast bunches of flowers, some clustered in vases as bouquets, some woven into garlands. A white runner on the floor ran across the parlor floor from the doorway to a table draped in folds of white satin on which lay a white gold-embossed Bible.

Pastor Pickett was seated next to the table in a posture of somber dignity. Every few minutes he looked at his watch. He'd given up offering words of comfort. There were none.

Most of the wedding guests had gone, eyes downcast, faces dismal, offering mumbled consolation to Sage on their hurried way out. The three piece orchestra had already been sent home. No one was in the mood for music. Priscilla, glowering, eyes snapping with anger, walked around the room extinguishing candles.

Doc Holden was at a window looking out, shoulders squared, spine stiff, hands clasped behind his back. Rigid as a board, he tipped slowly back and forth on his toes. His face was somber, his mouth set, eyes glazed in thought.

Odie sat tearfully next to Sage, alternately dabbing at her tear-swollen eyes with a lace-trimmed linen handkerchief and gently patting the back of Sage's hand.

Nervously chewing the inside of her mouth, Sage sat in profound silence, every once in a while inhaling deeply, then letting the air escape. When she woke that morning, she was sure nothing in the world could have ruined her joy.

She stared vaguely at her shoes. They were new, white satin with tiny crystals on the bow at the toe. What a waste of money. After only two hours, they were headed for the trash bin. She beat back a sob that was burning her chest, trying to explode from her throat. She would not cry in front of these people. Would not.

Oh, Bridger. How could you do this to me?

She looked over at Martha, Sven and Jenny huddled together, the little family churning with emotion. Jenny leaned her head against Martha's shoulder and sobbed softly. Sage had looked forward to being stepmother to the child, hoping to soon give her a brother or a sister. The disappointment and icy disgust showing on Martha's face sufficiently sent a message about what was going through her mind. Sven looked murderous.

Acer spoke. "Sage, why don't Honcho and I ride out to Bridger's spread?" It wasn't the first time he'd made that suggestion.

Sage repeated her terse answer. "I said no!"

"But then we'd know . . ." he persisted.

"No! Bridger is a grown man and he does or doesn't do what he wants. I won't have you going out there to persuade him to marry me. I won't have it. I don't need you or anyone else to speak for me. I can speak for myself, and take care of myself." Livid, she cast a steady gaze around the room. "I think I've already proven that."

Acer and Honcho exchanged a quick sidelong glance, pressed their lips, and fell back into silence.

Standing nearby, Rodney, who had so far exhibited the good sense to keep quiet, apparently thought now was a good time to express his opinion.

"She's right," he said to the deputies. He looked as smug and self-righteous as a school yard bully. "She doesn't need him. Turns out the good marshal has shown himself to be a first rate scoundrel after all."

Acer grasped Rodney by the front of his starched shirt, and threw his fist into the middle of the man's arrogant face. Rodney fell back against the buffet, sending dishes, glasses, and silverware scattering. He recovered quickly and came up swinging. Doc Holden grabbed him from behind. Honcho restrained Acer who tried valiantly to pull away and finish what he'd started.

"Mind your own damn business, you dough-faced jackass," spat Acer. "You don't know Bridger, and you have no right to call him a scoundrel. Maybe he's got problems, but he's a good man."

"Stop! Stop it right now!" Sage stood up and glared at the two men straining to tear each other apart. The force of her anger was palpable, almost suffocating. "I will not have violence in this house." She looked meaningfully at Acer. "Haven't we had enough already?"

Reluctantly, but not chagrined, the furious men backed down, shrugged off the restraining hands, but let their cold stare remain locked in place.

Sage peered around the room, deliberately meeting everyone's eyes, then spoke with unhurried purpose.

"I'm going upstairs to my room, and tomorrow my life will go on as it has before. For now, I'd like to be alone. I don't want company. I don't want anyone worrying about me or asking about me. I don't want anyone pitying me. I know I can't stop the gossip, but I've weathered worse and will survive this as well." She pressed her point into the silence. "We will *all* go on with our lives."

Then she rounded on the deputies, distress pinching her face. "And I mean it," she said, looking ominously at them. "If you dishonor my request and ignore my wishes by going out to Bridger's, I will never forgive you. Don't shame me further by doing such a thing. I've been humiliated enough."

At that, she gathered up her dignity and her broken heart, along with the yards and yards of glossy silk and lace that made up the skirt of her wedding dress. The hem dragged on the floorboards as she stalked out of the parlor, and up the curving staircase holding her head high. The slam of her door reverberated through the house like a gunshot.

She turned the lock and fell back against the inside of the door, squeezing her eyes to hold back the burning tears behind her eyelids. Painful spasms tearing in her throat choked off her air. To compensate, her breathing speeded up with the effort of taking in oxygen. A sob convulsed in her chest and exploded.

She hurried to the settee and collapsed on the cushions, burying her face in a throw pillow to muffle the sound of her breathless weeping. She doubted her heart would hurt any more if someone sliced her open and ripped it out of her chest. Her shoulders shook uncontrollably. Tears flooded, soaking the brocade pillow cover.

It was a long while before her tears dissipated, but not long enough. She felt no relief. She wanted to cry some more, and keep on crying until she had cried away every last vestige of feeling inside her. Until she was drained of all emotion. She didn't want to feel anything, and tried to restore the flow, but there were no more tears left to shed.

She hiccoughed one last shuddering sob, and released a shaky sigh. Her breathing returned to normal and she put the pillow aside and stared vacantly at the wall.

Abandoned on her wedding day.

Again.

It was unimaginable, and she shook her head regretfully.

It was her own fault, of course, fool that she was. She only had herself to blame. For giving herself so wantonly to Bridger. For trusting him without question. For actually believing he could ignore the fact that she had been a madam and marry her anyway. To many, she was still a madam, and she guessed she would never be able to live that down no matter how much time went by or how much money she had.

His touch had been so warm and enticing, his kisses so tantalizing. She loved his smile and his smell. She sniffed and purposefully hardened her heart against the memory of their lovemaking.

Exhausted, energy almost spent, she rose and began undoing the tiny buttons that began at her neck and trailed down to the small of her back. She couldn't reach them all. Melanie and Colorado Kate had together buttoned her into the dress that morning.

Agitated, she tugged at the opening, trying to pop the buttons, but the threads wouldn't give. She went to her clothespress, took a pair of scissors from a drawer and began cutting at the fabric. First the sleeves came off. Then she slit the bodice and cut it away around the waist. She snipped a deep slash down the front of the skirt, so she could pull it down over her hips, and suddenly she couldn't stop herself. The scissors flashed and snapped relentlessly until her beautiful wedding dress was nothing more than a heap of pearled and sequined scraps in a pile on the floor.

She wiped off all her makeup, washed her face, and wound her hair into a tight bun at the back of her head. She slipped on a pristine, high necked cambric blouse, then stepped into a dark blue skirt and tied it at the waist. Properly shod in sturdy low heeled shoes, she studied her resolute face in the mirror.

Never again would she allow herself to be shunted aside by a man, dismissed and discarded like so much trash without standing up for herself. She was going out to speak to Bridger, not to beg him to reconsider, not even to demand an explanation. She was going to give him a piece of her mind.

There was a light rap at her door.

"Sage?" Odie's voice, still hoarse from crying, called softly from the anteroom. "Miss Priscilla brought dinner. Can we come in?"

Sage threw the door wide and stepped back to admit them. Odie gasped and Priscilla stared aghast at the silky pile of fabric scraps on the floor.

"Oh, Miss Sage," Priscilla exclaimed, clutching a dinner tray. "What did you do?"

"I won't be needing it," Sage said. "Burn it."

"What? Oh, no!" Odie cried, horrified.

"Burn it . . ." Sage stalked out the door, but stopped at the top of the stairs and turned. "Will you please leave dinner on the warmer?" she asked. "I'll be back in an hour."

She hurried down the stairs leaving Odie and Priscilla openmouthed with astonishment and alarm. The house was quiet. Everyone had gone. On her way out, she snatched her shawl from the hook beside the back door and wrapped it around her shoulders. Cheveyo was in the barn cleaning a stall. He looked at her in surprise when she came in.

"Will you help me hitch Mandy to the rig?" she asked.

He stopped his work and studied her. She saw the questions churning in his eyes, knew he wanted to ask where she was going, but he didn't, and set about doing as she asked.

On the ride out of town, she thought about what she wanted to say to Bridger, ran words through her mind. She tried to picture the look on his face, what he would say when he saw her at his door. Part of her wanted to rage at him, to slap at him, and keep on slapping until he begged for mercy. She wanted to hear the satisfying smack of her hands on his face, on his chest, on his arms.

But what would that accomplish? It would do nothing but confirm that he'd made the right decision by not showing up to marry her.

She held a steady rein and clucked at Mandy urging her on.

When she arrived at Bridger's cabin, there were cloud capped mountains visible in the distance, misty fingers reaching down to touch the tops of the stands of good timber in the foothills.

She reined Mandy to a stop in front of the cabin and looked around. The cabin door was closed, the windows shuttered from the inside. No sound came from within, or from the long stretch of land between the cabin and the first rise where the mountains began their rocky climb to the sky. A wind came up setting tiny dust devils twirling across the field, miniature whirligigs that danced a while, then disappeared.

She lifted her skirt and climbed down from the buggy, and stood there a minute wondering if Bridger was peeking at her from inside the cabin. Somehow she couldn't picture that, Bridger skulking in the shadows, peering surreptitiously through the shutter slats. She knocked on the door, and when there was no answer, put her ear against it, listening. She heard no footfall, no intake of breath. Nothing.

The barn door was open, so she walked over and looked in. Bridger's bay wasn't there, and the saddle was gone, too. Fresh hay hadn't been forked in the manger and the watering trough was dry. It looked like he'd been gone a while, probably since yesterday morning after breakfast. They'd eaten together, then she'd gone for a final fitting of her wedding dress. Bridger said he had some paperwork to finish up so he could take a few days off for a honeymoon.

The memory spiked a dagger of pain through her heart.

Back at the cabin, she drew a deep breath to embolden herself, then tried the door. It opened easily and she went in. She didn't know what she expected to find, but the normalcy of the tableau jolted her.

His bed was unmade, but slept in, the covers in a heap at the foot. The trail coat she'd bought him was draped over the back of a chair, and her heart clutched to think he didn't find it worthy enough to take along with him. Did he detest her that much?

She tilted the slats of one of the shutters for light, and looked around. His wedding suit, spotless and well cut, hung on a peg. She stared at it a moment, then walked slowly to his bureau in the corner, and gazed at the photographs on top. In a silver frame, was a picture of a woman, pretty and petite, light colored hair framing a heart-shaped face. She stared. It could have been her twin, but she knew it was Elizabeth. She picked up another photograph, Elizabeth beaming with pride, holding a baby on her lap. Jenny, a few months old.

She put the frame down and opened a drawer. Bridger's underwear was there, skivvies, long johns, socks, a nightshirt, an extra belt with a silver buckle. Letters tied with a turquoise colored ribbon. Curious, she took a letter from the stack, unfolded it, and read. To Papa. From Jenny. The others were all written in the same childish handwriting. Heat spread to Sage's cheeks.

Something was not right.

Hurriedly, she opened the other drawers, and found them filled with Bridger's belongings. In the little kitchen, she threw open the cupboards and checked the pantry. She found them all full and stocked, or at least as stocked as one could expect of a single man.

She felt a bump of alarm, and her heart began to pound. She pulled a chair out from under the table and sat down.

Bridger wouldn't go away and leave all this behind.

Not the picture of Elizabeth.

Not the letters from Jenny.

A wave of panic engulfed her, but she shook it away so she could think clearly. Where was he? Did he have an accident? Was he lying somewhere hurt? Where was Tumbleweed?

Apprehensive, she stepped out onto the porch, and peered into the distance. Storm clouds were lower now, completely blocking the sun. Faraway, lightening flickered. Thunder rumbled low and close. Out of the corner of her eye, she saw something move in the trees that lined the empty field.

She waited for the movement to come again, straining to see. Tumbleweed emerged from the pine grove, head down, and stared at her forlornly. Somehow the latigo strap had loosened the cinch. The saddle had slipped around and was hanging under his belly. His legs were wet and covered with mud up to his knees. Fear smoldered in her chest.

She whistled and made kissing sounds to coax the horse to come to her, but he stood still. Slowly she walked toward him, speaking softly. He danced and whickered, nervous at her approach. As she got closer, she extended her hand, palm down, and he stretched his neck to sniff it. She sidled up close, and grasped his bridle.

There were bare spots on his neck and back where the saddle had rubbed his skin raw. How long had he been saddled? It wasn't like Bridger to neglect the care of his animal.

With slow, careful movements, she uncinched the belt, and let the saddle fall to the ground. Tumbleweed, relieved of his awkward burden, wheeled on his hind legs, and galloped off to the barn.

She could tell the horse had recently been in the river, the mud on his legs was still fresh, and she headed that way. The dirt path was marked by many hoof prints. It looked to her like more than one rider had passed through recently.

The river murmured in the distance. Fog was rolling, weaving in and around the trees. Gnarled shapes of branches could be seen through the mist. The air felt wet and thick in her lungs.

When she reached the clearing, she saw the river meandering around rocks and tufts of grass on its way downstream. It had rained in the night and the flow of water was everywhere. Runnels and tiny waterfalls spilled down the faces of the larger rocks. There were miniature rapids and placid stretches where the smooth brown stones were visible under the water. Further downstream, white foam rushed over rocky crags, then plummeted down with a roar to the rocks below. Overhead the trees formed a shadowy arcade that would have blocked the sun if the clouds weren't already doing so.

At the water's edge, she saw Bridger's boot lying in the mud next to a large boulder. Apprehension yanked her into panic mode as her eyes zipped back and forth taking in the scene. There was blood on the boulder. Blood on the ground. The river had overflowed its banks a little, but not enough to wash away a trail of blood leading into the tall grass at the turn of the river.

She didn't have to follow it far. A sobbing breath of relief escaped her, then a scream tried to fight its way out of her throat. Bridger was sprawled on his stomach in the undergrowth. Blood soaked the back of his shirt turning it crimson, and his eyes were closed. From the look of the marks in the wet sand, he'd crawled into the undergrowth seeking refuge. He wasn't moving. It didn't look like he was breathing.

Sage slogged through the mud to reach him, her breath coming in gasps. Kneeling beside him, she put her ear against his lips. She thought, prayed, she felt a tiny breath slip out.

"Bridger," she whispered. "Bridger. Can you hear me?" She stroked his cheek and forehead, and lightly kissed the side of his mouth. "Bridger, please, if you can hear me, say something."

His body that had been an intoxicant for her was now broken, damaged. He moaned as she embraced it, turning him gently on his side, pulling him to her bosom. She laid her cheek next to his. His lips moved against her skin, and she pulled away to study his pale face. He was trying to say something, but didn't have the strength to get the words out.

She didn't know how long he'd been there, how badly he was hurt, or how much blood he'd lost, but it must have been a lot. His skin was ashen. Blood was leaking out of a hole in his back. She pulled her shawl away from her shoulders and wrapped him in it, and gently pressed the palm of her hand against the wound.

A tremble ran through his body. His eyes opened part way and she could see enormous pain taking away his will to live.

"Bridger, tell me what happened." Her voice sounded shaky and she steadied it with effort. "Who did this to you?"

He struggled to keep his eyes open. "Don't leave me here alone," he whispered, his voice tortured, barely audible. "Please don't let me die alone."

"I'm not going to let you die at all," she promised on a sob. He slumped in her arms too weak to say more, but he kept breathing. Fear threatened to overcome her and she fought it off so she could think. He needed help. He needed a doctor.

Carrying him to the cabin was out of the question, his weight was too great. Struggling to keep her thoughts from spinning out of control, she studied the terrain. If she could get him to level ground, she might be able to bring Mandy in close enough so she could lift him into the back of the rig.

She put her lips to his ear. "Bridger, listen to me." He stirred. "If I helped you, do you think you could stand up?"

His nod was feeble, devoid of strength, the movement unconvincing. But she had to try. Kneeling in the mud, she wrapped her arms around his chest, grasped her wrists to lock her arms, and slowly got to her feet. He sucked a breath and hollered in pain when she lifted his shoulders. She began to tremble.

Fear was weakening her arms, and he was beginning to slip away from her, but somehow she managed to haul him to the flat ground at the beginning of the dirt track. Gently, she laid him on his side. He groaned a curse, but he was alive. She didn't know for how long.

"Try not to move," she said, rewrapping the shawl around him. "I'm going to bring the buggy down here. I'll help you get in, then take you to Doc Holden."

He blinked at her and began to shiver.

She put her hands on the sides of his face, and lightly kissed his lips. "I'll be right back." Even as she said it, she knew it was going to take more than a little time to maneuver Mandy and the carriage down the narrow dirt path.

It seemed like hours before she returned. Bridger hadn't moved and she put her fingertips to his neck checking for a pulse. It was faint, but it was there. She lifted his arm and draped it over her shoulder.

"When I say 'now', try to get your feet under you." She folded her arms around his waist. "Now," she said and lifted.

He squeezed his eyes and roared in pain, but he got to his feet. Nearly doubled over, he braced himself against the iron carriage wheel, his breath coming ragged and hoarse. He lifted agonized eyes to Sage.

"You have to get the bullet out," he croaked.

Sage looked at him, horrified. "I can't do that," she said, her voice a terrified whisper. "Doc Holden has to do it."

He shook his head feebly, barely moving it at all. "I won't make it to town." He coughed. "No time left to fetch him. I've lost too much blood. If you don't do it, I'll die." His knees buckled and he sagged against her.

Stomach churning, she stared at him, stricken.

"Do it," he said, and coughed again. A gurgling sound came from his chest, and her protest died on her tongue.

Steeling herself, she tightened her arms around him. "Come on, put your foot on the rail, then lean on me, and we'll step up together. I'll help you lay down in back." Her muscles ached with his weight, but she was able to boost him in. He groaned and cursed again, then fell silent.

By the time they got to the cabin, Bridger's breathing was so faint, she was afraid each breath would be his last. She helped him inside and face down on the bed.

"Where's your whiskey?" she asked.

His gaze directed her to the pantry.

She retrieved the bottle, poured an inch into a glass and held it to his lips. "Here," she said. "Drink this." He swallowed weakly, and she poured him another, then wiped his lips with a part of her skirt that wasn't stained with mud and grass.

"Tie my hands and feet to the bedposts, so I don't thrash," he rasped, then sucked a breath and groaned heavily as a fresh wave of pain tortured his body.

Without a word, she took a bed sheet from a shelf, scissors from a kitchen drawer, and hastily cut it into long strips just as she'd done earlier to her wedding gown. Time was running out, so she worked fast. By the time she finished, sweat dripped down her face, stinging her eyes.

When Bridger's wrists and ankles were secured, she twisted a towel into a thick rope, put it into his mouth, and shoved it between his teeth. Then she retrieved his knife from the bureau, lit a candle and held the blade in the flame.

* * * * *

"Cheveyo, can't you go any faster?" Odie snapped, her forehead wrinkled into an uneasy frown. She twisted her fists in her shawl and pulled it tighter around her shoulders against the chill.

He slapped the reins on the rumps of the two harnessed horses and they immediately picked up their pace. "The road's kind of rough, and it's gettin' dark," he replied. "Don't want to lame up the horses."

"No," she agreed with a huff, frustrated. "We don't want to do that."
Then, "Are you sure Miss Sage didn't say anything about where she was
going?"

"You already asked me that, ma'am," Cheveyo said. "Twice. The answer is still no."

"No need to ask," put in Priscilla knowingly. Her voice carried over
the sound of the team's hooves on the hard dirt pack. She was sitting
beside Odie in the wagon, her face also creased with anxiety. "I know
where she went. Same place we're headed now. The marshal's."

"Well, we can't be sure of that," Odie said, crossly. "We may very
well be wasting our time riding out there." Worry was making her
grumpy.

"We aren't," came Priscilla's self-assured reply.

They rode in silence awhile, then Priscilla leaned over to Odie and
whispered so Cheveyo couldn't hear. "You don't think she went out there
to kill him, do you?"

"Of course not," Odie said, but she hadn't checked to see if Sage's
gun was in her room or not, so couldn't be one hundred percent certain.
"Hush, now. She wouldn't do that."

When Sage didn't return, Odie and Priscilla sent Cheveyo to the livery to rent a team and a wagon. Heeding Sage's warning about wanting to
be left alone, they didn't tell the deputies or anyone else Sage hadn't
come home and so far had no reason to alert anyone. Instead, they went
looking on their own.

At the turnoff to Bridger's place, Cheveyo slowed the horses, and
headed them up the slight rise to the cabin. Lamplight showed through
the windows. Odie was relieved to see Mandy waiting patiently at the
hitching post. The two women and the boy disembarked and went quietly
up the steps. Odie put her ear to the door, then knocked. Footsteps

hastened across the wooden planks inside, and Sage opened the heavy door. She was wearing a pair of Bridger's pants, and one of his shirts.

"Thank God you're here," she said, throwing out her arms to hug each one.

Odie and Priscilla entered the cabin, Cheveyo following. Bridger was wrapped in a blanket on the bed. Bloody clothes were heaped in the corner by the wash tub. Odie gasped. For a moment, she thought Priscilla was right, and that Sage had murdered the marshal, but then he stirred and emitted a god awful snore.

Speaking hurriedly, Sage told them what had happened in the past couple of hours, the words spilling out one on top of the other. "I was able to get the bullet out," she finished, pointing to it at the bottom of a shallow pan of pinkish water. "But he needs to get to the doctor. I'm worried about infection."

It was easier to manage Bridger's bulk with the help of three other people. They were able to get him into the wagon with a minimum of pain and discomfort.

While Miss Priscilla held a lantern, Sage put a pillow under Bridger's head and propped rolled up blankets around his body. "Are you all right?" she asked.

"Yes," he answered weakly, "except for one thing."

"What?" Sage asked.

His smile didn't make it all the way, but a tiny sparkle appeared in his eyes. "For the rest of my life," he joked, "I'll be known as the marshal who had to be rescued by three women and a boy."

Sage grinned, then leaned over and kissed his lips. "I love you," she whispered.

"And I love you. Would it be all right if we sent those wedding invitations out again?"

"As soon as Doc Holden says you're well enough to walk down the aisle," Sage replied, settling in the back of the wagon with him. "Then I'm never letting you out of my sight again."

* * * * *

Sage and Bridger were married the following autumn in the newly built chapel of the Fairplay Creek Community Church. The ceremony was performed by Preacher Jared Pickett.

Sage wore an ivory satin dress designed by Chantal and Colorado Kate. The bride's white blonde hair was swept high up on top of her head, loose curls bunched together and held in place by a circle of gold and pearls.

A string quartet comprised of violin, viola, cello, and harp played the allegro from Handel's Water Music Suite. Odie was maid of honor, and all the former Honeys stood as bridesmaids. Acer and Honcho shared the position of best man. Jenny sprinkled rose petals down the aisle. Martha and Sven beamed from front row seats.

After the ceremony, a cake and champagne reception for family and friends was held in the Venetian room of the newest hotel to be built in Fairplay Creek.

Bridger silenced the music and called everyone's attention so he could toast his bride.

"I owe my life to you, Sage Cane Norwood. I want you and the world to know that I am a proud man to have you as my wife. I promise now and forever, that I will love you and honor you and keep you safe forever by my side."

Sage smiled with happy tears and returned a loving tribute to her husband.

"And you, Bridger Norwood, are a man of unmistakable strength and honor of the highest order. I will love you forever and always."

The room erupted in laughter and applause as wedding guests raised their glasses and everyone drank to that.

* * * * *

Sage, Bridger and Jenny stood on a grassy rise in the meadow behind Bridger's cabin. A thick stand of trees to the north were resplendent in fall colors: crimson, gold and orange. Snow fields covered the highest elevations along Hoosier Pass. The breeze blowing over the mountaintops carried a hint of the winter to come, though the sun was still warm.

Bridger extended his arms and grandly swept the air. "I thought this would be a good spot to build our new house. What do you think?"

Sage slowly turned in place, admiring the long views. "Oh, Bridger. It's perfect. It's so beautiful."

"Will I live here, too?" Jenny asked.

"Of course you will," Sage said. She put her arm around Jenny's shoulders and pulled her close in a hug. Taking the child's hand in hers, they walked up a gentle slope. "And this is where your bedroom will be. Maybe a window here and here," Sage said pointing left, then right. "Would you like that?"

Jenny's eyes sparkled. "Oh, yes. I'd love it." Jenny turned to Bridger. "Papa, you said I could have a pony when I came to live with you."

"And you shall," he said. He scooped her up with his big strong hands, and swung her around gently. "Just as soon as the house is built." He set her down and paced off a few strides, his face thoughtful. "Where do you want the kitchen?" he asked Sage. "Would this be suitable?"

"Perfect," Sage answered. "But I'd like it to be a big one. And a big dining room, too, with a big table so we can have lots of friends over for dinners and parties."

"Then you will have it," Bridger said.

"And extra bedrooms for when Martha and Sven come to visit. And for . . ." Sage paused and sent Bridger a warm gaze from under her lashes. "For a baby."

Jenny's mouth immediately fell open and her eyes lit with glee. She clapped her hands and jumped up and down. "A baby? When? Will it be a boy or a girl? Will I have a brother or a sister? Can I have a sister, please? Then I won't need the pony."

Bridger and Sage broke into laughter.

"Now just a minute," Bridger said, catching his breath. He held out his hands as if trying to tamp down Jenny's overabundance of enthusiasm. "Hold on just a second, Jenny. We don't know yet if it's going to be a boy or a girl," he told her. "We don't even know when."

Sage let a silence settle around his words, her smile and her gaze speaking volumes.

Bridger's expression froze in hopeful expectation. "We don't, do we?"

Sage nodded. "We do," she said. "This time next year we'll be holding our precious little baby."

Bridger whooped with joy and swept her up, swinging her around as he'd done earlier with Jenny. "You're going to be a Mama!" he exclaimed. Then he set her on her feet, kissed her palm and pressed her hand to his cheek.

Jenny watched them, her eyes still. "Are you *my* Mama, too?" she asked shyly.

Sage gathered Jenny to her side and nuzzled her face in the child's hair. She put her hands on the little girl's shoulders and knelt so their eyes were level. "Jenny, I'll never be able to take the place of your mother. But I *will* love you as if you were my own daughter."

Jenny's grin was heartfelt. She put her arms around Sage's neck and squeezed tight. "And I'll love you like you were my real mother."

"Have you thought about names for the baby?" Bridger asked.

Sage stood. "Yes, I have. If it's a girl, I'd like to name her Hannah Elizabeth. Would that be all right with you?"

"Yes," he said. "That would be fine." Gently he caught a loose lock of her hair the wind had blown free. He wound the end around his finger, then tucked the tendril behind her ear.

"If it's a boy, do you mind if we name him after you?" she asked.

"No," he said, and sighed contentedly. "I'd like that. I'd like that a lot."

He pulled Sage and Jenny to his side, an arm around each of them. Sage rested her head on his shoulder, her heart galloping with joy. This magnificent man had married her, this wonderful little girl loved her, and there was a baby on the way. A baby that would be part of him and part of her. A baby that would join them together irrevocably and make them a family.

She didn't know what the future would bring for any of them, what Fairplay Creek, the town she'd grown to love, would become. She just knew this was the life God meant for her to live.

Epilogue

Trip Mondragon hadn't yet been found, but Priscilla had no doubt he would be eventually. The arrogance of bad men didn't permit them to remain hidden forever. Their need to flaunt their villainy was greater than their fear of perdition.

She was sitting on the padded bench of her new two-seater runabout at the crest of a low hill watching workmen dig the foundation for the new stagecoach transfer station to be built at Hatchett's Draw. A stiff wind sent dirt into the air like spindrift.

Priscilla opened the basket on the seat beside her, took out a covered dish of cold herbed chicken and biscuits, delicately laid a napkin on her lap and began eating her lunch. She reflected on how much had changed in the last year.

Sage Cane's House of Grace and Favor was flourishing. The musical performances and poetry readings always drew a large audience. The writing classes and voice lessons were always full. There remained a handful of residence rooms that would accommodate any of the former Honeys who chose to live in, but none did. Only Odie and Priscilla had chosen to stay.

Natalie Bennett, who had saved her money slavishly, had chosen to invest it in a boarding house in town—a *real* boarding house—called Natalie's Plush Residence Rooms for Single Ladies, Fine Private Suites and Public Parlors. Most of the Honeys lived there.

Sage and Bridger and Jenny had taken up temporary residence in rooms at the hotel while their new house was being built on Bridger's spread. Sage was a well-liked town board member, and there was talk of electing her mayor even though no woman had ever held that position before. A baby was due soon.

Colorado Kate, who had begun calling herself Katheryne, had opened a dressmaking shop called Katheryne's Fine Fashions and Apparel. Chantal rented space next door and was now a popular corsetiere. Recently a controversy had popped up about, of all things, ladies corsets. The ladies loved them, but critics were claiming that corsets displaced internal organs causing injury. Chantal had a way of measuring around the waist that reduced such risk. Regardless, both shops were patronized by all the Fairplay Creek women and had prospered.

Cheveyo's parents never came to get him, and he'd left for California.

Sage had asked Priscilla to stay on to oversee the care of the house, but she worked fewer hours now so had time to herself. Most of it was spent away from the house. Mornings found her sitting at the windows of any one of the many restaurants along Main Street watching for Gladys. The child had run off when she was only twelve years old, and there hadn't been a day since that Priscilla hadn't prayed she'd be reunited with her only daughter one day.

The rest of her time was spent here, at the dig site where she came to watch the progress of the construction. It was only a matter of time before Shooter Riker's bones were dug up.

And when that day came, Priscilla wanted to be the first to know. She'd pictured it happening, and knew precisely what she'd do when it did. When that first shovelful overturned the remains, and the man holding the shovel shouted to the foreman to come take a look, Priscilla would turn the buggy around and go home to pack.

Even in death, bad men didn't stay down.

On Sale Now!

Winner of the 2019 Western Fictioneers Peacemaker Award

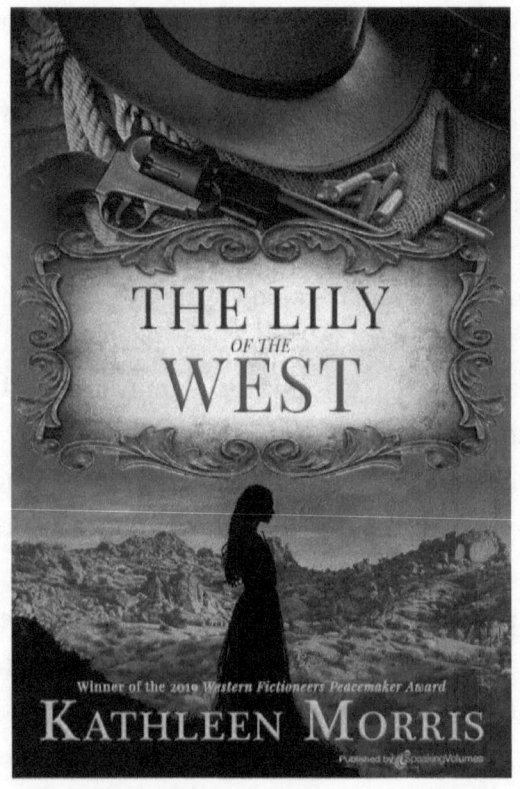

For more information
visit: www.SpeakingVolumes.us

On Sale Now!

For more information
visit: www.SpeakingVolumes.us

www.ingramcontent.com/pod-product-compliance
Lightning Source LLC
Chambersburg PA
CBHW050559260626
47157CB00002B/637